Praise for Horo

"Michael Freed-Thall's *Horodno Burning* is a beautifully textured, epic historical novel with an ending that will simultaneously break your heart and inspire you to live life to the fullest. With courageous, noble, and big-hearted characters at its center, *Horodno Burning* takes readers on a journey through turbulent and dramatic times and into a rich and stirring account of Jewish history. Readers of historical fiction who look for strong female characters at the spine will be enraptured by this exquisite debut."

> – Stephanie Storey, bestselling author of *Oil and Marble* and
> *Raphael, Painter in Rome*

"I love *Horodno Burning*, an unflinching, courageous book about loving great books during the horrors of the late nineteenth-century Russian pogroms. These foreshadowed the twentieth century, the waves of antisemitism, racism, and hate that still wash up on our borders and shores, the ease with which too many still project their shadows upon refugees and vulnerable others simply trying to live. Richly drawn, deeply compassionate, and moving—a book about how words and stories can change us, save us, give us hope, make us more human, more humane—*Horodno Burning* is truly a great book."

> – Lex Williford, award-winning author of *Macauley's Thumb*
> and *Superman on the Roof*

"Thoughtful, powerful, and tender, *Horodno Burning* brings to life the conflicts and contradictions of family life and political activism in the Pale of Settlement, beginning with the story of a religious boy who cannot read and a girl who loves books and wants equality for women. Living with the constant threat of violence in the late nineteenth-century Russian Empire, Bernard and Esther search for ways to resist the prejudice and hatred and build a family. Michael Freed-Thall offers a moving story about human persistence and hope despite brutality, and about the power of storytelling to fight injustice. *Horodno Burning* is both timeless and timely."

> – Ellen Meeropol, author of *Her Sister's Tattoo*

"*Horodno Burning* is a wonderful novel—rich and engaging and beautifully written. It moves so well, as details of locations, events, and personalities provide a vivid backdrop to the fiction. Estes, a free-thinking feminist before her time, and Bernard, a religious vodka distiller, will stay with the reader after the last page, along with the deep insights and humanity that emerge in the face of trauma and prejudice. A superb debut."

> – Bernie Lambek, award-winning author of *Uncivil Liberties*

"What is the price of courage in the face of antisemitism? I strongly recommend *Horodno Burning* for anyone interested in rich details of everyday life at a tumultuous time in Jewish and Russian history. This novel will also appeal to readers who wonder how to live a life with integrity when threatened with censure and violence, and to those who question whether love can surmount differences in faith and political belief."

> – Maryka Biaggio, author of *Parlor Games* and *Eden Waits*

"Under a cloud of looming danger in the late nineteenth-century Pale of Settlement, the vivid and sympathetic protagonists of Michael Freed-Thall's novel *Horodno Burning* try to build lives of safety, meaning, and purpose. As antisemitism and violence grow around them, Estes and Bernard face harrowing choices. This gripping novel brings history to life."

> – David Ebenbach, author of the novel *How to Mars*
> and the creativity guide *The Artist's Torah*

"What a tremendous book! The prose is brilliant and tender in this absorbing debut novel. The struggles of Estes and Bernard as wife and husband and as young parents are universal, yet *Horodno Burning* is an invitation into a particular place and time, placing the reader in the heart of a community on the cusp of a great migration. Epic in scope, intimate in detail, *Horodno Burning* is historical fiction at its finest. I was so very moved and astonished by this story."

> – Julie Christine Johnson, author of *The Crows of Beara*
> and *In Another Life*

"What an incredible novel! Experiencing these characters—their struggles and love for each other and their reverence for books—was a balm in this difficult time. I will never forget Estes and Bernard who show us that even in times of deep pain, precious books can speak to our souls. In *Horodno Burning*, Michael Freed-Thall has gifted us such a book."

    – Diane Zinna, author of *The All-Night Sun*

HORODNO
BURNING

For Rabbi Weisman

L'chaim!

Michael Freed-Thall

HORODNO
BURNING

By Michael Freed-Thall

Rootstock Publishing

Montpelier, VT

First Printing: September 21, 2021

Horodno Burning
Copyright © 2021 by Michael Freed-Thall
All rights reserved

ISBN: 978-1-57869-067-1
eBook ISBN: 978-1-57869-068-8
Library of Congress Control Number: 2021911160

Cover Art: Marc Chagall, *The Flying Carriage* (1913)
© 2020 Artists Rights Society (ARS), New York / ADAGP, Paris

Photo Credit: The Solomon R. Guggenheim Foundation /
Art Resource, NY

Interior design and maps by Tim Newcomb

Map of the Pale of Settlement based upon: Hundert,
The YIVO Encyclopedia of Jews in Eastern Europe (2008)
© Yale University Press

Author photo credit: Patricia Freed-Thall

Published by Rootstock Publishing,
an imprint of Multicultural Media, Inc.
Montpelier, Vermont
www.rootstockpublishing.com
info@rootstockpublishing.com

Printed in the USA

Author's Note

Real places, people, and events appear in *Horodno Burning* for fictional purposes. For historical dates within the Russian Empire, I have used the Julian calendar, which ran twelve days behind the Western calendar in the nineteenth century. Supplemental materials, including a glossary of the Yiddish and other non-English words and phrases in the novel, follow the last chapter.

The front cover shows a digital reproduction of a Marc Chagall painting. Born in the Pale of Settlement, Chagall drew on his early years in Vitebsk for artistic inspiration throughout his life. *Flying Carriage* (1913), with its blend of modernism and folk art, expresses both trauma and transcendence—interconnected and recurring themes throughout Jewish history.

For Marvin and Harriet

Pale of Settlement

Late 19th Century

From 1791 to 1917 the czars barred their Jewish subjects from the Russian interior. Nineteenth-century statutes delineated Congress Poland and the Pale of Settlement for Jewish residence. These areas of the Russian Empire roughly corresponded to present-day Lithuania, Belarus, Moldova, and Ukraine, a significant portion of modern Poland, and slivers of modern Latvia and Russia. This map shows the train routes that appear in *Horodno Burning*.

Horodno

Late 19th Century

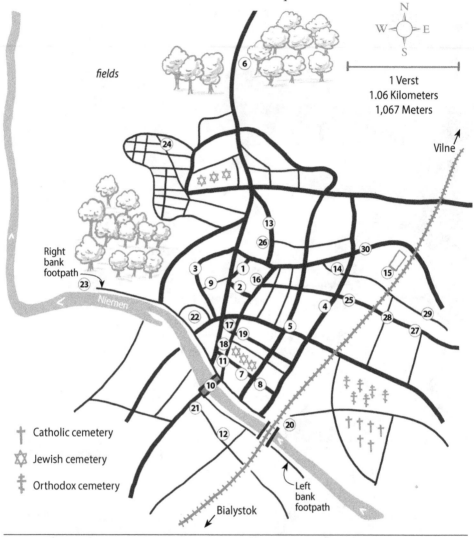

fields

N
W E
S

1 Verst
1.06 Kilometers
1,067 Meters

Vilne

Right
bank
footpath

Niemen

† Catholic cemetery

✡ Jewish cemetery

‡ Orthodox cemetery

Left
bank
footpath

Bialystok

Landmarks in Horodno are numbered according to when they first appear in the novel

1 Leving Shoe Shop and House	12 Garfinkle's Spirits	22 Old Castle
2 Market Square	13 Sophie Feinberg's House	23 Boris and Gleb Orthodox Church
3 Choral Shul	14 Leib and Shlomo's House	
4 Horodno School for Girls	15 Train Station	24 Eliza Orzeszkowa's House
5 Public Library	16 Professor Micah's House (Horodno Bookshop)	25 Rabbi Menshein's House
6 Garfinkle House		26 Firehouse
7 Great Wooden Shul	17 Catholic Basilica	27 Infirmary
8 Holy Land Kheyder	18 Sophia's Church	28 Jewish Old-Age Home
9 Chaim's House	19 Office of State Security	29 Jewish Orphanage
10 Foot and Carriage Bridge	20 Railroad Bridge	30 Rabbi Jacob Rosenblum's House
11 Shershevski's Factory	21 Efron's Sawmill	

PART I

ESTHER AND BERNARD

1860–1872

On the seventh day, before He rested,
God made the book and told his people to read.
— Rabbi Isaac Benjamin

I

A few days past her fifth birthday, in 1860, Esther Leving held still while her papa made a sand mold of her deformed foot, with its radical inward cant of the sole, twisted toes, and high Gothic arch.

"Next comes the cast-iron form from the foundry, Estes. We'll make new ones as your foot grows."

When he finished, Estes began to do small jobs in the shoe shop. At her little table, she pulled laces through brass eyelets and applied dubbin to new leather. She scraped her good foot along the splotches of wax, bits of thread, and leather scraps on the worn wood floor.

Papa, on his high stool, took a deep breath and cleared his throat. "Just six days until Pesach, Estes. This year, we need to give another child a chance to read at Seder. Tradition is tradition."

"Jacob Rosenblum was born a few days after you," he said before she could protest. "Tradition dictates the youngest reader recites the Four Questions."

"Five, Papa." Estes counted the question not used since the time of the temple.

He groaned, and she had no doubt—Avram Rosenblum's son would perform to the delight of their guests.

Reading: the only thing Estes did better than anyone else her age. Unable to run or dance, she stunned everyone whenever she read aloud from the *Mayse-Bukh*, the dense collection of religious stories and moral folktales filled with werewolves and dibeks, or when she recited old sayings from memory. She especially loved how proverbs hid a second meaning behind the first and the way they made foreheads crease. *Where there is no man, a herring is also a fish.*

Hadn't she read without error at last year's Seder, not missing a single word, so proud she wrote the Four Questions on her bedroom wall the next evening? When he discovered them, Papa spread his arms and lifted his eyes to the cracked plaster ceiling.

"Estes! Now you're writing on walls? You challenge everything I say, even the meaning of the prayers on Shabes. How will you ever find your place?"

"Herman Leving! What's her place? You pretend to be an enlightened man—a shame and a disgrace." Mama knelt and gently took the charcoal from Estes's hand. "Your father can't make up his mind."

The night different from all others arrived. Above Papa's shop, on the second floor of their brick house on Horodno's Market Square, the guests crowded into the dining room. Mama had adorned the Seder table with a hand-stitched blue cloth, her prettiest plates, silver candle holders, bottles of wine, bowls of symbolic foods, salt water, matzo, and a handmade Haggadah next to each setting.

Street cleaners had scrubbed the cobblestones in the square for the holiday. Indoors, the pleasant aroma of poached fish dumplings and stewed carrots filled the air as Papa signaled the start of the Seder. He took his place on Estes's right, reclining on a cushion like the other men. He whispered into her ear, "You're scowling."

On her left, Avram Rosenblum bulged like an overstuffed pillow. Jacob, well fed, blue eyed, and rosy cheeked, sat between his father and his tiny mother, Maida. Even now he rehearsed the questions with his parents. When Estes had the honor last year, she'd refused any help.

Across from the Rosenblums, closest to the kitchen, Mama and three other wives anticipated the Seder's sequence like coal stokers, intent on keeping the ceremony moving with the perfectly timed delivery of food.

Papa tapped his wineglass. Estes settled into a pout during the Holy Blessing, purifying hand washing, symbolic dipping of vegetables, breaking of the middle matzo, and hiding of the afikoymen.

She wouldn't feel so bothered if another girl had taken her place with the recitation. She clenched her fists when she thought about Jacob Rosenblum and the other boys marching off to kheyder carrying their books.

Jacob sang the first question without reading the Haggadah. Estes wished for a mistake or a stumble, but the second and third also came out perfect, and even worse, in a loud and melodic voice. When he faltered on the fourth question, she pushed on her knees and straightened her back.

Avram Rosenblum whispered to his son, "Why is it that on all other nights, we eat either sitting or reclining . . ." and Jacob finished, "but on this night we eat only in a reclining position?" The entire table, except Estes, chanted an answer in unison: "When a person eats on this night, he is required to eat and drink while reclining, as a sign of freedom."

When the boy finished, Papa poured more wine and raised his glass. "What a mentsh." Estes ignored the grape juice in her glass and pointed at Jacob. "You cheated!"

"Pesach is about freedom from oppression, Estes. Jacob did a fine job. Apologize!"

"Jacob doesn't even know they changed the fourth question." She glared at the boy.

Papa scooped her out of her seat and onto his shoulder. She twisted around and looked down at the nine startled guests.

"It didn't used to have anything to do with reclining at the dinner table!" she screamed.

Before Estes could say anything else, Papa carried her off into exile, causing her to miss her favorite part of the exodus story, the ten plagues: blood, frogs, lice, wild animals, pestilence, boils, hail, locusts, darkness, and the killing of the Egyptians' firstborn. Estes imagined a similar fate for Avram Rosenblum and his son. After thirty minutes of penance, she returned with Mama and made a tearful apology in time for the bitter herbs.

After the feast, the hunt for the afikoymen, and the final prayers, the guests departed. Mama massaged Estes's foot and tucked her into bed. Estes threw her arms around Mama and held on. Mama kissed her cheek, said goodnight, and left. A minute later, Papa's raised voice boomed in the hall and Estes stifled a sob.

"What have I done to deserve a disobedient daughter?"

One question.

"Do you expect an answer from the sky?"

Two. She hoped Mama poked him in the chest.

"We teach her she's as good as any boy, and now you're unhappy because she's taken our lesson to heart?"

Three.

"Is rudeness the same as equality?" Papa shouted. "Can't we take it one step at a time?"

Four and *five*. As she drifted toward sleep, Estes composed her own imaginary Haggadah, with all women characters and a female God.

✳

With the first partition of the Polish Commonwealth in 1772, Russia inherited hundreds of thousands of Jewish subjects. Alarmed Moscow merchants finally convinced Catherine the Great to eliminate these aliens from the Russian interior in 1791, and she forced them back into the seized lands. After the third partition, in 1795, nearly one million Jews, including some of Esther Leving's ancestors who had roots in Horodno from the fourteenth century, resided in the Russian Empire's western territories. They had no rights other than those specifically granted by the czar. By the time Nicholas I, a leader universally hated and feared by Jews for his thirty years of harsh laws, censorship, and forced conscription of children, died in 1855, this Pale of Settlement had become synonymous with misery.

After years of suffering, even a sliver of sunlight allowed into a prisoner's pitch-dark cell feels like liberation. By the summer of 1861, six years into his reign, Alexander II, the most benign of the czars, had ended conscription of minors, curtailed censorship, expanded educational opportunities, allowed limited freedom of movement into Russia proper for Jews with particular skills, and in his most dramatic action, freed twenty-three million serfs. Many Jews now called him "the liberator czar" with the same reverent tone they used when speaking of Moses.

Customers told Estes's father that Alexander aimed to bring Russia into the modern age, like those countries in Western Europe that had already emancipated their Jews. For proof of his intentions, just look at the nearly completed railway from Saint Petersburg to Warsaw which passed through their growing town. With twenty-four thousand residents, Horodno had transformed from a shtetl into a growing shtot.

In June, on this train route, Uncle Simon arrived in their small city, one hundred sixty versts southwest of Vilne, on the Niemen River. Estes couldn't believe that Simon, a first guild merchant who'd lived in the capital and traveled around Europe, and her father were brothers. Papa—

tall, modestly potbellied, full bearded, with a round, cup-sized bald spot on his crown—moved deliberately. He'd spent nearly his entire life in Horodno. Simon—short, plump, and bald as an onion—did everything with immense energy. As a young man, he'd become rich selling and buying for the nobility, a favored Jew until he began speaking about his socialist beliefs.

The last time she'd seen her uncle, a few years ago, he'd charged up the stairs. "Where's my little scholar? Just let me find her!" He pretended to look in the cupboards, under furniture, in jars of dried peas or flour. He searched the whole second floor until he found her shaking with suppressed laughter under the bed. He wrapped her in his arms and pretended to eat her. "Yummy, tasty little morsel, perfect for my afternoon snack."

Then, before he'd rested or unpacked after his long journey, she'd begged for a story. Now, when she met him outside holding her *Mayse-Bukh*, his shoulders slumped.

"I'm six, Uncle Simon." She threw her head back and swished her dress.

"Not too old for my stories, I hope."

She laughed at his exaggerated frown.

He settled into his "Horodno cell," a corner of the shop where Papa had placed a cot and strung a curtain. Later that afternoon, Uncle Simon and Estes sat on a bench in the square across from her father's handmade wooden sign, its red lettering prominent against a white background— LEVING'S SHOES, *travel in comfort.*

He told her about his recent travels, and after a while they leaned back and absorbed the warm sun. Neither spoke for about five minutes— their ritual. Estes waited for a signal. The day's commerce had dwindled. Peddlers pushed their carts out of the square. A broad peasant, his eyes bloodshot and cheeks flushed, approached, bent beneath the weight of a heavy sack. He wore mud-splattered boots, soiled work pants, and a wool shirt worn bare at the elbows. He raised his eyebrows. "Vodka, for just a few kopeks?" Uncle Simon waved the man off as if shooing a horsefly.

When a dirty gray pigeon landed in front of them and pecked at crumbs, Estes said, "Nu, Uncle Simon?"

"I told Hannibal not to take the elephants." Most of his stories started this way. Uncle Simon mixed in real history and science but claimed to have witnessed events that occurred centuries earlier. His tales snared her despite her new, grown-up skepticism.

"Consider human history as a broad sweep of ideas and forces—the grand perspective, Estes. Learn to watch civilizations expand and contract from the distance of the moon."

With dizzying speed, he pulled her out of abstraction, plunged her back to earth, and tossed her into the French Revolution. Estes travelled with the condemned on the way to the guillotine.

Each day, after he finished telling stories, they spent hours on German instruction, learning the language as natural for her as pulling on an old sweater.

"German has a different alphabet, but so many of the words resemble Yiddish without the gestures and inflections. The mother tongue gives you a head start."

Estes wanted Simon to stay forever, but after a week of late summer rain his knees pumped at the dinner table and he paced in the shop at night.

"What's wrong with Uncle Simon?" she asked Papa.

"The signs of approaching flight."

Who would teach her new languages now, or take her around the world without ever leaving Horodno? Two mornings later she awoke early to say goodbye and watch his carriage depart, leaving the square empty until the buying and selling began. Leaving her behind.

*

Jewish boys had many choices for their early schooling, and the best of these students continued their education in yeshiva. Almost all Jewish girls learned at home from their mothers or, if the family could afford it, tutors. Some, however, chose the Horodno Kheyder for Girls, the only one of its kind in the city. A month after Uncle Simon left, Estes prepared for her visit and wished it had a more inspiring name, like some of the boy's kheyders: Holy Land, Maimonides, Judah Maccabee. Still, the possibilities so excited her that she misaligned the buttons on her dress, undid them, and started over. While Mama braided her hair, she imagined new books and stimulating discussions.

The three of them walked the four blocks east to the drab, weathered building. When she looked back at the western skyline, she spotted the rounded tip of the massive Choral Shul, where the Levings went to services each week.

Inside, dusty windows dimly lit the classroom. They stood in the back, and Estes counted thirty-four pupils, sorted by age, on benches. Tongues pushed out cheeks, hands twirled braids, and legs bobbed. The youngest concentrated on writing the alphabet.

The stocky teacher, her gray hair uncovered, walked among the girls sitting shoulder to shoulder, encouraging them for their efforts. Estes doubted that she told stories like Uncle Simon.

"Do you want to try, dear?"

Estes shook her head.

"A lot of the girls come in not recognizing gimel from nun. Soon enough, she'll learn," the teacher said to Mama.

"She already knows how to read."

The surprised teacher led them to the tables of the oldest girls. Words and simple sentences replaced alphabet training. One of the girls whispered *cripple* as Estes walked past, and a familiar pain moved into her ankle. Estes declined to participate when the girls began to repair tears, patch holes, and fix buttons on the clothing they'd brought from home.

"Useful activity," Papa said, glancing at her.

On the return home, he sounded like the peddlers who failed to convince Mama to buy their wilted greens, soft potatoes, and overripe fruit. "Alexander's reforms will improve education for girls, but change takes time."

Dreariness in the girls' school and on the street. Bent under his load, a charcoal peddler wheezed as he neared them. Estes sought out color, and a young woman, dried flowers adorning her straw hat, stood out amongst the tattered blacks and grays of the bearded men.

When they arrived home, Estes said her foot hurt and went to her room. Her parents' subdued voices in the kitchen indicated a private conversation, but with her door open, how could she help but overhear?

"It's not right for her to spend time only with us. She should be around other children," Papa said.

"Imagine if you, Herman, a master shoemaker, had to start over as a cobbler."

A while later, Mama came in carrying a bowl of rapeseed oil and sat on the bed. Estes placed Uncle Simon's German-language book on the windowsill and leaned back against her pillow. Mama eased off the tight boot and dropped it on the floor. She unrolled the blue sock and, for an instant, Estes imagined her foot whole, instead of a twisted disaster.

Estes craved independence and for a time had tried to massage her foot by herself, but she couldn't match Mama, who spread oil onto the calloused outside edge that bore all her weight, worked the sensitive arch, and gently manipulated the chronically painful and swollen ankle. Mama stretched the hooked toes, but they curled back stubbornly into a claw as soon as she released them.

After dinner, Papa said he and Mama had a surprise. While Mama fastened a strip of cloth over Estes's eyes, Papa went down to the shop, his step slow and heavy on the return.

"Ready."

Mama guided Estes down the hall and removed the blindfold. Estes threw her arms around each of her parents and began looking through the books stacked on her bed.

"Your mother and I collected these for you. I hid them in the shop." He pulled one out. "Eugene Sue's *Mysteries of Paris*. Translated into Hebrew a few years ago."

Mama helped her arrange the books in the cabinet Papa had built, and Estes grinned at her modest collection. The ones in English, French, and Russian would have to wait. Why didn't they teach *those* languages at the Horodno Kheyder for Girls?

※

She and Mama won the argument: why attend that school when she had these books at home? First, Estes chose the Yiddish adaption of *Robinson Crusoe*, renamed *Robinson, the History of Alter-Leb*. It thrilled her to share the reading with Mama, though neither of them loved the story.

Alter-Leb survived in a world without women or girls.

Next, they spent weeks exploring the illustrated child's version of *Gulliver's Travels*. Estes did all the reading and practiced translating the German edition for Mama ahead of time. They reclined on pillows against the headboard and the bookmark moved forward several pages every night. The best part—Mama's arm around her shoulders as she read.

Estes stretched into the giant, stepped around tiny people in the streets, and squinted through half-mast eyelids at her father, the Lilliputian. When she and Mama went to market, they examined a horse's placid face for signs of intelligence.

Soon after Estes had begun to reread these books, the first public library in Horodno opened on the east side, between the girl's kheyder and the Great Wooden Shul. Mama took her to the inaugural celebration in the three-story brick building. Outside, a black-cloaked rabbi muttered, "An abomination to God." Inside, men in suits and women in colorful dresses held glasses of wine and talked in hushed voices. More volumes than Estes had ever imagined lined the tall shelves.

The librarian, a man her father's age with a thin mustache and gold spectacles, tilted his head and stared at her when she brought a book to him.

"Moshe Knorozovski at your service, miss. *Pride and Prejudice*, a rare German edition. Will your mother read this to you?"

"We read every night," Mama said, pride and annoyance mixed in her voice, "but I don't read German like Estes."

"Amazing." The librarian removed his glasses and pinched the bridge of his nose. "Too bad Jane Austen's books haven't found a wider audience, though Sir Walter Scott recognized her brilliance. Perhaps you'd prefer his *Ivanhoe*?" The librarian handed back the book.

Estes answered by reading out loud, embarrassed when she struggled with the first line. "It is a truth universally acknowledged, that a single man in possession of a good fortune, must be in want of a wife."

"Do you have any idea what it means?" The librarian put his glasses back on and leaned over the counter. His gray eyes narrowed.

"It means . . ." Why didn't she think to bring Uncle Simon's German-to-Yiddish dictionary for these grown-up words? She bit her lip. Some message in the author's airy tone hid just beyond her reach. "I'm not sure, yet. I think Miss Austen is poking fun, but I'll have to read more and talk with Mama about that."

After their first meeting, Estes anticipated Moshe calling her "My best little reader" when he greeted her each week. He always picked out several volumes and kept them for her at the desk. She loved the sliding sound a book made when she pulled it off its shelf, the way its neighbors on both sides fell into the vacated space, how they leaned on each other for support. She loved the organization of volumes into dozens of categories, with no particular prominence given to the religious ones.

Months later, the rabbi protesting outside had finally departed. Perhaps he'd scared away all the bearded Jewish men with their peyes, black cloaks, and hats. They could have their old shuln. The library was her temple.

One afternoon, she ducked behind a bookshelf when Avram Rosenblum's loud voice echoed in the silence. Father and son each carried an armload of books. She counted four in Jacob's arms, held against his chest.

"My best little reader," Moshe told Jacob.

Traitor!

"Top in his class," Rosenblum said. "And now Russian from a private tutor. He'll go straight through to yeshiva." When they left, Estes came out with five.

2

After spells of torrential rain had transformed the bumpy, rutted roads surrounding Horodno into boot-devouring swamps, stoic horses, motionless in their flooded fields, hung their heads. Even some of the devout Jews complained about the Lord's choice of weather.

"If this keeps up, the farmers won't have a grain harvest," Solomon Garfinkle said, gazing through the kitchen window at the downpour. Rivulets that flowed through their garden flattened tender greens and washed away unmoored seeds. "Then we'll have to make vodka from potatoes, like the peasants."

"It will be sunny again soon, Father," six-year-old Bernard promised. "We could say a prayer."

A few days later, on a cool September morning, the threatening skies finally cleared. Bernard wondered when God would hear his other, secret request—to help solve the problem that shamed him more than the rare occasions he wet his bed.

All the boys he covertly watched at shul read the prayers. He knew this because their eyes tracked the page. Like these boys, Bernard had started reading lessons when he turned four. Solomon taught him the alphabet, the sounds for each letter, and made Bernard read lines of holy text after hearing them several times. His father praised God when Bernard read back the prayers and passages with only minor errors.

Now Bernard listened as his father read from the Chumash before handing him the thick black book. The words on the page still blurred into meaningless, squiggly lines, so Bernard moved his finger right to left and pointed at the place he thought matched the end of the story. David defeating the giant Goliath with just a stick and stone clung to him like a spiny burdock pod. "The stone sank into his forehead, and he fell facedown on the ground."

After a breakfast of buckwheat kasha simmered in milk, Bernard and his father began the familiar walk, one verst south into the city and two more through town, for his first day of kheyder. He held his father's hand as they proceeded down the gentle incline. The knot in his stomach tightened.

When they reached the thick, blackened oak, a rickety horse-drawn cart carrying a steaming mountain of drek approached. The driver wore a floppy, wide-brimmed hat. Solomon had instructed Bernard never to cover his nose when they passed the night soil man. "God himself is a laborer."

One of the horses rubbed his neck against Bernard, knocking him back a step. "Easy, girl," the driver said. "The boy's not a scratching post."

"Sholem aleykhem, Mendel," his father said. "How's business?"

"Aleykhem sholem, Solomon. The czar and shit—the only things we can count on, eh? Taking the boy to kheyder? You best study hard, Bernard, otherwise you'll be tending this palace someday."

"Bernard's a born scholar. Hearing him read is better than any fortune. You know he was born one month after our czar Alexander began his rule."

Mendel's horses clopped up the road. Bernard welcomed the distraction of songbirds in a copse of birch, and his stomach knot eased. Children played in muddy yards and wood cook smoke drifted from nearby chimneys. A mixed conifer and hardwood forest backed a thickening cluster of dwellings on the east side of the road. Blue splashes of the Niemen River and fields of golden wheat and rye highlighted the western view, and to the south—Orthodox and Catholic church spires, shuln, intersections of roads and bridges, and new industry in their growing city.

Bernard and Solomon waved to Jonah and Clara Bloom as they neared their house. Bernard spotted his clothes surrounded by the Bloom family's garments on a rope stretched across the yard—clothes handed down from older to younger, until the last in line wore more patch than pant.

"A fair exchange, clean clothes for a bucket of vodka," his father said in a low voice.

In the city, they avoided Market Square with its shops full of meat, clothes, utensils, leather goods, and even jewelry. Instead, they turned left into the east side before continuing south toward the river. Peddlers pulled long-handled, two-wheeled carts piled with goods. Shopkeepers with hoarse voices announced items for sale, and men and women bent under overflowing baskets strapped to their backs. A few wagons moved slowly on the crowded street.

"If so many sell, Father, who remains to buy?"

"The same ones selling, Bernard, and new customers too. Markets must expand to survive."

Adjacent to their Great Wooden Shul—which everyone called a three-hundred-year-old miracle because fire had cooked most of the city to ash several times—Bernard spotted the two-storied kheyder and yeshiva.

Other fathers stood next to their sons in the narrow yard, waiting for the rabbi. Some wore a tallis katan under their shirt, a reminder of the commandments. All wore yarmulkes, and some of the boys held theirs on in the suddenly gusty wind. Bernard appreciated how the snug fit of his knit skullcap left his hands free.

"The Holy Land Kheyder and Yeshiva," his father said reverently. "Rabbis for teachers and real classrooms. You won't be squeezed like I was around a poor melamed's kitchen table. And the Hasids haven't taken over here. They can keep to their own school if they want to worship rebbes, like Catholics do their Pope." He clucked his tongue.

A stout boy with a shock of red hair approached. Bernard eyed his peyes and reached up to feel where his own black hair grazed the tops of his ears.

"God lives inside, too, Bernard," his father whispered. "Not just in Chaim's hair or the rabbi's beard."

The boy grinned and revealed a gap in his front teeth.

"Sholem, Chaim." Solomon patted the boy on the shoulder. "Are you as excited as Bernard?"

Chaim held up his book. "I've been practicing." He read for a minute about the baby Moses floating in the reed basket on the Nile. He didn't point or hesitate, and the knot in Bernard's stomach returned.

"Here comes Rabbi Menshein," his father said. The rabbi, wearing rumpled, black trousers, had a beard that reached his waist. He approached on stumpy legs and rang a handbell, stopping the conversations at once.

"Welcome to the Holy Land Kheyder and Yeshiva," the rabbi called out in a high-pitched voice, his gray eyes squinting behind thick glasses.

Bernard's father kissed him on the cheek and turned to go. The press of his lips and the brush of his beard stayed with Bernard as he got in line. The boys followed the rabbi into the building. Through one open classroom door, groups separated by age sat on the floor. A rabbi strutted through the din of simultaneous recitations.

"Some of you may go on to yeshiva." The rabbi pointed at the second floor. "Those who pay attention and apply themselves." He rapped two identical gangly boys with shaved heads on their shoulders with his stick. They stopped talking.

Leib, the louder one, stared at the rabbi. His twin, Shlomo, scratched his head.

"Lice," Chaim whispered.

At the end of the hall, Rabbi Menshein pointed out the lunch and prayer space before leading the boys to their classroom. Pencils and writing paper, neatly laid out on three battered tables, each with one wobbly bench, marked a spot for every student. The rabbi let them choose their seats, four to a table, and Bernard and Chaim sat furthest from their teacher's desk. The twins sat next to them.

"You will learn from one rabbi for all six years. One rabbi with boys all the same age. An experiment. Unheard of even for our modern kheyder. We'll start with a passage from the Chumash. Who wishes to read?"

Leib elbowed his brother in the side. The rabbi strolled between the tables, humming, his hands clasped behind his back. Bernard kept his eyes on the table and flinched when the rabbi tapped his shoulder with his stick.

"Come along, boy."

Bernard followed the rabbi to the front of the room. Rabbi Menshein opened a thick book. He flipped the smudged pages until he found what he wanted.

"We'll start with something you all know."

As Bernard pretended to read the prayer he and his father said every day as soon as they awoke—the only one they recited while sitting—its words enclosed in all the mezuzahs in Horodno, the other boys covered their eyes with their right hands.

"Hear, Israel, the Lord is our God, the Lord is One. Blessed be the name of His glorious kingdom for ever and ever." Bernard exhaled, relieved.

As the school year progressed, it became apparent Rabbi Menshein neither saw nor heard well. When he wanted students to read or explain a passage, he ordered them to speak into his ear and raise their voices. If they kept their voices low enough, they could murmur among themselves all day.

Leib was the first to test their teacher's auditory limits, increasing his volume until he drew Menshein's stick. Those whacks, devoid of wrath, failed to instill fear and obedience.

Another pleasant discovery: Menshein always let them decide which passage from the Chumash to read aloud.

"Choose your passage, Chaim."

"I'm Bernard, Rabbi."

"Of course. Isn't that what I just said?"

∗

In his second year, when lines bled into one another like paint spills, only Bernard's keen memory still saved him from disgrace. He suppressed a bitter resentment toward his classmates. Maybe God had given out a finite dose of literacy to the world. Why didn't he get an equal share?

One language would have been daunting enough, but they practiced Hebrew for the sacred texts and Yiddish for everything but prayer. Letters reversed, flipped, and switched positions. He couldn't find the key to their secrets.

But he did have Chaim. By then, they had become best friends. Bernard waited for his father after school every day at Chaim's house, southwest of Market Square.

One snowy afternoon, shortly after he turned eight, Bernard and Chaim arrived as Chaim's older sister, Mazal, round and cheerful like her mother, escorted two baby brothers away from Mrs. Bloomenfeld and her cooking.

"L'chaim and Bernard Adonoy," she teased, playing with their names and handing over two baskets, one full of wash, the other empty. "Unless you'd rather change diapers."

The boys removed the clothes from the line, brushed off the dusting of snow, and replaced the frozen shirts and pants with the new wash.

"Doesn't Mazal want to go to school?" Bernard asked Chaim when they went back inside and warmed their hands above the stove.

"Mama says she teaches her whatever she needs to know."

Mrs. Bloomenfeld was plucking chickens in the kitchen. Chaim's brothers escaped from Mazal, ran to their mother, and grabbed her apron.

"Boys, boys." Mrs. Bloomenfeld lifted one in each arm. "How will I get anything done with you hanging on?" One of the toddlers reached for her breast. The other lunged and sent the pile of feathers flying. The little boys yelped as the white floaters landed on the counters and floor. They wiggled free, ran in circles, and threw handfuls at each other.

Mrs. Bloomenfeld called Mazal for help. Feathers coated her hair and stuck to her dress. She flapped her arms and squawked, "Keep these barbarians out! Chaim, take Bernard into our bedroom to study." She handed Chaim a plate of freshly baked biscuits.

Bernard and Chaim closed the door to Mr. and Mrs. Bloomenfeld's room. They enjoyed the biscuits, and after a while, Chaim pulled out the Chumash. They'd progressed through Genesis, and God had created night and day, shaped all the animals, banished Adam and Eve, and sentenced the serpent to a slithering, despised existence.

Chaim read: "Then God said to Noah and to his sons with him, 'As for me, I am establishing my covenant with you and your descendants after you, and with every living creature that is with you . . .'"

Bernard repeated the same passage and passed the book back.

"Do you think God is perfect, Chaim?"

"He must be, or he wouldn't be God."

"But God created us, right? So why aren't we perfect?"

"We're not God."

"But in his image. We should be perfect too."

Chaim scratched his head and shrugged. "Let's read, Bernard." He took another bite of biscuit.

"Don't you want to talk about it?"

"Mmm."

"Why do you think God ordered Abraham to sacrifice Isaac?"

Chaim took a gulp of milk before objecting. "We're not up to that part yet."

"But you know the story. We've heard it in shul."

"He's God. He can do anything he wants." Chaim always struggled to interpret the stories.

Bernard rushed to explain. "It was a test. He never wanted Abraham to kill his son. When Abraham agreed, do you think he really would have done it? He was also testing God." He paused. "Chaim, can you keep a secret?"

Chaim looked at Bernard and put his arm around him.

He had to trust Chaim. "I haven't told anyone this," Bernard whispered. "I can't read." He'd thought about it for weeks, ever since Rabbi Menshein had started assigning their verses. The inevitable and disastrous call to read something he didn't already know terrified him.

"What do you mean? You read all the time."

"I just listen to what you say and recite the same words."

Chaim's brow furrowed. "You read in class with Rabbi Menshein."

"I only repeat Chumash passages I memorized."

"Is something wrong with your eyes? You should tell your father."

"No. My father thinks I'm a born scholar."

"What are you going to do?"

"I had this idea. You help me read in kheyder, and I help you think about the meaning."

"Like a trade at market, right?"

"A covenant—much more serious. We need to seal our promise."

"What does that mean?"

"You know how Abraham and the men circumcised themselves?"

"We're already circumcised. Can't we just promise?" Chaim blinked rapidly.

The next afternoon, Bernard pulled out a rusty horseshoe and worn yarmulke from a canvas sack and laid them on the bed. Chaim held the horseshoe up to his face, the upturned ends giving him the world's biggest smile.

"Now, your sacrifices, Chaim."

Chaim reached into his pocket, pulled out a folded paper with

Hebrew letters, and read, "Chaim and Bernard are best friends."

He handed Bernard his lucky stone, plucked from the banks of the Niemen. Bernard ran his thumb over the stone's smooth surface, and Chaim did the same, before they put all the offerings in the sack.

They climbed out the window, careful not to make noise. In fifteen minutes they arrived at the Niemen. They started across the bridge and stopped halfway. They waited until a stooped peasant pulling an empty cart crossed over to the left bank.

"Let's do it together." Bernard counted to three and said, "Chaim and Bernard are friends forever." They both let go of the sack, and their treasures dropped into the river.

✳

Weeks after the covenant, hordes of grackles began to cluster in the trees and fields alongside the Niemen. A false early spring had lured the birds back prematurely. Their noisy chittering, sudden flights, and unpredictable dips and soars entertained Horodno's winter-weary Jews.

For the ancient soothsayer known only as Widow Goresh, however, the angry birds filling the sky recalled the tragic past and predicted a grim future. Widow Goresh spent her days wandering the town, reading palms for a kopek, warning whoever would listen of approaching doom.

Bernard and his father spotted her occasionally along the river or standing on the bridge talking to herself, staring down into the water. One morning, as they approached the kheyder, the Widow Goresh stood on a crate in front of the Great Wooden Shul addressing passing religious men. They all ignored her. Bernard and his father paused for a moment, curious as she pointed to the deep creases in her age-ravaged face and recited a litany of ruination—the Lithuanian expulsion, Chmielnicki massacre, Russian and Swedish invasions—from one genocide to the next before she moved to even bleaker prophesies for the Jews in Russia.

Bernard had faith these calamities belonged to another age. He was too young to remember the bloody Odessa riots just four years ago, when men with metal clubs beat Jews and smashed the windows of Jewish shops. The greatest tragedy of his life, he believed, would be his failure to read.

Indeed, later that morning when the rabbi assigned Bernard a passage, Exodus, Chapter 23, the first time he couldn't rely on memory, he trembled with the immediate risk of exposure as a fake and the awful shame his father would bear. This felt different than practicing from Leviticus at Chaim's house. There, they'd perfected a dramatic pause after Nadbad's and Abihu's consumption in fire for disobeying the Lord.

Bernard moved slowly to give Chaim time to find the passage. A slate with a vertical lightning-bolt crack hung behind the rabbi's desk. Through their window, the dead stirred in their graves beneath the cemetery's ancient frost-heaved stones.

Some of his classmates had laid their heads on their forearms, others fiddled the pages of the Chumash. Only he anticipated his looming downfall, and the urge to run out of kheyder grew so strong he started to shake.

Rabbi Menshein leaned his ear close to Bernard and nodded. Bernard coughed, signaling Chaim who whispered the first verse: "You shall not accept a false report; do not place your hand with a wicked person to be a false witness."

Bernard waited for Chaim to stop before he repeated what he'd just heard. The tremor in his voice and hitch in his speech would surely bring the rabbi's furious denunciation. They continued this way until the final verse, which Bernard liked more than the first. "If you see your enemy's donkey lying under its burden, would you refrain from helping him? You shall surely help along with him."

When Menshein marched them off to lunch, all twelve classmates crowded together at one table. The rabbis always ate together, the boys relieved to be unsupervised. Leib and Shlomo Fetterman sat on one side of Bernard. Chaim, Daniel Zweig, and Joshua Bornstein sat on the other. Daniel, a dreamy boy, sometimes smiled to himself for no apparent reason. Joshua had come to kheyder on two occasions with blackened eyes. "An accident," he'd told them, but no one believed him.

Jacob Rosenblum, the best student, sat across from Bernard. Jacob, like Bernard, never laughed when Leib imitated Rabbi Menshein during lunch, calling each food by the wrong name. He wasn't amused, either, when Leib made his "Menshein bird" out of paper, flapped it under their classroom table, and repeated their teacher's name in a squeaky voice.

To Jacob's right—Daniel Pinkman, a bony boy with bitter breath who ate pickles and sauerkraut for lunch; Itsik Gilstein, his glasses as thick as their rabbi's; and Michael Kellorman, hands cracked like old leather from working with his father, a tanner. On Jacob's left—Joshua Goodman, his fingers always ink stained; Nathan Friedman, the youngest of ten siblings; and David Haukman, who Menshein rarely called on because he cried with nervousness when he had to stand in front of the class.

Bernard got along with his classmates, and much better than the others with Leib, whose sharp wit and insults drove the boys away, so only Bernard and Shlomo would sit next to him.

Leib looked around, rapped on the table, and said, "Nu, Bernard? We all heard Chaim read first, and you repeat the same verse."

Bernard had prepared for this. He shrugged. "I help Chaim understand the passages and he helps me with the reading."

"You've read before, and now you're telling us you can't, which means you've fooled everyone. Did you just memorize passages ahead of time? What's in it for us not to tell?"

"Because you're not a rotten snitch, Leib." Chaim's face had turned as red as his hair.

Leib continued to study Bernard, as they all did now. Bernard had decided to leave things in God's hands. He described his problem and what it would do to his father to find out. "That's why I have to keep this secret. Perhaps God sent me this affliction as a test of my wits, like the blind who have to learn to maneuver around obstacles."

Heads nodded and eyes glistened, but Jacob shifted uneasily on the bench. Leib asked, "What's that to me? My father's a drunken lout."

Days after he'd revealed his secret, Bernard sat across from Jacob again in the noisy lunchroom. He'd made progress gaining the other boys' sympathy. He'd helped several with math and others with interpreting the religious teachings, as he did for Chaim. Why would they turn on him now? But Jacob and Leib didn't need his help with math or analyzing the long, rambling stories the rabbi told—one because of his serious scholarship, the other because he didn't care.

Bernard pushed a triangular rugela his father had helped him bake across the table.

"I have extra today, Jacob."

Jacob took a tentative bite and licked the fruit jam residue from his lips. "This is delicious rugela," he mumbled, followed by a heartier "Thank you." Jacob leaned forward and briefly smiled. Bernard passed him another pastry and felt his classmates watching. He'd brought enough for everyone. Only Leib refused.

"I don't want your bribe, Garfinkle."

That night, his father complimented him for sharing with his classmates, and Bernard beat back his guilt. Didn't Father hide vodka from the tax farmers?

Bernard distributed the treats once a week. Give them too much of a good thing and it loses value. His father had taught him about supply and demand. Nobody questioned that he gave Leib's share to Jacob, or that he gave another to Jacob each morning as well.

✳

Several months after the start of his rugelach campaign, on a promising May afternoon, with cottons replacing wool on the wash lines, Bernard and his father prepared their Shabes stew. The meat, beans, potatoes, and barley, slow cooked for the next day, made his mouth water. At sundown, he lit the candles and recited kiddush over the wine his father permitted him to taste.

After dinner, as they piled dishes in the sink, Solomon said, "Many times, I thought I should remarry, Bernard, for you to have a mother after Deborah. Did I tell you she would sing in the kitchen? After a nightingale, how could I settle for a crow?"

"Don't you get lonely, Father?"

His father turned and wrapped his arms around Bernard, then retrieved their chessboard and placed it on the cleared table. They couldn't wash dishes or do unnecessary housework on Shabes, which didn't bother Bernard. The only loss—his father forbade stacking wood, his favorite job. Bernard forgot this hardship when the chessmen appeared. Separated by color, the pieces fit snugly in the compact, sturdy box his father had made.

When he'd first learned to play, he asked, "Why do we keep the crosses on the kings? Isn't that a potasy?"

"Apostasy." His father chuckled. "No, the rabbis ruled if it's not used as a religious symbol, the crosses get to stay on the king's head."

Solomon placed each of his pieces on one side of the board, and Bernard set up the other, centering them in their assigned squares. If only he could hold words in his hand and run his thumb over their surfaces, as he did with the worn wooden pieces—the jagged edge of the rook, the cone of the bishop, the curled mane of the knight. How would it feel to read books as effortlessly as he read positions on the board?

The next morning, instead of praying at home when they rose at dawn, they walked to the Great Wooden Shul. Its log first story with Gothic-style windows supported a second floor wrapped in vertical pine siding. Six overlapping roofs narrowed to a pointed triangular cap. Outside, the building's weathered gray coat belied the lush interior—a carved balcony for the women and girls beneath a soaring blue dome with magnificent illustrations of Samson chained in the temple, Jonah swallowed in the belly of the whale, and Daniel with nothing but his faith to use against the lions. The endurance of the structure through the centuries, despite the cycle of invasion, plunder, and occupation, made him think the superstition might be right: Jews would thrive in Horodno as long as this shul stood.

Bernard searched for his friends before the service began. Chaim fiddled with his peyes. Behind him, Leib rocked in his seat and spoke to Shlomo, who remained silent and gloomy. Their uncle put his hand on Leib, who settled back, miserable.

Leib had the same restless energy in shul as in kheyder. Some of the grownups, though, men Bernard knew one way in town, magically transformed as soon as they walked through the doors. Zalman the candlemaker, who screamed at his wife in front of customers, treating her like a misbehaving employee, now whispered lovingly in his grandson's ear. Lipman the bookseller, known for peddling books banned by some rabbis, carried his Tanakh as if he held the Messiah. Yankl the candy merchant, who ran children out of his shop with a broom if they were a kopek short, had the pious expression of a man who might be transported straight to heaven at any moment.

The service lasted all morning, with prayers they stood and sat for, recited and sung. Bernard loved the moment the rabbi lifted the Torah scroll from the ark and carried it throughout the shul. He and his father touched the burgundy velvet cover and kissed their own hands. When the rabbi took up his pointer, Bernard felt intense happiness. What did it matter if a boy across the aisle read along? The word of God lived in his heart, as Father said.

Following the service, they went home for the meal they'd simmered overnight. "But if we can't light fires, why is it okay to cook?"

"True, so we have to keep one going."

"If it's wrong to light one, Father, how can it be right to let one burn?"

"Wrong to light, Bernard, but also wrong to extinguish."

How can it be wrong to do something and also wrong to stop doing it? Bernard wanted to fix this inconsistency, and the ones he witnessed in shul, like a smudge on his best shirt.

Later, as the sun dipped below the horizon, Bernard leaned against his father on the flat rock in their yard. On cloudy days they had to guess when Shabes ended, but tonight they would wait for the first three stars. He craned his neck and searched for the twinkling light. "There's one, two, three." Too many to count.

On Sundays Bernard helped at the distillery. Upon rising, he prayed with his father. Occasionally his shame clamored for attention, as it did that morning. He used the Shema to hammer it back under the surface.

Before breakfast, Bernard went out to their small barn. Alte Ferd raised his head and snorted the air. Bernard had named him Old Horse, although he and the horse were the same age. They took Alte Ferd to the distillery for particular jobs and whenever his father wanted to smuggle unstamped vodka to his secret cache beneath the barn floor.

"Back to work today, old boy," Bernard said into the horse's ear. He carried over a pail of grain from a wooden bin, and the horse whinnied. He filled the trough with fresh water and made five trips behind a partition for armloads of hay.

After breakfast, they prepared two wrapped lunches. Bernard helped his father harness Alte Ferd and hitch the wagon. Church bells rang as they passed the western tip of Market Square in the town center. In some neighborhoods, Jews and Christians mixed like stones along the riverbank. Bernard compared the crosses of Horodno's churches to their own plain wooden mezuzah, which could fit in his hand, and thought about something his father had told him—God could take many forms. So, besides their shul, why couldn't He be in a peddler's cart, the noisy street, maybe even a church with its giant cross?

As they crossed the Niemen, Bernard wondered where the old soothsayer was this morning and if the covenant bag remained where he and Chaim had dropped it two months before.

His father tugged the reins when they reached the opposite bank and pointed back to the looming Shereshevski factory, built two years ago. "A reminder how fortunate we are."

Bernard felt sorry for Chaim's father, who worked there. He moved slowly and sometimes fell asleep in shul.

"Moses delivered us from slavery, but he forgot Shereshevski's workers. Foul air and no breaks for twelve hours. We wouldn't treat Alte Ferd that way."

"Yes, Father. Garfinkle's Spirits' first principle—treat the worker and customers as you want to be treated. Hillel said: 'that which is despicable to you, do not do to another.'"

"Correct. An eye for an eye, and we'd all stumble around."

"Father . . ." Bernard hesitated. He knew adult matters could be complicated. "Doesn't vodka make some people do bad things?" He'd witnessed a drunken man in the market waving a jug in one hand and dragging a woman by her hair with the other. The police had freed her and led the man away, but what would happen in the privacy of their home?

"Something good in measured quantity can turn evil in excess, Bernard. Gluttony is harmful, whether it's food, gold, land, or vodka." Solomon sighed. "So much has been forbidden Russia's Jews. We must work how we can or starve. Are you ready for the second principle now? Or perhaps we should wait until you're older. It might be too confusing."

"Test me, Father."

"Rabbi Hillel also preached, 'If we don't look out for ourselves, who will?' That's the second principle, Bernard. Isn't it the opposite of the first?"

"It doesn't have to be either the head or tail of a coin. When we treat our worker fairly, he returns our respect to the vodka. Good for him and us—principles one and two."

Solomon clapped. "Hillel added: 'If I am only for myself, what am I?' You must not think of a material payment for doing what's right. Kindness comes from the heart, not calculated from the head."

"Father, when will you teach me the third principle?"

Solomon smiled. "When you're ready."

"I'm ready now, Father."

"Look at the river, Bernard. Can you make it move faster?"

Another lesson, but not the one he wanted.

The distillery sat in a clearing, halfway up a gently sloping hill with a view of town. He leapt down from the wagon and strained to pull open the double doors of the barn attached to the distillery. He slipped each of the door hooks through two iron rings bolted to the building.

After they unhitched and settled Alte Ferd, Bernard tested his strength again. Only in the past year could he handle by himself the distillery's heavy sliding door his father had built. They greeted Melachim, their sole employee, and Solomon went off to tinker with the second still he'd recently purchased.

"My helper, just in time. Whew, my aching back." Melachim opened one valve, closed another, and grunted.

Bernard grabbed the undersized shovel his father had made for him. He struggled to reach over the high lip of a fermentation tub to empty his scoop of grain, so Melachim lifted him. "Don't drop me in, Melachim!"

"We'd really have Garfinkle's Spirits, then."

Securely suspended in Melachim's grasp, Bernard emptied his child-sized load. Melachim set him on the floor and began to jig. Quick on his feet for a beefy man, he kicked his legs out in a parody of the Cossack dance. He had a round cheerful face, and as he danced, he smiled at

Bernard and sang in a vibrant and spirited baritone:
Vodka cold and clear as ice,
Her eyes black as coal, Hey,
Vodka warms my feet and toes,
Her lips warm my soul! Hey!

Melachim stopped to catch his breath. "I'm a pretty fellow, eh?" Before Bernard could answer, Melachim began cleaning the still.

Bernard grabbed the broom from the corner and swept the floor. When they finished their tasks, they went outside and enjoyed two apples.

"Oy, Bernard," Melachim confided, "my wife no longer speaks to me. It's been almost two years since we've shared the conjugal bed." Bernard wondered what that meant.

"Do I ask for freedom, or do I carry this burden until I break?"

Bernard worried Melachim expected him to have the right answer. "Father always says, it's not about what feels right at this moment, but what will feel right years from now." Uneasy, he thought of his deception.

"For such wisdom, you get to light the fire. Who says our righteous deeds are rewarded only in heaven?"

※

One cloudless day during the summer of 1863, before Bernard's third year in Holy Land Kheyder began, a drumming of distant thunder wrinkled his father's brow as they labeled buckets of vodka.

"What is it, Father? The Polish Rebellion? Leib said the Poles fight for freedom, and we should be on their side." He had heard Leib talking of it the previous spring at school before Rabbi Menshein cut him off and declared it wasn't the Jews' business. The adults had so many whispered conversations now, and why did his father suddenly hire men to distribute their vodka instead of doing it himself?

"Czar Alexander has a good heart, Bernard. Look what he's done already. The Poles want their own country, to be in charge of their affairs as we do, but push too fast, too hard . . . Sometimes when people disagree about the right way to live, they succumb to anger and violence.

A grave sin."

"But the Torah . . ."

"Stories to teach right from wrong. Real punishment belongs to God."

Bernard dipped his brush into the glue bowl and coated the back of another label. His father centered it on a bucket and rolled it out.

"We speak Polish and Russian. Could we help them understand?"

"Not every problem has an obvious solution, Bernard. It takes great faith and trust to find one with an adversary."

That afternoon, walking home, his father guided him to the edge of the road as Russian soldiers in dirty uniforms and tired horses passed. Some eyed them without apparent interest; others swayed, half-asleep in their saddles. Bernard counted over forty riders and five wagons, four covered by tattered canvas, carrying supplies. In the fifth, the wounded, wrapped in bandages, reclined against the rails or lay prone. For weeks he dreamed about those men and wondered if they believed in their cause.

3

Something new in the Russian soldiers' faces worried Estes. They'd often come to Horodno from their nearby camp. They visited the market and entered Papa's shop. They spoke to her, not unkindly, and she gathered more Russian vocabulary with each encounter. Lately, though, it seemed they'd bitten something hard and cracked a tooth.

Trips to the library had always included stops. Now, Mama gripped her hand and they walked with purpose. There would be no lingering during these times.

"Mama, shouldn't we be on the Polish side?" she asked at dinner. "The weak against the strong?"

"It's not clear it would be better for us than Alexander's reforms."

"But don't the Poles want freedom, too, Papa? Isn't that what we celebrate every Pesach?"

Papa snorted. "The Russians will soon crush this uprising, and woe to anyone who supported their enemy. Why poke a wolf with a stick when he's cornered his prey? Better to stand clear. Anyway, I make shoes. Both armies need them."

The war never came any closer to Horodno, and six months later, the distant rumbles diminished and finally vanished. Papa said, "Good day," in his choppy Russian to soldiers in clean uniforms who visited the shop.

"We Jews have survived, Estes, keyn eynhore," Papa said. "Wait long enough, and all this will be forgotten like a bothersome guest."

✳

But three years passed and the bothersome guest lingered. The Russian garrison expanded. The once-boisterous Polish in the market had turned into secretive whispers. The Russian authorities seized Polish books in the library, executed, imprisoned, or exiled leaders of the rebellion, and fined those caught mourning their dead. The Jews of Horodno, however, had mostly stayed clear of the struggle. Belief in the czar's reforms remained strong.

In the Leving house, books lay open on Estes's bed, piled on the floor, and displayed in three bookcases filled with volumes from Uncle Simon or purchased from book peddlers. She cradled *Jane Eyre*, her favorite, which she'd just finished for the third time—a miracle, authored by a woman with a heroine at the center. She loved talking with Mama about Jane's sorrows and triumphs.

"My grazer has transformed into a carnivore," Mama said. "Today you're eleven, Estes. You have years to read and discuss all these. Come."

As Papa put a felt crown on her head and served her a piece of the babka, Estes appreciated that her family recognized yearly birthdays, when many Jews only celebrated particular milestones as significant. She opened the wrapped gifts—a collection of Charles Dickens in German from her parents, and a Russian translation of Jane Eyre in *Otechestvennye Zapiski* magazine from Uncle Simon.

She glanced at Papa. When she'd begun learning the Russian alphabet during one of Uncle Simon's annual visits, Papa had said, "First German, now Russian? It's not enough I taught you to speak it? You have to read and write it too? Next, you'll be on your knees, praying like a goy."

"I don't pray at all, Papa."

His eyes widened and he cleared his throat.

"And why shouldn't I have more languages than Jacob Rosenblum?"

Papa grumbled that she was worse than a yeshiva student with his Talmud.

At first, with the simple primers, she had pinched her lips in frustration—a concert pianist restricted to one finger. More complex books followed and never left her side. She stole glances at them during dinner, on her way to the outhouse, and in the shop.

Papa complained again when she began to write long sentences in Cyrillic, but when she corrected Uncle Simon's faulty grammar during his most recent stay, Papa had suddenly praised her scholarship.

"Two more gifts," Papa said. He held up her new boots. "See how the shaft fits your ankle? Inside, the nest is perfectly shaped for the foot."

Estes admired the polished brown leather. With Papa's artistry, the sole of her right boot would contact the ground, though she would always walk on the edge of her foot. But not even his magic could hide that she wore two different boots. "They're beautiful, Papa."

Papa stepped into the hall and returned with a cane, longer than the first one he'd made her years ago. Back then, he'd called it a walking stick—something a shepherd might use. It will help with the pain, he'd told her.

"It's for old people." Estes had refused to have it near her.

Last year, she gave in to the inevitable: her foot would never get better. A cane didn't identify her as a cripple any more than her lopsided gait already did. Now she rubbed the curved handle like a discerning shopper at market. She examined the straight grain lines and the shiny metal tip.

"Thank you, Papa." She poked him gently in the side.

The following afternoon, as she walked to the library with Mama, Estes leaned into the cane and let it take her weight. In the square, the remains of market day—clumps of animal droppings, feathers, fruit probed by too many dirty fingers, and general litter—had been cleared from the cobblestones.

One block east, an old watercarrier, his gray vest pulled askew by his yoke, bent under the weight of two full buckets. Nearby, a young man with a melancholic mustache and deep scar across his cheek called out sizes of the shoes draped across his chest and back. Estes noticed the mediocre quality of the leather and the wares other peddlers hauled in baskets and handcarts. Neither they nor the shoppers who clustered around these men noticed her in the crowd.

She brought her cane down forcefully. Estes didn't want to resemble the blind, who cautiously swept the ground in front of them, or the old and feeble, who trembled. So many people had visible defects—missing fingers, a purple birthmark covering half a face, a back curled with age.

She might bear her own if someone noticed the beautiful things too. In the library, when she read from *The Russian Messenger* for Moshe Knorozovski, he whistled and beckoned other patrons to listen. Estes paused for Moshe to tell her she read better than Jacob Rosenblum. Instead, he told Mama about the Russian reading class in the library and encouraged them to enroll. "Begins tonight. Once a week through summer. It came about quickly. It's mostly adults, but there will be another bright youngster—Jacob Rosenblum."

That evening she and Mama passed through the stacks of books and arrived first to the narrow classroom. Eleven sturdy wood chairs faced a narrow podium. An adjacent table with books drew her attention—Gogol, Pushkin, Turgenev. Famous names. She would read to Mama, of course. Would Jacob Rosenblum already have the books? She didn't want him to have a head start.

She and Mama sat close to the door in the second row. A young couple in front of them held hands. The man's side-whiskers flared out at the cheeks, and his companion's pinned hair formed an egg-shaped bump on the top of her head. Two young men in matching gray uniforms and cadet hats spoke Russian too quickly for her to catch every word. A woman around Mama's age and a man, considerably older, with a crooked cane, said sholem and filled out the first row.

Estes flinched when Avram and Jacob Rosenblum came in. Over the years, besides at shul and the library, she'd encountered him occasionally in the shoe shop. The two families hadn't socialized since that Pesach debacle years ago, and Jacob's singing had since led the Rosenblums to more prestigious Seders. He might have been a different species; they had so little to say to each other. In his male world, he would finish kheyder, then yeshiva, achieve rabbinical ordination, and along the way obtain a wife to cook, clean, and raise his children. With his bright blue eyes, sandy hair, and curly, shoulder-length peyes, Jacob remained a pretty boy, grown quite large, though, stuffed with his father's compliments.

"Ah, Doris, Moshe said you and Estes had signed up. Jacob's already begun reading the shorter stories by Gogol. His Russian is much better than mine. He may want to be a crown rabbi. We need good representation, you know."

Behold my son!

"Congratulations, Jacob," Mama said. "I'm happy you and Estes are in class together."

"Thank you, Mrs. Leving." Jacob blushed.

"We've been reading English writers—Dickens, Charlotte Brontë, and Jane Austen," Estes said.

"Women authors, how interesting," Avram Rosenblum said. He turned away from her and led Jacob to chairs at the end of their row, leaving an empty seat between them.

Moshe Knorozovski swept in, greeted them, and asked Estes and Jacob to help him pass around the first books. Estes laid her cane under her chair and limped to the table.

"Ah, our last student. Mrs. Feinberg has arrived. Welcome."

Everyone stopped talking. This woman drew every eye in the room. Her silky hair pinned back from her face and the white flower above her ear showed off her brown eyes. She wore two black necklaces, a white bodice, and an elegant burgundy dress with three columns of buttons. The lower of two frilled hems nearly touched the floor.

"Please call me Sophie," she responded in refined Russian, not mixed with Yiddish like Papa's, or clipped like the Russian cadets'.

Mama stood and Mrs. Feinberg squeezed by. Estes followed and passed her a book.

"Spasibo," Sophie said and gave Estes a warm smile.

"We'll start with Gogol's stories, 'The Nose' and 'The Overcoat,' followed by Pushkin's *Eugene Onegin,* and finish with the most tempestuous and controversial, Turgenev's *Fathers and Children.*" Moshe opened his book and began: "'On the twenty-fifth day of March, an extraordinarily strange incident occurred in Petersburg.'"

✳

The summer passed too quickly, slipping away like Kovalev's runaway nose. Farewell to Akaky, Bazarov, Madame Odintsova, Onegin, Tatyana, and the Rosenblums, neither of whom looked at Estes after the time she corrected Jacob's pronunciation. The boy and his father had reddened, one with shame, the other with anger. Although Avram Rosenblum had Jacob practice at home, he still stumbled over some words when he read in class, just as she occasionally did but undoubtedly less often than he.

Sophie Feinberg, who had lived in Petersburg her entire life until now, had acted as a second teacher with her perfect Russian and insightful knowledge of the literature. She invited Estes and her mother to her house, north of Market Square, following the last class at the library. Mama had invited Sophie to lunch and tea several times, but Sophie had always politely refused.

On this afternoon, Sophie poured three cups of tea arranged on woven place mats depicting scenes of rural life.

"Do you play?" Mama pointed to the old piano, the finish worn and scratched.

"Yes. In Petersburg I gave lessons."

"What brought you to Horodno?" Estes asked.

"My husband spent his childhood not far from here. He died last year." Sophie paused. "He was forty-five and I was eighteen when we married. After decades of army service he'd been elevated to colonel, even without converting. He had an iron will. The kahal turned him in when he was a young orphan."

Sophie told them about growing up in Petersburg with her father, a first guild merchant. She had a good marriage for four years, but when her husband died, the authorities ordered her expulsion to the Pale. "They said I lost the protection of my father's rank, since I had married. My husband's military service didn't apply anymore, as he was dead. We had friends, and I had many students. I'd never even visited the western territories."

Sophie massaged her temples and Mama reached out and touched her arm. "Desperation drove me to apply for a yellow card." Her hand trembled when she picked up her tea. "The state will grant even a Jew freedom of residence for serving on the battlefield like my husband, or in a woman's case, if she agrees to serve in bed."

Sophie shook her head. "I had planned to stay in our home under this pretense and continue teaching music. What a fool. When an official came and wanted me to . . . I refused, of course. He got quite angry because I didn't accommodate him, and I feared he would force me. Instead, he pushed me into exile."

Estes, embarrassed by her ignorance, didn't ask questions. She knew about yellow cards and the shame of prostitution but didn't exactly understand what the Russians expected Sophie to do. None of these particulars came out in *Jane Eyre* or her other novels.

"They drove me out like a criminal. That Russian official watched while I bought my ticket. I debated going through to Warsaw but decided to try Horodno first. Before I boarded my train, this man informed me he would notified the district governor's office and report me as an unmanageable prostitute. So, with one spiteful stroke, he would brand me as both indecent and disobedient.

"Horodno is a small city. A word here and there, and one might as well be a typhoid carrier. I hope enough time will pass soon without any repercussions, that perhaps he didn't follow through with his threat. But until I'm sure his slander won't become public knowledge, I don't dare teach music."

"We can help you find work now," Mama said, "until you're ready to take students again."

"I consider myself a seamstress," Sophie said. "I make my own dresses."

"You could cut and sew for Herman."

Sophie gripped each of their hands. Estes couldn't wait to go home and tell Papa.

When Papa lit his cigar after dinner, Mama told him about Sophie's problem and left no room for dissent.

He sat up and knocked his ash into a silver tray. "It would be bad enough to crowd the shop with unneeded help. Now we're in the business of employing prostitutes?"

Mama stood, grabbed a cup off the table, and flung it against the floor. Ceramic shards skittered across the wide pine planks, and Estes felt her heart racing. Mama never showed this much anger.

"If you had half-listened to me, you wouldn't refuse her a chance. You already hire out some cutting and sewing. She's more skilled than anyone else you use."

"Doris . . ."

"What happened to the kind man I married?"

Mama left the room and Estes followed. They sat on Mama's bed and waited. A few minutes later, Papa knocked softly on the door.

✳

Winter arrived early that year and snow framed the edges of the window facing the square. Sophie helped Estes clean up the shop at closing while Papa took care of their last customer.

That night at dinner Papa announced, "Three tables in the Leving

Shoe Shop. We're becoming a factory. Sophie is bright, and a hard worker with an excellent eye for detail. She not only cuts and sews to exact measurements, but her stitches rival my own. She's even learned how to make patterns, and if she went into business for herself, she'd be the second-best in Horodno. We're selling shoes at twice the usual speed. Hiring her was the best decision I've ever made."

Mama smiled but said nothing.

4

By the spring of Bernard's fifth year, Rabbi Menshein no longer required the boys to read aloud. A blessing, because Chaim had tried teaching him after kheyder, and a few of their classmates had joined in for a while, but Bernard still couldn't read. The letter sounds he tried to blend into words resisted like mismatched puzzle pieces. He couldn't bear the frustration and embarrassment.

The days passed with rote learning and long lectures on the Torah, which mirrored the section the rabbi had introduced that week in shul. Bernard and his classmates never complained about their teacher or the typical long day of dreary exercises because they heard the rabbinical oaths and sounds of justice from the other rooms. Theirs had a window, and Menshein allowed a fresh breeze to sweep over them.

Although his fear of exposure had diminished, Bernard's guilt, which intruded everywhere, gnawed at him, a sharp-clawed creature that scratched from the inside. Especially following the *thwaks* of the other rabbi's paddles and during prayers, he felt it digging, trying to come out.

During somber Yom Kiper the previous fall, Bernard thought he'd finally confess to his father and teacher, but he said nothing. For Sukkos, Bernard had searched the woods with his classmates to gather sticks and boughs for the harvest hut. While Rabbi Menshein stretched out in the leaves, the boys scurried back and forth, rescuing building materials from the mossy decay on the forest floor. Bernard's falsehood felt flimsier than the shed they built, roofed with ferns and bound with rope.

Then, when they'd put on a Purim play for the whole school a few weeks ago, Queen Esther's courage shamed him. So did Leib's, when he stepped forward to take the role of Haman that no one wanted and transformed himself into the ominous villain with his cotton beard and charcoal scowl. The hiss of the audience and the rattle of noisemakers had drowned out his voice.

Still, Bernard bore his guilt and did his best to conceal his defect. Chaim even transcribed Bernard's dictated commentaries in handwriting different from his own, not that Menshein would have ever noticed a gimel with a thicker top, an alef with a longer foot. When Bernard convinced Shlomo to be his emergency reader if Chaim was ever absent, Leib had given them both a carnivore's toothy appraisal.

But one situation Bernard never anticipated—he and Chaim called together, standing in front of the class, Rabbi Menshein between them with an unruly hair standing straight up out of his thick brow.

"Boys, here we have interesting statements on this topic. Why does God send us old age, sickness, and death?" Menshein folded one arm across his chest and unfurled it toward this calamitous end.

Bernard knew it wasn't this ultimate fate that caused his classmates to freeze, but rather his and Chaim's impending doom. Even Leib paid attention.

"Tell us your answers," Menshein ordered, waving their papers.

Age had drawn their slumping teacher toward the earth while the boys sprouted up around him. Bernard bent over and spoke into his teacher's hairy ear. Satisfied, the rabbi leaned toward Chaim and waited, so close to them both that detection would follow if Bernard tried to assist. As Bernard feared, once Chaim had written what Bernard dictated, it left his mind. How would Father take the news? Not only had his son been lying all this time, but, much worse, he was an idiot.

"God challenges us, so we grow stronger. Awareness of death helps us live the life he gave us more fully. Knowing of sickness, we are grateful for health. Experiencing loss, we appreciate abundance." Jacob Rosenblum spoke in a low voice. Jacob, who appeared to ignore the banter at lunch, but lit up when asked about a Torah passage, must have heard Bernard telling Chaim what to write. He threw a rope, and Chaim didn't let go.

Rabbi Menshein sent them back to their bench with a quizzical half-smile on his lips. Bernard tried to catch Jacob's eye, but his savior had bowed his head over the next assignment.

※

During the winter of 1867, Bernard's sixth and final year at Holy Land, two fevers spread throughout the city. One, a sudden recurrence of tension between the Polish Catholics and the Russian Orthodox rulers, and the other, a chess spectacle.

Most Jews ignored the first, referred to as the "Campaign for Morality." The Orthodox bishop, with the support of the district governor, publicly denounced Polish rebel sympathizers, prostitutes, and "undesirables." Only a battle between Christians, the rabbis and his father insisted, a fake moral inquisition.

As the governor posted the list of sins, Bernard and his classmates turned to the other obsession. Chess master Steinitz, a poor Jew and youngest of thirteen children, the best in the world, would visit in April to conduct a simultaneous exhibition. Boards appeared everywhere—on shop counters, the backs of carts, even in the shul. The bishops the Jews thought about were the ones carved from wood.

The rabbis would select the best player in the kheyder to join forty-nine other aspirants in testing their skills against the genius. Rabbi Menshein surprised them one day when he unveiled six chess sets. Now they played throughout lunch, ignored their food, and studied tangled positions.

*

Only Bernard and Leib emerged unscathed from the kheyder competition, and on the day before they would battle each other for the right to play Steinitz, the twins invited Bernard and Chaim over. The Fetterman home was even more cramped than Chaim's. Mrs. Fetterman shared a bedroom with her two older daughters. In the other bedroom, the twins had to cram into one bed while their grandfather snored insufferably in the other.

"It's a never-ending shofar, reminding us to atone for our sins," Leib told them. "Grandfather is with Mother and the girls now, pushing a cart at market. No news from our father for six months. We think he's somewhere clearing a forest for a new rail line."

Shlomo snorted. "Mom hasn't received a single ruble in all this time."

Leib tipped an imaginary bottle to his lips.

In the yard, chickens scratched around a weedy garden and a decaying wood fence. Leib caught one of the birds and held it up by its feet as it squawked and rotated its neck.

"You're next old girl, but not tonight."

He set the squirming captive on the ground, and it resumed pecking at worms. Leib led them into the kitchen and plunked two battered chess sets on the table made of four scarred planks nailed into sawhorses. "A bit of practice."

Tomorrow, he and Leib would play, and Bernard didn't want to give away any strategy. Chess is contested on the board, but the real battle takes place in the mind, his father had told him.

"Music first?" Shlomo asked, and without waiting for an answer took a battered fiddle out of its worn case. Leib grumbled but grabbed the clarinet resting on its flared end by the door. He licked the reed and played a few notes as Shlomo ran the bow over each string and adjusted the tuning pegs.

Shlomo played a few somber, pulsing notes. Leib played a minor scale and echoed the fiddle in a call to prayer. Suddenly the tempo quickened, changing the funereal tune into a wedding dance. Chaim bounced his head and swayed in his chair. Bernard clapped his hands in time with the lively beat. In response to a sustained note on the clarinet, Shlomo slowed the fiddle. Before the pace could pick up again, Leib held up his hand and broke the trance. "Chess."

Shlomo reluctantly put the fiddle away and sat across from Chaim. Leib faced Bernard, picked up one black and one white pawn, and held them behind his back. He thrust his two fists forward and Bernard chose. Black. Leib offered his hand and Bernard shook it. They wished each other a successful game, and Leib pushed his king's pawn forward two squares.

After a few moves, Bernard spotted Mrs. Fetterman through the cracked kitchen window. She gestured at the girls and the cart. The grandfather sat on a wood chopping block in the yard. Leib and Shlomo jumped up and replaced the chess pieces and boards on their high shelf. Leib grabbed a broom, and Shlomo darted to the door just as their mother entered.

Gaunt as her sons, Mrs. Fetterman reached out and caught Shlomo by the collar before he could escape. "What's this? You're entertaining guests?"

She scrutinized Bernard and Chaim. When neither of the twins introduced them, Bernard spoke. "Glad to meet you, Mrs. Fetterman.

I'm Bernard and this is Chaim."

She nodded, her eyes on the one white pawn left on the table.

"Chess?" She turned on Leib.

"Just a quick game, Mother. Now we're doing our chores."

"We push the cart, and the two men of the house sit and play a child's game. I sacrifice to pay your kheyder fee so that you might turn out more useful than your father."

She addressed her captive. "Help your sisters unload the cart and clean out the chicken shed." She let go of his collar and smacked him hard across the top of the head. Shlomo gasped and darted out before she could deliver another blow.

"You, Leib! Out to the root cellar. Bring six beets and two onions. Chop them for me. You can clean the kitchen and help grandfather with his bath after dinner."

Leib did not race out. His mother stood guarding the door, her hand raised. When he got within striking distance, he slowed, and when her hand shot out quick as a snake, he didn't try to move away. *Thwack!* on the left cheek. He offered his right. *Thwack!* Leib acted as nonchalant about these real blows, which left his cheeks bright red, as he did when Menshein delivered his harmless swats.

"Tomorrow, Bernard. For the championship," he said, then stoically received one more blow, this time on his backside.

✳

Every class gathered in the lunchroom to watch the contest. Leib played the king's gambit, full of danger for both players, but Bernard did not accept the offered pawn, instead aiming his bishop at white's exposed king. Leib had pushed for a decisive duel, but rather than pistols or broadswords, Bernard chose fencing sabers.

Leib launched a furious assault. Bernard would only survive with a counterattack. He didn't want to lose, not to Leib, not in front of the whole school. His chess skill didn't make up for his reading problem, but it helped.

The adversaries threw everything against each other—pawns, backed by rooks and the queen, supported by harassing knights and bishops—in a race to break through first. Pieces fell, and the stark truth on the board emerged as the two armies thinned out.

✳

The master traveled inside a perimeter of fifty-one chess boards set up in the Choral Shul. Glad that he faced the curtained ark, rather than the spectators along both sides and in the balcony, Bernard concentrated on his board. Next to him, Leib futilely tried to twirl his short hair. Holy Land Kheyder had admitted both of them to participate in Steinitz's exhibition when Leib had accepted Bernard's draw offer.

After withstanding Leib's siege of his castled position, Bernard had held a clear advantage going into the endgame.

"Why did you offer him a draw?" Chaim had asked. "You were up two pawns."

"This way Leib gets to play Steinitz too."

Bernard had finally found what Leib desired, a worthy reward for keeping his secret, though he'd known for years that Leib would never tell. Rabbi Menshein had praised both players and the spirit of generosity in their match.

However, Rabbi Horovitz, called Attila the Hun for his lectures and epic paddling, had something else to say when he stood over their lunch table. Stories had passed down over the years, and everyone knew what had happened when a boy once challenged Horovitz's authority.

"If God created man, Rabbi, who created God?" a foolish sixth-year student had asked him. Even if this was an honest theological inquiry, it was a grave mistake.

Horovitz bellowed, "The Lord God is one, you fool. He cannot be divided or diminished!" He ordered his class to recite the Shema before he chased the rebel from kheyder. The terrified boy ran into a Polish butcher shop and cowered behind a slab of ham.

The barrel-shaped rabbi had glared at Bernard, who hunched his shoulders. "Steinitz will offer you no respite. Nor the goys in Petersburg or the peasant with his blood libel superstitions. Eye for eye, wound for wound, life for life. We Jews must learn to be tough."

Steinitz approached on a crutch that supported a deformed leg. How could this surprisingly short man be the best in the world? Yet every Jew in Horodno knew that last year he defeated Adolf Anderssen, the maestro of the all-out attacking style. Anderssen, an older man who played his Immortal Game years ago, in which he sacrificed nearly all his pieces before finishing with an impossible checkmate, had collapsed against Steinitz's unrelenting pressure.

When the master stopped in front of each board, his opponent had to move immediately. Steinitz pondered for a few seconds, made his move, and stepped to the next challenger. He didn't make eye contact, smile, or react when Bernard took his knight with a bishop. Steinitz recaptured the bishop with a pawn and continued along the line. Precious time to think before the master came around again.

Follow the logic of each move. Consider every possibility without losing track of all you've already analyzed. Inside his concentration, only the percussive tap of the wooden pieces punctured the silence. Bernard leaned forward, put his elbows on the table, and made a shelf with his hands. He rested his head there.

Older, bearded Jews draped with prayer shawls sat interspersed among the twenty-six young players selected from kheyders and yeshivas throughout Horodno. As the match proceeded, challengers resigned by tipping over their kings, or Steinitz said without emotion, "checkmate," and the defeated joined the crowd and witnessed the continuing slaughter.

Twenty, then ten players still held on. Now, though, Steinitz stood at each board for a whole minute before grasping his piece and moving decisively. The ranks of the challengers continued to thin.

Bernard played carefully, but Steinitz built multiple threats until he broke through his defense. Bernard resigned on the forty-second move. By the time he worked his way to the balcony and stood next to his father and Chaim, only Leib and a yeshiva student remained.

This student, who continually rubbed his receding hairline under his yarmulke, gasped when Steinitz trapped his queen. He teetered to his feet, which left Leib, the only surviving challenger, facing the best player in the world among the empty chairs and tipped kings.

Leib gave Steinitz a hard stare after each move. "The stink eye," he'd explained to Bernard when they discussed how they would each approach the contest. "It's not exactly an evil eye; I don't want to give Steinitz bad luck in life. Just a few bad moves in the game."

A murmur swept through the crowd. "Down a piece." Now the master would have to make it up by complicating the position.

On the sixtieth move, Steinitz said something to Leib who appeared to study the board. He reached out his hand, and Steinitz took it.

"Leib drew the master," Bernard's father said, hugging him. "Fifty wins and one draw, and it's to a kid." Rabbi Menshein did a little dance and praised God. Only Attila the Hun complained among the rejoicing Jews of Horodno.

"He had him defeated and let him go. Feh! A draw is nothing. Bobkes!"

5

After the distraction of chess master Steinitz's visit had come and gone, most Horodno Jews still ignored the Russian Orthodox morality campaign. For Sophie Feinberg and her allies, the Levings, however, the weekly condemnations posted on storefronts and in the local papers made it difficult to think of anything else.

When the campaign had first begun, the rants printed in the *Herald* delivered a general reprimand that didn't target individuals.

DRIVE INDECENCY FROM HORODNO!

Mikail Alexevich, Grodno Gubernia's Holy Bishop, calls upon all patriotic citizens to root out the destructive behavior that threatens the moral integrity of Russia. With the full support of his excellency Ivan Petrovich, subversive foreign influences, immoral behavior, and prostitution are condemned.

By June, two months after Steinitz's visit and just days after a Polish veteran of the uprising tried to kill the czar at the World's Fair in Paris, Estes knew the campaign would not quickly disappear.

On one of the evenings the three of them walked to the library, Estes spotted the poster, written in bold Russian letters and repeated in Yiddish, fastened to the window of Wolfeld and Son's dry goods store. Bishop Alexevich called for public shaming. "Only by turning to the Orthodox Church is salvation for these sinners possible," the sign said, next to a list of names and street addresses.

Estes scanned the list as Sophie and Mama looked over her shoulder: *Horodno, Sophie Feinberg, Maimonides Street, Prostitution.* The general reprimand had turned into a threatening fist.

Sophie clutched her own shoulders, and the color drained from her face. "I pretended to be something I'm not in Petersburg, and now they won't allow me to shed that false label."

"We have to fix this mistake immediately," Mama said.

"Immediately? We had a saying in Petersburg: 'As likely as a golden plover whistle in January.' First, we'd need a written petition, then we'd have to wait for a response, bounced from one bureaucrat to another, and perhaps landing back with the same official we started with."

"Like Gogol's 'Overcoat.' I can rip all these down."

"They'll put up more, Estes, and I'm sure the papers will publish this," Sophie said. "The bishop is rabid about this matter, and he has the governor's support. We'll just have to wait it out."

＊

Six weeks passed, and the late-afternoon sun cast the back of the shop in golden light. Estes waxed thread and spied on Sophie, who concentrated at her own table near the entrance. Estes had become skillful at observing without Sophie noticing—a quick survey of the space with a brief pause at Sophie, or a sideways glance, and only when Sophie was absorbed entirely in measurement and cutting would she venture a direct stare.

Sophie had stayed for dinner every evening since the bishop named her an undesirable. Afterward, Estes and Sophie would read together and talk in Russian and German about books until Estes and her parents escorted their guest home. Often, Sophie would invite them in for a piano concert. Estes shivered with pleasure and imagined her hands over Sophie's as the Chopin pieces resonated in her chest.

This night, Estes and Sophie took turns reading *Adam Bede* aloud. How marvelous to hear Russian spill off Sophie's tongue and to enjoy the expression in her voice, to have this educated woman companion who loved books and language as much as she did. She could watch Sophie openly now, relieved when the familiar sadness and concern around her eyes withdrew for a while.

When they walked Sophie home, the Levings lingered for a bit outside her house, and Estes sank into her friend's embrace. They waited until she went inside, and Estes wished Sophie had accepted Papa's offer to move into the shop. On the way back, Mama and Papa linked arms as Estes enjoyed the full yellow moon.

If only they were the same age, she'd have a best friend. They would sit together in the shop, guess what each customer wanted, talk about the issues of the day, and share a bed when Sophie stayed over. Her friend would never turn away from her deformed foot as they talked about extraordinary things, such as the passage Sophie read in *Adam Bede*: "What greater thing is there for two human souls, than to feel that they are joined for life . . . to be one with each other in silent unspeakable memories at the moment of the last parting?"

She would ask Sophie about private matters, the intimate relations that went on behind closed doors, and perhaps Estes would wake in the middle of the night, entwined with her beautiful and cultured friend, so close that she could feel Sophie's breath on her face. If she dared, their mouths would touch.

In the morning, when Sophie didn't show up or send word, the Levings anxiously retraced the night's walk, this time in a chilly drizzle.

WHORE! painted on Sophie's blue door in sloppy Cyrillic, drove Estes up the steps in a sudden panic with Mama following. Glass from the smashed windows covered the porch. Papa ran across the street and stopped two black-coated Jews on their way to shul.

"Sophie!" Estes shouted.

Mama pounded on the door. "Sophie! It's us."

Papa joined them, his chest heaving. "They told me thugs harassed the people on the bishop's list last night."

"Why didn't she come to us?" Estes bit her lip.

"Let's see what we can learn."

They found no message, only the evidence of a hasty retreat: kitchen drawers left open, two dresses in a closet, boxes of thread, sewing needles, and piles of books scattered across the floor. A Chopin concerto drooped on the piano's music rack and a tipped vase of wilted flowers dripped water onto the table.

"Why would she leave these things?" Estes leaned into Mama.

"She must have been terrified. Maybe she's on a train away from this madness," Papa said.

"But she must come back. How could she go without saying goodbye?"

She and Mama returned home while Papa raced to the Horodno train station, a humble wood structure one verst east of Market Square. When he returned, Estes and Mama came to the head of the stairs.

"I have news. Sophie left at dawn." He waved a folded letter and placed it in her hand. "The old station master planned to send a boy to deliver this, but I got there first. It's in Russian."

My Dearest Herman, Doris, and Estes,
I write quickly now, until my train arrives. If not for the refuge of the shop and your attentiveness, I would have fled months ago. The terror of last night left no choice, and when you read this, I will be on my way to Warsaw. I will stay there awhile before I continue west. I am so grateful for your kindness, and Estes, for our shared love of literature. I will never forget you. With love, Sophie

Sophie would surely send them her new address in Warsaw and invite the Levings to visit. Mama placed paper, pen, and ink in front of her. With her eyes closed, elbows on the table, and hands on her cheeks, Estes imagined Sophie waiting for her train, scared, checking all the men for those who attacked her house. She picked up the pen and rolled it between her fingers. Now Sophie traveled west, farther away from Horodno every minute, but with her writing, Estes would keep her close.

✳

Two days later, on Friday morning, Papa went out after breakfast for the Petersburg paper, *Golos.* She read the headlines to him, a practice they'd begun when he finally accepted her Russian literacy. But how did the news prepare Papa for Shabes, any more than gorging on bad food readied him for a fast?

They spent the afternoon getting ready for the day of rest. At sundown Papa said a prayer for Sophie and they shared their hopes and reassurances. Estes estimated their friend had arrived in Warsaw the day before. Maybe Sophie had already sent a message back on the train. Estes would write another to mail with her first one as soon as she received an address.

Seven weeks passed, and the expected message still hadn't arrived. Estes reread Sophie's note multiple times, gradually understanding the finality of "*I will never forget you.*" Loneliness crushed her. "I don't know what to do, Mama."

"Papa and I are heartbroken too. Trust me, my daughter. Time and routine."

Estes searched for someone to blame: the men who'd driven Sophie out, the bishop, Governor Petrovich, the vindictive Petersburg official, the bureaucrats enforcing the injustices directed at Jews. She hated them all. Joyless, she resumed reading to Mama and visiting the library. Moshe offered gentle condolences.

The czar promoted Petrovich and recalled him to the capital. The new governor, a more reasonable man, suppressed the previous intolerance and the bishop's zeal, which he called, "a surefire way to generate another rebellion." But none of this would bring Sophie back to Horodno.

Estes did take one action, however. She refused to attend shul, and Mama joined her. Men, using religious morality as a club, had driven Sophie Feinberg out of Horodno. Not a single rabbi or Catholic priest had raised their voice against the crusade.

"Yes, men are imperfect, but that's why we need the purity of God," Papa said.

"I will not give a shoddy craftsman my business, Papa."

"Doris?"

"My daughter is far more important to me than the rabbi's sermons, Herman."

"But when will you return?"

"When women sit with the men."

"What will I tell Avram Rosenblum and the others?"

"The truth."

6

"Who do you think will go on?" Chaim asked no one in particular. The four friends stretched out in Bernard's yard, one day after Rabbi Menshein had reported a sad fact—that only a few from their class would continue their studies in yeshiva.

"Jacob Rosenblum will advance for sure," Leib said. "He's the most serious student in the entire kheyder. But what a dull life he'll have surrounded by his holy books."

"Our future's sealed," Shlomo said glumly. "Behind the cart or in the tobacco factory."

"At least with the cart, we'll be free men." Leib mimed playing his clarinet. "And we can get out the chess board whenever we want."

Shlomo grimaced as he considered this.

"What's wrong with Shershevski's?" Chaim asked. "We'll always have enough to eat." Bernard glanced at the twins. Leib's ribs showed through his thin shirt.

"Would Moses have taken the Jews back to Pharoah even if they had just one piece of matzo left?" Leib's imitation of Rabbi Menshein startled them. Chaim and Bernard laughed, and even Shlomo managed a slight grin.

"Besides Jacob Rosenblum," Leib said, "Bernard always has the right answers."

"An illiterate yeshiva master," Bernard said.

"I could still read for you."

"I won't go to yeshiva, Chaim, not even if all the rabbis are as hard of hearing as Rabbi Menshein."

"Just don't confess now, so close to the finish line," Leib said. "Besides, we're all implicated, though it's not like we plotted to overthrow the czar. Think about all the planning and rugelach just to get through kheyder."

While his three friends debated the merits of honesty, Bernard chewed on a stalk of grass. A lone cloud drifted across his line of sight.

✳

Bernard, like most Jews in Europe, knew the story of Sabbatai Zevi, the self-proclaimed Jewish Messiah in the seventeenth century, who had thousands of disciples. The Messiah who promptly donned a turban and converted to Islam when the Turkish Sultan gave him the choice of keeping his head or his faith. Every Jew in Horodno had also heard about the martyrdom of Eleazar Ben Solomon, a local Jew falsely accused of murder at the end of the last century who chose torture and gruesome death over conversion.

On the day of the dreaded meeting with Rabbi Menshein, Bernard carried over a bench and faced his father and teacher, seated on their wooden chairs. He wavered between self-preservation and principle, between Sabbatai Zevi and Eleazar Solomon.

His father covered his mouth with a handkerchief and coughed for several moments. The rabbi waited for him to recover. The occasional throat-clearing and sniffles had progressed in the past few weeks to spells of violent hacking. "It's nothing," he'd told Bernard. "Fresh air and hard work are all the medicine I need." He'd finally agreed to consult a doctor after the conference with Rabbi Menshein.

"A brilliant mind, this one, a compassionate boy, perceptive and resourceful," the rabbi said.

Solomon smiled, patted Bernard's knee, and coughed again.

"Bernard would do well in yeshiva, but I always ask the student what they want. Long hours of study involves more than ability." The rabbi settled back and waited.

If he'd only told them years ago, he wouldn't have to face this colossal shame now, because the deception had gathered interest and grown immense.

"I won't go to yeshiva. I've broken a commandment. I've lied!" The falsehood he had carried and protected for years, torn down with a few words.

"Bernard, we all make mistakes." Solomon told the rabbi, "He thinks he needs perfection to go into yeshiva. Our vodka comes out pure, but never goes in that way."

"Do you want to explain, Bernard?" Rabbi Menshein asked.

"I can't read."

Rabbi Menshein opened and closed his mouth, then tugged on his beard. Solomon asked, "Do you need glasses? Why didn't you tell me?"

"No, Father. I lied to you and Rabbi Menshein all these years." He wiped his eyes.

"Of course you can read. You read perfectly."

"I just repeated verses after you, Father. Or I recited those I knew from shul."

Solomon started as if stuck with a pin.

"Ah." Rabbi Menshein took off his glasses and rubbed his eyes before replacing them. "I suspected you helped Chaim with his interpretations, and once, while you read aloud, I thought your eyes were closed. Had you memorized so much of the Chumash, I wondered? Impossible!"

Bernard confessed all of it. His father's shoulders sagged.

"Incredible!" Rabbi Menshein smacked his cheeks. "We've witnessed two miracles—a voluntary unmasking today and no one telling for six years. A fragile balloon. Any of the other eleven could have knocked it down with a single word, an anonymous note. What a tactician. You won them all over with kindness and rugelach. Now, the one who has the most to lose throws the dart."

The rabbi paused, then reached out and lifted Bernard's chin until their eyes met. "You've been Chaim's brain. He's been your eyes. I've seen this problem before, and I know a rabbi, not for the timid, who might teach you to read. We'll appeal to the rabbinical court for both of you to attend yeshiva as one. We had a blind boy accepted with his personal reader some years ago. How is this any different? No need to decide now."

After his confession, Bernard felt raw and naked as a peeled turnip. On the way home, he worried that the weight of his sin now resided on his father's shoulders, which heaved when he coughed. His father squeezed and released his hand, their only communication.

When they arrived, his father excused himself. He would lie down for a bit, not more than an hour. Bernard stayed outside, stacking a pyramid of split wood in their yard. Crosshatching the ends of each row, he made one solid wall and covered the top with an old oilcloth. While he worked, the anxiety about his father's persistent cough hammered against his chest.

He had started on a second row when the clean-shaven and neatly dressed doctor arrived by carriage. The driver waited while the doctor examined Solomon, who had propped himself up with pillows. The doctor pressed a wooden stethoscope to Solomon's chest, made him stand up, and repeated the procedure for his sides and back. He tapped, asked questions, produced a glass and had him pee, swirled the urine, held it to the window, and frowned as if it were sour wine.

Bernard prayed silently for a positive sign, waited for the doctor's concentrated look to break into a smile of reassurance, for his pronouncement—"nothing more than a chest cold." But with one word, "consumption," everything changed. A death sentence, Bernard knew, because no one ever afflicted spoke of that disease in the past tense.

"Are you sure?" his father asked.

"Your chest spoke, and I listened."

Bernard wanted to argue with the doctor, but when had his strong father, now weakened, spent an afternoon in bed?

"The disease doesn't always follow the same course. Some have a year, others much longer."

Hope.

The doctor glanced over his glasses and frowned. "You should have seen me earlier. If you can't make it to the sea, take rest and lots of fresh air. Get someone to take care of you."

After the doctor left, Solomon said, "It could have been worse. It might have been better."

For his father's sake, he needed to find strength. "I'll check on Alte Ferd and make tea."

Bernard went out to the barn, dropped to his knees, and sobbed. Alte Ferd came over and nuzzled him. *A year.* This horse would outlive his father. Bernard would be thirteen. A man. What would he do? *Others live much longer.* He wiped his eyes, made himself stand, and walked back toward the house. Before going inside he turned, shielded his eyes against the low western sun, and looked to the distant Niemen River.

In the kitchen, he washed and dried his face, prepared strong tea, and returned to his father's bedroom. He pulled over one of the chairs they used when they prayed the Shema.

"I'll take care of you."

"Yes, Bernard, you'll be my nurse."

The slanted sunlight divided his father's face into half-light and half-shadow.

"I'm sorry I lied. I didn't want to disappoint you."

"Just sit with me for a while. I have something I want to confess too." His father shifted in bed and looked directly at Bernard. "This isn't easy for me either. When I was a boy your age . . . You know the general history, but I never told you about our neighbors, Hannah and Mordecai."

He had another coughing spell.

"Drink, Father."

His father drank and put the tea on the bedside table. "You and Chaim have been good friends. I'm glad. I had a best friend at your age—Saul."

He paused, closed his eyes, and put both hands on his chest, his breathing a low, moaning wheeze. "Hannah and Mordecai lived for Saul. He loved to help push Mordecai's cart, and when they made a sale, he scrambled through the piles of old clothing, tools, religious books, and even vegetables from their garden to pull out the bought item. I would go along sometimes, and this is how I got to know him.

"They accepted almost anything in return, sometimes getting back the same items they'd started the day with. I remember a time Saul took a live rooster as payment. Mordecai grabbed that bird, gave its neck a quick twist, and threw the dead fowl on the cart. Saul picked up the dead rooster and wept. He had a sensitive heart.

Solomon paused for a drink.

"Do you want to rest, Father?"

"After. As you learned today, the hard part is starting a confession. That requires courage, and now, the poison must come out." He closed his eyes and sighed. "I've told you conscription into the czar's army meant a death sentence for us, and how they took some Jewish boys as young as six. Now I'll tell you my whole story, Bernard.

"Our leaders did everything they could to shield us from military recruitment, unlike some other towns, but when we fell below our quota the Russians responded by sending officials to investigate. These men threatened to add two recruits to our requirement for every one we lagged behind. No one would be exempt anymore, not fathers with large families to support, old men, invalids, even members of the kahal.

"I wasn't aware at the time that my parents had paid the town leaders to keep me on the bottom of the dreaded list. Now, I see what that meant for others without means, like my friend Saul's family. Some parents sent their boys alone to Vilne where they could hide. Others cut off some of their son's fingers."

Bernard glanced at his father's hands.

"By claiming his son had died, Mordecai kept Saul away from the authorities for a while. One night he dragged an unpretentious granite slab to the cemetery. Saul showed me his gravestone, etched with a crude tool: 'Saul Brodskoy, 1821-1832, Beloved Son of Mordecai and Hannah,' it read.

"We heard that someone had informed on them, and Mordecai begged my father to let Saul move in with us until the danger passed. He agreed, and my mother and I practiced hiding him just in case. She did her best to make it fun, and Saul enjoyed the attention, but I understood the deadly seriousness. Then my mother had the idea to pass him off as a girl. He was almost twelve but tiny enough to pass for eight, with long hair and delicate features. The dress my mother bought him completed the disguise.

"One day, those two officials came to our house with their list. A spindly, pockmarked fellow tried to project a friendly expression, but his crooked smile made him look more wolf than lamb. The other, who did all the talking, affected a pleasant tone, but his voice dripped with deceit. We understood enough of his Russian. They asked us about Saul, son of Mordecai and Hannah."

Solomon began to shiver, and Bernard reached for the blanket at the foot of the bed.

"I'm not cold. It's the memory, Bernard.

"The agent asked about the young lady, and my mother gracefully introduced her niece. Saul kept busy playing with two dolls. Soon after this encounter, these men left to spread misery among the neighboring towns, and we didn't see them again for months. We grew hopeful they'd gone for good, and Saul returned home, but when we fell even further behind the quota . . .

"It was Shabes. Hannah, Mordecai, and Saul had joined us for the evening meal. I remember his delight when my mother served the apple cake.

"Four men entered our house without knocking this time, the same two officials and two soldiers who stood on either side of the door. 'This must be him,' they said. 'The one they dressed like a girl last time.'

"Mordecai struggled to pull the agents' arms off of his son, while Hannah fell to the floor and held Saul's thin legs. The men struggled to separate them from their only child, and the soldiers stepped forward, holding their rifles with fixed bayonets. My father shouted they'd made a mistake. This boy was Ezekiel, a nephew visiting from Warsaw.

"The Russians let go, and Hannah pulled Saul into her arms on the floor. They shifted their eyes to me. I suppose they thought I would be a better recruit. I was only a year older, but twice Saul's size. They started tugging me out of my chair.

"I'll never forget what they said: 'Okay, if that's the way you want it. We're here for Saul Brodskoy, but one Jew kid is the same as another. Come along, lad. We'll make you into a man.' I clung to the edge of the table."

Solomon gripped Bernard's wrist and didn't let go.

"My father told them I was his son and searched among the papers strewn on the desk behind the table. I thought I was about to be dragged out of our house and taken away from my family. You see, Bernard, the first and second principles were at war. In his place, what would I have wanted from Saul? To protect himself or to save me? When one's hair is on fire, we hope for a bucket of water, not lamp oil.

"I pointed at my best friend and said, 'He's Saul.'" Solomon held up his right index finger. "I've thought many times I should cut it off, a reminder of my sin." He began weeping.

His father never cried like this. The sobs brought on a coughing fit, and he struggled for breath. Bernard put his hand over his father's, which still clasped his other wrist, and wished his touch could cure such a deep wound.

By the time his father stopped coughing, the Niemen had grayed in the dusk. Solomon took another deep breath and slowly exhaled. "But still, the scales must be balanced. Yes, a third principle, Bernard. I only survived this guilt by having a chance to be a good man, to be your father. Still, I think this consumption must be my final cleansing."

When his father said nothing for some time, Bernard asked, "What happened to Saul?"

"My father offered to pay the men, but they wouldn't listen. Saul burrowed into his mother's lap and she screamed, 'You won't take my son!' The two agents tried to pry Saul away, but Hannah held on. Mordecai charged into these men and all three crashed to the floor next to Hannah and Saul. One of the soldiers trained his gun on my parents. The other clubbed Mordecai and then turned the rifle butt on Hannah. Saul begged his parents to save him, but they lay bloody and helpless on the floor.

"I ran to the door as they shoved Saul into the wooden cage built on their cart. The two soldiers stood on the back lip, holding onto the stockade; the two officials rode in front. As the horses trotted away, Saul screamed for his parents.

"My father gave Hannah and Mordecai much of his savings to buy Saul's freedom, and they left that very night to find him. Perhaps they didn't blame me, because they never mentioned my betrayal. My mother forgave my weakness and always loved me, but my father and I . . . Our mutual shame ripped open a permanent breach that day. The papers he sought would have saved me and sealed Saul's fate, even if I hadn't condemned my friend. Whatever happens, Bernard, you and I must never let guilt drive us apart.

"In my imagination, Hannah and Mordecai pursued rumors and interviewed other devastated parents to get some hope. For years I told myself they lived as a family in some faraway village. In my fantasy, Saul had not grown and still scrambled over Mordecai's cart, but they never came back, and I know better now. Ill-fed and poorly clothed, many child recruits died before they turned eighteen, when their twenty-five-year service officially began." His father studied the worn lines on his palms like roads on a map.

"You were young, Father. It's natural to want to live. Rest now."

That night, blood appeared on his father's handkerchief for the first time. He coughed until a thick wad of red mucous tore loose. Bernard felt his father's forehead and winced.

*

Three years after he and his father had both revealed their secrets, Bernard removed the wooden slats and set the bottles they'd brought home last night into the dug-out earth. He replaced the cover and spread hay across the spot. Alte Ferd stretched his neck over the barn's half-wall.

"You won't tell anyone, will you, old boy? You know who takes care of you, right?"

Though the state commanded vodka be sold only by the bucket, some, including army officers and even the same liquor officials charged with enforcement, wanted a more sophisticated drinking experience. Bernard's father provided bottled vodka, without the customary state stamp, to those customers.

"A bargain for them and us. Why should the state take half when we do all the work?" his father said after Bernard brought Alte Ferd out of the barn. "If we don't look out for ourselves . . ."

"Who will? I wish we sold it all this way."

"What would we tell the inspectors when they come to tag our product?"

His father coughed, and Bernard hurried to his side.

"Rest today, Father. Save your strength."

"You take the horse. I'll join you this afternoon. The walk will be good for me."

Bernard led Alte Ferd along the Niemen's right bank, in and out of shadows. So much had changed since his father's diagnosis. When he'd shunned yeshiva, Bernard also rejected reading lessons. He told Rabbi Menshein he needed to remain available to care for his father, though he admitted to himself that he would be too ashamed, blundering along lines of print, lines the other boys sped past. God had something else in mind for him, even though for his thirteenth birthday he'd memorized a Torah section and recited perfectly in front of the full congregation at his bar mitsve.

His father's illness progressed, then retreated, and Bernard's emotions cycled back and forth, too, between despair and elation.

"He's doing remarkably well," the doctor told him after the last visit. "You've given him a few extra years, but you can't expect a miracle."

"A short time for all of us, doctor," his father said.

Bernard chose to ignore the doctor's pessimism. Why not expect a miracle? So he prayed these 'extra years' would continue, and the clock would start over each time the doctor visited.

7

Ten months after Sophie fled, Estes and her mother had not returned to shul, but her melancholy had passed. Time.

"Did you ever want to do more, Mama? I mean, some other kind of work?"

"I used to wish I had some special talent. You know I learned to read from my father. He taught me Hebrew, just as I taught you, but he never allowed a real break from tradition. I sometimes dreamed about what I might have done with an education."

"Did it make you angry?"

"Yes. But when our troubles arrived, I only had time to worry about survival."

"What about now?"

"I have you."

"I'm afraid I'll forget Sophie, Mama. It's so hard wondering what happened to her and why she never contacted us, but some weeks I hardly think about her at all, until we light the Shabes candles."

"Every person has their own story. Sometimes our paths merge for a long stretch, sometimes for only moments. Sophie's life is completely detached from ours now, but she will always remain an important memory."

"Like your parents?"

"Yes, and my brothers."

After they said goodnight, Estes turned up her lantern again and leaned against the headboard. If only she were as strong as her mother. Mama called her youthful sorrows "our troubles," a phrase too ordinary for such trauma. How had she survived, when Estes teared up just imagining such loss?

She had asked Mama many times about her days on the north side of the Kodyma River in Balta. David, her father, a strong man with intense eyes and a thick curtain of beard that hung to his chest, traveled the countryside and performed ritual slaughtering. Her mother, Bella, short and stocky, nearly matched him in strength. Her calloused hands sliced meat in the butcher shop attached to the family's house.

Mama took care of her baby sister, Freida. She changed diapers and pulled Freida about town in a wagon. Late each day, she switched places with her mother and scrubbed the shop floors and stained wooden counters.

Estes picked up her bound leather journal, and Mama's tragic history tumbled out.

May 20, 1868

Her older brothers, Baruch and Benyamin, attended yeshiva and studied throughout the evening. Mama resented that they did nothing else at home, but when she complained, her father said, "The honor their scholarship returns to the family is our blessing. Women have their work, as do men." They read Talmud while she emptied dirty buckets behind the shop.

The past lingered in Balta, and the elderly told Mama stories of those slaughtered in the Haidamak massacres. On dreary days, fog hugged the Kodyma, and those tragedies clung to her like chimney soot.

In the fall, the whole town prepared for the three-day Trinity Fair. Narrow wooden bridges and dirt roads bore tens of thousands of visitors who brought grain, cows, chickens, horses, cheese, vodka, tools, and useful craft items. When released from tending her own family's booth, Mama wandered through the maze of tents and wagons clogging every street and listened to stories, watched jugglers, delighted in a traveling magician's sleight of hand. The town emptied and debris from the fair found its way to the riverbank. Mama returned to her routine—caring for Freida, cleaning the shop, doing household chores.

Terrible events happened without warning. When the rabbi came into the shop on that awful January day, one look at his tearful face dropped Bella to the floor. Her two sons had walked out to the countryside with three other classmates after yeshiva, despite warnings not to leave town. One of the boys made it back and gave the alarm.

"Khapers!"

A search party scoured the road where the boys had been seized and posted rewards in adjacent towns. For weeks, Mama and her father traveled the countryside, stopping at inns within a day's ride of Balta. They sought information, a chance sighting, some hope to offer Bella. Nothing.

The shock drove Bella into bed, and when a cholera epidemic swept through town, she died calling out for her stolen sons. David mourned Bella for a year and gave up hope that his sons would ever come back. He took his family to live near his brother in Kiev, but on a lonely road outside Uman, death arrived again.

She stopped writing and closed her eyes. Mama wouldn't talk about some events, and Estes only knew that the two sisters survived. Orphaned, they'd settled with their uncle's family just before Czar Nicholas decreed all Jews must leave Kiev. Estes sighed and resumed writing.

Mama was eleven, on the move again to Minsk, where she lived with her new family until she met Papa. She was eighteen, he twenty. Papa came from Horodno to apprentice with the best shoemakers in the Pale. She entered his shop one day, and after he measured her foot, neither of them slept until they met again. They married and moved back to Horodno.

Mama's aunt eventually arranged a marriage between Freida and Hirsh, the son of their old neighbor in Balta. Freida returned to Balta and had two daughters. She and Mama exchange letters every month.

It's strange, but if Mama hadn't lost her family, she never would have met Papa, and I wouldn't exist to write in this journal now, to write about ancestors I can only know through Mama. So I collect her memories and make them my own: Bella's laugh with a snort at the end; Baruch and Benyamin bent over their books, arguing about a question the rabbi had posed; David holding the worn prayer book he read before dinner; the pungent smell of blood in their butcher shop.

✳

Uncle Simon arrived along with summer. "Now that you're thirteen," he told her after he settled in, "it's time for you to learn the language of Shakespeare."

Estes worked hard, and they stayed up late every night, long after Mama and Papa went to bed, two lanterns on the table as they bore into their studies. By the end of August, when only a week remained of his three-month stay, Estes's voice cracked when she asked him at dinner, "Why do you have to leave, Uncle Simon? I'm making so much progress with the language."

"America is a better place for Jews." His voice rose and he folded his arms.

"We have always gotten by," Papa said. "This is where our people belong. Nothing of value arises from moving about." He looked at her and Mama, then he pointed at his brother. "And how do you live with yourself? A rich socialist is worse than a pork-eating Jew."

"Damn comfortably," Simon replied, helping himself to another serving of cake. "When the revolution comes, everyone will have whatever they need, but in the meantime, why should I suffer?" He jumped up and bounded down to the shop, returning with a book. "This one will have to be in Russian, Estes. Chernyshevsky's *What Is to Be Done?*, my favorite."

Estes tore through it in two days and concentrated as Simon spoke about it on the landing, halfway between the shop and the second floor, where Papa had banished him for spreading claptrap. "It will be as influential as Marx's *Das Capital* on the upcoming revolution," Uncle Simon said.

Estes moved in with her analysis. "*What is to be Done?* is wonderful regarding the status of women." She interlocked her fingers. "Chernyshevsky calls for nothing less than full equality."

"Exactly, Estes. He links social and economic progress . . ."

"But Uncle Simon, the writing is terrible."

"Estes . . ."

"I'm not finished. Placing these worthy ideals within a poor novel? Why serve wedding cake in the outhouse?"

Simon lifted his index finger.

"And why do we need a man to teach us about emancipation?" she continued, then delivered her coup de grace. "I grant you, Uncle Simon, he's a marvelous advocate for women, and I admire his courage in going to jail for his beliefs, but he shapes his story with a hatchet instead of a craftsman's chisel."

"You don't need a teacher. Continue to read and tell your parents to stay out of the way."

After Simon departed for America, Estes and Mama searched for the rubles he always hid like the afikoymen.

"We can't tell your father. Herman has never forgiven his brother for buying the shop and house for us years ago."

Uncle Simon left a clue—*Unlike me, this benefactor is anonymous.* Estes limped to her room and pulled *Great Expectations* from her shelf. The middle of the book bulged with a thick wad of money. He'd left a brief note. *Buy books, Estes, my not-so-little scholar.*

✳

She did buy books, and Uncle Simon's generosity also helped pay for eighteen months of tutoring. Estes asked her third instructor, the dour Melamed Freidkin, who had none of Simon's intellectual passion, to listen to her read English. The old man studied her through puffy eyes. She regretted he didn't have a table for her to work at as she sank deep into his battered sofa, and that when he sat across from her in his orange, stain-covered chair, his poisonous breath lingered in the air. But she wouldn't have minded any of this if he'd taught her well.

Once, after Estes asked a question, he stared into his hands. *What does she want from me?* Maybe he preferred a student who would nibble gratefully at what he offered, allowing him a more relaxed morning. Instead, she surgically extracted his French, with its throaty Rs, and more English with its strange grammar rules.

He called her, without affection, "Little Inquisitor." When she persisted, asking him if he believed Gogol's *Dead Souls* was a scathing indictment of serfdom or too ludicrous for that purpose, he snapped at her: "I'd rather be on Torquemada's rack than endure any more of your questions."

Still, if she had to spend three hours in his claustrophobic house with its stench of wet socks, she might as well make the most of it. Melamed Freidkin had lived in England for a while as a young man before his family came east, which could have made him unique and mysterious. Perhaps he'd fled a failed love affair, or killed someone, or driven by loyalty to family had left a comfortable home for the troubles of a Jew in Russia. No, quite impossible to attach romantic notions to this humorless man with his scraggly beard and dusty black coat.

Papa counted kopeks into Melamed Freidkin's outstretched palm, and Estes vowed to herself this would be the last in the succession of failed experiments. She renounced the tedious instruction, her wit unappreciated, her status as a girl reflected in his disappointed tone and averted eyes.

"He's emptier than a Shabes wine bottle," she told Papa on the way home.

"You're finished with this one so soon? Why don't you collect pollen without killing the plant?"

"Papa, how can you expect me to make honey from an old, dried flower?"

The next day, during a lull in her shoe shop routine, Estes traded the worktable for her favorite chair, blue and overstuffed, with heavy wooden arms. Instead of picking up her novel, she studied Papa punching holes with compact swings of his wooden mallet, followed by the familiar thumps against the metal awl. Russian officers, stationed in the area since the rebellion, raved about Papa's work and condemned their army-issue, factory-made boots. Papa, outspoken and friendly with most of his Jewish customers, adopted a reserved demeanor around these men. He switched from Yiddish to the required Russian. Afterward, he always sat down on his wooden stool, his lap-stone, pincers, and nippers idle for a moment on the workbench beside him.

No other shoemaker in Horodno made a pair of boots with sixty stitches per inch that precisely matched the shape of the customer's foot. Only Sophie Feinberg might have equaled him.

Papa looked up at Estes with a smile. She knew he had a riddle for her.

"Children and shoes, Estes—they come in different shapes and sizes, but they all . . ."

She thought for a moment. "Get underfoot. Not bad, Papa. But most children come one at a time, and shoes come only in pairs."

"How did I get such a daughter? Two weeks until you're fifteen. You've worn out the tutors, so it's time for a matchmaker."

"A matchmaker leads to marriage, Papa."

"Think of courtship as an exploration of the possible."

Cooking and washing with children draped from her waist like flowers from a broken stem? He could do whatever he wanted, but she would decide her own life—not God, Papa, or a matchmaker. She resumed her work waxing thread. She had tried to develop her skills working with leather after Sophie left, despite lacking natural ability, but that ended when she nearly sliced off her finger.

All morning customers came in, and she hoped for a story or interesting bit of gossip. They reported on life since their last pair of shoes and left their joys and sorrows in the shop, entwined like tangled laces.

"We had another baby. Six weren't enough already? But so smart, six months and trying to stand. He'll be learning Talmud in no time."

"Finally, our Masha has a match. He's not much to look at but quite the head for business."

"We were sitting shiva for my mother, and I swear, Herman, her voice came from the next room. And would you believe it, she criticized me for not having enough food for the guests."

Her father laughed and lamented along with his patrons. When alone again, he asked, "Estes, why do Jews tell so many stories?"

"That's a long story, Papa." They both smiled.

When she completed her morning's work in the shop, he gave her instructions for several deliveries, and Estes bundled up against the March wind. Papa walked with her to the door, but before she could leave, the Rosenblums, father and son, entered. Months had passed since their last visit to the shop. Surprised to see them, she paused in the entry. To leave now might seem rude.

"The last pair of shoes, Herman—perfection. I'd like another just like them," Avram Rosenblum said. And without pausing to take a breath, he continued, "The other reason we stopped by is to tell you about Professor Micah. He taught for years in Petersburg and recently returned to Horodno. He lives right over there." Rosenblum pointed a beefy arm toward the other side of Market Square. "He speaks many languages, an expert in the classics."

Estes suspected Jacob's father didn't know anything about "the classics."

"He might accept students. Perhaps even a bright girl like Estes. Of course, after yeshiva, Jacob will be going on to the State Rabbinical

School in Vilne. He has a keen memory for Talmud. You heard him sing in shul last week." He gave her a hard look: *You would know about this, too, if you attended.*

Jacob glanced at her as though waiting for more praise. She answered by excusing herself to make the two deliveries. She didn't care what the Rosenblum's thought, but why didn't Papa brag about her? She allowed the fresh air to wash away her resentment.

She carried the shoes in a basket with one hand and gripped her cane in the other. Maybe someone would notice the book she'd wedged upright in the basket, its spine showing. They might comment and engage her in a spirited literary exchange.

The first customer, an older woman still in her nightclothes and sleeping cap, didn't notice the book. "My pain was so bad yesterday, and today I hardly leave the bed. Two weeks without a visit. What kind of son is that?"

The second, a woman Mama's age with four grandchildren tugging at her dress, inquired about Estes's parents and commented on her appearance. "What a sheyn ponem, and the gorgeous hair."

This kind of attention made Estes uneasy. Surely this woman noticed her cane and limp. She exchanged the shoes for money, hid the book in her bag, and headed home.

✳

A week after Estes had renounced tutoring, Papa's widowed older sister, Miriam, who had recently moved back to Horodno, paid them a visit. Mama removed one cookie tray from the oven and replaced it with another. Estes, her book open beneath her, leaned on her elbows and bent over the butcher-block table in the center of their kitchen. She sensed her aunt's gaze but didn't lift her eyes from the book. What had happened to make her aunt so disagreeable? Papa said everyone carried burdens. Uncle Simon had changed the subject when Estes fished for more information.

"Look at you, always working—in the kitchen, with Herman in the shop. You could use more help. Besides, reading won't get her a husband. And she still refuses to go to shul, and you go along with this madness?

Who's in charge here? She's spent too much time with our wandering brother, Simon, and he's filled her head with nonsense. Estes could end up an alte moyd. Daughters need to be trained."

She has three grown sons. What does she know about daughters?

"She could be an author, a scholar. Miriam, she writes in six languages."

Aunt Miriam threw up her hands. "Nu! Have it your way, Doris. I hope I don't have to say I told you so." Miriam pecked Estes on the cheek on her way out. They both smiled when she left.

"I could do more to help, Mama. You sacrifice too much for me." They both knew her heart wasn't in following kashrut; it lived with the books Mama always allowed her to keep open.

Mama took off her apron. "You're my miracle, Estes." Three miscarriages. Life is uncertain.

Estes cleaned the kitchen and waited for the cookies to bake when Mama went down to the shop.

Before bed, she sat in front of the full-length mirror in her parents' room. Mama brushed Estes's waist-long, wavy, black hair. Mama's own hair was shoulder length and almost completely gray. Estes tried to quiet her mind, but her parents' conversation flared up in her memory, the one she'd overheard last night with her ear pressed against the door between their adjoining bedrooms.

"She has no friends."

"She adored Sophie, Herman."

"Her own age."

"She will when the time is right."

"How will she ever find a husband? She's so opinionated."

"That's a good thing. Besides, what's the hurry? Let her grow up."

"What match can be made when all she wants to do is read?"

"She's shown me her journal. Our daughter is wise beyond her years. A scholar will understand."

Feeling the brush and the snags coming free, Estes looked at her mother's reflection.

"Where did you go, my Esther?" Mama asked.

"I'm right here, Mama."

The very next day, Papa invited three other families of prominent tradesmen with daughters her age for dinner. He expanded their table as he did for Seder. Estes sensed Papa watching her throughout the meal. When she joined the girls and women in the kitchen to clean up, her father and the other men stayed in the dining room, their privileged assumptions and cigar smoke hovering above the table. Later, the girls all crowded into her room, away from his snooping.

Feeling alone and restless, she listened to their conversations about courtship.

"Poor Golda Pulski. Nathan Goldstein is not the right match for her."

"True, he's much older."

"And he lives with his parents. Golda will be taking orders from his mother."

She tried to break in: "Listen to this passage from *Pride and Prejudice*." She recited from memory: "'There are few people whom I really love, and still fewer of whom I think well. The more I see of the world, the more am I dissatisfied with it; and every day confirms my belief of the inconsistency of all human characters, and of the little dependence that can be placed on the appearance of merit or sense.'"

"Oh Estes, that's just a make-believe book."

She leaned back against her wall, as welcome as the town's tax farmer.

✳

Papa must have considered that sad event a huge success, because he continued his attempt to manage her social relations. He pursued his interest in matters of her courtship by taking on the matchmaking job himself.

When he told her about the first suitor, Estes put both hands on her cheeks. "Oy Vey. Why Jacob Rosenblum? He's arrogant and never talks to me."

Papa rubbed his brow. "There's an order to these things. Who benefits by insulting the Rosenblums? It never hurts to have friends well placed." He cut her off before she complained again. "Do it for me."

Estes tried not to watch Jacob across from her. Still handsome with the beginnings of a beard, especially if he didn't act so superior. She wasn't the one wasting her talents on religious pursuits. She reminded herself the job of wife would never be hers.

Jacob's waistline had expanded over the years. Perhaps his parents viewed such abundance as a sign of wealth. He moved on to his third helping of kugel before Estes had finished her first. Maida Rosenblum beamed at him. "A growing boy," she laughed. "Jacob loves to eat almost as much as he loves to study."

Once, when their eyes met, Estes smiled and Jacob stopped chewing. Papa broke his trance when he filled the wine cups. After Mama served dessert, Jacob stood, looked at Estes for a moment, then closed his eyes and, in a rich voice full of emotion, sang the blessings. How did something so angelic come from him?

When he finished, everyone remained silent. Avram Rosenblum spoke first. "Have you ever heard such a voice?"

Jacob, his eyes still closed, shifted from foot to foot.

"You sing beautifully, Jacob," Estes said. His eyes opened and she waited for some acknowledgement.

"Thank you."

She wanted him to say her name, compare their language skills, describe what the boys learned in yeshiva. But a serious conversation, with the adults looming? Impossible. Besides, Avram Rosenblum never stopped talking. She had not been unkind, though, and Papa took this as encouragement to bring in the other candidates.

Abe Lebowitz came next, a handsome boy of sixteen whose knees knocked incessantly. Max Rosenfeld turned beet red when Estes asked what he thought about the Brontë sisters. Mendel Farbenstein had a coughing fit and couldn't speak. Harvey Zeitzman never took his eyes off her chest, and when she turned, he tracked her breasts in a trance. Hershel Blonsky cut her off mid-sentence to ask if she'd always been a cripple. And Harold Pintovsky, with a reputation for intelligence, talked only of Talmud. When Estes asked if he believed God cared about such silly rules, he opened his mouth, speechless. None of them sang like Jacob Rosenblum.

✳

Thankfully, the array of suitors paused for her fifteenth-birthday trip to Vilne. When she and her parents boarded the train, Estes turned at the third whistle and watched the white-coated porters hauling luggage. Behind the bustle on the platform, a brick station with arched windows and a parapet circling the roof had finally replaced the original three-sided shed.

Aware of the furtive glances of grown men—traders and artisans who leaned across the aisle to strike up conversations with Papa while Mama knitted—Estes kept *Persuasion* in her lap throughout the eight-hour trip. Her armor. A soap and candle manufacturer with pink hands, a pocket watch on a chain, and a suitcase full of perfumed samples got off the train, and a thick-bearded furrier with a sable coat and callouses like Papa's took his place. A goldsmith replaced a cattle dealer, men came and went, and the car filled with cigar smoke and shop talk.

With her cane concealed under the seat and her foot partly hidden beneath her long dress, they didn't suspect she had a club foot. Would they still be so fascinated by her if they knew?

An hour outside Vilne, a young man boarded and sat across from them. His wire-rimmed glasses, delicate hands, pale complexion, and German book—Hegel—marked him as a man of letters. Estes wished she'd brought something more intellectual to read. Unlike the merchants, the young man never looked at her, too absorbed scribbling notes in the book's margins. His hand blocked her attempt to read his written thoughts upside down. She longed to say something in German and wondered how he'd respond, but squeezed between her parents, she could never be so bold.

When they got off in Vilne, the Levings trailed behind him as they exited the train. Once outside, he moved away quickly, the book tucked under his arm. A man with another life, wholly disconnected from her own, except for the book.

They had arrived in time to stop at a bookshop before dark. Estes made Papa promise she could browse by herself. Her parents waited outside while she chose a new writing journal, a set of three Jane Austen novels, and the same Hegel book the young man had carried. She tucked another among these—the scandalous and widely banned *Fanny Hill: Memoirs of a Woman of Pleasure*. Who could fault her that a copy had found its way into this bookshop, or that it resided on the shelf just below the Austens?

She passed two rubles to the old clerk with glasses halfway down his nose. He returned a handful of kopeks. She waited for him to hold up the licentious volume, fix her in a baleful glare, and demand to see her parents.

"Enjoy."

Estes hid *Fanny* in her coat and kept her expression innocent. Papa approved of the Austens, scowled at the Hegel, and never suspected the deception.

They walked to the Vilne Splendor, the spacious inn close to the train station. The contraband remained hidden, and the next day they explored the busy streets, shopped, and put on their best clothes to attend an evening piano concert in the hotel lobby. The Russian attempt to crush the Polish language and culture did not extend to Chopin's compositions, and the young pianist, who played like Sophie Feinberg, swayed with feeling, eyes closed, fingers caressing the keys. The Nocturne in E-flat major, which finished the performance, broke Estes's heart with its soulful longing, and she wept silently.

Home again the next night, Estes explored a different kind of art—*Fanny Hill* and the fleshy fifteen-year-old eponymous heroine of her forbidden acquisition. Estes ran her tongue over her lips with the revelation about the creaking bed and low grunts which sometimes escaped her parents' bedroom. Mama had alluded to carnal relations between a husband and wife in love, but never in enough detail for Estes to visualize the act. And what would Mama think about sex between unmarried couples, strangers, or two woman, all without any pretense of courtship.

"Encouraged by this, her hands became extremely free and wandered over my whole body," Estes read, "with touches, squeezes, pressures, that rather warmed and surprised me with their novelty." It shocked and excited her. Before the trip to Vilne—she called it "B.V."—her body had existed only to consume food, eliminate waste, and sleep, an inconvenience she hauled around that interfered with the life of her mind. Now, it was "A.V.," and Estes moaned into her pillow and imagined the hands on her breasts and between her legs belonged to the young scholar from the train.

She could never talk to Mama about this physical pleasure—about the exploration of one's own body, about sex without a partner and love, but with imagination and pleasure. Now that she had a better idea what men and women could do, she imagined how Jacob Rosenblum might manage carnal relations. He and all the rabbis would undoubtedly consider what she did a grave sin—another reason to never go back to shul.

Two weeks later, Estes returned *Fanny Hill* to her shelf and took down her new hardcover journal. A hint of the dusty bookshop remained when she held it to her nose. Perhaps resting on a shelf in proximity to masterpieces had imbued the pages with magic.

April 20, 1870

After Papa arranged a few more disappointing meetings with young men and their families, my ardor for Fanny Hill flamed out, doused with arrogance and stilted conversation. Men make so many rules, even about what we do with our bodies. How do they put one foot in front of the other without lengthy discussion—right or left, drag or lift, hop or skip? Fanny, a gross parody, written by a man of course, now repels me. A.V., I reject her lack of intellect, the raw carnality without tenderness and love, all the penetrating, plunging, and skewering!

Estes waited until she and Mama had carried the dinner dishes into the kitchen to tell her father. "I'm not interested, right now, in meeting anyone else, Papa." She'd felt more alone than ever after dinners with those boys.

"What? Avram Rosenblum came in again today. He thinks you and Jacob should see each other again."

"Is Jacob interested?"

"Avram said that, with your Russian and German, you'd be a perfect assistant for him. Jacob's a scholar, Estes. There has to be a reason you've acquired those languages and spent so much time with your books."

"Oh, Papa." Stung by the worst thing he'd ever said to her, she turned her back on him and folded her arms.

"So, now you're shutting out the world? How will an intellectual such as yourself find support?" he yelled. "Will our grandchildren appear magically out of one of your stories?"

Estes refrained from arguing and only turned to face him again when Mama shouted, "Herman!"

Mama placed the tray of cutlery, plates, and cups on the butcher block and put her hands on her hips.

"Doris, I'm just saying . . ."

Mama pointed her index finger and nearly poked his nose. "I know what you're saying. Don't you care what she wants? She's fifteen, you numbskull!"

Papa eyed the tray and backed out of the kitchen.

For three days, Estes and her father did not talk to each other, although she continued to prepare thread and polish boots in the shop. When she finished her chores, and each evening, she built a wall with her books.

Glancing at him as lunchtime approached, she waited for an opening, but Papa never stopped working. He hadn't come upstairs to eat with them since the confrontation, but at noon Mama carried down a pot of tea, three cups, and sugar. After she served them, Mama poured her own cup and sat across from Papa. A minute passed without a word.

"Well, Herman, this silly silent treatment affects me too. I'm tired of carrying on two separate conversations at dinner. Enough already. Estes wants you to talk with this Professor Micah. He's a sophisticated man from the capital, different from the others. Are you going to do anything about it, or do I need to go over there myself?"

Papa looked over at Estes.

She managed a weak smile.

They rose at the same time and embraced.

*

Professor Micah's house in the square sat in a row of narrow, somewhat elegant shops for Horodno, separated by one road that slashed from Market Square out past the railroad tracks. Estes and Mama had wandered by several times during the previous week. They couldn't afford the new dresses, engraved silver candle holders, herbal medicines, or leather bags, but Estes hoped for a chance encounter with the professor. She would have introduced herself to him in English and thrown in some German, French, or Russian, and he'd extend an invitation to browse his library.

Now, on the way to their appointment, she completely ignored the shops, interested only in his living quarters. A housekeeper with a red headscarf and double chin greeted the Levings in a disinterested manner and led the way through the professor's book collection—a labyrinth of floor-to-ceiling volumes in many languages, like the public library's collection, with barely enough space to squeeze through the dusty aisles. A door at the back of this wondrous room opened to a narrow staircase.

"Go up and knock. He's expecting you."

Thin, as if rolled and stretched from a coil of clay, Professor Micah welcomed them with a bow and backhand sweep of his arm. If she squeezed her two hands around his waist, Estes thought her thumbs would meet at his belly button and fingers on his spine. His bony knees and sharp elbows stuck out when he sat and crossed his arms. His round head seemed attached to the wrong body, but his shock of white hair, thick mustache, and wisp of beard beneath his mouth made him rather handsome.

Around his dining table, Professor Micah studied them through glasses perched on an aquiline nose. He had piled books—some oversized and imposing, others that would fit in her hand—on every surface in the apartment.

He addressed Estes directly, which surprised her. "I instructed young men, mostly in Russian. We never used Yiddish or its better-dressed cousin. What can I do for you?"

Estes described her lessons with Uncle Simon and frustration with the other tutors. Then she handed him the three journal entries she'd chosen for the occasion. She'd rejected those that simply reported what happened on a particular day and others full of the emotion this professor might expect from a fifteen-year-old girl. She wanted him to see that her language ability and intellect could match any man's.

April 22, 1870

It could be argued that all great literature is about one thing—loss. We must give up everything, even our memories. The only trace we leave behind is what we create, or what is said about us after we depart. Living must be preparation for this final separation. What other purpose a parent's decline, a sunset imbued with aching sadness?

April 24, 1870

If we could look back at our time from a distance, step away from estate, religion, and gender, would we see that flawed men, not gods, created convention and hierarchies?

The women's question—why do half the people in the world deserve only a question, not an answer? The pathetic portrait men draw of us in literature—capricious characters, kept or pure, with little to do except wait for marriage—and the Jew, conniving, greedy, fixed in the Russian imagination like a toothache.

May 3, 1870

The Judaism of the most religious men, the rabbis and their devotees, is as much a part of them as their heart or lungs. They're different from Papa, who puts on and takes off his practice like an elegant spring coat. Sometimes it hangs in the closet, forgotten until Shabes or High Holy Days when it's brought out and proudly displayed.

Professor Micah read the Yiddish without comment but smiled at these same passages translated into Russian, German, English, and French. "All these languages—if you were a boy and studied Talmud—an Ilui," he said softly. "We start in one week, meet six days, off for Shabes. You will be here by eight, and we finish each day at noon.

"There are more ways to approach literature than through the portrayal of Jews and women. Your first assignment—bring me your idea of characters who show us something original and defy the quarantine of convention."

As soon as she got home, Estes began searching her books. She stopped only to eat before she dived in again. Characters tumbled onto her bed. Emma Bovary dreamily contemplated Bazarov, who argued with Chernyshevsky about what was to be done. Prince Myshkin stroked Raskolnikov's hair, while the underground man, who hated them both, cornered Faust. Akaky shivered, comforted only by Elizabeth Bennett.

She recited her favorite passages aloud, thrilled again with Brontë's *Jane Eyre*. "I can live alone, if self-respect and circumstances require me to do so. I need not sell my soul to buy bliss."

✳

Estes's heart pounded as she traversed the cobblestone square on market day, dodging horses and their droppings, maneuvering around wagons full of goods, avoiding peddlers fighting for space. Professor Micah, an exotic bird with his bright red scarf, waited for her in front of his house.

"My housekeeper resigned. Here's a key. You'll let yourself in from now on."

To her disappointment, he took her papers, folded them, and slid them into his overcoat pocket. "Later. Now we explore." He gave her a notebook and pencil. "Observe and record."

Estes's cane tapped in unison with the professor's as they walked south toward the Niemen on Police Street, the only name besides Market Square that Poles and Jews agreed upon. The Catholics had Saborna, Zamkovaya, Dominikanska, Stephan Batory. The Jews clung to Maimonides, Rambam, Jerusalem. Mostly, one navigated Horodno by landmarks.

The tallest of these, the Catholic basilica with three spires, soared above its neighbors. A brick wall sealed off the grounds from the street. The church had iron-hinged front doors next to the largest crucifix in the city, a four-arshin-long savior carved of oak. Most Jews turned away from the sad-eyed Jesus splayed out on the cross, but not Estes, impressed by the intricate details—the carved beard and hair, the bright red of

Christ's wounds, and the sea-wave folds of the loincloth. Its smaller neighbor to the south, the Orthodox church, Sophia, had five green domes, each with a gold cross.

Across the street from these churches, uniformed men entered the Office of State Security. A line of petitioners waited outside. Passing Jews who spilled out of shuln after morning prayers had beards which tangled into dense forests, not neat and defined like Jesus's on the cross.

Estes and the professor turned east for a block and then south toward the river. As they passed peddlers with laden carts, Professor Micah greeted strangers with a quick wave of his hand. He paused in front of the Great Wooden Shul, which dominated the neighborhood. He pointed to the adjacent cemetery. "My parents."

Through the rusty, iron gate, a hill of black dirt had not yet settled at a fresh grave. Weathered stone markers, the carved names washed out with age, crowded newer, upright monuments.

Next to the shul, Jacob Rosenblum's Holy Land Kheyder and Yeshiva looked insignificant. None of his rabbi teachers had as much education as Professor Micah.

They soon arrived at the Niemen. They followed the path which dipped to the right bank. In five minutes they passed the foot and carriage bridge and met a young man coming the other way leading a sway-backed horse.

"Gut morgn," the professor said.

"And to you," the boy said, bowing.

Estes smiled at his courtesy, and he smiled back. His luminous brown eyes ignited a hot spot on her skin.

"Who is this stoic creature," the professor asked, running a hand along the horse's flank.

"This is Alte Ferd, though he's no older than I am."

"Has he been working for Pharaoh?"

The boy grinned. "You'd think from his posture he hauls granite blocks from the quarry, not light wagons about town." He pointed across the river. "We're on our way to Garfinkle's Spirits, the vodka distillery. My father's the owner. I'm Bernard."

Estes turned from the river and their eyes met again. Bernard blushed but did not look away. Even with his strong hands, he did not seem to Estes like someone who made vodka. He had the look of a scholar.

The professor said goodbye and started along the path. Estes hesitated a moment, gave the boy an awkward nod, and followed. If only Papa had asked him to the house instead of all the other suitors. But could such a boy, with his chiseled cheeks and pretty eyes, be interested in a cripple? She glanced back as Bernard led his horse onto the bridge.

The professor stopped and pointed to Shereshevski's Tobacco Plant, which dominated their side of the river. "This three-story behemoth didn't exist when I was a boy. The biggest employer in Horodno."

"They even have their own shul," Estes said. A worker who came in for a shoe repair had told Papa that they prayed there for a better wage and some fresh air in their pungent hell.

Upstream she spotted that boy and his horse. He moved along the left bank toward the railroad bridge, farther away from her. Directly across the river, men unloaded a barge at Efron's sawmill. Estes and the professor resumed their journey.

A woman trudged by, bent under the weight of a bulging sack hanging over her shoulder. A girl clutched the woman's coat, trailing behind like a kite's tail. The professor strolled along with Estes by his side. Sticks and debris in the river twirled in isolated eddies before floating away. A family of ducks bobbed on the water and paddled off into tall grass.

They came upon a rock piling, the scant remains of an ancient bridge, where they turned north, away from the river. They labored up stone steps cut into the side of the steep bank, emerging into the ruins of Horodno's thousand-year-old castle. Only the Boris and Gleb church downstream, just before the Niemen flexed like a muscle before turning north, came close to the castle's longevity. A stone arch, blanketed with creeping vines, connected the original structure to the newer version, a grand palace built for a Polish king in the last century.

"Time and the works of man," Professor Micah sighed. "What is eternal?"

Estes floated along his dreamy melancholy and didn't answer until he turned to her.

"Perhaps the question?" she finally replied.

They remained still for a while before heading back to Market Square. When they arrived, Professor Micah claimed a bench. While he closed his eyes in the morning sun, Estes observed the familiar scene before her and began to write.

Horodno has no protective mountain range, sea, or desert—a crossroad of languages and culture, settlers and invading armies. Now Jews, Poles, White Russians, Lithuanians, and Russians sell and buy, back and forth with different words and accents, the din of simultaneous conversations challenging to follow without the gestures—a rag peddler's dismissive wave, a squat peasant with both hands thrown into the air, an old man blowing breath through compressed lips, spittle coating his beard, head nods, shakes, eye rolls, hands in pretend prayer, balled into fists. We don't even have the same name for our city—Horodno, Grodno, Hrodna, Gardinas. It's a miracle we communicate at all.

A few fashionable women in bell-shaped dresses ignore the balebostes with their slack, colorless clothes, the maze of wagons and tents, and the tumult of bargaining. They stroll past at their leisure and stare into shop windows.

Two old men play chess. One strokes his gray beard as if searching for the right strategy hidden there. The other sits—a sphinx, arms folded, staring intently at his opponent. A crowd presses around the board, chatters about the position, argues about who is winning.

"White has the upper hand. Let me tell you—mate in five moves."

"Ha, that shows what you know about chess."

"Meshugener!"

"Feh!"

I can see into the back of the nearest wagon. Salted and smoked beef and lamb hang on two rods:

I watch as you haggle with the butcher,
knowing you know where this will end,
right in the middle of your low and his high.
For years you buy his kosher beef,
yet you repeat the same ritual each week,
an invitation to dance you can't refuse.
You both know the exact steps—

"Oy, such a high price this week?"
"So little you offer for such wonderful kosher beef?"

Professor Micah peered over Estes's shoulder. "Strategy. Who will prevail?" He pointed to a Russian official in a blue uniform who pulled out a bottle of clear liquid from one of the wagons. "Looking for vodka without the official state stamp. *The Communist Manifesto* tells only part of the story. The real struggle isn't just about class, but between control and freedom."

For a moment, Estes had returned to the young distiller on the trail, and she had to write quickly to catch up with her tutor's animated comments. A yeshiva student stopped in front of their bench and started to translate the professor's Russian into Yiddish for the Jewish men who had clustered around them. These men, with their black hats, cloaks, and long, dangling forelocks, looked suspiciously at the few Gentiles—laden with overwintered potatoes, spring parsnips, and eggs—who had also stopped to listen or perhaps to rest. The peasants glared back at the Jews. An old man, his wooden cross swinging on a chain as he shuffled by, pulled a bottle from his coat and took a long swallow, muttering something about the Yid's evil eye and magical spells.

One of the Jewish men pretended to spit, then complained about the corruption of young innocents with dangerous ideas before he walked away. The chess game concluded, and its disputatious players and observers migrated to the professor.

"I tell you, Marx had it all wrong. There's a necessary order in nature. Rip out the foundation, and the whole structure crumbles. Who would keep the Cossack from his murderous rampage? Kaput for us all!"

"Meshugener! You have done for Marx what a blind, drunk moyel does to a putz. You want us stuck in the czar's Pale, helpless as fish in a tank. That's your order of things."

A crowd assembled around the combatants, who continued to argue as Estes and Professor Micah departed. Delighted by her first lesson, even though they hadn't yet opened a book, she already anticipated the next.

8

That night Bernard lay in bed and conjured the girl by the river. The old man must have been her grandfather. She'd walked with a cane and had waist-length braids. Her olive complexion, full mouth, and alertness had stunned him a moment, and when Bernard acknowledged the old man's greeting he sensed her watching him. He smiled when she smiled at him and he'd stood as still as Alte Ferd on the trail.

The old man broke his trance when he asked a question about the horse. While they chatted, Bernard stole more glances at the girl, who had turned toward the river. He would have stayed as long as she did. He remembered how her eyes flashed again and met his, how the blood rushed to his face.

When the old man had said goodbye and resumed walking, the girl kept her eyes on Bernard for another instant, gave him a nod, and followed behind the old man. As she walked away, he noticed the severe hitch in her gait and club foot. A shame. From the middle of the bridge, he had spotted her again, downstream. *Turn around.*

Bernard sighed. He didn't even know her name.

His father hadn't told him much about marital relations, only: "When you fall in love, Bernard, you give both body and soul to the other."

When dogs mated, nothing in their frantic humping felt sacred. Nor when boys his age addressed each other variously as putz, shmok, and shmekl. But their reverent discussions of shmundies, yentzes, and knishes, where they fantasized they would one day plant their shvents . . .

His erection grew rigid and refused his efforts to pull up the energy from his swollen flesh and offer it back to God. Jewish law forbid touching oneself. In the *Torah*, God killed Onan for spilling his seed on the ground. When his fingers drifted closer, he remembered the prohibition in the Talmud: "In the case of a man, the hand that reaches below the navel should be chopped off." He thought of Adam reaching for the apple extended by Eve, and the girl's image filled his mind, her voice ringing in his ear. He undressed her, and his erection responded with the intense pressure and pleasure of release. The rabbis must be wrong. How could God not bless a miracle? The girl's lips barely curled in a curious smile.

*

The following winter, a few weeks after master distiller Melachim left Garfinkle's Spirits and moved to Odessa, Bernard walked toward the bridge to meet his old classmates. Just released from a twelve-hour shift at Shereshevski's tobacco factory, Chaim and the twins waited for him midway across the bridge. Before Bernard reached them, he searched the bank, as he always did now, for the pretty girl with the crippled leg. But she never appeared.

His friends bent over the wood railing and stared at the icy river. A crow landed nearby and pecked at the slippery planks. Leib kicked at the bird, which skittered away and resumed its search for food.

Chaim managed a wan smile. He'd lost weight since he started at the factory. He asked about Bernard's father.

"He's a tough old goat," Bernard said. "We argue about his need for rest, but he hates to slow down. How's factory life?"

"It's not so bad, Bernard. At least we're always warm."

Shlomo grunted. "Geese in the oven."

"We got your summons, Bernard," Leib said. "Tell us quickly so we can go home and sleep. We'll be back here too soon."

Bernard spoke quietly. "Melachim's off to Odessa, and with the new stills my father's bringing in, we'll make a lot more vodka. What if you didn't go back to the cigarettes and instead came to work for Garfinkle's Spirits?"

Chaim covered his eyes as if in shock, Shlomo's mouth opened and shut again like a beached fish. Leib grabbed Bernard by the shoulders and whooped.

"When do we start?"

"As soon as you can give notice."

Leib shook his fist at the sprawling plant. "Did those bastard bosses give notice that our pay would always be late, or that it wouldn't be enough to keep the meat falling off our bones? Did they give notice we'd work for hours on our feet without a break, and our raw fingers would ooze blood?"

Chaim and Shlomo put their arms around Leib and Bernard, and the four huddled against the freezing wind.

✳

Over the next two months his friends completed their training and helped Bernard renovate the distillery. On a chilly, damp spring morning, his mates already had the stills working when they greeted him in the barn.

"Hey, Bernard. Ready to make some vodka?"

"Gut morgn, Chaim."

"How's Alfred this morning?" Leib asked. "A goy name for a Jewish horse."

Bernard laughed, and Shlomo's dependable frown relaxed for a moment. The boys stabled the horse and carted in the buckets they would fill today, stacking them near the three eight-foot, double copper tubes. With the new Coffey Stills, Garfinkle's Spirits could expand production from twenty to sixty thousand buckets a year. In theory, as his father had explained when he sold off the older single-batch cookers, the new stills could run continuously, producing an endless drip of vodka, as long as the distillers supplied the fermented raw material. His father preached, however, that cleaning and restarting the stills each day was a devotional act, similar to donning their prayer shawls and tefillin.

Steam rose to the ceiling. Bernard inhaled the vapor and the grainy odor of the malted rye mix, delivered already cooked. The day before, Alte Ferd, walking in a circle, had driven the pulleys and gears on the chute that transferred the raw material from the barn's silo to the distillery's new raised floor.

Bernard bent his knees and pushed his flat-bladed shovel into the pyramid of grain. Straightening his back, he deposited his load into one of the steel fermentation vats. He and Chaim worked in rhythm; the twins mirrored them on the other side, alternating scoops as they counted to five hundred.

Bernard walked to a saucer-sized valve and turned it with both hands. He opened another, and the water, preheated by the cast-iron jacket on the woodstove, mixed with the grain.

"What do you think of my water today, Chaim?"

"The best well water in Horodno makes the best vodka, Bernard."

"Our water tastes so pure my father won't let the rabbis bless it. Impossible to improve God's perfection, he says. We're lucky we have a hill, so gravity works for us. Imagine if we had to haul buckets?"

"They'd call you Alte Chaim and Alte Bernard," Leib said.

"Imagine the process of creation, Leib—sunlight, earth, and water transformed by fire."

Leib chuckled. "Bernard sounds like Rabbi Menshein. Who needs yeshiva with Reb Garfinkle to guide us?"

Shlomo peered into the second fermentation tank. The yeast had completed its work, and a lush odor wafted out. He turned a fist-sized handle, and the wash flowed through a mesh filter, then down into the top of the steam-heated column.

"Fermentation takes us only partway," Bernard told them. "God created a miracle when he made alcohol boil before water. Remember, we don't want the head or tail . . ."

"We go for the heart, just the heart," the crew repeated back in unison.

"Why don't we use a charcoal filter, Leib?"

"Because our ingredients are perfect."

"Is that all?" Bernard glanced at Shlomo.

"Our stills take out the impurities, but leave a hint of personality," the dour twin intoned.

Bernard admired the haze of steam rising through the roof vent and the full buckets ready for sale. Enough space to add more columns.

When his father arrived on foot, Bernard went with him to the cramped office behind the wall of vodka. In two hours they reviewed the books, orders, and distribution details. Since the time of the rebellion, they'd had a reliable partner to deliver their product. They'd continue with Saplestein and Sons, who picked up the vodka and brought it to the province's taverns. The taciturn father and his two boys, after nearly eight years, still communicated mostly with head nods, half-raised hands, and brief observations about the weather.

Bernard's pride in his management of the distillery turned to worry as soon as his father began coughing. When Solomon could speak again, he said, "There's one other thing you need to know."

Bernard expected something profound, like what his father had told him that morning after prayers, although it wasn't clear if he'd meant their vodka or their souls or both: "A master distiller discards the treyf until only the holy remains."

"We search for the spirit in our spirits, Bernard, but we must be practical too, for who will revere God if we don't survive? Call it a special case of the second principle for us Jews." He took Bernard's hands in his own. "Alexander's reforms have improved our lives, but we Jews must remember that deadly encounters in the Pale still flare without warning."

"Vigilance will save us, God willing."

His father smiled. "You're ready to run Garfinkle's Spirits."

9

"How can I concentrate with such an irresistible enticement?" Estes and Professor Micah sat in his tiny dining area, their classroom on the second floor. She wanted total freedom to browse the immense library beneath them.

"You choose one, and I pick two. The men I taught at university did precisely what I ordered, but we started three weeks ago and you're already in charge? And besides, what's this reading for entertainment?"

"You wanted me to hunt for characters who surprise us, yet at the same time you praise obedience?"

"You pick out my flaws like fish bones."

Professor Micah gave in, as Estes knew he would, and allowed her to choose whatever books she wanted. "With one caveat. You have to complete my assignments first. Otherwise, we'll have complete anarchy."

Texts in ten languages. Estes wanted to race downstairs at once, but he shook his head.

"What happens to a cup if you keep running water into it?"

"Our minds aren't a finite cup, more like an elastic sack." She blew her cheeks out to demonstrate but laughed and lost all her air when he smiled.

"See, fill up too fast and you'll pop. Where should we go next with our studies? Enough testing. Hebrew? Only if you want to be a rabbi. The few translations from French and English novels are pale imitations, like an official's stamp after it runs out of ink. Vivid expression defies capture by a language untested in the streets for nearly two thousand years. Polish? We'd have to be circumspect in public." He went on this way for several minutes, debating himself.

"Alas, some practicality is called for. When will you ever use Greek? No, translations will have to do for Homer. Russian must come first, followed by English. Yes, yes, you showed me you speak, read, and write both with some accuracy, but your grammar is haphazard." He grimaced. "Followed by more German and French, with Latin throughout.

"We will read *Metamorphoses* in Ovid's tongue, and if we have to make time for modern writers"—he scrunched up his face, making Estes laugh again—"let us not become trapped by emotional reactions to plot and characters. Perspective is required of the scholar."

✳

A full year later, she struggled to find Professor Micah's scholarly perspective, and at their first-anniversary celebration asked him, "What if I end up stifled and despondent, like other women?" She tried to suppress the anxiety in her voice and handed him her journal.

May 9, 1871
I chewed the nails on both hands as Frankenstein's monster staggered to his feet. He wobbled forth, created by a man who had taken for himself the one role solely owned by women as a matter of biology—giving birth. At least Mary Shelley didn't pretend to be a man, like other women afraid to publish under their real names, not out of fear of a failed effort, but to avoid the shame upon their families of a successful one.

Professor Micah read her journal and suggested a walk, so they took their discussion into the street and switched from Russian to English.

"How have we come to be property, ostracized for straying from rules men made for their own benefit? If I could steal freedom for women the way Prometheus stole fire . . ."

"But, my Estes, we do not want an eagle to eat your liver for eternity."

She followed him north and west, past a Jewish cemetery and into a Polish neighborhood with tight streets and alleys. A woman with a red headscarf and blue dress hauled two water pails from a well with stiff arms. Shoppers ignored the language ban and bartered in Polish.

Estes glanced through the picture window of Kobeleski's Meats. In kosher shops, the bearded rabbi or an assertive baleboste carefully examined every cut. They knew what they wanted and how much to pay—serious business. Here, two bare-headed men smoked pipes, lounged against a meat case, and chatted with the butcher. A peasant couple pulled a slab of raw beef off their pushcart and held it up for inspection.

One-story wood houses crowded in on them. These houses hid most of the privies from view, but families shared a few communally, built on the thin, muddy strips between dwellings. They appeared rooted to the ground, the rotten boards sunk into earth. Young girls held babies while mothers hung wash. Worn linen waved in the breeze.

Boys ran around the small yards and used sticks for swords. One called out, fell to his knees, looked up at the sky, and collapsed. Another staggered back and forth, spun around, and sagged to the ground. As the battle raged around them, the corpses twitched and moaned, then resurrected themselves to resume the fight.

Open doors of meager churches revealed dim interiors lit by candles. Estes and the professor had walked just twenty minutes from Leving's Shoes, but here no one conversed in Yiddish.

They emerged into a neat square bordered by better homes. Professor Micah knocked on the door of a cheerful yellow cottage with a single dormer. Smoke floated from the chimney. A woman around thirty with a regal appearance opened the door. Her erect posture, prominent nose, hair pulled back from her face, and penetrating eyes commanded Estes's attention.

"Eliza Pawloska, allow me to introduce my student, Esther Leving."

The sharp features relaxed when she smiled. "The young lady you've told me about."

"Most pleased to meet you, Pani."

"Are you going to stand on the doorstep like lost cats, or come in for tea?"

Their host took the professor's overcoat and hooked it on a peg by the front door. Flames crackled in the stone fireplace, and Estes took off her sweater and leaned her cane against the wall. They sat at an oval table with a charcoal samovar centered on a copper tray.

"Please, you must call me Eliza," she said, reverting to Yiddish. She lifted the red ceramic teapot from the polished silver urn, which had flowers etched on the sides and two handles. The thick infusion trickled into their cups perfectly centered on matching saucers, until they signaled Eliza. Professor Micah, who hardly thinned at all, took three-quarters of a cup. Estes went halfway, as did Eliza.

Eliza topped each cup off with hot water. "Each tea drinker must find the right strength for themselves, as mood and habit dictate. My Yiddish is worthy, no? I will not speak Russian, at least not while they have banned my language, a failed attempt to control our minds, for language is not a uniform one takes off when required."

Estes glanced at a desk with neat stacks of paper.

"Ah, are you a writer, Estes?"

"I want to be, but right now, I'm more of a reader."

"A prerequisite to produce your own work."

"You have so many books." Volumes covered every wall.

"Come, let me show you my collection."

Estes pushed back her chair, bumped the table, and nearly tipped her cup over.

Professor Micah chuckled. "With this much enthusiasm you might think she's deprived, like a barn-fed calf waiting for spring."

Eliza guided them through the floor-to-ceiling display. Estes compared this library to the professor's, arranged only by language with books rarely returned to the same spot. Eliza organized her books the same way Estes organized her modest collection, by language, but also by topic, each topic arranged alphabetically by the authors' names.

"Professor Micah told me of your interest in women writers." Eliza pulled out a leather-bound book, and they returned to the table. "*Hertha*, by Fredrika Bremer, an English copy. Crafted not only to tell a story but to challenge the established order."

She slid the book to Estes. "I accept the tendentious style, for art and beauty alone will never bring political rights and new laws. It's no surprise the authorities fear a liberated press. Imagine writing a book debated throughout our country with ideas powerful enough to lead to new laws protecting women."

"Chernyshevsky's book inspired me," Estes said, "though I criticized the style to my poor uncle. But why do we need men to tell us how to be liberated? They must simply treat women as their equals." Estes turned to Professor Micah, who nodded and smiled.

"Yes, if all men acted so reasonably, they'd be worth keeping around," Eliza said.

"You must include your own work, Eliza," the professor said. "My Estes has spent too much time in the thrall of dead writers, but you are here with piles of drafts on your desk."

"Dear professor, wait at least until I have something worthy."

"My Polish friend is too modest." He stood and retrieved a book from his overcoat.

"My work in no way should be compared to *Hertha*."

"True, Fredrika Bremer initiated a revolution in Sweden, and you only triggered a debate on emancipation in Poland."

The professor passed Estes *A Few Words About Women*.

Estes examined the book and the author's name, Eliza Pawloska Orzeszkowa.

"At sixteen, I entered an arranged marriage with a man ten years older, not at all interested in discussing the major issues with me. When I argued about rights for women and Jews, he called me crazy. Just a phase, he believed, convinced I would settle into the comfortable life on his estate—a well-fed cow. I kept my married name, though they exiled my husband to Siberia, and I had the marriage annulled."

"I'll never agree to an arranged marriage," Estes said.

"You are quite determined. I learned from failure. My husband had no respect for my support of the rebels during the January Uprising. We had nothing at all in common."

They didn't speak for a few moments. Professor Micah glanced from Estes to Eliza. "I think we have what you novelists call a perfect setup to tell us your whole story, Eliza Pawloska Orzeszkowa."

"Yes, please," Estes urged.

✳

When they left, Estes pressed Eliza's two books against her chest and willed them to fill her with courage. She noticed a pig nosing in the dirt, a blind man led into church, and the suspicious stares, but none of these distracted her from the deep shame of her shaky reaction to Eliza's story.

It had started well—Eliza's battle with her conformist mother, her study with the nuns in Warsaw, her father's Enlightenment library, which now resided in her own home—all safe territory. But when the Polish writer told them about her staunch support for the rebellion, with vivid descriptions of injured men, Estes's imagination had betrayed her.

How could she ever become a writer if she couldn't handle stories from real life? Eliza ran a field hospital in the war. She had risked everything when she tried to transport the leaders to safety. Estes condemned her own soft existence. What had she ever sacrificed for any cause? A coward. She blamed Papa for his pragmatic neutrality. Eliza's narrative had left no opportunity to reclaim her composure.

When Eliza had described a young man, Janutz, who talked about returning home to see his family even as his guts flowed from a bayonet wound and his eyes glazed over, Estes feared she might vomit. Before she'd fainted, Eliza reached out and grasped both of her hands between her own.

"Oh dear, you're quite pale. You're right there with me, aren't you?"

The next moment, Estes lay prone on the floor. Voices came from a great distance as Eliza elevated her feet and Professor Micah placed a water-cooled towel on her forehead. When Estes could sit up, Eliza gave her water and watched while she drank.

Eliza censored the rest of her story.

Led into battle and found unworthy to serve.

*

That night, Estes read to her parents from Eliza's book. "The status of women in both family and society is low and unsatisfactory and ignores women's importance. Man has an unlimited power and control over woman, and he holds the privileges of being her judge and master. By law, the woman is totally subject to and dependent on her husband."

Mama said Eliza spoke for so many women, but Papa didn't say anything at all. Estes couldn't marry someone like him. Eliza had given her hope she wouldn't end up in the banal, predictable existence Papa would impose on her. She would be different.

After she said goodnight, Estes sat up in bed and forced herself to study an illustration in Papa's history book depicting the Battle of Borodino—penance for her faint. She read the caption: "Seventy thousand killed or wounded in the first real battle against Napoleon." The carnage given no more significance than the bushels of wheat consumed by the armies.

This time, the portrayals of violence and death didn't make the room spin or cause lightheadedness, but it still repulsed and shocked her—men cut apart with sabers, rifles, cannon fire. How could they have shared her wonderment at life or her belief in the permanence of its passing?

Estes had seen and touched a lifeless body just once—her last grandparent, laid out on her parents' bed, her earliest memory, even before the one of writing Hebrew script on her walls. She had asked Papa why Grandma kept sleeping, impatient to play the rhyming game with her bobeshi while they both rocked with laughter.

"She'll wake up later with God," he told her.

The arrival of Uncle Simon and Aunt Miriam convinced her that Grandma had to wake up now. She put one hand on Grandma's lifeless skin and the other on her own warm belly.

She pressed her ear to Grandma's chest—silence.

"Grandma, everyone's here," she whispered directly in her ear. "Please wake up, Grandma, please." She kissed Grandma's cheek and hoped for a sign of life—a twitch of the fingers, a flutter of an eyelid, a movement of the lips. But Grandma had left her body.

She ate with the gathered family, then went back to her parents' bedroom. Three women, dipping cloths in a water basin, washed the body. They dressed Grandma in white linen while a fourth stood to the side, chanting about God. Estes turned and buried her face in Mama's dress.

Before they traveled to the cemetery, Mama explained the rending and gave her a choice whether to participate. She let Mama nip her blouse with a knife. Still, it startled her when the grownups grabbed their collars and ripped their shirts at the graveside. Then Mama tore Estes's.

Papa, Uncle Simon, and four other men used ropes to lower the wooden box. When the rabbi spoke, Estes asked Mama, "Why is he talking about God? Did he die too?"

"God never dies, and now Grandma is with him."

"They both fit inside?"

When the rabbi started to sing, a line formed behind Papa and Uncle Simon. Each mourner grabbed dirt from the excavated pile and tossed it on the box. When her turn came, Estes picked up two handfuls but didn't throw them at once. Instead, with her arms out straight, she sifted the earth through her fingers.

That experience of death had no blood and no struggle. The rending, and later the shiva, convinced her something important had happened, unlike this gory war illustration.

May 14, 1871

So many bodies rotting with no names. In place of songs and prayer, there are crows hovering over the dead. Nameless soldiers. Did they believe in their cause? Where is the French farmer's enmity to the Russian peasant sprawled across his chest?

*

Estes worried Eliza wouldn't want to see her again after the faint, but the following day the Polish writer invited them back to discuss literature and read aloud. Neither Eliza nor Professor Micah mentioned the incident, and Estes vowed to leave it behind as well. On their return home, she wondered aloud if Eliza had other friends in Horodno.

"Anyone who defies convention scares people."

"I don't understand. Many sympathized with the rebels." Before her teacher could react, she repeated one of his favorite phrases: "Not understanding is the beginning of knowledge."

"Progress. As for Eliza, her involvement with the uprising didn't mark her for social exile. She had the misfortune to marry a man she didn't love and to fall for a married man who had an invalid wife, confined to bed."

"Like poor Rochester?"

"Yes. But *Jane Eyre* is fiction. You will find, my Estes, unlike novels, real life lacks these convenient endings. But we must lift up our mood." The professor reached into his overcoat and pressed a book into her hands. "From a scholar friend in America."

Estes read *Waldon Pond* that very afternoon and imagined walking those woods with Thoreau in complete freedom. In the following days, however, she couldn't imagine freedom for her neighbor, Mrs. Sablestein, who sobbed in their kitchen—a woman with a drunk and abusive husband and eight children to feed. Or for Papa's customer, Eva Forgins, younger than Estes and forced against her will to marry a much older man. And especially after the shocking four days of vicious attacks against Odessa Jews, the idea that Jewish freedom might be attained with this czar felt as deluded to her as the emancipation of women.

In the *Moscow Daily*'s hateful article, "A Scourge on Blessed Russia," the author blamed the Jews for the condition of the peasants and the disturbance. He quoted the notorious Jacob Brafman—a converted Jew turned antisemite—who warned about the "Jewish conspiracy against the rest of humanity."

Estes raged to her parents and Professor Micah. "If we remain silent, these lies will pass unchallenged."

"It's to be expected," Papa responded. "We make some progress, and the knives come out." He looked at Estes with sad eyes and counseled patience.

Mama suggested she write in her journal.

Professor Micah took her to Eliza Orzeszkowa.

Estes's letter to Czar Alexander II, which challenged the system of privilege upheld by the economic and political repression of peasants, Jews, and women, would remain concealed in her journal. Her poem, however, first appeared in the Hebrew Jewish weekly, *Ha-Melits*, in Odessa. Subsequently, the *Moscow Daily* translated and reprinted "A Russian Notion."

> *Aristocrats in gilded parlor*
> *discuss their very nasty plan.*
> *Their wives, alas, they also harbor*
> *a Russian notion they call grand.*
> *This czar, less harsh to Jewish people,*
> *concerned ministers not so gleeful.*
> *The time is right to set things straight,*
> *to anger peasants, stir their hate.*
> *This strategy, it leaves them smiling:*
> *"Let's blame the Jews for poverty!*
> *Then deftly, by bitter degree,*

from us to them send what's defiling.
We'll keep our peasants in the dark.
The voiceless Jew—an easy mark!"

Estes studied her gefilte fish while her parents discussed the poem.

"Who could have composed this?" Papa asked.

"It's wonderful, don't you think?" Mama said.

"They say the author used a style called the Onegin stanza. Now they're questioning writers in Petersburg."

"Whoever it is, they spoke for all of us." Mama touched Estes's knee under the table.

Professor Micah later told her, "The bureaucrats will stamp their reports, accumulate stacks of paper, and soon forget this matter. Alexander and his advisors have a dam about to burst. They don't have time for these diversions."

As the professor had predicted, the authorities did not confiscate the presses or arrest the publishers. Instead they warned them not to print extreme antisemitic invective or radical sentiment, and the most virulent attacks stopped. Estes never claimed credit for her work, but the weight of injustice lessened a bit, and she continued with her studies. Neither she, her mother, Professor Micah, nor Eliza mentioned the matter again.

IO

The riots in the spring of 1871 surprised the Jews of Odessa—known for their literature, music, and vibrant culture. It had caused some in the Pale of Settlement to question their future in Russia because the attack, the second targeting in twelve years of the center of Jewish enlightenment, seemed a sign that even modern, educated Jews would never be secure. The antisemitic mob had stolen possessions, raped a woman in front of her bound husband, and beaten six Jews to death. Now, who could know where or when the next assault would occur?

Bernard, however, wholly consumed with keeping his father alive and vigilant only to every turn in his condition, paid little attention to this isolated incident of horror in the south. Besides, Odessa, perched on the Black Sea, was more than one thousand versts from Horodno. Another world.

By late fall, despite Bernard's prayers and nursing, his father's consumption had changed from a cranky guest—soothed with fresh air, baths, and good food—to a dangerous intruder. He ran high fevers and his cheeks hollowed out. His already pale skin blanched further, and his once-solid frame dwindled. Weeks had passed since his father felt well enough to ride to the distillery and watch the men work for a few hours.

Bernard prepared breakfast and helped his father to the table.

"Smart to get me out of bed." Solomon shuffled like a much older man. "Once the eating and sleeping areas lose their distinction . . ."

"I'll stay home with you today, Father."

"How will we keep the distillery going? Unless you want to put Leib in charge." His laugh at the expression on Bernard's face set off a coughing spell.

"Until noon, Father. They can manage without me for a few hours."

"See, Bernard, you're already a skilled negotiator."

Solomon's fever rose all morning, and Bernard didn't leave his side. As his father slept fitfully, Bernard recalled a story about their first house—how it filled with vapor whenever his father cooked vodka. In the winter, water condensed on the windows and puddled on the floor.

His father had saved to buy property for their distillery, and when prospects improved, he built this house, close enough to walk to work but removed from the town's gossip. Bernard had lugged and dumped tiny pails of dirt away from the foundation trench his father and two helpers dug. They rejoiced when the house emerged from the earth.

"Everything needs a solid foundation," his father said.

Bernard watched as his father covered field stones he'd collected with gray mortar. The men set adze-squared timbers into place on top of the leveled rock wall.

"New life," his father said as the house rose.

The disease, first diagnosed four and a half years ago, entered its final stage. Solomon, delirious in his sleep, mumbled incoherently. He sat up and stared at Bernard with glazed eyes. "Saul, you came back. Where have you been?"

"I've returned." Bernard eased him back and massaged his father's feet and hands until the agitation passed. He professed his love and gratitude, wept and prayed.

✳

Rabbi Menshein conducted the graveside service, and Bernard led the assembly in the Mourner's Kaddish. He progressed through the prayer, though he felt stuck like an oared boat mired in shallow water. After the service, guests overfilled their house and spread out into the yard. Leib, Shlomo, and Chaim stood next to him. Bernard wanted to run until he collapsed.

For the seven days of shiva, he didn't eat much. He sat on a low mourner's bench for hours at a time and received guests. Jacob Rosenblum appeared each morning and sang. His sonorous voice lifted Bernard above the house, and he watched himself pray. Bernard vowed to attend shul three times a day for the next eleven months once shiva ended. He would visit his father's grave and say hello on the way to the distillery.

Chaim's family offered to take Bernard in, but he wanted to stay in his own home. Rabbi Menshein didn't intrude on Bernard's grief or offer platitudes to fill the emptiness, only saying, "Come visit me anytime."

When the stream of guests ended, Bernard opened the front door, and fresh air swept in.

"Why do we have only one door in the whole house?" he had asked his father.

"And what do we possess to hide behind doors? God would see it anyway."

Bernard walked around the tidy, well-stocked kitchen. Wooden spoons, cast-iron pans, and copper pots hung from hooks. In the dining area, he ran his hand fondly over the Chumash and prayer books. The second shelf held the rest of the collection—philosophy, history, and annotated chess games.

In his father's bedroom, neatly stacked clothes waited in a cramped closet. From the top shelf, Bernard pulled down a heavy crate full of abandoned items with no purpose except to mark the passing of time: a couple of clay sculptures, one a voluptuous nude, the other a praying man with a missing leg; old cutlery and dishes from grandparents, some chipped like bad teeth; a delicate wooden box containing his mother's thin, scratched wedding ring; a water-stained letter signed, "love Solomon"; a horseshoe with a few bent cleats; an empty Garfinkle's Spirits bottle; a pair of Bernard's first shoes.

He tenderly fit all the items, like little birds with broken wings, back into their crate. He took his father's wool coat down from its peg, buried his face in the collar, and wept.

❊

For weeks, when he got home from the distillery, Bernard put on his father's coat. Then he sat at the table and sobbed without restraint until he felt empty. Afterward, his father's absence refilled the void until the next evening, when Bernard wept again.

He had a morning routine as well. Upon waking, he splashed cold water on his face, stirred the wood fire and added a log. Then he put on his yarmulke, wrapped himself in his tallis, and strapped on his tefillin.

With the Shema bound to his body, he recited his prayers. After packing his breakfast and lunch, he walked to shul. Following the thirty-minute service, the rabbi called those who had lost a parent to join him. Bernard and the other bereaved led the Mourner's Kaddish, with the congregants echoing, "And we say amen."

After six rounds in a loud, clear voice, the service ended, and Bernard went to the cemetery. He imagined his father, who rested on the street edge of the shul's ancient plot, rejoining the bustling chaos of Horodno.

He finished a morning of vodka production, then left midday for the twenty-minute walk back to the shul for another service, before returning to the distillery to make more vodka. In the evening, Chaim, Leib, and Shlomo joined him for the recitation, and he walked home alone.

Three weeks after the funeral, Chaim put his arm on Bernard's shoulder. Leib, who had ceased his joking and teasing, except for the occasional poke at his brother, patted Bernard on the back.

Shlomo's dolorous words, meant to comfort, matched the slow, sad songs he played on his fiddle. "This will pass in time, Bernard." But Bernard heard the unspoken, "and something else will take its place."

All this reminded Bernard of his loss. The shul lessons about the Torah and the parables hadn't prepared him for the finality of death. He felt angry at God for withholding the gift of literacy and now taking away his father. He even felt mad at his father and his principles, as though the universe had any governing laws except chance and loss.

Bernard feared he might drown in his sorrow and doubt. In desperation, he began boring into the Shema—in the morning, before bed, whenever he was alone. *The Lord is our God The Lord is One The Lord is our God The Lord is One The Lord is our God The Lord is One The Lord is our God The Lord is One The Lord is our God . . .*

At the distillery, he managed with effort to concentrate on production and to carry on conversations. But even there, the Shema droned on in his mind as he shoveled grain, rotated valves, drew vodka from the still, ate lunch. *The Lord is our God The Lord is One.*

At home, the droning continued, driving him out of bed on a January night, two months after his father's death. He threw wood in the stove, prepared for prayer, and sat next to the warmth.

Was he going mad? He dispatched the thought and the fear, wielding the Shema like a scythe. He cut through the memories, guilt, loneliness, and grief that rose up. He did not cling to joy when it filled the emptiness. *The Lord is our God the Lord is One The Lord is our God The Lord is One The Lord is our God The Lord is One* . . . The air vibrated. Bernard's mind split open and filled with brilliant light. Had he died? Stunned, ecstatic, he stumbled outside. The moon, an orange half-crescent, hung motionless in the dawn-streaked sky.

He needed to tell someone. He removed his prayer accoutrements and raced to the rabbi's house. He ran along the empty road past his blackened oak, the laundry hanging in the Bloom's yard, and the snow-dusted fields sloping down to the Niemen.

Bernard pounded on the rabbi's door and heard shuffling. Rabbi Menshein appeared, Chumash in hand. In the tiny kitchen, the rabbi listened closely, without interrupting, as Bernard described his experience.

"Many study Torah for sixty years but see only the reflection of God's manifestations in the created world. You have experienced Eyn-Sof, God's pure essence."

"Tell me what to do now. How do I keep it from becoming just another memory?"

"How would I know? I'm just a poor rabbi. You could spend every moment on the Zohar for the next fifty years and still see only God's shadow. But do we need to stare straight at the sun and burn our eyes to experience its warmth? All I know is that you need to live, Bernard."

After Clara Menshein served them eggs, toast, and tea, Bernard ran to the shul. For the first time since his father's death, grief did not choke his voice or tear his heart. The other mourners stared at him like he didn't belong—a songbird perched among a conspiracy of ravens.

On the way to Garfinkle's Spirits, Bernard noticed the worn clothes hung over the sides of carts and squat houses crowding each other. *Manifestations of God.*

He slid the distillery door open. The shiny column stills rose like arrows poised to fly. The fermentation vats bubbled with life. His three workers went about their jobs with purpose.

"Gut morgn!" Bernard shouted. His friends froze in place for a second, before gathering around. "Let's make vodka!"

II

On a February day in her second year with Professor Micah, Estes moved carefully across the icy square, deserted in the frigid wind except for one fish peddler and his customer. As she passed, she noticed the peddler's red nose and the customer's hands pinned under his crossed arms. Both men stomped their feet.

"Ten kopeks? I'll give you eight."

"Haven't seen this kind of winter since I was a boy. Make it nine, and it's yours."

"Done."

She fumbled with the key to get into the first-floor library and resisted the temptation to browse since Professor Micah would be waiting for her. Sometimes, when she left for home and he didn't follow her down, Estes borrowed a book, denying him the pleasure of advising her.

Professor Micah usually met her on the landing before she could knock, and she expected him to open the door before she reached the top of the stairs. Her approach must be unmistakable—the beat of the cane followed by the lighter touch of her foot. Today, however, she waited on the landing. She tapped the door, then knocked harder.

"Just one moment, Estes."

Professor Micah's appearance startled her. Ordinarily impeccably attired and groomed, this morning he wore yesterday's rumpled clothes, and white stubble covered his cheeks. The lantern on the table, surrounded by books and papers, had blackened with soot.

While he went to change clothes, Estes turned down the wick and extinguished the flame. She cleared the table and prepared the tea. None of the professor's cups or saucers matched in color or style. In the winter, he kept two teapots on the stove, one for hot water, the other with concentrated tea, always a different strength. In warm weather he used the battered and tarnished copper samovar.

The professor joined Estes at the table. "Both the tea drinker and the scholar must keep a flexible approach. Look how much thinking you've accomplished already."

"You must promise you won't let your lantern get this hot." She frowned at the smudged glass. "Why was it lit this morning?"

"I was engrossed in my work and must have dozed off. I overslept and deeply regret being late for my favorite student."

"I'm your only student, Professor Micah."

"Yes, and also my best."

"Your best student cautions you about working late at night, but since you're repentant, here are my geometric proofs." She handed over a few sheets of paper. What would she ever do with this useless information?

While Estes cut the cake, Professor Micah added sugar and a bit of milk to each cup. In no hurry to resume mathematics, she chewed slowly as her fingers and toes thawed in the delicious heat from the woodstove.

Except for one visit from Eliza, they'd spent the past two weeks working alone in his apartment. She rubbed the familiar, worn surface of his small table. The windows rattled as the wind howled.

After they cleared their plates, Professor Micah tapped on the stack of problems he placed in front of her, and Estes went to work. She completed a few, fiddled with her pencil, and stared with desire at his weighty volume of *War and Peace*.

"Literary research," he told her.

"Why am I doing this meaningless work instead of exploring Tolstoy with you?"

"Every scholar must have some mathematics." He turned back to his book. A few minutes later, Estes put her pencil down.

"What now?"

The blackened lantern gave her the advantage. "I promise I'll complete these tonight. But now, please tell me a story, Professor Micah. Tell me your story." She knitted her brow, and he closed the book.

"Incorrigible. What is to be done with you?"

Estes nudged the geometry problems a bit farther from herself, refilled both cups, and waited.

"Hmm, what to include? Tolstoy leaves out little in his stories, but for you, I will edit mine."

"But how will you choose what's important? Why not tell me

everything and I'll make up my own mind." She glanced again at the mathematics.

He shut his eyes and remained so still he might have fallen asleep. When he finally spoke, his voice, softer than usual, invited her into his childhood, when his family lived south of the Niemen in shtetl Horodno.

✳

Days later, Estes showed him her proofs, now relegated to evening work, her ticket to his continuing adventures. As with her favorite books or Uncle Simon's stories, Professor Micah had drawn her in. She'd suffered in an icy rain among the sick Jews of Horodno, who waited to see Micah's father, the shtetl's doctor. A young mother cuddled her wheezing, glassy-eyed baby. Two daughters supported their old father, bent double in pain. A young man coughed up blood. The professor's father had replaced the faith healer's incantations and fetid concoctions with science.

Estes's stomach bubbled at the foul smell of human waste that hung over the river town, and when Professor Micah told her how his parents had succumbed to a cholera epidemic, she'd wanted to move closer and reach for his hand. Instead, she fumbled for words and sagged into her chair.

When the town's head rabbi also fell sick and died, a rumor spread that his disembodied voice continued to recite Torah. Professor Micah credited this period with his lifelong rejection of religious belief. She, too, had turned from religion because of its ignorance. They had so much in common.

Estes traveled with the orphaned Micah across the empire to join his wealthy uncle in Petersburg. Villages rolled by in an expansive countryside with peasants hunched over planting potatoes, wagons full of early spring greens, and baskets of soft onions left over from the fall harvest. The immensity of Russia made her life in Horodno feel so confined.

He'd shared details: how he arrived as a young orphan in Saint Petersburg with its broad, crowded streets, men draped in fancy clothes carrying valises, ladies in white dresses strolling arm in arm with medaled officers, soldiers frozen in position guarding the grand palace along the Neva, beggars on street corners, blind, crippled, or drunk, with tales of woe and outstretched hands. And Napoleon's hubris—if not for Russia's winter, *"Nous pourrions parler en français ma jeune amie."*

Estes had shuddered at his history of the violent, backstabbing czars, patricide, and deadly coup d'états, but cheered for Catherine the Great, who died fourteen years before Micah arrived in the capital city. Brought to Russia as a child, Catherine perfected her Russian, forged alliances, took lovers, and waited. She waited and watched, then seized the throne, had her husband strangled, and ruled for thirty-four years.

Steam rose from the professor's tea, and his glasses fogged up when he took a sip. Estes eased them off, wiped them on her sleeve, and returned them to his nose. "Now you can see."

"Not necessary for telling my story, but I'll know if you yawn at my tale."

Professor Micah, once a boy her age, that young man still present when he smiled. Would she have loved him then too?

"You're flushed, my Estes." He sighed, suddenly lost in reverie. His narrative might twist away from the main route, perhaps run parallel a while, before rejoining the story, years later. Or it might wander along a secondary lane, following tangentially related topics, before coming back to where it had veered off.

"The deaths and ugliness I experienced by the time I turned twelve spurred my life-long interest in aesthetics. Perhaps if I had been raised in a time of peace, or my parents had not died, I would have become a soldier."

Estes tried to imagine his thin frame and delicate hands wielding a rifle. "As likely as sturgeon living in trees. And who would teach me about the decadence of the czars?"

"Let me skip forward a bit to my appointment at Petersburg University, as a professor of the classics and philosophy. By 1825, fifteen years after I left Horodno, heartbroken, I had mastered my new world. With the help of my uncle, I had an apartment a comfortable distance to the University and Nevsky Prospekt.

"Alexander I, the savior of Russia, died that year. He had no children, and his successor, younger brother Nicholas, viewed dissent as a weed to eradicate, not a tree to prune and shape. A momentous time had arrived in Russia, Estes. On one side, despotism and the ideology the presumptive czar would soon adopt—orthodoxy, autocracy, nationality—on the other side, the abolishment of serfdom and a constitutional monarchy, modest demands by today's standards. When I think about what happened, though, I see that struggle has shaped Russia's history for the past half-century."

The professor continued: "A group of us, students and faculty, walked across the frozen Neva to a demonstration of military officers. A few thousand gathered at the Admiralty and the statue of the Bronze Horseman."

"I want to see a demonstration like that." Estes balled both of her hands into fists.

He offered a slight smile. "Some of the officers who had refused to swear allegiance to Nicholas mingled with the friendly crowd and explained their demands. I fell in with one of them, a cadet about my age. His name was Ivan Thominavich, and he doffed his hat at me and spoke of his desire to advance through merit, rather than patronage."

"But if this Ivan wanted to give up his lands and privileges, why would he need permission?"

"Do revolutions happen by acting alone?"

"A single ball of snow grows as it rolls downhill."

Who else could she talk to this way? They each took a sip of tea. The wind gusted, and Estes turned to watch the falling snow for a moment. She offered to top off his tea, but he declined, so she prompted him to continue his narrative.

"Tell me more about Ivan Thominavich."

"The number of protestors didn't change, while Nicholas's forces grew. Still, an air of optimism rose among us. Ivan told me December 14th would be forever known as the turning point. These young men represented Russia's hope for the future.

Would she look back, years hence, to find a moment when time bent, making a sharp separation between what came before and what came after?

"The vapor froze in our mustaches and eyebrows as we talked for hours. I was quite taken with him."

Professor Micah had never looked so melancholy. Her throat thickened with loneliness.

"I remember a few older men as well, somber fellows without Ivan's enthusiasm. Men of action, a bit sour standing around in the cold, Ivan told me. Now I know it wasn't impatience but foreboding on the faces of those veterans.

"When I asked Ivan whether the czar would even consider their petition, he laughed.

"'You're a pessimist, my dear friend,' he told me. Ivan acted not as a mutineer, but as a guest who expected to be invited in for a pleasant exchange. Even when the rebel leader abandoned the cause, Ivan did not waver. But when a Decembrist shot and killed the military hero Nicholas sent to negotiate with the officers . . .

"Ivan suddenly grasped their critical situation. He promised me we'd continue our conversations after the demonstration, then he joined the military formation near where I stood. I kept my eyes on him. My new friend stood with bayonet and rifle poised.

"When a rebel regiment tried to enter the Winter Palace, my hope for a peaceful resolution vanished. Indeed, Nicholas ordered a cavalry charge, but it failed when the horses slid on the icy cobblestones."

Professor Micah paused. Most of the literary conflicts that kept Estes up at night resolved with time—love requited, the innocent set free, heroines and heroes wiser after suffering. Now, though, she knew something horrible would happen, but one can't change history after it's already passed by. Before he resumed, she knocked over her tea, apologized, and mopped it up with a rag.

"If we could change the outcome by spilling tea, I would fill the entire house, cup after cup, to undo that sorrowful event. When the shooting began, I couldn't tell where it came from, but I saw Ivan's chest burst crimson. He collapsed, an empty sack, and lay faceup in the snow. Ruthless cannon fire ripped apart the rebel lines, and I ran with the crowd away from the slaughter. We went a distance on Nevsky Prospekt before we felt safe and stopped."

She pressed the floor with her good foot.

"The Decembrists battled their way clear of the Admiralty and regrouped on the icy river. The boom of artillery was deafening and shattered the ice. Later, we learned the explosions threw many into the frigid waters."

Estes shivered.

"And the friendly crowd of moments before? What of us? Did we rush back to aid the men at this moment of decision for Russia? The surprise of the devastating assault had sent us racing away. Who wouldn't bolt from an angry bear's den? But after we'd saved ourselves and looked back from a distance at the massacre, not one among us attempted to organize and aid the reformers. Not a single one."

What would she have done? Return, to place her body between the wounded and the czar's army? No. She doubted she would willingly die for any cause.

"They dragged the survivors off to the Winter Palace and exiled most of them to Siberia, but five received a death sentence and public execution I did not attend. Friends told me each man fell to the ground, bruised but alive because of defective ropes—a sign from Providence. According to custom Nicholas should have ordered reprieves. Instead, he demanded stouter rope. In Petersburg, God also had to follow orders."

Estes imagined her tipped cup righted itself and received its spilled tea. Bullets returned to their rifles, swords to their scabbards. Ivan rose from death and returned to life, hopeful about the future, talking to the young professor who now sat in front of her, an old man.

"Ah, Estes, all this talk of the past. These events, so real as they unfolded, turned out to be as ephemeral as spring snow. Yet I still recall them from half a century away, as if they'd occurred this morning."

"And this moment," she said, "will pass also."

Estes wanted to shift away from the mood of that sad story. "When you retired, why didn't you go abroad?" She imagined Professor Micah in Paris or London, stopping in bookshops, speaking his accented French and English.

"Oh, I didn't have the energy for such an adventure, and how natural to come back to where it all started. Besides, I have my books, and the one I'm writing."

She pressed her lips together. He hadn't told her about this project.

"Estes, my dear, I write in the evenings, and I've been sharing some of it with you these last days."

"Do you give Eliza your drafts?"

"When I'm ready, both you and Eliza will be my first critics, the two women I most admire, but first we have to think about your future. You cannot go on with this old man indefinitely."

"But what else can I do here?" Her voice broke. "I'm happy with our arrangement, and you have so much to teach me."

"You must have a plan with your parents. Eliza and I will advise you, of course. When better than the imminent return of spring, when this wretched ice is gone, to talk about new growth? The czar's reforms have completely derailed. Everything is in reaction. Nihilists who could gather openly in Petersburg a few years ago, the young women with clipped hair smoking cigars with the men—they're all potential assassins now, exiled to Siberia. No one is satisfied with a little freedom, and I fear a violent clash is unavoidable. When things turn bad, they'll get worse for the Jews."

Ten days later, Estes strained to pull a weighty box of Professor Micah's literary magazines across the square. At least he felt guilty about bringing up the end of their academic work together. Otherwise, he'd never have allowed these precious *Sovremennik*s to leave his house. The censors had shut down its publication in 1866.

The sled she'd retrieved from Leving's Shoes slid smoothly on its wooden runners. She rested halfway. Two men offered to help, but she politely declined. Once home, she carried an armful of the journals through the shop, limping, with the cane hooked loosely on her arm.

"More books?" Papa asked. "Why not donate them to the library?"

"*Sovremennik*s, Papa. I have to return them."

She said hello to Mama, went back to the shop, and hauled the remainder of the journals to her room in three trips. Papa joined her and Mama for lunch.

"This just arrived." He held up the dinner invitation. "In four days, we're having dinner with Professor Micah and Eliza Orzeszkowa to talk about your future. How long have you known about this?" he asked Estes.

"How wonderful," Mama declared. "Don't you agree, Herman? I feel I know Pani Orzeszkowa already."

Papa spoke carefully, "The Polish writer has been very good to the Jews, but her involvement in the '63 revolt, and personal matters, have caused her some difficulty."

"A principled woman, Herman. Horodno's famous female writer, and she'll have dinner with us because of our daughter."

That night she spread the *Sovremennik*s on her bed. Thrilled to find Professor Micah's name as a contributing editor, she chuckled. He'd pretended—not very effectively—to disparage the modern novel, while for thirty years he'd challenged his intellect working for Russia's best-known literary magazine. She browsed the contents for famous names, then read a George Sand piece, some back and forth between Turgenev and Chernyshevsky, and a remembrance of Vissarion Belinsky.

This is what she'd wanted when she asked Professor Micah for his story—his intellectual development and tales about authors: Pushkin and his duel, Belinsky's famous letter, Chernyshevsky writing from jail, Dostoyevsky's arrest and mock execution, which Professor Micah had learned about from the brooding writer himself.

March 24, 1872

Six men marched to the prison yard, three of them tied to a post, blindfolded, Dostoyevsky next in line, not the queue one finds waiting to see some imperious official when time is a burden and the impatient petitioners jostle for position. No, instead he prayed for time to stop, would have gladly stepped aside and let others push to the front. "Take my turn, I can wait," for that moment of waiting was the entirety of life remaining, and to go on waiting forever would have been a gift, except anticipation and dread knocked him to his knees, his senses on full alert, the sounds and movements surreal—the awful command of the officer, the rustle of rifles lifted on shoulders. Then the last second commutations! The drowning men plucked from the sea, their troubles afterward weighed against those few seconds, which had spread out like eternity, and I, too, had nearly drowned in the tumultuous waves of Professor Micah's narrative.

"Think about those writers," he urged me, "and the risks they took.

If only Belinsky were here. What a debate we could have. Eliza Pawloska Orzeszkowa and Vissarion on one side, Professor Micah and his protégé on the other."

He called me his protégé and urged me to illuminate the past with my pen! Now I see that all his stories have been pointing me toward boldness and courage.

Estes extinguished the lantern, got out of bed, and located Professor Micah's house through her window. The dimly lit first-floor library said he must be up late working. She considered getting dressed to visit him now. Maybe he'd allow her to read his manuscript before anyone else and advise him. He might acknowledge he needed her as much as she needed him. She should also make sure he had not fallen asleep with the lantern lit again but didn't want to treat him like a child. She yawned and realized how tired she was. She would talk to him tomorrow.

PART II

L'CHAIM

1872–1881

Nothing is so necessary for a man
as the company of intelligent women.
– Leo Tolstoy, *War and Peace*

Van Gogh. *The Novel Reader* (1888). Oil on canvas 73 x 92 cm. Private collection.

I

The newspaper called for young men to volunteer at the Horodno Firehouse. This struck Bernard as something that would honor his father, so with his rekindled spirit, he entered the old barn with its attached observation tower, north of Market Square.

A stout boy with hazel eyes, blonde hair, and a pale face grasped his hand. "You'll have to meet the captain. He's a former Polish officer. Fought in the rebellion. I'm Joseph."

"Bernard Garfinkle."

Joseph didn't try to crush his hand or lock him in an iron grip and hold him captive, nor did he keep his hand limp and offer nothing of himself. His grasp, like Bernard's own, was firm but not intrusive.

"I come here for two overnight shifts each week. Days, I work with my uncle, cutting saw logs for Efron's mill." Joseph dipped a rag into a bucket of grease and knelt next to a wagon with its rear wheels removed. "We need to be prepared, though we've had no fires since I joined. Are you connected with Garfinkle's Spirits?"

"My father started the distillery." Bernard rocked from one foot to the other to get some sensation back in his toes. Six horses huddled in the yard, their breath vaporizing in the frigid air.

"What's this, a recruit?"

"Captain Stanislav Boraski, this is Bernard Garfinkle."

"You look able-bodied, and a handsome lad, but the girls might not find you so pretty with one of these across your face." He rolled up his sleeve and tapped an ugly red blotch running from wrist to bicep. Bernard smelled whiskey.

"Litvaks, Poles, even Russians—we'll try them all. There are no Jew fires, Russian fires. Flesh is flesh, and it burns faster than wood. This is a private operation, Garfinkle. Wealthy merchants paid for the building, but the city gives us nothing. My friends in Petersburg donated this Shand and Mason engine.

"We fight okay if we discover our foe in time. At least our lookout tower gives us some sight in all directions. Without the churches blocking our view we wouldn't be so dependent on warning bells. Someday, before everything is ash, the idiots on the council will listen to me and build a four-story stone tower."

Boraski ordered Joseph to train Bernard. "Lucky you Jews are snipped. Less to burn."

Bernard left the distillery early on his firehouse days and learned how to set up the steam engine. He and Joseph took dry runs to imaginary fires. They practiced their fireman's carry from the tower to the street below.

After a month, Joseph told Boraski—who sat on his horse, a cigar in one hand, a glass of whiskey in the other—that Bernard had completed his training. They'd responded to three fires in that time, perfect for building his confidence. They'd drowned a chimney fire, containing it within the brick flue before it spread to the walls. When vandals torched an abandoned warehouse along the Niemen, the blaze died naturally, starved of fuel. A few embers drifted harmlessly into the river with a hiss of steam. The most serious one occurred when a family burning brush had ignored high winds. Flying ash ignited in a circle about the original blaze, setting other piles on fire though snow still covered the frozen ground. Bernard, Joseph, and the other volunteers couldn't maneuver the steam engine close enough to do any good. With their gloved hands and rakes, they separated the smoldering stacks. A pile divided could be defeated.

"Welcome aboard, son," the captain said. "Try not to catch yourself on fire."

On his first overnight shift, Bernard and Joseph took turns on watch, alert for renegade smoke or fire, a warning bell, or the arrival of distraught citizens. When not in the tower, Bernard tended to the equipment and fed the stove, which heated water circulating through the five-hundred-gallon steam engine tank.

✳

By the time spring lilies should have emerged, harsh winter still lingered, and Bernard drew his fifth overnight shift. He'd never spent time with a Christian boy before meeting Joseph, who reminded him of Chaim—guileless and kind spirited—except for the cross displayed on top of his coat.

"I haven't known any Jewish boys until now." Joseph blushed. "I don't believe what they say about Jews in church."

"My father taught me a principle from Hillel, one of our brilliant rabbis. 'That which is despicable to you, do not do to another.'"

"That's also preached in our Bible."

"My father died three months ago. Consumption."

"I'm sorry, Bernard. My father's gone too. The '63 rebellion."

Joseph went down the tower stairs and into the barn. They'd switch every hour in this cold.

Bernard peered through the field telescope. Smoke curled from chimneys. Church spires rose above surrounding buildings. Market Square, illuminated by a bright moon, lay under a thin blanket of snow. He thanked God for this gift of new responsibility. In the silence, he sensed his father's presence. Half-turning, he expected him to be there. When he looked through the scope again, a light flickered on the east side of the square.

"Fire! Joseph, Fire!"

Bernard raced down the stairs and into the barn as their fire bell rang. A few seconds later, the bell in the square sounded. He harnessed two horses and opened the doors. Joseph disconnected the hot water pipes, put a torch to the engine's firebox, and opened the damper all the way. Bernard grabbed the reins and Joseph took his position as brakeman on the rear running board. They raced toward the fire.

※

Awake and restless, Estes retained only a few scraps of her unsettling dream. The sole passenger on a train, she'd spied her parents, Eliza, and Professor Micah on a distant platform. They gestured to her, but she couldn't tell if in greeting or farewell.

Sleep now elusive, she got out of bed and pulled the curtains aside. Across the square, flames and smoke—Professor Micah's house! A distant bell sounded, followed by another in the square.

"Fire, Fire, Fire!" She limped over to the adjoining door. "Professor Micah's!"

She put on her boots and grabbed her cane. She rushed down the stairs with her parents just behind, and they pulled coats from the stairwell hooks. In the square mothers held young children, some still asleep in their arms. Others rubbed their eyes and cried.

Papa joined the neighbors who had already formed a bucket line that stretched from the well in the square to the blaze. Jews and Poles usually separated by customs and religion, women and men by role, rich and poor by privilege, united against their common enemy. The first in line emptied a bucket, then rushed to the back of the line to refill. The water steamed off the fire without effect, and they couldn't reach the second floor.

Estes strained against Mama's firm grip on her arm. *He must have gotten out!* Flames sprouted from the shattered downstairs windows. "Professor Micah! Professor Micah!" No answer. *All his books, burning!*

The fire engine clattered into the square, spitting steam and smoke. A volunteer unharnessed the rearing horses and pulled the animals away from the falling ash.

An armload-sized pile of books lay on the ground a few arshins from the professor's house. *He got out!* "Professor Micah! Has anyone seen Professor Micah?"

"He's alive, Estes. Neighbors took him to the infirmary before we formed our line." Jacob Rosenblum swung two buckets forward to his father. It was the first time he'd ever spoken her name.

※

As Bernard and two volunteers pulled a hose toward a water wagon, a distraught girl with a cane and an older woman holding her arm brushed past him. Two years ago, the Niemen, the old man, his beautiful, lame granddaughter. What could he do now? He submerged one end and raced back to the piston intake valve. He spotted the girl again, limping out of the square.

Joseph tightened the metal fitting of a second hose to the discharge and opened the valve. It pulsated and wriggled like a giant snake. Stanislav

Boraski arrived on a coal-black horse, which skittered to the side when he pulled hard on the reins.

Boraski shouted commands: "Smash a window. Water to the second floor. Ladder on the roof, over there." He pointed two houses away. "We need a hole." He grabbed a volunteer and pulled him to the ladder. "This is war!"

The fire reached the second floor. It wouldn't give up easily. The crowd gasped as a window exploded into fragments. Another volunteer fed the engine's firebox while Bernard and Joseph directed the stream through the opening.

Boraski made it to the roof and scrambled across the slope until he arrived above the fire. The volunteer passed him an ax. Their leader attacked the wooden shingles until flames and smoke shot out of the jagged hole. They made their way back down to cheers from the crowd. Bernard and Joseph aimed the hose at the opening as water wagons continued to arrive. The emptied ones raced off to refill.

After four hours of steady water, the fire fighters finally had control. No wind had come to aid the blaze, which had consumed the house and nibbled on two others. Bernard learned from a neighbor that the old man who lived there had misjudged the fire. *That must be the source of the girl's distress.*

"They took him to the infirmary," a middle-aged woman in a yellow nightdress and moth-eaten wool sweater told him.

"Will he be all right?"

The woman frowned. "He risked his life to rescue some books. Can you imagine? Books?"

✳

The fire had burned off Professor Micah's mustache, eyebrows, and half his hair. Bandages covered one of his hands, both legs, and part of his face and torso. Estes stifled a sob, went to his side, and gripped his one unburned hand. He wheezed, and when he tried to talk only a hoarse croak came out. Mama went in search of writing supplies and came back with paper, a book, and two pencils.

"How do you feel?"

He scrawled an answer with his undamaged hand.

"OVERCOOKED"

"Would you like me to read to you?"

"YES"

Estes told Mama which books to bring and where to find them. Eliza Orzeszkowa arrived and scrutinized the swath of bandages on Professor Micah's thin frame. She put her arms around Estes then left to speak with the doctor.

She returned with her lips fixed in a tight line. "My dear friend, books can be replaced, but where will we find another like you?"

"LIMITED EDITION"

In the hall, Eliza explained to Estes the probability of infection from this kind of severe burn.

"He'll live, won't he?" She leaned into Eliza's strong embrace. "He has to finish his book." When Estes pulled away, she read the answer in Eliza's face.

An hour later, her parents returned with books, and Estes introduced them to Eliza. The three of them sat on a bench Papa dragged in from the hall and listened as Estes, sitting on the uncomfortable wooden chair by his bed, read to Professor Micah.

He won't die while I'm reading. When he slept, she continued with the Russian translation of *The Odyssey*, an early birthday gift he'd given her. *If Odysseus struggled for ten years to return home, I can do this forever.*

As dawn appeared, her voice grew hoarse, and she stopped to drink some water. Mama urged her to take a break at home while he slept, but she wouldn't leave him now.

"We'll come back with clothes and food in a few hours. Is there anything else you need?"

To turn back the clock. Why didn't I go over and make sure he was okay? "No, Mama."

Eliza departed with Estes's parents to learn more about the fire.

Alone with the professor when he awoke, Estes read until his eye caught hers. She held a sponge to his lips and squeezed some water into his mouth.

She resumed reading until he signaled her with his fingers.

He wrote slowly: "READ AT MY FUNERAL"

"You're not going to die." *There are over three hundred pages I have to read to you!*

"NOT MY CHOICE"

Estes wept and kissed his hand. "What do you want me to read?"

"SURPRISE ME"

After a long pause, she said, "What will I do without you?"

"GO WEST"

✳

Bernard and Joseph returned the fire engine to the shed, cleaned the equipment, and tended the horses. For the first morning since his father had died, Bernard didn't go to the shul to mourn. Instead, he avoided the sodden ruin in the square, crossed the train tracks beyond Rabbi Menshein's house, and passed the Jewish old-age home.

He hesitated before going into the infirmary. Soot coated both hands. He hadn't washed his face, and his clothes stank of smoke. At the front desk, he inquired about the burn victim and headed away from the common ward.

Bernard stood at the open door as she read in a firm voice. Russian poured from the girl, and he wanted to go in, but doubt turned him away. He stopped a gray-haired nurse. "The girl, his granddaughter?"

"Esther Leving, his student. Who are you?"

"A friend," he croaked before walking out into the new day.

✳

Professor Micah lay still, one eye staring at Estes. When Eliza and her parents returned, she did not acknowledge them. Instead, she continued to read the epic poem, composed two-and-a-half millennia ago, as if it contained the most profound revelations. When Mama pried it from her grasp, she collapsed into her arms.

*

Over twenty neighbors and shopkeepers Professor Micah had regaled with anecdotes about the capital came to his funeral near the Great Wooden Shul. Two years ago, on her very first day with him, he'd pointed to this same cemetery, where Estes now stood with her parents and Eliza Orzeszkowa in a freezing drizzle.

From Eliza, she had pieced together most of what happened that awful night and imagined the rest—how he worked late at his first-floor desk surrounded by his precious library until he dozed off and knocked over a lantern. He awakened to flames already climbing the curtains. He might have delayed his escape to rescue books as the fire bit into dusty volumes amassed over his lifetime. Perhaps he also made a desperate dash upstairs to save sections of his manuscript, although Eliza reported she had found no remains of his final project.

Professor Micah made it out of the house, a staggering torch, the damage already done before the fire bells had even rung. Neighbors had dowsed him with water and rushed him to the infirmary.

Estes struggled to find the right, elegant note of pathos to please her teacher, her voice strange in her ear, as if she lay in the plain wooden box, too, about to be lowered into the earth.

> "*Orpheus,*" *she cried,*
> "*What madness has destroyed my wretched self, and you?*
> *See, the cruel Fates recall me, and sleep hides my swimming eyes,*
> *Farewell, now: I am taken, wrapped round by vast night,*
> *stretching out to you, alas, hands no longer yours.*"
> *She spoke, and suddenly fled, far from his eyes,*
> *like smoke vanishing in thin air, and never saw him more,*
> *though he grasped in vain at shadows, and longed*
> *to speak further.*

Eliza Orzeszkowa spoke next, but Estes was shivering and caught only pieces of her eulogy—"brilliant scholar . . . supportive friend . . . loyal teacher."

As the Levings and Eliza passed the ruins of Professor Micah's house on their way home, Estes wobbled from the stench of wet ash and charred brick.

Her parents invited Eliza to stay for dinner, but when Mama felt Estes's forehead, the plans were postponed. Her fever raged for five days. Mama gave her sponge baths, and Eliza visited twice with soup. Estes managed to swallow a bit of broth and a boiled potato.

In her delirium, she imagined her own gravestone engraving—*His Best Student.*

My Estes, it's not your time. Didn't you learn anything from our work together?

I should have made sure the lantern was out. You would still be alive.

He shook his head sadly and said nothing more.

2

S he recovered in time for her seventeenth birthday. The remaining snow had melted, and when Papa pried open her window, fresh spring air swept in. After breakfast, Estes went downstairs to read and watch her father work.

"Now that you're feeling better, Pani Pawloska says she has important news. She'll join us for your birthday dinner tonight. You've had another visitor, too, a young man asking after you. The persistent fellow stops in every day. He'll come by this morning."

"Oh, Papa." She didn't want to talk to anyone.

"His name's Bernard Garfinkle."

She recalled the young man with the distillery. She had searched Market Square for weeks after that encounter, hoping for another glimpse, until her work with Professor Micah had pushed her childish fantasies aside.

"Yesterday, he delivered those for Jacob Rosenblum." He pointed to the wilted bouquet in an unglazed vase with two storks etched into the clay.

Jacob had spoken directly to her for the first time at the fire. Now he sent flowers? He should have come himself.

When the shop door opened, the young man who entered had just the beginnings of a beard. He was taller than she remembered, but still wore the same wool yarmulke.

"I'm sorry for your loss. I'm Bernard Garfinkle."

"Estes Leving."

"I know. I found out from the nurses at the hospital." His cheeks flushed. "We couldn't salvage any of the books in the building. I brought the two in the best shape among those he dropped in the square. I thought you might want to keep them."

Bernard took a leather bag off his shoulder and reached inside. He stepped forward and handed her Tolstoy's *War and Peace* and John Stuart Mill's *On Liberty*.

Estes ran her hand over the Tolstoy. "While I struggled with geometry proofs, he read this." She set them both on the floor beside her chair. Her eyes watered.

He reached into his bag again and pulled out a fist-sized, round rock, black with a red ring around the center. "It's worn smooth by years of weathering in the Niemen." He set it on the floor, next to the books.

"My studies with Professor Micah focused on languages, literature, and history."

"I wonder if I could see you again. When you're stronger, of course." Suddenly exhausted, she shrugged and studied her empty hands.

"Stop by tomorrow, and we'll set a date for dinner," Papa said with hope in his voice. She hadn't frightened this one away yet.

❋

Professor Micah's will named Estes as his sole beneficiary. That night, Eliza Orzeszkowa read the notarized document to the family. The first item, his vast library, which she would have prized above all else—now smoke and ash.

The professor had also left her his house, soon to be reduced to an empty lot. Still, in the square, this was a prized location for an ambitious merchant. When Eliza added ten thousand silver rubles, without stipulation, to the list, a small fortune, eight times her father's yearly income, a deep pool of grief opened. She would give it all plus her right arm to have him back for a minute. She wept, embarrassed, because Eliza, who carried her own sorrows, remained composed in front of her.

"You will need to manage the estate for Estes," Eliza told Papa.

Mama added, "With her involvement, of course."

"Her interests are my primary concern."

Her hopes for an intellectual life had risen with the professor, then collapsed with the fire. Now, he'd left her a lifeline. When she regained her strength, she'd start pulling.

❋

The next day Estes made a decision and told Papa she had no interest in having dinner with Bernard or any other men.

This time he stayed calm. "Sometime in the future, you might?"

"Maybe, Papa."

When Bernard stopped by each morning on his way to the shul and the distillery, Estes stayed in her room and couldn't make out what he and Papa talked about. Stray words floated up the stairs: "time . . . tomorrow . . . loss." Afterward, the young man always lingered outside. She tried to ignore his presence but couldn't resist peering discreetly around the curtain. When would he give up?

He came every day for a month, waiting for a sign that Estes wouldn't give. On some days he leaned against his sorry, swaybacked horse. On others, he stood by himself, oblivious to the people who stopped next to him. They stared up, too; perhaps he'd discovered something of value in the facade of Leving's Shoes. One day, Bernard took up his position facing Estes's window as wind and rain drove people indoors. Twenty minutes passed before he turned away and left Market Square. It felt like hours to Estes. But when he didn't show up for two days, her satisfaction with outlasting him mingled with disappointment.

Finally, he'd given up, as she knew he must, but then he appeared again. Estes nearly called out to him in relief and then concern when he blew his nose and sneezed. His persistence wore her down, and when she came into the shop, her father also chipped away at her resolve, asking the same question but expecting a new answer. On a mild spring day, he handed her a message from Bernard. Convinced that they'd conspired, Estes glanced at Bernard's neat Yiddish penmanship: "We must celebrate life, Estes, for the living and the dead. Your friend, Bernard Garfinkle."

※

"She's beautiful and brilliant," Bernard told his friends as they bottled vodka. "Spends all her time reading. Probably wants to marry a scholar." He stroked his beard.

"You have your own business, Bernard. That must count for something," Chaim said.

"Are you going to make a list of every possible difficulty?" Leib asked. "Who else but you would endure standing in the rain outside the shoe shop? Take her father our vodka."

"But what should I bring Estes?" During the five days she lay with fever, and throughout her refusal to receive him again, he'd visited with her parents. Their description of her passion for books worried him. What could he offer someone so literate?

"A river rock isn't enough?" Leib laughed. "Take a chess set and teach her to play."

"I meant a gift."

"So did I."

Bernard's friends spent an hour heaping suggestions on him, though they had no experience with such matters.

"Perfume and flowers."

"No, she doesn't want trifles."

"Candy and chocolate."

"She'll eat them and forget me."

"Books."

"Yes. Her father suggested this. But what if she wants me to read?"

He settled on paper, ink, and steel nibbed pens. "For the journal she keeps," he told his friends.

"To write about you," Leib said.

Bernard changed into clean clothes before leaving with two bottles of vodka and his friends' encouragement. He would stop for the writing supplies on the way.

✳

Herman sipped from his glass of Garfinkle's Spirits and Doris moved around the kitchen, cleaning up after the dinner of fish and scalloped potatoes. Estes smiled when Bernard presented the writing materials.

"So thoughtful. Thank you."

He wanted her smile to stay, but it retreated. Still, he had to accomplish only one thing—persuade her to meet him again.

Herman and Doris hovered, and Bernard wished this didn't feel like a performance.

"Since my father died last fall, I lead the Mourner's Kaddish for him three times a day. Do you want me to include Professor Micah?"

"No. He wasn't religious at all. Neither am I. Religion holds women back. Superstitious beliefs . . ."

Herman coughed. "What Estes means is . . ."

"Papa likes to finish my sentences."

"If not with our religion, how are you passing through this hard time?"

"I read."

Bernard swallowed, and his eyes flickered away for an instant.

"Do you live with your mother?"

"No. My mother died. I live on my own. I'm seventeen."

Her eyes fastened on his.

"After kheyder, I went to work for my father. I manage the distillery now."

"Is it alchemy or science?" she asked him.

He considered this. "I don't claim our vodka to be a universal elixir, but it's more to me than just chemistry."

"If someone else copied your exact procedures, the product wouldn't be the same?"

"The human element must matter—the dedication and love put into the work."

"I see. One part chemistry, one part love."

At their next meeting, he asked if she'd like to play chess.

"I've never learned." Women didn't play, and the sets in the market, surrounded by commenting, bearded Jews, reminded her of the shul.

"Would you like a lesson?"

Nobody had ever offered to teach her before. "Of course." She wanted to explore his world and forget her own. She mirrored his setup and learned the names of the pieces and their basic movements. The bishops and pawns were rather phallic. On the other hand, the queen was the most powerful piece.

After several more meetings with Bernard, Estes solved the puzzle over the aim of the game—checkmate, not capture. "It takes planning. A player can't carelessly stumble into victory," she said. Pleased with the complexity, she wanted to play.

The first few games ended with most of her pieces stripped away and her king running from Bernard's army. She studied how he finished checkmate.

"I'll take my queen off the board," he offered.

"No. How will I become better?"

Bernard beat her game after game, but Estes found satisfaction in the collection of his pieces she captured on the way to defeat. She observed his furrowed brow while he concentrated on the board.

He joined them for dinners every night now, like a member of the family. Estes regained her energy, though sadness reemerged when she went to bed, without the distractions of chess or the presence of her handsome friend.

May 28, 1872

If I could resurrect the dead with haggling, what would I offer? When I'm with Bernard, I feel like a book he wants to read. I must be written in another language; he studies so intently. He shared his father's three principles tonight, and I challenged the idea that everything must be balanced. The scale is never static, in the middle, unmoving. Just look at Catherine the Great, Napoleon, the Decembrist revolt—the ferocious randomness of events.

We agreed the Hassidim cling to their masters like moss on river rocks. I imagine Bernard with his tefillin when he prays at home. I told him I would wrap myself with the leading minds of the Enlightenment, but free thought cannot be squeezed into a box and bound to the body. He kissed me tonight when he was leaving. His lips tasted a bit salty. Mama watched, so it was brief.

June 3, 1873

Eliza shocked me with her proposal. She wants us to build a bookshop on the professor's lot, which I would run, and open a publishing business in Vilne, which she'd manage under an associate's name—her own might bring unwanted surveillance. We'd be equal investors and partners.

"We'll publish stories of women who must be heard," she promised. She looked at me as if I was one of those voices. Mama said it would honor Professor Micah's memory.

Going west will have to wait. I look east instead, one hundred arshins across the square, at the professor's burned-out home.

Estes put aside the journal and glanced at *Fanny Hill* on her shelf. Bernard had never read anything like that, she guessed. She pulled out *De Figuris Veneris*, guilty she'd taken it from Professor Micah's library without his knowledge, the explicit details hidden from her parents by the Renaissance Latin. The writing had the same objectivity scientists used to classify plant phyla.

Fanny, a heroine without intellectual drive, had disappointed her, but *De Figuris Veneris* reduced love to a catalog of ninety sex positions and other erotic techniques. Still, better to be informed about these things.

✳

Estes glanced up at Mama, who was watching her and Bernard through the kitchen window. Papa must also be spying from his workbench. At least they couldn't hear the conversation.

A peddler pushing a cart waved a brush and several scarves in front of Estes and commented on her beautiful hair. A peasant family stopped, and each of the four young children held up a carved serving spoon with chisel marks visible on the thick handles. The moon-faced wife's colorful dress touched the ground. Her husband wore a battered felt hat.

"A deal for a nice lady and man?"

She shook her head. Any other response and this family would treat them like nibbling fish.

"Can you imagine living someplace else, Bernard?" What if the censors seized the books and press she and Eliza planned to purchase?

"What, a village nearby?"

"I mean far away—America. How wonderful to live wherever you want and have the freedom to speak your thoughts."

"My parents are buried here. I recognize individual trees and greet the night soil man by name. And all the stories my father told me, our history, my friends."

"And the czar, Bernard? What has he done about the attacks last year in Odessa? The restrictions on women and Jews?"

"But Alexander has made reforms, Estes. Since our fathers' time, it has improved so much. Don't you agree?"

*

Estes's chess game had improved steadily, and she threatened Bernard's castled position with her queen and knight. He had to promote a pawn to defeat her. If her parents, in the kitchen to give them a little privacy, would leave the house, she might sweep the pieces away and wrestle him to the floor.

Despite her growing ability, she wanted a break from losing. There must be another battle she might win—perhaps a debate about religion. She'd accepted that Bernard believed in God, even though she didn't, but she had more to say.

"What I object to most," she told him, "is the form belief takes when it coalesces into religion—the subordination of women and persecution of non-believers." She moderated her voice. She didn't have to checkmate him and would settle for a draw.

Bernard told her about experiencing Eyn-Sof after his father's death.

"God is everywhere and nowhere?" she asked him. "Like Hegel's 'Everything is inherently contradictory.'"

"Yes and no."

She laughed and they stopped talking. Papa rustled his paper in the kitchen.

"I wouldn't ever want to be responsible for observing all the Jewish laws about food, Shabes, and the holidays . . . I have plans, too, Bernard."

"I can manage religious observance, Estes."

Why did it have to be managed at all? She wanted a life without any orders from God. Still, Bernard said it would be his responsibility.

"How can you justify shul when women have to sit like children, away from men. How does that fit with your father's first principle?"

Bernard chewed his lower lip, looked away, and didn't respond immediately. Her stomach turned over. She hadn't meant to push so far, to challenge the core of his practice, not when she'd begun to believe she wouldn't always be alone. Why did it come out that way? She waited for him to stalk out.

Bernard looked at her again with a furrowed brow. "I'll be back in two hours. Can you wait that long for my answer, Estes?"

She nodded, not trusting her voice. Better to find out now before this went any further. Bernard left without another word.

❋

When he arrived back at the Levings', Estes came out of her room and led him back to the table. Her parents stopped talking and returned to the kitchen. After he'd prayed in the Great Wooden Shul, on the same bench where he had sat next to his father every Shabes and holy day for their entire life together, he'd gone to the cemetery and put his hand on his father's stone.

Tell me what to do, Father.

Why do you even bother to ask, Bernard?

"After the four months remaining of Kaddish for my father, I won't attend services until you can sit beside me. I'll pray at home."

Estes accompanied Bernard downstairs when he left that night. She leaned against him, held her lips to his, and put her hands on his hips. She didn't care if her parents watched. He made no move to break free and wrapped his arms around her shoulders. The kiss ended, and before Estes could move in again, Papa, who had followed them down, coughed. "Goodnight, Bernard. We'll see you tomorrow."

3

The following evening, Mama worked her thumbs into the pad of Estes's deformed foot. "Would you like to try, Bernard?" She stood up and motioned for him to take her place.

Bernard sat on the relinquished chair. Estes placed her foot on his knee, smiled at him, and closed her eyes. She breathed deeply and kept her hands folded in her lap. Mama brought more oil, which he worked into her foot, ankle, and underdeveloped calf. Bernard was now the only one besides her parents to see and touch her deformity.

"How does it feel?" he asked.

"To walk with my foot twisted on its side?"

"I meant the massage. Is the pressure good?"

Bernard's touch felt different from Mama's, and heat moved up her leg. She opened her eyes, afraid if she kept them closed she might sigh with pleasure. What would Mama think?

"Yes, you're hired, Bernard." Just one more test. Now they'd read to each other.

She scanned her bookshelves while he remained in the dining room. She passed over the contemporary Russian novels, including Dostoyevsky's *Crime and Punishment*, and instead chose her old favorite, *Jane Eyre*.

She took off her other shoe and put on slippers. She'd have to walk out naked to match the intimacy of what Bernard did with her foot.

Mama had retreated into the kitchen, and Papa retired early. Estes and Bernard remained at the table. She felt his eyes on her as she read the first chapter. "He bullied and punished me; not two or three times in the week, nor once or twice in the day, but continually: every nerve I had feared him, and every morsel of flesh in my bones shrank when he came near."

Bernard leaned forward when little Jane threw herself at her tormentor, and back when they cast her into exile.

"Take her away to the red-room and lock her in there. Four hands were immediately laid upon me, and I was borne upstairs."

Bernard's dark eyes flashed with energy. "Jane has no allies."

Estes held the book out to him. "Would you like to read chapter two?"

He hesitated.

"Of course, how thoughtless of me. The rabbis don't teach Cyrillic. I'll pick another book in Yiddish."

"I must tell you something, Estes." He took a deep breath. "Reading has never been easy for me. With the help of friends, I faked my way through six years of kheyder until I confessed to my father and rabbi. I will never read effortlessly, like you."

She would have been no more surprised if he'd slapped her. He must be joking, but what Jew would say such a thing? How did this happen? Impossible. Estes couldn't conceal her shock and dismay, and a rush of shame stifled her voice. The color drained from Bernard's face.

He explained his ability to memorize and interpret text. His voice broke when he asked if she wanted some time to think, and Estes searched for the right thing to say. Seconds ticked by heavily, and she feared her delay might break something irreparable between them. Bernard did not choose this flaw.

"I'll read to you, Bernard." She locked his hand in hers and resumed the tale of the spirited Jane Eyre.

⁕

June 30, 1872

I love a boy who can't read. If I hadn't gotten to know him first, he'd be a book returned to the shelves unopened. Single words aren't the problem, but when they gather, all talking at once, he lurches forward, pauses, sounds out, only to lose his way and backtrack. It exhausts him. I try to imagine the awful frustration of a plodding pace for a sharp mind. It breaks my heart, so for now, I read to him. But I will solve his problem, trace letters on his skin, fill him with words and wonder until he cries, "I can read, I can read!"

✳

She said yes! They would wed in his yard—no ketubah, shul, or dowry, according to Estes's wishes.

"All signs of a double standard, Bernard," she'd told him, and he didn't argue. He only requested that Rabbi Menshein preside over the ceremony, and took her, Doris, and Herman to meet his old teacher.

When they walked through the market, he held her warm hand, and Estes responded with a surprisingly firm grip. Both sculptor and clay, Bernard waited for a double, "hmm hmm" from Herman, strolling with Doris a few steps behind, but he remained silent.

Her parents had certainly relaxed since the marriage proposal. Bernard had asked Estes before seeking her father's permission, which he knew would please her. They'd already made plans for the Horodno Bookshop with her mentor, Eliza Orzeszkowa. Bernard and his friends would organize the cleanup and start rebuilding in August.

A rose bush bloomed beneath the only window of Rabbi Menshein's tiny house. Bernard knocked, and Bella Menshein threw her arms open and welcomed them. A green headscarf completely covered her hair. She wore a shoulder-length blue apron, stained with a record of decades of marriage and work in the kitchen—a splotch of some ancient sauce, a splash of Shabes wine, a wet patch of the chicken soup whose welcoming fragrance permeated the house.

Bella took Herman and Doris into the kitchen for tea. Bernard and Estes sat with Rabbi Menshein in the dining area, separated from the kitchen by a wall of books. Imposing volumes rested next to short, thick ones, and the uneven line of their tops resembled the battlements of a fortress to Bernard. Estes studied the titles and only stopped when the rabbi took her hand. He held Bernard's hand also.

The rabbi's thick glasses enlarged his eyes. "What do you expect from marriage, Bernard?" The rabbi squeezed his hand.

"I love being with her . . . It's not some kind of business arrangement. I agree with Estes. We don't need a ketubah. A righteous man doesn't need laws."

Estes didn't need priming.

"Complete equality, Rabbi, between two best friends."

"A wonderful thing." The rabbi paused. "Have you considered conjugal relations and children?"

Bernard did not tell the rabbi he'd imagined Estes without clothes. Nor did Estes reveal what she dreamed about doing with Bernard, nor about *Fanny Hill* or *De Figuris Veneris*. What rabbi read Latin? And why did conjugal relations usually involve babies? She wanted to do more with her one life and would never be one of those women who pumped out children, one after another, until the mothers were too old, or worse, died in childbirth.

She also didn't mention the specific methods she'd investigated to prevent pregnancy. *Leave it to the woman.* "Large families lead to poverty. I enjoy children. I also love chocolate cake but not so much after the first piece." She braced for a challenge, but none came. She told the rabbi about the bookshop.

"Excellent. We need female scholars. Deborah, one of my favorites, made the wicks for torches to encourage Torah learning."

Estes frowned. With Professor Micah, she had researched the woman of the Hebrew Bible and Talmud. "She also saw motherhood as her greatest role."

"How about Queen Shlomtzion, who recalled learned men from exile and rebuilt yeshivas?"

"Isn't she known for bringing fertility to Israel?"

"Okay," the rabbi said, sounding exasperated. "Beruryah in the Babylonian Talmud. She cleverly reinterpreted law and taught her husband to pray for the eradication of sin, not the sinner."

"The same Beruryah who mocked the sages for calling women light-headed, then hanged herself after a student sent by the rabbi seduced her?"

"But that's a much later interpretation by Rashi not found in the original text and . . ." Rabbi Menshein stopped mid-sentence, rocked back in his chair, and covered his mouth. He regained control but started laughing when he tried to speak. At first, Estes struggled to maintain her composure in case she needed to refute another one of his weak examples, but then she laughed along with him, and Bernard joined in. Like hungry travelers coming upon the remains of a sumptuous meal, her parents and Bella Menshein joined the levity as the paroxysm of laughter subsided.

4

One hundred and fifty guests stood in Bernard's yard on a perfect midsummer evening. Under the chupe, Estes circled Bernard slowly, without her cane, and he locked his eyes on her and imagined God's hand sweeping away the void, calling forth night and day, sky and sea, land and plant, sun and moon, fish and birds, animals and mankind. She returned his gaze, her dress a comet's tail. As she passed behind him, he did not turn around, but waited until she completed her revolution and reappeared in front of him again. His heart filled with joy. Day existed only with night. Nothing existed without duality, except God.

Estes did not think of biblical passages as she held Bernard within her orbit. She did not analyze or reflect on the proceedings or feel self-conscious about her foot. During her seventh and last revolution, the day of rest, the wonder of simply walking on the earth filled her, and she stopped by Bernard's side, facing Rabbi Menshein.

Silence lingered for an instant, until the rabbi chanted the seven blessings. Bernard put a ring on Estes's right hand and said, "Behold, you are betrothed unto me with this ring, according to the law of Moses and Israel."

Rabbi Menshein pronounced them husband and wife, and Bernard smashed a glass with his foot, symbolizing the destruction of the temple, as shouts of, "Mazel tov!" erupted from the assembly. Guests gathered around, kissed Estes, and clasped Bernard's hands.

They received everyone—relations, friends, and acquaintances like the Blooms, who still did Bernard's laundry, and Mendel, the night soil man. Estes's parents came first in the long line winding through the yard. Papa wrapped his strong arms around Bernard, squeezing as if to shape him into the perfect fit for his daughter. Mama kissed both his cheeks and fiddled with the flower in Estes's hair, a splash of yellow in a dense black forest. Papa stood to the side grinning, until Estes threw her arms around him, hanging on to retain her childhood a bit longer.

"Why so relieved, Papa?"

"You're going to a good man, Esther Leving." He hardly ever used her full name.

"You're not giving me away," she told him. "A daughter is not property."

He said nothing. He'd learned some things at least.

Yiddish congratulations replaced the Hebrew of the wedding ceremony. So many well-wishers needed to be received, each an expert, and she and Bernard a captive audience. Women offered prescriptions on pleasing a husband, kosher preparations, and much more she vowed to ignore.

How could she rush Uncle Simon, who'd traveled from America? He'd delivered a crate of books and wanted to talk about them all. He barked out the names of authors—a herald announcing honored guests: "Emerson, Thoreau, Fuller. They call them Transcendentalists in America. And you must read Whitman, Estes, if you are to understand the ferocious debate about individual liberty and artistic expression."

He would have continued, oblivious to the line behind him, naming scores of new writers and the significance of their work, but Estes promised they would visit and discuss everything before he sailed off again to his America. He moved on to engage Eliza, his high-pitched voice rising above those of the other guests.

Estes wished her aunt Freda, Mama's only surviving sibling, could have made the long journey from Balta. From her aunt's letters, Estes imagined a strong and kind person. Her other aunt, Miriam, required no imagining at all. She disapproved of Estes's ideas about the emancipation of women. Now they exchanged a hug, not her uncle's open-armed and warm embrace, but a brisk tug to her aunt's chest, trapping Estes against a sagging bosom, followed by three taps on the back. One didn't choose blood relatives.

An image of a grief-stricken young boy traveling to Petersburg came to Estes. Professor Micah, gone. And Bernard's father, who had moved more gradually to the grave, dead just the same. A fallen birch leaf swirled in the breeze before landing again. Existence spreads out with a voracious appetite. We run around feeding it, then . . . poof.

The procession continued, leaving no time to linger with ghosts. Bernard's best friends from kheyder and the distillery waited their turn.

Estes had met them weeks ago when Bernard took her and Papa to Garfinkle's Spirits. Chaim had blushed and reached out his hand to hold hers. She didn't need to tell him she would take over as Bernard's reader. The new covenant, husband and wife, would replace the old. Shlomo's long face brightened somewhat, and Leib shook her hand like a merchant closing a deal.

Papa had stayed to watch the boys distill vodka while she and Bernard went out to the barn to visit Alte Ferd. "Fine old horse," Bernard said, running his hand over the thick mane.

He turned, and they'd kissed. She would have stayed attached to him, but Bernard broke away and led her back to the others.

What will happen when Papa doesn't hover nearby? She turned the ring on her finger and started when the next person in line stepped in front of her.

"Hello, Jacob Rosenblum." She resisted asking him how he fared, because she knew from his father's bragging, from the gossip of customers, and from Papa, that cantor Jacob sang every week in the Choral Shul. Rabbis flocked to Horodno from other cities to hear his voice. Soon he'd be studying in Vilne to become the youngest crown rabbi in the gubernia.

He reached out a hand and congratulated Bernard, much too loudly. Why had he come? So arrogant, even at her wedding, to walk away without acknowledgment.

Estes put aside her old grievance and smiled when the last guest in line bowed to her.

"My friend from the fire station, Joseph Brodkowski."

Joseph's yarmulke sat crooked on his head like a jaunty beret. He'd stuffed his muscular body into an ill-fitting suit, and his bare ankles showed below the legs of his black trousers.

"How do I look, Bernard?" He centered the yarmulke and tried to tug his jacket sleeves over his wrists.

"You make a perfect Jew, Joseph." The boy beamed as if a teacher had held up his work for praise.

Finally, Bernard and Estes could move among the guests, accepting more toasts as they went. Rabbi Menshein's belly laughs, at whatever

Uncle Simon and Eliza Orzeszkowa, two non-believers, had said, made Estes smile. The wine made her dizzy.

Leib and Shlomo played a lively dance tune, and a line circled the musicians. The dancers reversed direction, pressed into the center, stepped out again, and strained to keep the circle intact. She clapped for the dancers, the familiar longing to join replaced by anticipation.

"I want to be alone with you," she whispered into Bernard's ear. When they walked toward the house, a cheer went up. "L'chaim! To Bernard and Estes!"

5

He didn't offer to carry Estes across the threshold. "I'm not helpless, Bernard," he imagined her saying. Instead, they put their arms around each other. Closed curtains had kept the house cool but only slightly muffled the whoops of the dancers. Estes led him around two bulky sacks of her possessions. She stopped in front of his bedroom and tugged him inside, as though she had lived there all her life, and he was the guest.

Bernard still couldn't believe his good fortune, that she hadn't chosen someone else, especially a scholar like Jacob Rosenblum. The day of the fire, when Bernard left the hospital, he intercepted Jacob who had arrived with books for Estes. Bernard told him the family wanted privacy.

Then, during Estes's illness, Bernard stopped Jacob again, this time outside the Levings' house. He told his former kheyder mate that Herman had already invited him, Bernard, to dine with the Levings that evening. It surprised him how easily he lied to Jacob a second time, without remorse. He did take Jacob's flowers and promised to deliver them. Perhaps he'd held them a bit too long in the cold.

He lit a candle, and Estes pressed against him, her ear to his chest. "Your heart is beating so fast."

"Are you sorry you didn't marry a bookish man, Estes?"

She stepped back and undressed in front of him, until she stood naked in the dim light, her wedding dress bunched on the floor.

Though he'd imagined her without clothes, his mind had produced a poor imitation.

"I want to see you, too, Bernard."

He took off his yarmulke and put it in the top drawer of a scratched dresser. Starting at the top, he unbuttoned his best white shirt, fumbling with the tiny buttons. Next, his shoes, socks, and pants. He stood facing Estes in his black and white checked underwear.

"Like a chessboard," Estes observed.

His last piece of covering came off.

Estes tried to keep her eyes on his and resist the desire to peek but failed. She stepped into his arms. They kissed and clumsily groped their way to the bed and dropped as one. The way she'd imagined this moment—skin to skin, extended caresses, eyes locked and professions of love when he entered—vanished as Bernard fumbled and poked, the bed creaked and shook, and he made frantic painful thrusts. He moaned and called her name.

He pushed himself up. "I'm sorry. It was so quick."

At least it hadn't hurt too much.

"I feel your heart, Bernard. Heart, I'm your commanding officer, and I order you to be true and never stop beating."

"If you had to pick one or the other, to be true or continue beating, which would it be?"

A dilemma Estes resolved by kissing him, this time in no hurry, excited by his touch and the realization he would ignore rabbinic laws about virginal brides for her. She stroked his back and felt him grow inside her. A pleasant sensation had just started to build when he shuddered again.

He rolled off beside her and she nuzzled into him. "Tell me your father's principles again."

"Now, Estes?"

"Now, Bernard."

"Treat others as you want them to treat you."

She licked and pulled on his nipple. He reciprocated.

"The second one, Bernard," she said between moans.

"If I'm not for myself, who will be?"

"Touch me like this." She took his hand and guided him. She kept her hand on top of his. "Too much pressure, Bernard. Mmmm, just right. What's the third one?"

"Everything must be balanced, Estes."

She grabbed his right shoulder and pushed him back on the bed. She straddled him and guided him deep into her. She rocked back and forth as the pleasure deepened and spread.

⁕

Estes woke first to the chittering of birds. One of her arms lay across Bernard. She lifted the sheet he had used to cover their nakedness in the night chill. About the same height, but where she flared in hips and breasts, his lines were taut and flat, his penis relaxed and innocent.

She slipped from the bed and pulled a robe from one of her bags. She limped into the yard barefoot and went around back to the outhouse. Its wooden door groaned when she pulled it open. Although it had a window for fresh air and a pipe from the pit through the roof to carry odors away, Estes momentarily caught her breath as she latched the door behind her. Last night she'd stood naked in front of him, shameless, but in here, impossible. *Perhaps a time came in a marriage when even this . . .*

She pulled up her robe, removed the cover, and sat over the hole. The wedding night's ecstasy now replaced by ordinary bodily functions. *Without our nine openings, nothing enters or leaves.* She investigated the Yiddish *Kol Mevaser* newspaper folded beside her.

The headlines—a censored glimpse of Imperial Russia and the world beyond the Pale—had been stripped away. She read the poems, disappointed there was no literary criticism in this edition. Then she skimmed a story about the Belgium-built passenger locomotive hauling six cars which smashed into two British-made 0-6-0 freight engines in the Warsaw station. Fatalities and dismemberment had occurred— who, how many, as well as the cause of the accident, unreported—only *unfortunate mistakes were made.* She imagined drunk brakemen failing to engage the circular brakes on the car roofs, a distracted engineer forgetting to employ emergency procedures, a yard worker who threw the wrong switch before the awful collision. The Rail Commissioner declared Russian trains to be a safe mode of transport.

Estes shuddered and moved on to the activities of the czar ensconced in the Summer Palace, society marriages—Nickolai so and so had wed the daughter of a German baron—drought in the southern provinces. After using the paper, she scooped ashes from the metal pail with the rusty trowel and added them to the pit.

Back in the front yard, Estes surveyed her new home. She felt daring, naked under her robe, even though thick woods shielded her from the closest neighbors, and the road had no travelers at this hour.

On one side of the house, the vegetable garden had beans winding around eight-foot poles, potatoes mounded with dirt, cabbage and other greens ready to pick, and two frustrated rabbits seeking a breach in the fence. On the other side stood Alte Ferd's barn and the attached woodshed, the ends of the stacked fuel cracked like aged skin. Oak, pine, birch, and thickets of brush competed for space and light in the forest. When Estes faced south, as she had when Rabbi Menshein pronounced Bernard and her husband and wife, the open vista pleased her. Closer to Horodno, buildings clustered together like bashful boys at a dance. She spotted church towers and stretches of the Niemen, and beyond the river valley, green fields and woody patches into the distance. When the front door opened, Bernard emerged, smiled sheepishly, and disappeared behind the house.

Estes tilted back and found two faint stars. She attempted to observe the instant they melted into the morning light, but her concentration broke when Bernard returned.

"My father and I used to stand on that flat rock, waiting for those same stars to appear. I've started a fire and water's heating inside. If you want, I'll heat enough for the tub." He had bought a cast-iron bath to replace the battered copper tub he and his father had used. Chaim, Leib, and Shlomo had helped move it into the kitchen.

"A full soak would be wonderful later. Basins will do for now." Estes linked her arm through his, and they went inside.

In the kitchen, Bernard scooped warm water into two deep ceramic bowls with a silver pitcher. He gave her washing and drying towels, a glass jar of tooth powder, and a wooden box filled with soap flakes. "Did you pack a toothbrush? This has never been used." She had, but preferred the new one, with a bone handle and straight bristles unbent by wear, like their marriage.

After bathing, Estes joined Bernard in the dining room. He sat at the table chopping apples and smiled when she came in.

"Would you help me with my hair?" She had washed it before the wedding but wanted to break through the privacy that separated them.

"Of course. We have more hot water." He put on two leather mittens and took the blackened pot from the small stove into the kitchen. He set the pot in the deep cast-iron sink and worked the pump until cold water mixed in. "Tell me when it's just right."

"Perfect," she told him. Bernard lifted the pot from the sink and set it on the idle cookstove, which he never used in the summer just to heat water. Estes lifted her waist-long hair from the nape of her neck until it hung in front of her face. She bent over and bowed her head while he dipped and poured warm water over her.

"A Jewish baptism," she laughed.

"Such thick, beautiful hair. Enough to cover all the bald heads in Horodno. Do you want me to lather?"

"Yes, please."

He worked up a lather in his hands with a bar of lye and tallow soap and massaged the suds into her scalp, starting at her crown, careful not to pull when he reached the ends. Estes, hidden within her thick wall of hair, kept her eyes closed.

"You're gentler than my mother."

"Rinse." He poured water until no trace of soap remained and dried her hair with a towel. She wanted to embrace him and return to intimacy, but he had begun dipping the remaining warm water into the two basins she had used. She wished he had long hair or something else he needed her for.

While Bernard washed, Estes added the chopped apples to the pot of soaked oats and put it on the stove. When he joined her, she held a spoon in one hand and Bernard's hand in the other.

After they ate and cleaned up, he wrapped his arms around her waist. Without turning, Estes relaxed back into him. Neither of them moved for a minute before she led him to the bedroom, removed his yarmulke, unbuttoned his shirt, and caressed his chest. She took off the sash holding her robe closed and held out her arms. After he lifted the garment off her shoulders, Estes stretched out on the bed while Bernard removed the rest of his clothes, more quickly than last night.

He laid beside her. "Estes, you're so . . . How do you know . . . ?"

"I trust you, Bernard. Also, imagination and books." She told him about smuggling *Fanny Hill* back to Horodno, and *De Figuris Veneris* with its catalog of positions and techniques.

"With those books instead of the Chumash, I would have learned to read."

"You can read. I'll show you. Read this." She hovered over him and traced a letter on his chest with her finger, keeping her eyes locked with his and raising her eyebrows.

"Estes, I . . ."

"How about now?" she asked, drawing the same letter with her tongue, she the artist, he the canvas.

"Lamed?"

"Excellent work, Bernard," she murmured before placing a yen on his stomach and beys below his belly button. "Just one more letter, shaped like this." She held his erection and painted the last letter.

"Nun!"

"Can you read now, Bernard?"

"Lebn, Estes. I can read!"

6

few days after the wedding, Bernard walked to the fire station at sunset. The chief had one bloodshot eye, the other swollen shut from a "misunderstanding" with a tavern keeper.

"You want to spend all your nights with the new wife? When she's ready to throw you out, remember you're still a firefighter."

Bernard and Joseph stepped outside. "I'm going to miss our time together, Bernard."

"Would you consider coming to work for me? Do a trial week and see how you like it."

Joseph grinned widely, exposing the gap between his front teeth.

When his Polish friend arrived at the distillery the next day, Bernard pulled him aside and pointed to the cross hanging outside Joseph's shirt. "That could arouse passions. Once they know you, it might be different."

Joseph tucked the cross inside his worn flannel. Chaim, polite but reserved, greeted Joseph without comment. Shlomo nodded shyly. Leib looked sharply at the newcomer.

As Joseph's training progressed, he and Leib only worked together when they shoveled grain. When they fired the stills, drew off vodka, or cleaned up, neither could outpace the other, which made them try harder. Joseph, stocky and muscular, Leib, lean and drawn, both wheezed with exertion.

Bernard worried their competition might impact the vodka's quality, but the perfect taste reassured him. Didn't dogs who snarled at each other one day hunt with their pack mates the next? Still, he tried to calm the conflict by assigning Leib to the labelling job for a day. The others enjoyed their turns centering the rectangular Garfinkle's Spirits label on each bucket, a break from frenetic distilling, but not Leib, whose knees bounced as they had back in kheyder. When he finished the last bucket, he charged around, leveled off vats, turned valves, and hurled orders at Shlomo, who looked like a man caught in a violent storm.

Next, Bernard encouraged the twins to bring their instruments and play during lunch breaks. Instead, Leib set up a chessboard and asked if anyone wanted a game. He stared at Joseph.

"Sure, let's play," Joseph said.

Three quick massacres followed. Joseph had no effective strategies. He pushed out all his pawns—a peasant army with pitchforks and clubs fighting armored knights. Leib cut them down using coordinated attacks and creative flourishes. He sacrificed pieces and followed up with forks, skewers, and checkmate.

Leib didn't wait until the games finished to declare victory. He was omniscient.

"You call that a defense? This game's over in four moves." He finally brushed his hand through the air, swatting away some imaginary insect. He sauntered a few steps away and stretched.

Leib and Joseph didn't play again, and their frantic work pace eased. Several more weeks passed with an undeclared truce, and whether he forgot or thought they knew him well enough now, Joseph's cross reemerged. Chaim stared as it swayed back and forth on its chain. Shlomo turned away, but Leib immediately pulled a yarmulke, which he never wore except during those years his mother forced him to attend shul, from his pocket.

During the morning break, Leib retrieved the Tanakh from the office, glared at Joseph, and read aloud about how Samson, his hair cut and eyes gouged, prayed one last time for strength. Joseph appeared to be enjoying the story and rooted for its spiritually flawed hero. How did he miss that Leib, with his own hair shorn, didn't need a higher power for one final surge?

"It's too soon, Joseph," Bernard warned him, away from the others.

"But, Bernard, we're all friends now, yes? Is it my Yiddish? I miss some words, and my Polish mixes in."

"No, Joseph, and we understand most of the Polish too."

"I won't try to convert anyone, Bernard. People at my church call me a friend of the Christ-killers, but I tell them Christ was a Jew, and we all worship the same God, so we have to love Jewish people."

"Do you think I could change their minds, Joseph, about Jews?"

"They're trained dogs, Bernard."

Bernard waited, but Joseph's brow remained furrowed, unlit by insight. "For some Jews, that symbol will always be a poke with a sharp stick."

The cross, Leib's yarmulke, and the bible stories vanished from Garfinkle's Spirits.

7

"Only a few at a time," Estes assured Bernard, as she delivered six bricks to Chaim. The work on the professor's house had proceeded into a late, mild fall. She wanted to be helpful despite the bulge of new life that made the dress tight across her belly. The passion of the wedding night had overwhelmed her determination not to have a child so soon. She wouldn't make that mistake again.

Bernard and his friends had dumped the most fire-damaged bricks and salvaged others from the professor's devastated house. "We'll make the walls level and plumb, so the roof sits like a well-tailored hat," he told her.

Chaim added Estes's six bricks to the tray until a load of thirty bricks waited to ascend. He tied the rope dangling from the scaffold pulley to the tray and grasped the loose end from a thick coil. Stepping aside, he shouted, "Hey, ho, heave away."

"Fired from the earth, hoisted to the sky," Leib shouted as he peered over the edge of the scaffold.

Chaim pulled, and the bricks rose, slow and easy. Six arshins above the ground, the one-hundred-fifty funt load swayed before Leib settled it on the arm-width platform.

Their mason, an older man, stooped from years of bending and lifting, tapped the bricks carefully with his hammer—too forceful and they'd crack, too timid and they would only skim the top of the mortar, a weak bond. He scraped off the gray ooze, deftly buttering the end of the next brick. A load of mortar Chaim had mixed waited its turn to rise. Street peddlers, merchants, and shoppers watched the building's resurrection.

"A girl is working with them."

"She's pregnant and lame."

"Her father and husband allow this?"

Estes treated the judgments with no more consequence than banal market exchanges. Hot coals only burn if picked up. She turned away from the scaffold and locked eyes with a girl holding a baby in her arms.

The girl blushed and averted her eyes. Estes pulled another six bricks from the pile.

Bernard had split his crew into two groups. Shlomo and Joseph made vodka while he, Leib, and Chaim worked on the building. They would join their mates after dinner and work into the evening at the distillery.

Bernard moved around the site, ready to jump in if she faltered. He traded places with Chaim and climbed the scaffold ladder to assist the mason.

Though her arms ached, Estes found satisfaction in the physical effort and the line of red clay rising. When she nearly tripped with her load, Bernard sounded like a foreman. "Enough for today, Estes." She did not resist. He came down, they embraced, and she walked across the square. She'd clean up before beginning a different kind of work.

✳

Estes sat on her childhood bed, and through the window and partial curtain of trees she glimpsed Bernard at work on their project across the square. She stretched out to rest a bit before her meeting with Eliza and Gesia Gelfman, a representative of the Society of Narodniki. Estes hoped she and Eliza could publish something about this group. Advocating for literacy shouldn't draw the censor's ire, not when others wanted to blow up the czar.

It felt strange to stretch out in her old bed without her books. Alte Ferd had carted all her remaining possessions up the hill, so now her cough, the barking of dogs, and the distant sounds of commerce seemed louder in the empty room. She dozed until Mama opened the door.

"Eliza and Gesia have arrived. They're in the shop with Herman. You'd better hurry before he puts them to work."

Mama had abandoned the kitchen today to cut leather. Papa's reputation drew more orders and required longer working hours, but he never wanted to hire an assistant after Sophie left. "Quality, not quantity," he said, then complained about the punishment of success.

Estes went downstairs and kissed Eliza's cheek, then greeted Gesia. "I hope Papa has not asked too many questions."

"Only about my family, work, and plans." She surprised him when she stuck her hand out and gave his a vigorous shake. Papa's eyes drifted to the floor and Gesia's boots.

"Your left heel's wearing unevenly. You do a lot of walking. I can build you a much better pair."

"Oh, Papa. We should go now before you have us all waxing thread and delivering shoes."

She led Eliza and Gesia up the narrow staircase to the second-floor hall and into the dining room. Estes sat next to Eliza and across from Gesia. She served the tea Mama had prepared.

Gesia had thick black hair pulled back in a bun, heavy eyebrows, a dark complexion, and an earnest expression. Eliza's age, status, and erect bearing enforced a formal boundary with Estes, but Gesia, with her eager smile, felt instantly like a friend.

"We want to show the peasants possibilities for a real life," Gesia began. "It's nearly twelve years since serfdom and the master's lash, yet they remain imprisoned by ignorance. Eighty-five percent of our population labor on farms, but the gentry still take most of the benefits."

She leaned across the table. "Russia will emerge from its primitive state only by elevating those working the land. We must teach the peasants to read and write. We need simple materials—alphabet books, reading primers, fables, stories. You can help by publicizing our activities."

"What about the emancipation of women?" Estes asked. "Does the society have a strategy?" She had witnessed peasant men berating and slapping their wives at market. "Will teaching peasants to read stop the abuse?"

"If women have the education to take better jobs, it's a step forward," Gesia replied.

"Why do we have to move a mountain one pebble at a time? Czar Alexander could issue a decree. Emancipate woman in Russia immediately and put us on an equal footing with men."

"What use is equality if we have to beg for food or suffer in hellish factories like Shershevski's?" Gesia's cheeks flushed, and she kept her eyes on Estes. "You must not be discouraged." She spread her arms. "Come to the countryside and see for yourselves. You'll have a story to publish, I promise. Please come. We'll work with the children, girls as well as boys."

"I'll have my carriage and driver," Eliza offered. They would go the next afternoon.

"I'm so pleased," Gesia said. "Now, Estes, I've had midwifery training. Do you have plans for the delivery?"

Why did Gesia notice what she forgot? What kind of mother would she be?

"I've completed some of my coursework in Kiev at university and shown mastery of obstetrics. I'll do the same with pediatrics and gynecology when I go back. I found a physician in Horodno who will only interfere if a birth becomes difficult and I require his assistance. You must be past three months?"

Estes nodded. "What brought you to Horodno?"

Gesia laughed. "Of course, you want to know more about me before you open your thighs—a courtship."

Estes's smile felt lopsided.

Eliza stood to pour more tea. "Women helping women shows our liberation is not an abstract idea."

"I come from a well-off Jewish family in Mozyr. My father made his fortune in the forestry business and never paid much attention to me until I turned sixteen, which left me free to educate myself. At my uncle's house in Berdichev, I developed friendships with young Russians who taught me the language, and with Jews who believed in the Haskalah.

"When my father demanded I marry one of his friends, a Talmudic scholar, I refused. He called me disloyal, a disgrace, and said he would force me. The night before the planned wedding, he ordered me to shave my head and take a ritual bath. These superstitious practices and the unwanted marriage drove me to my uncle's and then to Kiev. I haven't seen my father or stepmother since I left, nearly three years ago. That woman never stood by me, but I don't blame her. She's my father's servant, not his partner.

"Through my uncle, I procured my father's permission to enter university. Perhaps he hoped I'd fail and come crawling back, because he never sent one kopek. I found work in a sewing factory and joined a cooperative because Chernyshevsky had his free love influence on us all. With new friends from school, we started a discussion group and planned to reach out to the peasantry. The police watched us constantly, so we temporarily dispersed. We vowed to learn from experience and bring back fresh ideas about what worked. I chose Horodno, and at this moment, I'm speaking with two new friends."

"I do need a midwife, and if you will be staying for a while . . ."

"Splendid! We must shake to seal the arrangement."

＊

They crossed the Niemen on an unusually warm fall day. South of Horodno, the wheels churned up a cloud of dust. Fields with cut corn stubble broke up the rolling hills. Peasant women and children stacked sheaths of bound grain and glanced up as Eliza's bright blue carriage drove by.

On the outskirts of a settlement, they passed dilapidated log houses, the walls chinked with straw instead of mortar, a family on its knees working in a garden, and men on a bench sharing a bottle.

Peter, Eliza's driver, slowed the carriage and stopped in front of a long, narrow building surrounded by shacks. "Here we are," Gesia said. "The community house, our temporary school."

Two women with nine children approached. The women and girls all wore colorful headscarves, patched dresses, well-worn white cotton blouses, and boots up to their knees. The boys wore similar boots, baggy pants bunched like accordions, and woolen shirts.

Gesia greeted the women and knelt, eye level with the children. Two smiled when she said their names, five others bobbed their heads, and two clutched their arms like they expected a beating to follow.

Inside, four long tables occupied each corner of the room, leaving the middle of the hall open. Six women sat at the table closest to the kitchen and sliced parsnips and onions. In the kitchen, a woman shoved split firewood into a cookstove, then picked up a ladle and stirred a grimy, black pot.

Gesia assigned three students each to Eliza and Estes and passed out the reading primers. Eliza tapped the Polish title, *Joseph and Marie on the Farm.* "Dictates from Petersburg mean little in the countryside."

Estes steered her students to a table, repeated their names, and introduced herself. She read first, then had each of them read and noted the types of errors they made. Could anyone care about reading this barren story? A farmer plants, harvests, and eats his crop, from one activity to another without a single illustration or surprise—no shifts in the weather, no jokes to laugh over, no pictures—as dry and humorless as a bureaucrat's report. She tried to engage the children with questions.

"What do you like to plant?"

"Corn."

"Do the crows eat the seed?"

One of the boys held an imaginary rifle and said, "Bang!" The other flapped his arms and laid his head on the table.

When the lessons ended, Gesia collected the books. Estes blinked in the sunlight and spotted Peter by the open carriage door. Three men waited for the women and children on one side of the carriage, chatting among themselves. They stared indifferently at her for a moment. Two other men stood on the opposite side and drank from a bottle. They kicked at the dirt and little swirls of dust rose from their shoes. One, bald with a pinched face and close-set eyes, raised his voice. The other—taller, bearded, and wearing a worn leather cap—slapped his companion's cheek and grabbed the liquor. Eliza stepped forward and stood next to Peter, her back to these men, shielding Estes and Gesia. As they entered the carriage, the word struck her like the click of a gun hammer, "Zydzi," not merely identifying her and Gesia as Jews, but a snarled denunciation, a curse thick with hatred. Eliza turned and approached the men.

"How dare you! We've come here to teach, not for your insults. What are your names?"

The men mumbled something unintelligible. Their downcast eyes said Eliza, with her gentrified Polish, would not be challenged. Class still ruled here. Peter, with his brute-force glare, stood beside Eliza.

"A bit suspicious of outsiders," Gesia said breezily on the way home. "It will take time to win their trust."

Estes sat pensively. Those attitudes wouldn't change by teaching a few children to read.

Gesia must have read her mind. "It will be a generational fight on several fronts, not a sudden upheaval. Yes, reading will open doors, but also, when these children are older, they'll remember our kindness."

"Suspicion we work with, hatred we must fight," Eliza said, "whatever class it comes from."

8

One morning, the winter sun still below the horizon, Estes awoke to the baby kicking. Bernard had risen first to feed the cookstove, and now he prayed in his old bedroom. She made a quick trip to the outhouse and began her most important daily chore at the kitchen worktable.

She translated a page of English into Yiddish for him. Bernard took liberties to drop prayers intended for a minyan and she left out or substituted words and phrases to find the right level of difficulty for him.

As Bernard recited the Shema, Estes yielded to curiosity about his daily practice. Papa only worshipped on Shabes and holidays. From the hall, she observed him swaying back and forth in a chair, the tefillin bound on his left arm and as a third eye above his forehead. He stood and exclaimed the greatness of God and asked Him to bless their home, marriage, and the baby in her womb.

Estes had an impulse to stand without clothes in front her husband. *It's God or me, Bernard. You have to choose.* She caught herself. *Jealous of an imaginary being!* How ridiculous she was. She vowed not to spy on him again.

✳

When Bernard arrived at the distillery, Joseph, partially hidden in vapor, greeted him first. Six months after Bernard's Polish friend had started, Joseph distilled with confidence. He filled buckets, and Chaim lidded each one with two latches.

During their lunch break, Leib told them how his mother, sisters, and demented grandfather went to join their father in Kishinev. "She took everything, including the chickens—minus their heads. Poor Shlomo. Before they departed, she arranged his marriage. Passed from one boss to the next. 'What will become of you without a woman?' our mother asked him, and to me, 'What woman in her right mind would settle for you?'"

He poked his brother, who stared at his potato kugel, trying to read his fortune on the wrinkled surface.

"Ha, I'm glad to see her go. No more slaps!" Leib's eyes brimmed a bit, and he spoke quietly. "Now he's moving in with the in-laws. It's okay, Shlo, you'll eat better than a king." Leib reached out and patted Shlomo on the back while Chaim and Joseph added their congratulations. Bernard retrieved five glasses from the office and opened a bottle.

"To my brother Shlomo and his happiness. L'chaim!"

"L'chaim," Bernard, Chaim, and Joseph echoed.

"Better drink up now, brother, before the mother-in-law gets your leash."

"How about you three?" Bernard asked. "Esteemed employees of Garfinkle's Spirits must be irresistible matches."

"I have a sweetheart," Joseph said. "She's my grandmother's cousin's granddaughter. We're waiting until she turns sixteen. We'll move into our own house," he hastened to add.

"Third cousins," Leib said.

"We're meeting with the matchmaker soon." Chaim blushed. "I wish I could find someone myself, like you did, Bernard."

"Well, I'm in no hurry," Leib said.

Shlomo snorted, but Leib ignored him. Bernard looked at his friend's long, bony face and didn't say anything.

"I have a few things to do before I leave," Bernard told them after they cleaned up. Behind the half-wall of buckets, he sat on a bench and spread out the cards and the page of Estes's translation.

"What are you doing?" Chaim held his wool coat in his hands and stared at the cards.

Bernard moved over, embarrassed by Chaim's lasting devotion to him since their kheyder years. His friend held up one word at a time, as instructed, and made a separate pile of the ones Bernard did not instantly name. After several passes, Bernard had them all.

"Now listen to me read and tell me when I make a mistake. We'll circle it and practice with new cards tomorrow. Estes says fifteen at a time like this is perfect."

Bernard read, and Chaim, with his perfect recognition, gathered the missed words—a joyful retriever bounding after a pheasant, never tiring of the repetition, nor understanding the meaning of the story.

✳

If part of Bernard's mornings belonged to God, reading ruled his night. They sat in bed propped against the headboard, each with a book as their table.

Estes ordered him to read the page he'd practiced with Chaim. "Too perfect, Bernard. I want you to memorize common words, not whole passages. That isn't reading, it's avoidance." She isolated the words in those lines, grouped them to practice similar sounds, switched one or two letters to make new words, and exhorted him to recite them multiple times until he could blend word parts without a painful pause.

"Estes, one shouldn't have to work this hard in bed. It should be a time of rest."

"Would you rather sit at the table?"

"Old Rabbi Horowitz—even he wasn't this tough." Bernard touched her belly and the soft skin on her inner thigh, but she removed his hand and held it in her own.

"Repetition, Bernard. Read. You're a pot of simmering water that never came to a full boil. I'm building a hotter fire."

"What will be left of me but dissipated steam?"

He read several paragraphs from *Middlemarch*, which Estes had procured in eight installments, with real fluency this time. He tossed the pages aside and mounted her. She wasn't ready for him, but he moved slowly, matching the pace of that book, until teacher and student cried out simultaneously.

"Is the book still too dull, Bernard?"

"My unmerciful reading teacher caused the fever, not George Elliot. Dorothea Brooke is no Jane Eyre, and her marriage to old Casaubon lacks excitement. Not like when Jane marries Rochester."

"That's romanticized love. Most books end with the marriage, but Elliot shows us reality—relationships that work and ones that don't."

"Why read about those failures? Romance is important, don't you agree?" He nuzzled her belly bulge and rested his head there.

"Yes, as long as both partners have satisfying work. Do you want me to read now?" He responded with light snoring, his final word on *Middlemarch*.

9

E stes tried not to laugh when Gesia pressed the flared wooden tube against her belly. The midwife put her ear to the instrument.

"Strong and fast, much faster than the mother's."

In three months, she'd be a mother. Gesia told her she was larger than other women at this stage but assured her she heard just one heartbeat and felt one baby. A good thing, because Estes was determined to have only one. Who else in Horodno had ever purchased two varieties of condoms? One, called a rubber, supposedly lasted a lifetime with careful washing and storage. Gesia described it as armor, which sounded promising. As an alternative, Estes also had skins made from the intestines of sheep.

Gesia put oil on her hands and lubricated Estes's protruding belly. "Beautiful."

"Do you have other women today?"

"One more back in town, but I have time. I'm working with a few in the countryside too. Scientific beliefs about childbirth are as difficult to instill as literacy."

Estes had heard about peasant midwives who stuffed a rag in the delivering mother's anus to make sure the baby didn't try to sneak out the wrong hole. She rolled on her side, sat up, and reached for her cane.

"The extra weight puts more stress on my foot." She put on her robe. "Come, I'll make some tea and lunch, and you feed the fire."

In the kitchen, Gesia put a few pieces of wood into the cookstove's firebox and adjusted the damper. On this winter day, the smaller stove in the dining room also crackled. Estes removed a thick glove from its hook on the wall, then carried out the kettle and two servings of tea packed in silver dipping spoons.

She went back to the kitchen and opened the cold box, packed with ice Bernard had chipped from a sawdust-covered block in the barn. Before spring melt, he'd cut more from one of the ponds. From the dairy side of the divided container, Estes brought out cheese. She added a loaf of oat bread and delivered their lunch on a wooden board. From a china cabinet drawer, she took out a knife. *Left dairy, right meat.*

"Tradition," Bernard answered her yesterday when Estes had playfully questioned the practice of keeping a kosher kitchen.

"A logical fallacy Bernard—*argumentum ad antiquitatem.* And religious absolutes are another form of the tradition argument. How can anyone challenge the moral authority of an all-powerful God?"

"Our traditions are full of questions and interpretation."

She sighed. "Questions about fine points, though, fiddle-faddle, not the underlying assumptions."

Bernard did better with a more personal argument, so when he added that following tradition brought him close to his father, she embraced him.

Gesia poured and Estes smelled the mint she and Bernard had gathered and dried last fall. They ate, quiet for a bit before talking about the Horodno Book and Publishing Company.

When Eliza had taken them to Vilne for the launch of the printing business several weeks ago, they'd stuffed their ears with cotton as the rotary press produced twelve hundred copies of Estes's work in just one hour. She had included her name as author of a pamphlet about reading instruction and what Russia could become with a literate populace.

"You wrote about teaching reading with immense passion," Gesia said. "I'm so grateful you and Eliza still go to the countryside with me each week."

Their pupils had made progress, which elicited more smiles and eye contact. She had teased Bernard he would have to work harder to remain her best student.

"Those two surly men nod to us now."

"See, they've changed for the better, Estes."

"Dogs obey when the master is home. I wonder what would happen without our noble Polish woman."

"You're my darling pessimist, but I'm thrilled with the books you've made for the children. I wonder when you'll write about how marriage between one man and one woman perpetuates our second-class status?"

"It depends on whether the union is voluntary, arranged, or in your case, forced."

"Yes, of course, but even in these so-called voluntary situations, all our laws support the supremacy of the husband over the wife, the son over the daughter. Free love allows us to choose our partners without becoming a type of property."

Estes stroked her restless friend's hand and refilled their cups.

IO

On a beautiful day in early May, with the window opened to the earthy smell of the turned garden, Estes went into labor. Hours passed with increasingly intense contractions and pain from the bottom of her rib cage to her tailbone. The sledgehammer blows to her lower spine made it impossible to hold on to anything she'd heard from Mama or read in her books. One wave of pain after another, with the briefest respite between. On fire. Split open. She would die.

Other women survive this . . . Other women survive this. She clutched this thought until it tore away too. She gripped Mama's hand and began to grunt. Gesia finally commanded, "PUSH! This baby needs to come out now. Here's the head, don't stop. PUSH, PUSH, PUSH!"

The baby emerged bawling, and Gesia placed the boy, his face bright red, on Estes's chest. Astonished, Estes watched her son search for her breast.

"Another head," Mama shouted.

The second baby slipped out in the wake of the first and Gesia placed the girl next to her brother.

"Where did this one come from?"

"You've got perfect twins, Estes."

Gesia opened the door and Bernard rushed in. He knelt and wrapped his arms around his family and kissed each newborn on the head. The boy had already found a nipple, but the girl continued to cry and shiver.

Mama came early each morning and didn't leave until nightfall. She cooked, cleaned, and held her grandchildren—Seraphina, the fiery one, and Solomon, the wise, after Bernard's father. Papa joined them in the evening for dinners, and Gesia visited every afternoon. She rocked both babies and whispered revolutionary slogans into their ears.

Estes remained silent about the planning for Solomon's bris, although she questioned the entire premise of a covenant with God. She didn't protest Bernard's wish to have a minyan, though it was not required. Neither she, Gesia, Eliza, or Mama counted among the ten. She didn't place her hands on her hips in defiance about the shul chair Rabbi Menshein brought to their house for the prophet Elijah, with its red upholstery and elaborately carved legs and arms. *Didn't prophets have more important work than a boy's circumcision?* She didn't cling to her baby when Papa took him from her arms and passed him to Bernard, who placed him on the chair. She observed impassively in their cramped dining room, not part of the proceedings, while her husband held Solomon on the cushion, and the moyel, an ancient Jew, said various prayers. Only when he took the sharp knife from his ceremonial box, and she noticed the old man's tremor, did she react. Gesia caught her before her head struck the floor.

She recovered in bed. Bernard, on one side, held Solomon, who sucked on his pinky. Gesia, on the other, swaddled Seraphina, who wailed as if she, not her brother, had been wounded.

They slept with the twins between them. Estes learned to breastfeed in the middle of the night in a dream state, rolling on her side and pushing her nipple into Seraphina's mouth before her daughter grew too upset to nurse. When Seraphina finished, Estes coaxed Solomon to her other breast and nudged Bernard, who got up wordlessly for the first diaper change.

Despite her exhaustion, Estes insisted on continuing Bernard's reading lessons after dinner while her parents held the babies. Conjugal relations were another matter. Her body had turned into baby food, and twelve weeks passed without physical intimacy. Bernard never asked when she'd be ready but reached for her hand in bed and wrapped his arms around her in the kitchen. When her body finally responded, they left the sleeping twins and went to the other bedroom.

Estes instructed Bernard on the use of the condom. It excited her to take control as she did when teaching him to read. She had tested the rubber with water, held it up and inspected it for leaks.

"It's washable, Bernard, and the manufacturer claims that with proper care it will last a lifetime."

"I'm your husband, Estes, not a shopper." He reached under her nightgown for her swollen breasts. She squirmed away.

"Well, this is a new coat, and we have to make sure it fits."

Bernard inspected the thick rubber with a worried look.

"I have oil for lubrication," she assured him. "You might prefer the skins. They're more expensive, but we can afford it." *Best to let Bernard decide some things.*

After he tried them both, she asked him which he liked more.

Bernard stroked his beard. "Hmm, difficult question. More testing might be necessary." He reached for her again, but Seraphina's crying in the next room ended further experimentation.

II

June 8, 1874

Solly and Sera turned one last month. Thanks to Mama and Bernard, I survive, but why did children have to come so soon?

Bernard's the one with the natural parenting instinct. He'll stop whatever he's doing to play with them, while I look forward to handing them off. I won't miss diapers, wailing, body fluids run amok, the lack of sleep, the challenge of getting anything done in short bursts of freedom.

Solly is the calm, happy child I imagined. Sera is often inconsolable, and I'm afraid sometimes I might start screaming too. Mama is never impatient or desperate. She told me Sera would be my teacher. But of what?

Estes put the pen and journal aside and, after she and Bernard delivered the twins to her parents, she walked across Market Square to her second home. The bookshop had a cathedral ceiling in place of a full second floor and attic. Posts and beams supported the wraparound walkways almost wide enough for her to lie across. On the third floor, along the eaves, shoppers had to keep to the inside edge to avoid bumping the rafters. She'd shelved the religious texts on the gabled ends.

She sat for a moment in the old chair they had moved from Papa's shop. Everything else was new. Nothing remained from before the fire. Still, she felt Professor Micah's presence, and some days when the door chimed, she expected to see him enter.

"What have you done with the place, my Estes? Where are the important books?"

Seated behind the counter with her hair pinned up gave her the look of a real merchant. What better advertisement as customers entered than having the proprietor immersed in a book? She surveyed the full shelves, with thousands of new and used volumes, several lifetimes of reading, even for her.

Rabbi Menshein, who often came to browse, started calling Estes "The Horodno Bookshop Lady," and it caught on with other customers.

An old man, bent with age, and a young boy around ten entered. They wore matching white shirts, black pants, and identical caps. "Good morning, Horodno Bookshop Lady. Do you have a recommendation for my grandson?"

With brief summaries, she ran through a list of titles. The boy frowned and commented, "Anything more exciting, a bit harder?"

The old man bragged about his grandson's German, so Estes pulled out a translation of Edgar Allan Poe's stories and opened to "The Pit and the Pendulum."

Sometimes she had the reader try a page. Like a new pair of boots, the fit had to be right. She showed him where to begin.

He read: "I was sick, sick unto death with that long agony; and when they at length unbound me, and I was permitted to sit, I felt that my senses were leaving me. The sentence—the dread sentence of death."

Hooked by death. "If you survive this without nightmares, try 'The Telltale Heart.'" Estes thumped the counter.

Two old men on the second level stopped to explore the philosophy, science, and history books on their way to the religious texts on the third floor.

Make them experience the Enlightenment.

A rabbi approached the other two, all old crows dressed in tattered black. "The answers you want are above." He continued his climb to the third floor.

The two browsers returned the secular volumes to their shelf. Estes smiled at their forced nonchalance. On their return from the religious texts, would they walk by that section without stopping, or, once the rabbi left, resume their illicit browsing?

Jacob Rosenblum had completed his studies in Vilne in record time and occasionally came to the bookshop with his father. This day, he appeared by himself and headed up the stairs. His accomplished singing and religious achievement hadn't troubled Estes at all, but recently customers had begun speaking of his reputation as an intellectual—a renowned Maimonides scholar. But why did he want a crown rabbi job? A puppet of the Russians.

Almost two years after their wedding, she still bristled at how he'd ignored her, but maybe, without Avram Rosenblum looming over him,

Jacob would talk to her on the way out. The Horodno Bookshop Lady was a scholar too.

He ascended, ignoring the French literature section Estes loved, not even glancing at the seventeen weighty volumes of Balzac's *Human Comedy*. An hour later, Jacob reappeared with a commentary by Rashi. Estes took his money and their hands met. He pulled away as if scorched, and when she sought his eye, he stared past her shoulder. She had an urge to test his Russian. "How have you been, Jacob? I've recently read Darwin's *Origin of the Species*. Natural selection is a perfect theory, don't you think?"

"I'm preparing a series of lectures on Rashi. Maimonides is my specialty, though." He spoke breathlessly. "His work is so voluminous and deep that I haven't had time to consider minor scholars. If you read nothing else, explore his principles of faith." He continued as if advising a student, ticking off all thirteen principles. He finally stopped and looked at her. "He valued science, of course, a preeminent medical doctor of his time."

Jacob speaking so much shocked her, but to call Darwin a minor scholar? She tried to keep her tone objective, because she wanted to refute his precious Maimonides's principles with logic, but her voice filled with emotion. "A belief system that requires blind faith instead of science at its core already has a fatal flaw. I'm a positivist, Jacob. Darwin's work proved that species evolve over eons and can't possibly have been created as described in Genesis. It's ridiculous to believe the Torah is of divine origin, dictated by God to Moses on Mt. Sinai."

Jacob turned scarlet and shook his head.

Her resentment and anger rose. "Vot Vasha sdacha," she said, then, "do iz dayn kleyngelt," in Yiddish, as if he couldn't understand the Russian. She returned his change and Jacob watched her for a moment, but this time she didn't meet his gaze. He left without another word.

Five yeshiva students came in toward the end of the day and gawked at novels, like food snitchers on Yom Kiper. One kept his eyes on the door and watched for any rabbi or authority who might catch them with their impure impulses exposed.

They grabbed each other to read a passage, ready to bolt for the third floor if the alarm sounded. The lookout hissed, "Rabbi! Wait, it's only Menshein."

Bernard's teacher, his shoulders sagging like autumn ferns, said, "Good afternoon, Horodno Bookshop Lady."

Estes cupped both hands and spoke directly into his ear. "Good afternoon, Rabbi Menshein. How are you?"

"Never better," he laughed.

"What are you interested in today?"

"Why does my beard continue growing, but I keep shrinking? Why would God create a species and allow it to become extinct? Why is there something instead of nothing?"

"Wait here." She returned with Kant's *Critique of Pure Reason* and pulled her copy of Darwin, in German, from the counter shelf.

"Regarding your philosophical and biological inquiries, read these."

He took them in his gnarled hands.

"As to the growth of your beard compared to diminishing overall height, allow me a day for research."

On slower days, she read aloud to him, but today he had to manage with his failing eyesight and rustic German. After ten minutes of Darwin, he fell asleep in her chair, the open book on his chest heaving like the *Beagle* in rough seas.

When he awoke, Rabbi Menshein stood with effort. Estes tucked Darwin and Kant into his bag and walked him to the door. He turned, and his moist eyes stared into the open peak of the shop. She kissed his cheek, and he shuffled away, listing to his cane's side.

Merchants and peddlers usually entered just before the shop closed. Today, two came in; one with a basket of apples, the other hauling a crate of newspapers. They didn't come for the books, but for the customers they coveted. When they yelled about their end-of-the-day sales, she ushered them out. The yeshiva students, who would have nested all night if she'd let them, were next to go. Estes hoped to read for a few minutes before her daily meeting with Gesia, but when she turned the Open sign around, her aunt Miriam appeared.

"So many books in one place! Who could possibly need all this information?"

After her aunt left with stationery, Estes locked up and resumed reading Flaubert. She wanted to improve her French, rusty for lack of practice, but soon her friend rattled the door.

Gesia sank into the other chair. "I need you, Estes. Lately, the letters have turned into strangers to the children. Where did the tall one with the scarf come from, the lady wearing the strange hat, or the fat man and his potbelly?"

"Progress is not always a straight line, Gesia. One step at a time, lots of repetition."

"If it were a circuitous route to the peak, traversing the slope, I'd be fine, but some days we find ourselves right back where we started."

Gesia wanted her to come to the country to teach again. The Horodno Bookshop Lady, in her spacious palace, surrounded by books organized by topic and author, went to the children's section and brought back an armload of stories. "Read these with the children."

"Thanks, but how will we carry out a revolution without women like you? Your mother loves watching the twins, and you could get someone to manage the bookshop for an afternoon."

"I'll make you some more stories for teaching too."

Gesia moved from their impasse to the daily outrages she collected from the papers and her contacts: the czar's secret police infiltrated collectives throughout Russia; a minister in Novograd beat a peasant to death for not bowing to him; a milling machine swallowed two children in Odessa; women still barred from attending classes with men in Petersburg; Bakunin declared equal to Marx as the most dangerous enemy of the state . . .

Gesia paused. "You care more about Emma Bovary than what's happening right in front of you."

"When I was a young girl, I sometimes explored the power of volition. I don't have to turn the page now, I thought. Or I held my foot above a predetermined mark but dropped it down in another spot. I told myself I was in control. But Russia is too immense. Perhaps pick one thing, the reading program, and make that your purpose."

Gesia ignored her comment. Suddenly, she leaned over and brushed her mouth softly over Estes's lips. "You practice freedom when it comes to choosing books. Why settle on just one lover?"

The kiss startled her and left a question burning on her skin.

Gesia smiled but didn't look away. She reached out and brushed back some strands of hair from Estes's forehead. "I've stayed in Horodno much longer than I'd planned. My comrades from school have gathered again in Kiev. It's your fault, you know. Why do I visit you every day? Of course, I enjoy talking about books, but it's you I love. Some think Chernyshevsky's free love applies only to male and female relations, but why can't we choose any partner based on mutual attraction? Should men sanction what types of relationships we have?"

Estes, nineteen years old now, only one year younger than Gesia, studied her earnest companion. "I love you, too." She took Gesia's hands. "I wasn't close to other girls in childhood. You're my best friend."

Gesia's features darkened an instant before she smiled. "As you wish—best friends."

12

What a fool. Bernard had given up shul until she would be allowed to sit with him. And now, how does Estes respond? Tomorrow, on the holiest of days, Yom Kiper, instead of spending the day with him, she would ride into the countryside with Eliza and Gesia.

"My relationship with women friends takes nothing away from you, Bernard," she told him again as they cleared the dinner table.

"Does it have to be on this one day, Estes?" He didn't expect her to pray or fast, just to share the day with him.

"Did you want something in return for doing what's right?"

He turned his back on her and went outside, directing his fury toward weeds in the garden.

※

September 21, 1874

Eliza orders Peter to pull over. She can be quite imperial. I have my journal and pencil in hand. Bernard looked so hurt this morning; I almost changed my mind. He always had friends, so how can he know what it was like for me, all those lonely years—and now I have two.

My attitude toward religion hasn't changed. It's not just about the seating arrangements at shul. And I don't believe in this compulsion to purify ourselves. Bernard bends on most things, but when forced to stretch too far, he's afraid he won't snap back into recognizable shape. Mama has the children today while Bernard, Papa, and many other men in Horodno atone for their sins.

We watch peasants work a field alongside the road. Their scythes whoosh back and forth, and the grass drops in bunches. Eliza scribbles some notes and makes a drawing, her eyes on the scene in front of us.

She dispassionately observes and translates what she sees into pictures and words. I try also to attend to this picture as it is, but comparisons and metaphors seep into the stillness.

Gesia steps out of the carriage and walks into the field. A thin scarecrow of a man in a broad-brimmed hat hands her the scythe and stands aside with his hands behind his back. The long-handled blade in his hands, a tool—in Gesia's, a dance partner. She sways gracefully, dips on the backswing, pauses for a second, then glides her whole upper body forward, and the grass gives way. Four other men come over, lean on the top handles, and watch the exotic woman from town work their field.

✳

The next afternoon, when she met Gesia at her parents' house, they put the twins in their wagon and walked north.

"Will your foot be okay?"

"If we take our time. It's a gentle rise home. Thanks for hauling the wagon."

They traveled in silence for a while and stopped when Solly cried out. Sera had grabbed a handful of his hair. After Estes peeled open her daughter's fist and released the hair, Sera climbed out of the wagon and began toddling back toward town.

"Take the handle," Gesia told Estes. After a few loping strides she caught Sera and hoisted the escaping child onto her shoulders.

"She does this only when you and I walk together," Estes said. "Her scheme to sneak onto your shoulders. See how happy she is now."

"Rascal. Sixteen months."

Solly had stretched out and stared dreamily at the sky. By the time they arrived home, the children had fallen asleep. Gesia laid Sera in the wagon next to her brother. Estes held her breath, but her daughter didn't wake up.

Estes gripped Gesia's hand. "I never believed I could settle down here, but Solly and Sera are thriving and so is the bookshop."

"How will we ever emancipate the peasants and workers when you're so complacent?" Gesia asked without her usual lightness. "We need a call to action for all the oppressed. Literature and articles for the bourgeoise are no substitute."

"Oh, Gesia."

"Forgive me. I'm jealous, my friend, and so restless. I've been away too long. It's time I return."

"Kiev's over six hundred versts away. When will I ever see you again?"

"Run away with me," Gesia said. "We'll live in a shack and teach peasants the principles of Bakunin while we pluck chickens."

"Or pluck the peasants and teach the chickens the principles. The birds would make wonderful anarchists. They peck away, follow their own path, reject state planning."

Gesia sighed, and spots of color rose on her cheeks. For true revolutionaries, unlike mere philosophers, some things are too sacred to satirize. Estes felt the same way about the emancipation of women.

"You're so brave. I'll worry about you."

"And I'll worry about you, too, Estes. How will you manage without me?"

*

On the eve of Gesia's departure from Horodno, Estes and Bernard invited her for their last dinner all together. They fed the children first and finally got them to bed. After dessert and tea, they remained at the table, and Bernard casually mentioned an invitation to the wedding of one of his kheyder classmates.

Gesia responded in a tone a parent might use to admonish a child, "Can't you see, Bernard? Marriage is another form of tyranny to serve the status quo."

"You're the one promoting tyranny, Gesia. Anyone who doesn't conform to your ideas must be wrong."

They went back and forth before Estes said, "Come, it's a beautiful fall evening." She held both Gesia's and Bernard's hands in the yard, the silence interrupted only by the last chirps of songbirds. Gesia kissed Bernard on the cheek and gave Estes a long embrace, then departed for town in the gathering darkness.

When Bernard noticed Estes's tears, the resentments he'd driven out on Yom Kiper returned to his chest. She should enjoy the company of women, but did they have to hold hands so often? And when Gesia embraced her, it resembled an intimate caress.

Some of Gesia's ideas, expressed with words like "overthrow," "revolution," "destroy," frightened him. What would be the counterweight to her extreme sentiments? He compelled himself to enjoy her finer qualities, but his mind ached from the effort.

"I'm jealous of Gesia," he said, looking toward town and not at Estes. "I want to be the one you're closest to."

"I feel the same way about your God, Bernard." Estes kissed him hungrily. "Stay right here." She hobbled into the house and after a few minutes came back with their love-making supplies and two blankets.

She guided his hand beneath her dress and laughed at his surprise that she had nothing on underneath. She spread out one blanket and pulled him down. He covered them with the other. Afterwards, they studied the stars, dozed, awoke to light rain, and went inside.

13

Autumn and winter passed with many letters between Estes and her friend. Gesia had resumed her university training and described her cooperative—the intellectual arguments, their optimism about changing Russia, the loves and struggles of her four closest comrades. She found something kind to say about each of them, and her intimate details helped Estes feel part of this circle.

During spring, however, Gesia's communications seemed hastily written. The interval between letters lengthened, and months passed without a word. When one finally came, Estes opened it eagerly.

July 18, 1875

My Dearest Estes,

I haven't forgotten you, and it makes me happy to imagine you looking up when the shop bell rings, reluctantly putting aside your book. The old men gazing in the windows—I wonder what they think about a twenty-year-old Jewish woman and her Polish mentor having the most extensive private book collection in Horodno.

Here, progress is hard. Hundreds of us have gone out to live among the people, organize against the aristocracy, join the peasants to work the land. I am determined to do more than skim the surface. How will we overcome centuries of oppression and ignorance with the teaching strategy I tried in Horodno?

I live with my four idealistic young friends from the cooperative. Has anyone ever had more loyal comrades than Olga Markinova, Ivan Karlovitch, Mikail Petrovitch, or Ekaterina Tumanova? You will be pleased to hear we are much too tired after working in the fields to explore free love. But if you were here, my darling . . .

I talk to the farmers about Bakunin's idea to share ownership of the land and keep the profits of our labor. They listen quietly, but as soon as I mention any action to force the czar into meaningful reform, their mistrust rises like the steamy haze off our sun-baked road after a sudden storm. I think about moving back into the city to organize workers not rooted in centuries of tradition. That's my life for now. The children sound lovely. You must give them kisses from me. Your best friend, Gesia

August 5, 1875
My Dear Gesia,

Bakunin himself could do no more than you and your comrades. I understand now why my mother shakes when she receives letters from her sister. It's been too long between, and I imagine you happy and safe, but as time passes and we hear about arrests in other cities, what am I to do? Bernard says the crackdown will end, and the reforms will resume. He's an optimist, like you, but puts his trust in magic. I had a dream you visited the bookshop and stayed until we read and discussed every book. Sera and Solly send kisses and so do I. You're in my heart, Estes

October 15, 1875
Dearest Estes,

I hope this letter finds you, Bernard, and the children well. You must give my warmest greetings to Eliza also. The police detained me for passing out revolutionary literature. You must not worry. They say we will be kept in Petersburg's House of Preliminary Detention until our trial, with a view of the luxurious Peter and Paul Fortress across the Neva. They suggested pardons for several of us, but my father denied having a daughter, and they withdrew the offer. No matter—they wanted us to betray our comrades and give names. The loyalty among us is unyielding, and not one faltered. We are engaged in a heroic struggle. A few reap all the riches while the many languish in desperate poverty. Only direct resistance will now change conditions in Russia. I love you, Gesia

Estes had read this letter twice when she received it at the bookshop. Now she read it again at home, her elbows resting on the table, her hands on either side of her head. The envelope had a script different than Gesia's. Perhaps she'd passed it to an ally to address and send later.

Solly and Sera pulled Estes's arms, and she rose from the table. When Bernard came in from the garden with a few cabbages and a winter squash, she told him about the arrest. He put down the vegetables and hugged her, and the children slipped inside their embrace.

Later, after the twins fell asleep back-to-back, each embracing a stuffed bear, she and Bernard went to their own bed. Estes blew out the lantern and spoke into the dark.

"If anything happened to you and the children, I . . . I'm not Gesia or Eliza. My heart bruises too easily."

She felt for the reliable beat when Bernard pressed her hand against his chest.

❋

Rabbi Menshein died the following spring, five months after Gesia's arrest. It had seemed the old man would live forever. Now, the Great Wooden Shul drew hundreds. Funerals and marriages provided exceptions to Bernard's vow, and he located Estes in the balcony next to Doris. Solly sat calmly in his grandmother's lap, and Sera squirmed restlessly in Estes's. The twins' high-pitched voices carried down to him above the quiet murmuring of mourners.

"I want to sit with Papa."

"We have a better view here, Sera, like birds in a tree."

Birds in a cage, he imagined Estes thinking.

A few old men looked annoyed, but others smiled when Sera yelled, "I don't see the cake. Where's the cake?"

Bernard and Estes had often stopped by Rabbi Menshein's on their way home, and Leib had usually joined them. The old rabbi would stroke his beard while they read to him—not scriptural stories, but tales of moral uncertainty.

On their last visit, several days before his death, the rabbi had shouted, "What's all this about confession and making peace with God after a horrible crime? It's not that easy. If only Raskolnikov were a Jew."

He explored their faces with his hands, marveling at Bernard's soft beard, Leib's prominent jaw, and Estes's smooth skin and long, thick hair. He joked that he used to be a tall, handsome man, but now God taught him a lesson about vanity.

At the gravesite, Leib sobbed without restraint as Rabbi Menshein was lowered into the earth. When Jacob Rosenblum sang, Bernard didn't understand how Estes could deny God's existence. What else could be the source of that voice?

14

On a foggy morning, seventeen months after Gesia's last communication, Estes met with Eliza in the bookshop before opening. She wished to write something personal about Gesia's passion to improve Russia and the harsh treatment of political dissenters. Abstract arguments had their place, but a real story would have more impact.

Eliza disagreed. "They watch closely now in Vilne, waiting for us to reach too far."

"But it's been so long. I don't even know if she's alive."

Eliza prevailed. Reason versus passion. For once, Estes wanted to be on the side of the fearless—the Vissarion Belinskys, Gesia Gelfmans, and the young Eliza before she grew famous.

Between helping customers, Estes wrote about the lack of representation, long confinements before trial, and dismal prisons. But she didn't blame any officials or say anything about the injustices that had compelled Gesia and the other prisoners to act.

Later, after closing the shop, Estes skimmed the Jewish and Russian papers. Before she could plunge into the seventh serialized installment of *Anna Karenina* in the *Messenger*, Eliza knocked—a single, sharp thump and two taps. Through the window, Eliza waved Estes off and entered with her own key.

"I have important news." Eliza held up the illustrated weekly periodical, *Niva.*

On March 5, 1877, the Trial of the Fifty, sixteen women among them, concluded with convictions for all but three of the defendants.

Estes raced through the article until she found Gesia's name.

Gesia Gelfman, convicted as an agent of Land and Liberty, sentenced to two years in the Litovskii Castle to be followed by exile to the province of Novgorod. Gelfman, born into a prosperous Jewish family in Mazr, was not offered a pardon, as she'd abandoned her privileged status to hand out revolutionary pamphlets to workers in Kiev factories. She is reputed to have been unmanageable by her father, running away on the day before her scheduled wedding. A midwife, Gelfman also practices free love.

"A light sentence compared to some of the others," Eliza said. "But how will she survive that awful prison?"

15

Two more years passed by after Gesia's sentencing without any updates about her situation. At last, on a rainy April day in 1879, a letter addressed to the bookshop arrived. Just this one, in all that time, despite the score of letters and supplies Estes had sent her. But Gesia had survived!

Locked up with prostitutes, beggars, and thieves—all rabid antisemites who blamed Jews for their condition, Gesia made light of the inedible food, slop buckets, her assignment to the worst jobs, and the slurs. She claimed she won them all to her side by sharing everything she received from Estes and other friends on the outside.

The tea and sugar sweetened them, the verbal abuse stopped, and they became my friends. Now I'm teaching them how to read and write.

Gesia's moral strength astonished Estes.

I'm happy to report, my dear Estes, that prison has not yet broken me, though, to be entirely honest, there is less of me to break, courtesy of the cuisine and the severe stomach ills that abide in this disgusting place.

Estes sighed. What could she do? Recently, the dormant GO WEST fluttered in her heart again, despite her intoxication with these walls of books. Her literary cave. Gesia would call it a lifeless tomb. Uncle Simon in America beckoned, but how could she leave Russia before the authorities freed Gesia? Even then, would Mama put an ocean between herself and her sister in Balta? If she agreed, could Papa be brought around? Yes, she could convince them, but getting Bernard to emigrate would be harder than prying a badger from its burrow.

She distracted herself from these uncertainties with covert observations of her children. Solly, outgoing and friendly, shared book illustrations of sea creatures with three other boys clustered around him at one of the tables on the first floor.

Sera, at the second table, spoke through her drawings and made several for girls her age who gathered to watch her work—two portraits and one evocative sky over Horodno, the clouds like black smoke, that brought her many compliments. She drew with such dramatic detail and sharp lines.

Forceful with Estes, Sera turned quiet around other children unless she perceived an injustice. Recently, when she and Solly had crossed the square, two Polish boys around their age grabbed a book from Solly's arms. They refused to give it back and called him names. Solly later told Estes how Sera wrestled the book away and shoved one of his tormentors to the ground.

Estes rejected kheyder for Solly because Sera couldn't have the same opportunity. Besides, she taught them better than any rabbi. But if they remained in Horodno, how would she explain the injustices to her children?

That evening, after Estes showed him the letter, Bernard still insisted that Alexander's reforms had simply stalled like a steam engine waiting for coal. The revolutionaries' determination to assassinate the monarch had not stalled, though, because just the week before, a student had fired multiple shots which the czar survived by running away in a zigzag. How could Bernard not see that the frightened autocrat and his Department of State Security, with their new powers of surveillance, had finally ceased wavering between reform and repression?

Although he shocked her when he offered a prayer at dinner for the czar's safety, Estes didn't protest. She understood, as any Jew paying attention to national affairs, that Alexander's namesake and heir, a brutal man, possessed none of his father's modest instinct toward compassion. But was a less lousy alternative the best Bernard hoped for? Estes didn't believe in fate. Still she sensed Russia's inexorable momentum toward the crisis that Professor Micah had predicted.

Before they put out the light, she followed his reading in bed. "It's challenging keeping up with a bibliophile like you, Bernard." He'd progressed to reading Yiddish without practice, and she worked hard to stay ahead of him as a translator.

"Are you tired?" he asked.

She tapped his foot with hers and yawned. "It's late, and yes, I'm exhausted. She turned down the wick. "Do you ever worry about staying in Russia?"

"We have the distillery and bookshop. People will always want vodka and books."

"But what if the children need more, Bernard? Or something different?"

"Do you want more?" he asked.

"Some days, yes. And I wonder what it might be like on the other side."

He rolled away from her, and she was disappointed when he didn't turn back to wrap an arm around her waist.

※

When their spring garden filled out in lush summer, rows of beans dripped succulent, slender pods. Abundant mustard and kale greens shaded the soil, and curled chard held pearls of dew in the mornings. The roots—potatoes with their thick tuber foliage, carrots with feathery greens, beets already popping above ground—waited for the fall harvest.

One evening, Estes told the twins about Gesia, her brave friend in prison. Solly asked what she did to get into so much trouble.

Sera clenched her fists. "Where is she, Mama? Can we visit her?"

"Gesia fought to improve Russia. One thing we need to change is the freedom to travel wherever we want."

Writing Gesia would give the twins a chance to show off their progress. Sera drew a picture showing the bars of Gesia's prison smashed to pieces; two figures held hands and smiled; birds flew overhead. Her daughter wrote, "Sera breaks the prison and saves Gesia."

Solly's prison bars remained intact with Gesia still in her cell. Another figure outside the bars reached out an elongated arm and fingers to touch the prisoner. "Solly visits Gesia."

One revolutionary, one rabbi. Estes added her thoughts and sent the letter off, though by now, she didn't expect a response.

16

Jacob Rosenblum, Horodno's Crown Rabbi, Renowned Cantor at the Choral Shul, and Eminent Maimonides Scholar, will speak on the Jewish Philosopher at Horodno's Public Library, September 18, 1879, 7:00 p.m.

The lecture hall on the library's second floor had already filled when Estes arrived. Bernard had picked the twins up at her parents' house, and she'd stayed in town to attend this event. For weeks she had stared at the announcement pinned on her community board by yeshiva students, next to advertisements by melameds, items listed for sale, and help wanted notices.

Estes had forced herself to attend, after complaining to Bernard about the unfairness of Jacob's followers lauding his achievements in her bookshop. It didn't help that Bernard couldn't understand how Jacob's success took anything away from her, nor why she wanted to go if it made her angry.

Estes scanned the crowd for a familiar face among the sea of beards in the hall and recognized some from the bookshop. She eavesdropped on the men around her talking about Jacob—how his scholarship and voice made up for his position as one of Russia's crown rabbis.

Maida, Jacob's mother, the only other woman present, sat in the front row of the packed hall with Avram Rosenblum. Even from the back, Estes could see him beaming as attendees stopped to say hello. Her old friend Moishe, who'd remained at the library all these years, made the introduction. He praised Jacob's scholarship and told stories of his intellect as a child.

When would women be described as "renowned eminent scholars?" She made herself rise along with the enthusiastic crowd when Jacob came to the podium, but she didn't clap. He spoke for an hour and, she had to admit, delivered an impressive analysis of Maimonides's work. She felt sure she could do even better, teaching about her writers. While audience members gathered around Jacob after his talk, she slipped out.

Jacob's talk drove her forward, and she wrote more essays that Eliza published. With a sense of desperation and voracious appetite, she read. With renewed vigor, she committed herself to the bookshop and teaching the children.

Several weeks after Jacob's talk, she approached Moishe at the library, and he enthusiastically agreed to host her lecture on female authors. When the date arrived, Eliza, her parents, Bernard, and the children sat in the front row of the half-filled hall.

Startled when Jacob came in and sat by himself near the exit, Estes turned her attention to Moishe, who called her a brilliant voice for women writers. She spoke for more than an hour, illustrating her comments with readings from Austen's witty, ironic comedy of manners, Brontë's dark Gothic romance, and Elliot's realistic and psychological dramas. Several times during her lecture, she smiled at her family and noticed Jacob's eyes on her. When she finished, her family led the enthusiastic applause. What else did she need? Still, she couldn't help searching to see her rival's reaction. Perhaps he'd congratulate her, but Jacob had already departed.

17

Neither the mass arrests of reformers in Saint Petersburg nor the execution of sixteen men suspected of terrorism quelled the growing unrest in the capital. In October 1879, Land and Liberty split into two factions. The majority formed the People's Will and favored a policy of terror and assassination.

One month later, radicals tried to destroy the czar's train with nitroglycerin but targeted the wrong train. A plan to blow up the czar as he passed over the Kamenny Bridge also failed.

In February 1880, a member of the People's Will, who'd found work in the Winter Palace as a carpenter, smuggled in dynamite and constructed a bomb in the basement. The explosion, two floors below a planned state dinner, killed or wounded sixty-seven sentries and workers in the vaulted room above but did only minor damage to the dining area and completely missed the czar, who had arrived late. The People's Will promised to call off the assassination if the czar granted the Russian people a constitution with free elections and an end to censorship.

Estes was speechless when, with all this turmoil roiling the empire, Bernard pointed to a release of a few political prisoners as a hopeful sign.

✳

In August, when a post arrived for Estes at the bookshop, she thought it must be another advertisement for America from Uncle Simon. The old postman, wearing his stiff leather cap and blue uniform with double rows of six silver buttons, complained about his ever-growing delivery route.

"They'll have us trekking to Siberia before long."

Gesia! She resisted tearing the envelope open right away, afraid she would rip it to pieces in her eagerness. The seven-kopek stamp, with its coat of arms placed cockeyed in the corner, indicated haste, confirmed by Gesia's scrawling script when Estes took out the single page.

August 25th, 1880
My Dearest Estes,

I have escaped exile, but the police take more of us away. The people will soon realize this tyrant hides behind a façade—all pomp and prestige, a flimsy veneer over a deep well of brutality. He lives in his palace while the poor crowd together like pickled eggs in a jar. It seems so long ago I believed pamphlets and words or teaching peasants to read would change a country. I won't waste these days of freedom. I sincerely wish I could see you again, my love. Gesia

On March 1, 1881, the very day Alexander II signaled his intention to pursue a constitutional monarchy, Horodno's towering Catholic basilica rang its bell midday, the mournful reverberations spaced seconds apart.

Estes left the bookshop and stopped a peddler wearing a jacket with multiple pockets, each one stuffed with an item—socks, handkerchiefs, scarves, gloves. He looked at her with solemn eyes. "The czar has been assassinated. A bomb blew his legs off."

She learned more from others. Unhurt after the first bomb, Alexander had stepped out of his carriage to tend a wounded soldier, when a second assassin tossed the fatal explosive. They had already crowned the new czar. Estes locked up and headed across the square to her parents. Some Jews wept or sat on benches, stunned; others talked among themselves; a few rushed out of the square.

Two days later, the police arrested Gesia Gelfman, labeled the "Jewess Conspirator" by the *Verdomosti*. The *Vilenskii Vestnik*, published in Vilne, claimed, "This is the Jew's Affair." Provincial publications did not hold back. Antisemitism exploded with the ascension of Alexander III.

During the short trial, Gesia steadfastly refused to give up comrades. The court showed no mercy and sentenced her to death but postponed the execution when she revealed her pregnancy. Her five co-conspirators were hanged on April 3.

The *Jewish Razvet* in Petersburg wrote, "A squall is coming, thunder is breaking, lightning is flashing and everything in nature is as if it is standing still . . . For the present everyone is hiding, lapsing into silence, until the deep echo of the bursting storm gradually dies down."

Estes pushed herself to read with the children. Her customers didn't talk about books anymore, but what the assassination meant for the Jews. When she walked to her parents' house for lunch, the familiar square felt immense and exposed.

Papa winced when anyone mentioned Gesia's name. "It would have been better if that woman had never come to Horodno. And to think she delivered my grandchildren."

Mama did not denounce him. She must have sensed his fear. "Our poor Gesia, cut off from her family, alone and pregnant."

The storm did not pass. On April 15, 1881, riots erupted in Elisavetgrad, and a general assault upon Russia's Jews began.

PART III

POGROM

1882

*We must never forget that the Jews
crucified our Master and shed his precious blood.*
– Czar Alexander III

Trip to Balta
March 1882

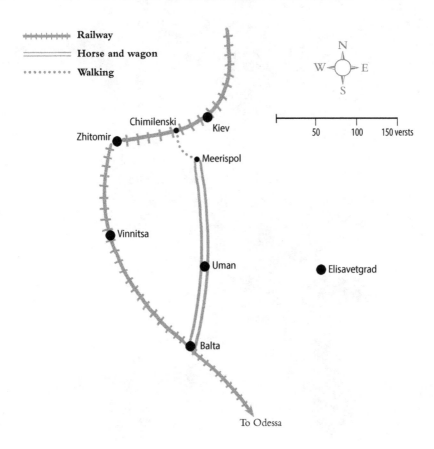

I

The new czar brought back the ideology of Nicholas I, his grandfather: Orthodoxy, Autocracy, Nationality. The czar's former tutor, Konstantin Pobedonostsev, became his influential advisor. A gaunt, pale figure Jews called Haman's corpse, Pobedonostsev believed any attempts to bring democracy to Russia represented a crime of violence against the state. This included misguided efforts to gain more rights for Jews. Those aliens, with their religious beliefs, insular communities, and strange customs didn't belong in Russia.

How could Estes concentrate with everything falling apart? She put her book aside as ice pellets bounced off the bookshop's window. Two young boys tugged on their weary mother's dress as closing time neared; she struggled to balance a bag against her chest as they steered her to the children's section. Isaac, an emaciated man with a belly-length beard and curved spine, shuffled past them on his way out. He muttered to himself and glanced at Estes with feverish eyes. His two clenched fists held his buttonless overcoat closed. She suspected he'd hidden some obscure religious text again. A rabbi would notice it missing and bring a replacement.

When he reached for the door, a thick black book slipped out and thudded on the floor. Isaac froze, so she got up and retrieved the book. He held out two shaking hands, and she placed the book there. He pulled it back against his tattered coat. Estes held the door and he left without a word of acknowledgment. The overcoat's tails flapped wildly as he shuffled away.

Isaac stealing a holy book almost made her smile. She tried once more with *Anna Karenina*: "Kitty felt a special charm in being able to talk with her mother as an equal about these most important things in a woman's life."

The first time she'd read the novel, caught up in the panoramic sweep of the story, she'd overlooked the limitations of Tolstoy's women and what they considered vital—how one made jam, treated the servants, arranged a suitable match, attained a marriage proposal, and so on. When Anna gives up these essential things for passion—disaster!

She'd done the same with Flaubert's *Madame Bovary* and the capricious Emma, because the intricate prose, a painting in words, astonished her.

Now, despite her effort, Tolstoy's words, like the hail bouncing off the window, refused to stick. If these crimes against Jews happened in cities like Kiev and Warsaw, no one was safe: not scarved wives in the market, their bearded husbands on the way to shul, or shtetl Jews with provincial concerns; not Hasidic masters with thousands of followers, Yiddish poets, leaders of the Haskalah, or radicals; not the bloodied refugees and frightened children who now streamed into Horodno.

Estes closed the door behind her last customer and sank back into her comfortable chair. Events played in her mind, and she dug at her wounds.

In the months after Gesia's death sentence and the outbreaks, Bernard had played chess and read to the twins, and, as usual, he made everyday household chores fun—stacking wood, cooking, even cleaning—but Estes could not summon the same steadiness. She had wished to shield her children from these atrocities, but how could she when information traveled in print, in conversations on the street, and in family Shabosim with prayers for the victims?

Solly, who used to stretch out in sleep like a sultan on a divan, had nightmares and screamed himself awake. Sera seemed to appraise Estes with some unspoken accusation.

One evening in late spring, after the assassination, Estes had found her daughter cross-legged on the floor, rummaging through the newspapers stacked by their kitchen stove. "I want to fight the people who do these mean things. We should do to them what they do to us."

Estes sat next to her and put her arm around her shoulders. Sera leaned against her. "Mama, why don't you do something about this besides reading books and writing stories?"

She heard the bitter accusation beneath the question. *Coward.* "You don't understand the power of writing, Sera. What else keeps the censors so busy?"

Sera didn't answer and they remained on the floor as daylight receded.

When Bernard arrived, Sera and Solly both embraced him. *What about your father? What action has he taken?*

The immensity of the violence overwhelmed her. Many said the authorities organized the assaults against the Jews, but these pogroms seemed more like random, deadly lightning strikes to Estes. What did Sera expect her to do? She might as well have shaken her fist at the sky or stood in front of a flood, waving her hands. Saving Gesia became her obsession.

The ice storm ended. She sat in the dark and shifted in her chair. Professor Micah hovered about the bookshop.

Why are you still in Horodno?

Didn't I publish five articles, printed by Eliza, advocating for clemency? Weren't my essays picked up by the foreign press, including the London Times?

Jews need to go west, my Estes.

But listen, my Professor, to the words of Thomas McQueen: "Any person of principle has to admire Esther Leving Garfinkle's poetry of compassion in her brilliant series of compositions."

Who's this Thomas McQueen? Never heard of him.

"She deftly brings in examples of mercy, culled from literature, history, and religion to make her case. She writes so viscerally that readers feel Gesia Gelfman could be their sister, Gesia's unborn child their son or daughter."

Newspaper clippings—ephemeral as spring snow. And what did it matter in the end?

What difference had she and the others made by writing? The resulting outcry in Europe had prompted ambassadors to petition the czar in favor of mercy, and even Victor Hugo had sent a letter to the Russian government. Still, troubling news came from Gesia's lawyer, who reported to the press, "Gelfman looked like someone utterly worn out or recovering from illness."

In June, three months after her arrest, the authorities refused to grant Gesia a reprieve. They also denied her request for a midwife and for the medical treatment she so obviously needed. Who else in all of history had known that the birth of her child would start a forty-day countdown to execution?

Then, late summer brought immense relief. They commuted her death sentence to a life of penal servitude.

It would have been less cruel to have no hope. What good is a life raft in rough seas if it sinks to the bottom?

Are you still here?

Stop holding your hand over an open flame. You did what you could. Now look to your future.

I will. I promise. Just let me finish.

The lawyer's lurid, final account was made public. Gesia had suffered unspeakable conditions during childbirth, and the male prison doctor had refused to attend to the tearing that occurred during the delivery. Gesia managed to nurse her little girl despite the growing infection.

Estes's idea to raise Gesia's child was a sudden inspiration. "On humanitarian grounds, please allow the innocent baby a chance for a life," she petitioned the new Czar. So did others, including the family of jailed People's Will radical Nicolai Kolodkevich, Gesia's common-law husband.

Until Gesia's eventual release, Estes could care for her friend's daughter. She had imagined a curly-headed girl, as intelligent and strong as her revolutionary mother. Bernard agreed, but this plan abruptly ended when the authorities ripped the three-month-old from Gesia's arms.

They sent the infant to an orphanage with a number instead of her mother's name. Little chance a foundling would survive such circumstances. This was the final blow, and Gesia lingered for just six more days. They'd killed her friend, not with the hangman's noose, but through neglect and heartbreak, away from the public eye. A deep sigh and the turning of a page came from the classical literature section.

2

Bernard left the distillery and walked to the bookshop. Attentive to potential threats—drunks, loud talk, eyes following him—he crossed the bridge. It had been this way since the attacks spread like a wave from Elisavetgrad westward. A wagon full of peasants leaving town approached and the driver tipped his floppy hat.

He told himself Horodno and the Northwest Provinces represented a distant and more secure shore. The governor had vowed to keep order and the Russian garrison a few versts east of town remained on alert, but Bernard began to worry about something else. Could Estes have fallen out of love with him? Maybe it started after the assassination a year ago. He couldn't imagine anything that would pull him away from her. Six weeks since Gesia died in prison, six weeks since they'd made love.

The unlit bookshop looked empty. Maybe Estes hadn't waited for him. He tried the door, and it opened.

"Here, Bernard. Sit a moment before we go."

He eased into the creaking caned rocker next to her silhouette.

"I haven't been a good mother. Solly and Sera . . . I try to keep things normal for them with our lessons, but our daughter has turned against me."

"We've all been under such strain. Can you find peace again, Estes?"

"Now that Gesia . . . What's holding any of us here? In America, we'd be full citizens, without pogroms. They have bookshops and distilleries there, too, Bernard."

"This is our home, Estes. Why should we always be the ones to run away?"

Estes refused his offered hand as they walked across the emptied square to her parents and Shabes.

They made their way through the shoe shop and mounted the stairs. Each tread creaked as they ascended, and when they reached the second floor, Solly ran to meet them, jumped into Bernard's arms, and reached out to include Estes. They huddled for a moment until Bernard put him down.

Solly wanted a report on their new chestnut workhorse.

"Young Ferd's almost ready to pull our wagon. He learns at the hooves of the master."

"Alte Ferd's an old Hasid, Papa. Every day is Shabes for him. We miss driving, and it hurts Mama's foot to do so much walking."

These days, Estes dragged her leg as if she pulled a weight behind. "A little exercise won't kill me, Solly. In a few weeks, we'll ride back and forth to town again."

Five lit candles on the blue Shabes cloth illuminated the guests, a pot of onion soup, and potato pancakes. They hadn't celebrated all together for months, and Bernard wanted the sorrow and anxiety permeating Horodno to lift for one night.

Sera sat next to Leib and laughed at something he said. Shlomo sat on her other side, impassive, as his wife, Reina, made some point and gestured. Chaim and his wife, Rose, cooed to their infant girl, swaddled in Chaim's lap. Herman and Joseph bent over a paper. In the kitchen, Eliza huddled with Doris, who held a letter in one hand and had raised the other to her forehead.

Eliza walked around the table, exchanged kisses on the cheek with Estes, and murmured something in her ear. Estes went to her mother and brought her to the table. After Herman's prayer, the room quieted but for the clink of silver and murmured appreciation.

"If we wait, it might be too late. I'm going to Balta," Doris said. Eating stopped. Eliza reached across the table and passed the letter to Estes. Her mother nodded and she read aloud.

My Dearest Sister Doris,

We're so frightened. Everywhere animosity—the churches, Christian merchants, and now the men who ride the train from Kiev looking for work. We're isolated and afraid to stay, but more afraid to leave. Stories of assaults on fleeing Jewish families are too terrible to repeat. In Elisavetgrad and Kiev people were burned out, everything they owned destroyed or stolen. I won't tell you what has befallen some women and even young girls. I keep my daughters attached to me. We don't feel secure in our own home anymore. Pray for us. Your loving sister, Freida

"This time, the authorities will be ready for any attack, and so will the Jews," Herman said.

Joseph glanced at Doris. "If there's anything I can do . . ."

"It will spread to Horodno," Shlomo said.

Leib stood and announced, "We have to fight back with weapons and a plan."

Sera stood next to him. "I agree with Uncle Leib. I'll go with you, Grandma." She looked defiantly at Estes.

Herman raised both arms and lowered them. "Let's not be ridiculous. If anyone goes, it will be me. Please sit." Leib hesitated a moment but did as requested. He tugged on Sera's arm and pulled her down beside him.

"No," Bernard said. "Doris needs you here, Herman. I can be there and back in a week with any luck. A train to Kiev, then the line to Odessa that stops in Balta."

Herman started to argue.

"Shush, Herman," Doris said. "Listen to Bernard."

Chaim, Leib, Shlomo, and Joseph all spoke at once, offering to go.

"I need Chaim and Shlomo to manage the distillery."

"I'm traveling with you," Leib said.

"You're not going without me," Joseph added.

"Make your preparations. I'll buy the tickets. In three days, we leave for Balta."

※

The night before his departure, Bernard and Estes tiptoed into the children's room. Solly and Sera now slept in their own beds. Estes stroked her daughter's hair.

Sera had been demanding that evening. "But why can't I go?" she'd asked Bernard. "I'm almost nine."

When Solly told her they had to stay home and help Mama, Sera turned on her father. "Why would God allow these pogroms?"

Before he could answer, she'd stormed off to her room.

Estes led Bernard to the table and trimmed his beard and hair. They double-checked his trip items, and Estes lifted a black wool hat from the clothes set aside for tomorrow's travel.

"This will be your yarmulke, Bernard." She pulled it over his ears. "Now you pass for Russian." She kept her voice light and stroked his forearm. "Take enough money to buy a horse and wagon." They'd heard the reports about vandals tearing up sections of track. She picked up the lamp, and he followed her to the bedroom.

Estes closed the door Bernard had built when the children began to come into their bedroom in the mornings. She remembered the narrow escapes, uncoupling when the quiet padding of feet in the hall had alerted them, with barely enough time to pull the sheets and blankets around their nakedness.

They lay in bed facing each other. Bernard put his hand on her hip, and she stroked the back of his neck and shoulder.

"Thank you. You didn't have to say you'd go instead of Papa. Are there conditions attached? Does this mean we have to stay in the Pale until our teeth fall out?"

"No conditions, Estes."

"I have one for letting you go." Her hand traveled below his waist.

He reached for the drawer in the bedside table, for what she called "their love paraphernalia."

As soon as he was ready, Estes pulled him in. He began to move the way she liked, but she wanted something else. She rocked him back and forth, tried to pull his whole body inside hers. She pressed tight against him and groaned into his chest. Her pleasure triggered his own. She kept him pinned against her.

"I'm sorry we haven't done this as often since the pogroms began."

"Almost a year ago," he said, sounding aggrieved. "Not at all since Gesia died."

"I've been so distracted."

"Our love is an antidote to the hate."

When he began to grow again, they both laughed. She ran her hands up and down his back, made him stop while they kissed, then start again, and measured his excitement against her own. She absorbed his taste, smell, and the feel of his nakedness.

*

On the railroad platform at first light, Herman and Doris embraced the three travelers. "Be safe and come back soon," Doris said, and handed Bernard a cloth sack filled with cheese, dried fruit, and bread.

"I'm glad you've got each other—the three musketeers without the swords," Estes said.

"Swords, who needs swords?" Leib waved his index finger at Solly until he found an opening. Sera joined her brother and repeatedly jabbed Leib's belly. Leib laughed so hard he collapsed on the platform, and the two climbed on top of him. When the train approached from the west, they tried to keep him pinned down, but he stood with the children still clinging on for a moment.

"I could still go and carry your things, Papa. See, I'm strong enough." Sera grabbed the strap and strained to lift his bag. Solly grabbed part of the strap, too, and they held it in front of them until Bernard slipped it over his shoulder.

"Yes, and because you're so strong, you've got to protect Horodno while we're gone. Promise me."

"I promise," Solly said.

When he reached his arms wide, a secure circle for Estes and the children, Solly rushed in and wrapped his arms around Bernard's waist. Sera stood by herself. When he separated from his son and wife, she approached and surprised him. Instead of an embrace, she stuck out her hand and squeezed his.

"You can count on us, Papa."

3

Seated across from Leib and Joseph, Bernard opened his bag. He shared a handful of dried pears, pulled a folded knife from his pocket, rested the brick of cheese on its paper wrapping, and cut several slices. He tore off a piece of bread and passed the loaf to Joseph.

The train rumbled for hours across the mostly flat, occasionally rolling countryside. First they travelled northeast to Vilne where they changed trains. On the next leg, they headed southeast to Minsk, switched engines, and continued toward Kiev. They passed farms with leaning barns, thatched-roof shacks, peasant families clustered on porches, and scattered estates in decay.

Bernard had traveled with his father to Vilne, and once to Warsaw, but never such a distance from home. Leib and Joseph had never gone farther than an hour's ride from Horodno. When Leib took his time at the window, he dozed or spoke with Bernard. When Joseph got his turn, he never took his eyes off the landscape. Even as the sun went down, he cupped his hands over his eyes and peered intently into the fading light.

"Why do you stare at these endless fields, woods, and miserable peasants, at these tiny stations with a couple of passengers boarding?" Leib asked.

"The forests have changed, Leib. In the west, spruce, birch, and oak mixed in with the pine. Now the spruce has disappeared and there's black alder. We've crossed so many rivers and streams. Did you notice all the swamps and the white stork nests?"

Leib hit his forehead and groaned. "Haven't you ever seen a tree or a bird?" He yawned and stretched his long legs.

Bernard studied the new passengers whenever they pulled into a station. In Bobruisk, a family boarded, the man dressed in clothes one might wear to a wedding. His black suit and vest had no wrinkles. Bernard admired the strength of the threads that contained his sagging belly. His wife's long dress with its upturned collar left only her hands and a bit of neck exposed. Their son, around Solly's age, wore his hair slicked back. In Gomel, around the middle of that long night, a Russian officer, his awards displayed on his uniform, had stared straight ahead when he passed by. Sometimes no one got on, and the conductor hopped off to speak to the stationmaster.

Why did he volunteer to go? He'd promised Estes he had no conditions, but now he allowed himself to hope his bravery might balance the scales and allow his family to remain in Horodno.

4

March 22, 1882

Tomorrow, Pesach, the first without Bernard since we married. It's been four days, and we're all hopeful they will return soon. We moved in with my parents while he's gone. It's good to be with Mama, to distract us both.

Sera works in the shoe shop and shows no interest in joining Solly for our lessons. She gives Papa ideas on how to make women's shoes more comfortable. He crows that she's a natural and gives me that look.

When Solly tried to explain how fossils proved that giant reptiles once walked the earth, she considered this for a moment but said, "You could be doing real work instead of reading science books with Mama."

"I am working—in the distillery."

"But only a half-day." She held out a hand and told him to smell it. When he pressed his nose tentatively into her palm, she said, "Leather and oil. I bet yours smell like musty old books."

She's what Darwin called a "mutation." She has such artistic talent but seldom picks a book up on her own and doesn't share my love of language—how writing has a cadence, how one can insert sadness into empty space, how words adhere, one to another, like individual bricks in a solid wall.

Estes stopped writing when a young man in a blue uniform entered. Soldiers had visited before, but instead of heading off into the shelves, this one approached her. He removed his cap and bowed.

"My name is Nickolai Melenkov. General Borishenko wants to meet with you, Mrs. Garfinkle, in two days, at 5:00. I'll escort you." The soldier gave her a card.

General Borishenko, Chief, Ministry of Public Order
Grodno, Grodno Gubernia
Special Appointment by his Excellency, Czar Alexander III

He bowed again. "The general meets all personages of note in his jurisdiction." He turned and departed. Eliza, with her regular habits, would visit the bookshop before closing. Estes would find out what she could from her.

＊

"Borishenko has a vicious reputation among Poles. I'd heard several months ago that he came back to Horodno, so last week when he summoned me, I wasn't surprised. We're acquainted from the days of the rebellion."

"You met with him?"

"In my case, he wanted to make sure I was now a harmless older woman, transformed from revolutionary to writer of pastoral novels. I think I convinced him, although he seemed obsessed by my association with Gesia. No point speculating until we gather more information. We've avoided criticism of the czar in your articles. They haven't made any moves yet in Vilne to shut us down."

Estes hated the idea a man could summon her, and, without recourse, she had to appear like a marionette. "'I am no bird; and no net ensnares me. I am a free human being with an independent will, which I now exert to refuse him.'"

"Ah—the example of *Jane Eyre* for courage." Eliza smiled grimly. "*Richard the Third* describes Borishenko—'No beast so fierce but knows some touch of pity. But I know none, and therefore am no beast.'"

Estes coughed to hide her fear.

"He is quite literate. Don't be fooled by his veneer of civility. He executed leaders of the Polish resistance and sent my ex-husband to Siberia. He spent years in Petersburg, though the western provinces are where he made his name. After the assassination, they appointed him the gubernia's army commander and leader of a secret police unit. It's probably no coincidence he waited until Bernard's trip to call you in. What time is the interview?"

"Five."

"I'll close up that day and wait for you. You'll listen but speak as little as possible and find out what he wants."

✳

Estes hid the summons from her family. *Stay busy.* They celebrated Pesach with a subdued Seder, and she was able to get a few hours of sleep despite her scheduled appearance the next day. She dropped off, soothed by Solly and Sera's breathing from the second bed her father had crammed into her old room and the mysterious yet familiar creaks of the old house. *Perhaps Bernard reached Balta and is on his way home already. Be well, my husband.*

The morning passed with Solly and science. In the afternoon, she recommended and sold books, traveled back and forth from French to Russian literature, Balzac and Zola to Tolstoy and Turgenev, with side trips through the poetry of Keats, Shelly, and Baudelaire. She waded into dense volumes of Roman history and even delved into Talmudic tracts and books by current rabbis about the writings of ancient rabbis, stories about stories, smudged by the eager, ink-stained fingers of yeshiva students.

Eliza took over the checkout, and Estes moved among customers.

"Do you need help?"

"Do you have books about America?" The thin man with black, curly hair sticking out from beneath a knit yarmulke lowered his voice. "Enough with this czar, his rules, the pogroms, Count Ignatiev and his puppet council." He snorted. "You'll see. They'll blame us. We're going to New York. They say the western border will open for Jews. We're leaving before the czar changes his mind."

Estes retrieved a book Uncle Simon had sent her with pictures of New York's crowded neighborhoods. The man flipped the pages and tapped one showing a crowded street, men in business suits and a teeming outdoor market. "What a place for a cart! A single block with more people than our entire town. And we think Vilne is a city. We leave in one week." He bit his lip. "We lost everything in Elisavetgrad."

Estes lifted an imaginary glass. "To your new life."

✳

Estes left the shop with her escort. They walked in silence in the direction of the river, the same route she and Professor Micah had taken on her first day of tutoring, half her lifetime ago.

Nikolai stopped in front of the solid brick building on Police Street, across from the giant bleeding Jesus. He led Estes up the granite steps and opened a heavy door, its white paint curling away from the wood. He ushered her into a foyer where a self-important-looking fellow— with glasses halfway down his nose, lank, greasy hair combed over a bald head, and jowls sagging—sat at a desk in the corner. Benches lined the walls. Estes guessed from the unhappy faces of the occupants that they'd been here a while.

"You won't wait with these petitioners," Nikolai said. "General Borishenko left instructions to bring you straight in." She followed him into a narrow hall with offices on each side. He stopped at the fourth door on the right and tapped three times.

"Come in." *A deep voice comfortable giving orders. Listen but say little.*

Nikolai opened the door. "General Borishenko," he said, bowing from the waist, "may I present Esther Leving Garfinkle."

A short man, her father's age, with cropped gray hair, a hawk-like nose, thick mustache that concealed his upper lip, and unsympathetic blue eyes stood behind a desk. A window framed the crucified Jesus across Police Street. Two rows of medals dangled from the general's chest. One sleeve, folded and pinned to his shoulder, indicated a missing arm. He stepped around his desk and surprised Estes when he took her hand in his.

"Mrs. Garfinkle, or may I call you Esther?"

"Mrs. Garfinkle is fine, General Borishenko."

"Of course. Please have a seat, Mrs. Garfinkle." He continued to hold her hand with a firm grip after she sat down. He studied her as seconds ticked away. Estes didn't want to look vulnerable. He released her hand and dismissed Nikolai.

Borishenko lifted a teapot from the copper samovar on his desk. He removed the lid, opened a spigot on the barrel of the urn, added hot water, stirred with a spoon, and filled two white ceramic cups. He passed a cup to Estes and their fingers met, her instinct to pull away foiled by the tea she balanced over her lap. General Borishenko replaced the lid and teapot and sat across from her.

Estes expected a formal interview, yet he drank in silence and watched her. Self-consciously, she sipped her tea and glanced at the floor-to-ceiling bookshelves.

"You like my collection? Perhaps you can make some recommendations." He put his cup on the desk, stood, and pulled down a thin volume. "Pavlova achieved renown in the '40s but is forgotten now. She lives in Dresden, I believe. *A Double Life,* her only novel."

"Yes, I've read it." Estes kept her voice flat. A review of the novel in *Sovremennik* had steered her to the book.

The general returned to his chair. "And what did you think of it?"

"The structure is a bit contrived."

"How so?"

"The separation of Cicily's traditional roles from her true desires into awake and dream states."

"You advocate for a more straight-forward rebellion?"

"In the case of women's literature, yes. I suppose looking at this work in context, it was advanced for the time."

He set the book down. "What did Pani Orzeszkowa tell you about me?"

Estes froze.

"You can speak openly. Your friend's a Polish nationalist. It wouldn't be surprising if she harbored resentment toward one of the men who helped crush the rebellion." He looked at her expectantly.

Best to give him something. "That you executed rebels and had a reputation for ruthlessness among the Poles."

He laughed. "Losing sides nurture resentment, Mrs. Garfinkle. Easier than examining their own flawed cause. And what if they'd won? Every nationality in the empire would be clamoring for autonomy. We'd have chaos and violence."

He reached past the samovar to retrieve a thin file. He held up a collection of newspaper clippings. "Your letters advocating clemency for Gesia Gelfman. Very impressive, Mrs. Garfinkle. Did you compose these on your own?"

"Entirely. Is that why you brought me here, General?"

He put the articles back in the file. "More tea?"

"No, thank you."

"These editorials did bring you to our attention. Many high-ranking state officials also believed it wrong to execute a woman. Even Sophia Perovskaya had her supporters." He tilted forward, and Estes recoiled.

"You're quite a beautiful woman, Mrs. Garfinkle. You have two lovely children. Solomon and Seraphina, twins. Your husband's name is Bernard?"

"Yes."

"Distillery owner. Excellent vodka, by the way. You must give him my compliments. And these boots, the most comfortable I've ever owned." He lifted one leg to show her. "Let your father know I said so."

"Of course."

"Your husband boarded a train for Kiev with two companions six days ago. Please tell me the purpose of his trip?"

"My aunt lives in Balta. He's gone to make sure she and her family are safe."

"The pogroms, a nasty business. Without law and order, Russia can't survive. You're quite out of danger here, I can assure you. I've given the garrison orders to crush any disturbances." He made a fist and rapped his desk. "I'll keep you and your family safe. You have my word, but will you do your part too, Mrs. Garfinkle?"

She nodded, not sure what he expected of her.

"Good. Now, concerning the articles you wrote. Taken alone, I might accept them as innocent pleas for mercy. You're quite an effective advocate and should be proud of what you accomplished. Still, it's my job to judge your situation in its entirety, considering the security needs of the state. These are dangerous times, Mrs. Garfinkle." He shifted in his chair and lifted his fist off the desk.

"There are other aspects of your case that concern me. Your friendship with Eliza Pawloska Orzeszkowa. He held up a finger. "Your involvement with her Vilne printing business." A second finger joined the first. "The possibility of radical literature housed in your bookshop." Three fingers aimed straight at Estes's bosom.

The fingers lingered, motionless, waiting for her response.

She pressed her tongue against the roof of her mouth, a sealed vault.

"Most troubling of all, Mrs. Garfinkle: we also possess evidence you had direct correspondence with Gelfman before the assassination, as well as a relationship with her during the time she resided in Grodno." His fourth finger and thumb joined their mates.

"All my actions were motivated by friendship and compassion. She was my midwife."

He put his hand on the table and smiled at her. "Of course, Mrs. Garfinkle.

❋

Nikolai walked her back, doffed his cap, and left. The setting sun streaked the sky pink. She stood on the street for a moment before going into the bookshop. Eliza had lit a single lantern.

"He thinks I have information and wants to see the letters Gesia sent me."

"Do you still have them?"

"Yes, but I told him I didn't. I don't think he believed me. His threats aren't explicit. 'I'm sure you'll be fine, as long as you cooperate, Mrs. Garfinkle. We might ignore your trips with a known revolutionary and Polish nationalist to the countryside to spread propaganda among the peasants.'"

The disgust and fear she'd suppressed during the interview made it difficult to speak now. "Before I left, he held my hand again, not in an iron grip, but as a suitor. He said he looked forward to our next meeting. 'Please bring your children; I'd like to meet them.'"

"He won't arrest you as long as he believes surveillance is more effective than prison to achieve what he wants, and in this case, the bookshop protects you. Like the library, a perfect place to observe liberal trends. But if he learns you deliberately withheld evidence . . ."

"I have to burn Gesia's letters tonight."

"It might be best to tell him you were mistaken and hand them over. Are you implicated in any way?"

"No, but Gesia named comrades, associates from Kiev."

Eliza looked at her steadily, her expression grim. "He'll find ways to pressure you, Estes." Eliza took her hand. "The assassination of a czar. Letters from one of the conspirators. I'm afraid he won't let this matter go. If only Borishenko were a solipsist, like many in state service, it might be possible to manipulate him. He believes in what he's doing, and a bribe is sure to go awry. He does fancy himself a paramour, and sex is the only thing he wants from attractive women besides information. But he won't force himself on you. At least, he hasn't in the past."

After Eliza left, Estes remembered Sera's words: "Can't you do something about this besides reading books and writing stories?" But what good would direct resistance do if Borishenko seized the bookshop and she rotted in jail? She raised the hand Borishenko had held much too long. She spread her fingers, concentrated, and willed away the tremor.

5

After traveling for twenty-two hours, the friends arrived in Kiev before daybreak. Bernard bought tickets to Balta from the bald station master whose wine-stained shirt stretched tightly across his chest.

"Most folks head north out of Balta and the southern towns these days. Business there?" He peered over his glasses, which perched on a red bulbous nose. Behind him, a half-empty liquor bottle sat on a shelf.

Estes had helped him memorize some essential Ukrainian words but assured him officials and city dwellers would speak Russian. He understood this fellow.

"Family." Bernard kept his tone neutral.

"Hope you're not Jews," the agent said. "I don't have anything against them. The riots last spring—families burned out, beaten—awful, truly awful. You know, it all comes from mixing types. You don't serve Russian borsht with kosher pickles. Give them their own land, I say. The Poles too. Let them ruin their own country."

His friends, busy arranging their bags, thankfully did not hear this conversation. Leib had a hard time letting anything pass. When Bernard had talked to him and Joseph about blending in to their surroundings, Joseph said, "Sure, camouflaged, so we don't draw unnecessary attention."

Leib had shaken his head. "The males of many species, avifauna, for example, are draped with color, not disguised in grays and browns. If every *pogromshichiki* got a punch in the jaw, the attacks might stop."

"In chess, we have one goal, right?" Bernard had asked him.

"Sure, checkmate."

"And our one goal on this trip?"

"Make sure Estes's aunt is safe," Joseph said.

"I know what the goal is," Leib had hissed at Joseph. "I'm talking strategy. If you learned some yourself, you might not play like a putz."

While they waited, the station gradually filled with families, some pulling carts loaded with battered suitcases, others with no luggage, holding crying children.

A young girl in a man's arms pointed at them and began to cry.

"Sholem," Bernard called out, which calmed her. "Where are you going?"

"Away from hell with my daughter," the father answered. "And you?"

"Balta, to see about a relative."

The second whistle of a waiting westbound locomotive smothered the father's words. He carried his daughter to their platform.

When their train arrived, Leib clapped one hand on Joseph's shoulder and the other on Bernard's. "Well, what are we waiting for?"

"Chimilenski, end of the line," the conductor shouted down the corridor. "Migrants tore up sections of my track all the way to Vinnitsa—a week of repair, at least."

They walked away from the stranded train. "That bum should have told us before we bought tickets." Leib punched a fist into his open hand. "One stinking hour of a ride, only thirty-five versts. Chimilenski! Ha. Why give a dung heap a name?"

"It's a fine day for a walk," Bernard said. For a verst or so, the road paralleled the train tracks. A repair crew placed fist-sized rocks on the rail bed and pulled supporting timbers and new rails from those spread along the route.

"The same ones repairing the track by day probably vandalize it at night," Leib said. "Make sure they never run out of work."

They came to a dusty intersection and Bernard pointed to the lesser path. "The track continues west to Zhitomir. We go south toward Uman."

"Are we going all the way to Balta by foot?" Joseph asked.

"It's almost three hundred versts, dummy."

"Thirty versts a day . . ." Joseph wrinkled up his brow.

"Ten days." Leib looked up at the darkening sky. "Assuming we can keep up this pace in bad weather."

"The conductor said a day's walk and we'll come to the turnoff for Meerispol. He thought we could buy horses and a wagon around there. Two workers will haul us and our bags."

They quickened the pace, walking a relief after so much sitting. The empty road in front of them wound through shorn fields bordered by clusters of trees. Leib swung his arms and took long strides. He whistled a melody and began to sing.

> *Stand up, damned of the earth,*
> *Stand up, prisoners of starvation,*
> *Reason thunders in its volcano,*
> *This is the eruption of the end.*

"Come on. Join me. It's called 'The Internationale.'"

Bernard instinctively checked behind them. Other rutted paths cut into their own, and along some of these he spotted smoke from isolated settlements.

Leib introduced other verses, changing the melody to whatever suited him. When they had mastered the Yiddish, he launched into Polish, then Russian. The day passed, Bernard's voice grew hoarse, and they entered a forested stretch. When a wagon rumbled behind them, he nudged Leib and Joseph off the road.

The driver, one cheek smudged with soot, the other displaying a long, angry scar, wore a wool hat pulled down to his eyes. Timber bulged out the sides of the wagon. He stopped alongside them with one hand on the reins. The other held a metal bar across his knees.

"Jews, right? Can't be too careful these days. No telling where migrants will show up with the tracks ripped out. Not from around here?"

"We're headed to Balta. Any chance of finding some horses?"

"Balta?" He spit on the road. "Climb up. I'll take you to the village."

He turned onto a narrow potholed lane. Trees formed an archway, and the riders ducked under bare, hanging branches. The logs creaked and shifted when a wheel dipped into a hole, and they kept their hands and feet clear, wary of being crushed.

They came upon a cluster of weather-stained houses surrounding a small shul. On the other side of the muddy street, Bernard noticed a second shul and more homes. Gardens and chicken coops dominated yards. Scrawny horses and cows mingled in the fields behind the settlement.

"Welcome to Meerispol. This side Misnagdim—" he pointed a finger "—the other, Hasid. I live just out of town, non-aligned." He laughed. "Good luck."

Bernard and his friends clambered down. The horses pulled away, and a moment later doors opened on both sides of the road. Two older men approached and stopped an arm's length away. Strange for a tiny Ukrainian village to have both Hasids and their opponents. Back home, their bitter religious war had eased years before with the arrival of the hated Enlightenment thinkers. But in Meerispol, secular thought, the unifying common enemy, couldn't possibly have penetrated the centuries of tradition and the sea of mud. Even the boards laid everywhere had partially submerged beneath the ooze.

The Misnaged wore a wool yarmulke and a long, black, mud-spattered coat with a frayed hem. He held a book to his chest. His white beard and braided peyes contrasted with his black, unruly brow.

"I'm Mordecai. On behalf of Rabbi Shearson, a master of hermeneutical discourse, I invite you weary travelers to join us for dinner and prayer. Make whatever offering you can afford." He stared at the bag slung over Bernard's shoulder.

Food particles speckled the Hasid's gray, fuzzy beard and his worn cloak. He clutched a bottle of wine and hummed to himself. "I'm Israel." He bowed toward the house he'd emerged from. "Our most esteemed and beloved master, an illimitable spiritual guide, doesn't waste his time eighteen hours a day, sinking into obscure and unimportant matters." He gestured at Mordecai. "After you finish dinner with them and the long and tedious discussion, our Rebbe Isaac extends the honor of his company."

Without looking at Israel, Mordecai hissed, "Apostasy."

Israel held his wine bottle aloft. "My brother—I mean this Misnaged—mistakes his own ideas for God's. A sorry Jew indeed."

Bernard shifted and swung his bag from one shoulder to the other. Israel walked to his side of the muddy intersection; Mordecai walked to the other and beckoned them to follow. It began to drizzle.

"Too late to walk any further tonight," Leib said, "but this is almost as bad as being between my mother and drunk father. Still—food, warmth, and a floor to sleep on."

"Yes, and an early start tomorrow."

They walked toward the dimly lit log house.

✳

Bernard opened one eye. Ordinarily, he loved this time of early morning illumination, when the void slowly refilled with the stuff of the world. Now, though, the light hurt, an unwelcome intruder. Joseph lay curled on one side of Bernard, his black wool coat draped over his shoulders and several shirts tucked under his head. Leib lay on Bernard's other side, snoring, a clarinet on the floor beside him. Empty wine bottles lined the windowsill.

Bernard's head throbbed from the night before—the prayers at the Misnagdim dinner, the rabbi's penetrating blue eyes and silken, combed-out beard, Leib, full of shpilkes, his legs bouncing the bench, the slurping and chewing. Wine. Later, across the street to the ancient Hasidic rebbe with the wide fur cap, the ring of dancers stomping, yelling, reversing, springing up back-to-back. More wine.

When the rebbe, with a face like old parchment and peyes braided to his shoulders, raised his fingers, the dancing had stopped. He beckoned the travelers with the slightest twitch and stared into each of their eyes. Joseph blushed and looked at his shoes. Leib quietly hummed. Bernard had kept his eyes on the rebbe and felt his entire life in Horodno, drawn out and exposed in front of his friends and these strangers, sanctified.

Bernard shook his companions. "It's time." Joseph rose and stretched. Leib opened his eyes and mumbled, "Fire up the stills," then sat straight up, blinked, and scratched his head. He arched his back and rolled his neck. "Enough hocus-pocus for an entire lifetime. The rebbe has them all hypnotized." He scrutinized Bernard.

"I felt it too," Joseph said.

Leib snorted.

After visits to the outhouse, they left wearing the clothes they'd slept in. The faster they completed this mission, the sooner he'd be back with Estes and the children.

"What about horses?" Joseph asked.

"We'll get them at the next settlement heading south. It's not far." Bernard wanted to get moving. In Meerispol they'd have to buy one from the Hasids, the other from the Misnagdim, and how would they ever pull in the same direction?

The bright orb of sun appeared above the horizon in a cloudless sky. Clusters of Misnagdim with tefillin and fringe murmured prayers as they traveled to shul. A woman with a baby on her back collected eggs from a leaning hen house. The flat land was broken only by a copse of lindens. Bernard imagined the fragrance of their yellow blossoms mixing with the earthy smell of village mud.

When they passed Meerispol's last house, Mordecai the Misnaged pulled up on their left and Isaac the Hasid on their right.

"The Misnagdim offer you a ride eight versts south. You can buy horses there," Mordecai told them, beckoning toward the wagon.

Israel coughed. "Rebbe Isaac instructed me to take you myself." He glared at Mordecai.

The argument about which conveyance would be more comfortable and who drove better ended when Bernard said, "Leib and Joseph travel with Isaac. I'll go with Mordecai."

"The wisdom of Solomon." Leib laughed and pulled himself onto the Hasidic wagon.

Bernard worried about the narrow road. "Mordecai, what will you do if someone approaches from the south?"

"Hypothetical. Do you see anyone?"

"Not yet, but if I did, would you ease up and pull behind Israel?"

"Misnagdim don't follow Hasidim. He'd have to let me pass."

The two wagons raced along, dangerously close to each other, neither able to pull ahead. Bernard searched for places to jump to safety, said a prayer for one of the brothers to show some sense, and prepared to grab the reins.

When the wagons finally pulled up to a farmhouse with a dilapidated barn, he blew air and tension from his mouth. Mangy cows wandered in the yard and nibbled on sparse patches of brown grass. Aggressive chickens pecked at the churned-up mud.

"A friend of the Hasids lives here. Tell him Rebbe Isaac sent you."

"Wrong again! The owner is a follower of our blessed Rabbi Shearson."

The three travelers grabbed their bags and said goodbye. Their escorts continued to argue as they turned around and headed back to Meerispol.

An ancient fellow hobbled out the front door. "Haven't spoken to anyone in two moons. Look at me," he said, indicating his bowed back. "Carrying the weight of Russia." His head bobbed with a bitter laugh.

"Travelers used to pass through, before the czar finished the rail line to Odessa. I'd pick up the news from Kiev, Petersburg, Meerispol, and the other shtetls. All the tales of woe added up. I'm Sam Sheranski."

Bernard introduced the three of them. "We're headed to Balta. How much for two horses and a wagon?" He didn't want to waste time here.

"Balta! No place for Jews now. Centuries in one place and we're still outsiders. Some go to Palestine and America but not Sam Sheranski." He laughed and spewed spittle. "So, they said I might be able to sell you horses? Which brother—Misnaged or Hasid? Doesn't matter, I'll pay tax to both. Follow me, lads."

The barn door dangled from one hinge and banged against its frame in the wind. Sam Sheranski ducked through the triangular opening, and they followed. Two swaybacked horses nudged strands of hay on the barn floor. The wagon missed one wheel.

"These nags must be leftovers from the Crimean War," Leib said. He went up to the dappled white. "You gals up for pulling us to Balta? What do you call them?"

"Slow and Slower, ha, ha. Or Bathsheba and Delilah, if you prefer."

Joseph set to work greasing the axle and replacing the wheel. Bernard and Leib took the horses for a walk.

"Well, it might work if we go easy, early starts, rests." Bernard pulled out a map and they reviewed their course.

When they returned to the barn, Sam Sheranski was asleep, nearly hidden in a pile of dusty hay.

"He dozed off telling me a story," Joseph told them.

Bernard gently shook the old fellow, and they went back to the house and bargained. When they pulled out of the old man's dooryard, he called after them, "Balta, who goes to Balta these days?"

Bathsheba and Delilah reminded Bernard of old men in Horodno who no longer lifted their feet on the way to shul but shuffled along, conserving energy for prayer. Herman claimed he could know the essence of a person just by looking at the sole of their shoe.

"This one's a stepper," he'd say. "See the wear at the point of heel impact. A fellow with prospects, in a hurry." Or, holding up another shoe, "Scuffer, worn out all over."

Bernard had inspected the shoed hooves before the purchase. He held Bathsheba's thick foreleg up and chipped away at the dried mud with an iron hook. He probed for soreness as Bathsheba sniffed his hair and ran her rough tongue over his neck. Definitely a scuffer.

It would be another week until they reached Balta at this pace. Bernard prayed the railroad men repaired the track soon for a quick trip home. He took his turn as driver, sentry, and sleeper. They'd bought several bales of hay and sacks of grain from Sam Sheranski, which left just enough space for one of them to stretch out. The other made sure the driver stayed alert.

For several days they stopped only to water and feed the horses and grab food for themselves in villages the size of Meerespol. On the first night of Pesach, clear and cold, they hobbled the horses and pulled everything off the wagon. They stretched out on the wagon bed under their wool blankets and passed around a bottle of Garfinkle's Spirits.

"Like peasants," Leib said.

Bernard swallowed the last of the vodka and lay back. His two mates had fallen asleep. The chirp of early spring frogs and distant barking mingled with Leib's occasional mumble and Joseph's shifts from back to side. Bernard's mouth watered when he imagined the Leving's table. He envisioned Estes lying in the hay next to him, reading aloud. She smiled playfully and he buried his face in her hair, the earthy smell ballast against his lightheadedness. *Stay awake while I read, Bernard.*

They continued their southward journey. Dogs announced their arrival as they passed through more desolate Jewish shtetls, separated from peasant settlements only by muddy fields. In one, a young girl hung wash, peered around a flapping sheet, and pulled back like a child playing peekaboo. In another, peddlers lined the road and beckoned. They sold knit hats, farming tools, leather work gloves, maps, eggs. All had hungry eyes.

In Uman, they stopped for food. A weather-stained wooden shul on one side of the square faced a Russian Orthodox church with a dreidel-shaped steeple and silver cross on the other. Morose peddlers eyed them suspiciously. Four men, their arms linked, knocked over one of the peddler's carts. A crowd gathered, peasants on one side and Hasidic men coming out of shul on the other.

Bernard grabbed Leib's shoulders and pulled him back when he started toward the scene. "Balta, Leib."

Two policemen pushed their way through the crowd. The sides dispersed, but not before one of the peasants yelled, "Your time is coming, Jews."

❋

Joseph leaned over the front of the wagon. Leib stretched out next to him, twirled a hay stalk in his fingers, and said, "A train journey of one day lasted for ten."

"Another Jewish miracle," Joseph said.

Leib laughed. "There's still a chance you'll make a decent Jew, Joseph."

Bernard held the reins and prayed this would be the last ride with Delilah and Bathsheba. They should reach Balta today. The horses' steady pulling had been admirable, but the slow pace and Leib's nervous energy gave him a headache.

The night before, weary from sleeping out in the cold, they had stopped at an inn. Bernard anticipated a cooked meal, a hot bath, and a bed, but inferior, cloudy vodka, served with greasy chicken and over-cooked vegetables, had completely flattened his spirits.

The tavern keeper, a nosy fellow whose long arms and fingers gestured as he spoke, also did not help with his dire report. "Lots of migrants and track workers around Balta. Word is, a pogrom has already started, and if it hasn't, tomorrow's Easter and that will surely be a spark. If I were you, I'd turn around and head north, or go northwest toward the track. The line is clear now from Vinnitsa all the way to Kiev. Go back to Horodno."

They'd left before daybreak, driven out by bedbugs and the wife and husband's shouting in the adjacent room. What had Bernard led his friends into?

As the morning passed, they received more news from the sparse traffic on the road. A farrier making his rounds said he'd heard a peasant and migrant army had attacked the Jews in Balta. A farmer with a wagonful of spring grain seed claimed no one could enter or leave. A father walking his family to church clucked his tongue and called it a nasty business.

Both of his friends kept watch now. Leib stopped talking.

Despondency and anxiety squeezed Bernard's gut like a cinched belt, but why cling to despair? These were only rumors. Whatever awaited in Balta had already been determined. They'd arrive by afternoon, find Aunt Freida, and bring her family or hopeful news back to Doris. He sat up straight and shook the reins. Delilah swung her head to the side and Bathsheba snorted. The old horses trotted for a few seconds, then slowed again.

Nearing Balta, they had the road to themselves. Leib turned his head side to side, and Joseph peered through an eyeglass similar to the one they used at the fire station.

"Whoa, girls." Distant screams and the scent of smoke reached them. The horses took one more tentative step and stopped atop a gentle rise. Joseph and Leib jumped down and Leib shielded his eyes against the sun's glare. He grabbed the eyeglass and studied the town like a complicated chess position.

"There, in front of the church."

He passed the glass to Bernard, who stood on the wagon, confident the horses wouldn't lurch and throw him off. Uniformed men milled about in front of the blue spires of an Orthodox church. Across the river, farther south, fires spread black smoke across the town.

Bernard took a deep breath. To push forward despite hearsay was one thing, to charge into real danger, another. He was afraid he'd run if attacked, afraid he'd arrived too late. They could turn away until this trouble passed.

"Separate fires." Joseph crossed himself.

"See what he does when things get rough?" Leib said with a smirk. He pulled a black object from his bag.

"Here's my prayer." He held the small pistol aloft.

"Leib! Put it away. It won't help to have you shot." Russian soldiers carried revolvers strapped to their waists and rifles slung over their backs. Peasants killed crows and hunted game in the fields around Horodno, but Jews and guns felt as foreign to him as leavened bread at Pesach.

Leib tucked the weapon into his coat pocket. "All right. Only a last resort."

"Meshuge! We'll ride closer and continue on foot. Freida lives North of the Kodyma, on Benzary Street. Keep an eye out for a place to leave the horses and our bags."

The road narrowed, curtains parted, and scared faces stared out at them. Smoke from the fires drifted overhead. Twenty or so men stood in front of a cluster of shops—a blacksmith's, kosher butchery, dry goods store, and tannery.

Bernard halted the horses and called out, "We're looking for Freida Gottman on Benzary Street. Her husband, Hirsh, is a scribe."

A brawny man, with thick muscular arms bared, approached. He towered over Bernard. Stubble covered his chin and cheeks. He wore a grease-stained leather apron and gripped a blacksmith's hammer in a huge hand. "Who wants to know?"

"She's my wife's aunt. We came to see if she's safe."

"Safe? I know them, but you'll be lucky to find them alive."

If they had left Horodno immediately . . . If the tracks hadn't been torn up . . . With better horses . . . If only they had traveled at night instead of stopping to rest. How would he explain to Doris?

"We had it under control yesterday, until the army stepped in. Krapukhin took our weapons and let the pogromshichiki keep theirs. He spread the rumor that we planned to attack the church. He stationed his men there and called in five hundred peasants with cudgels and axes to suppress the riot. Oil thrown on a fire. Held us back and let the goyim cross the bridge. The Jews south of the Kodyma are trapped. Stay here and make a stand with us."

"We have to reach the Gottmans."

"Not a chance with the wagon. You'll be arrested by the police or beaten to death by the pogromshichiki. When they finish on the Turkish side, they'll come back. We'll be ready." He grimaced and spat in the road. "Damn town officials are watching the whole thing from chairs and blankets along the riverbank, like it's an afternoon at the theater."

"Let us leave our wagon here, and we'll be back to help. I'm Bernard. This is Joseph and Leib."

"Benjamin." The blacksmith's hand swallowed Bernard's. "It's your funeral. You can put the horses and wagon around back."

Bernard led Bathsheba and Delilah through a narrow passage separating the shop and house, unhitched them, and put several scoops of grain on the ground. Benjamin went into his shop and came back with three iron pokers.

"Take these. Stay away from the church. Cut across to Benzary—that way." He pointed to the narrow side street.

Bernard rejoined his friends and gave each a weapon. These tools felt heavier than the one he used to stir the fire at home, as though their grim purpose added heft.

6

Estes kept the bookshop open Sundays, but not today, on Easter. Before dawn, the rest of the household still asleep, she made tea in the kitchen, but that didn't slow her thoughts.

Bernard must be travelling home. She wished they could have faced these trials together. She should have gone with him to Balta because she couldn't bear another day of not knowing where he was or if he faced danger.

And Borishenko had summoned her again. She felt so vulnerable and exposed, which obviously the general intended, because this time Nikolai delivered the note to her parents' house on Shabes, a blatant intrusion of both her privacy and the Jewish holiday.

General Borishenko requests the pleasure of your company on Monday, March 29, at 9:00. He would also like to meet your children at that time.

Tomorrow. A pleasure indeed! Borishenko was a fiddle sustaining one discordant note. If he watched her here, he might have her followed if she went to see Eliza. She knew what her mentor would advise anyway—appear compliant, make plans in secret.

The children, though. She'd have to give them a reason for the meeting without divulging what was really going on. Solly would be fine, but Sera was unpredictable if she sensed anything amiss.

They spent the day thoroughly cleaning the house and shop, and she even found time to read with Solly. After dinner, she reassured her parents again. "It's mostly about the bookshop."

."This is also about Gesia, isn't it?"

"Yes, Mama."

"I'm going with you. I can tell this Borishenko your association was innocent."

"And I made that fellow a pair of boots."

"Hardly makes you intimate confidants, Papa. Let me handle it."

That night, after Solly and Sera jostled for space on their bed, Estes invited their questions.

"Does the general have a sword? Is it strapped to his belt?" Solly asked.

"He wears a fancy uniform and only has one arm."

"Did he lose the other in battle?"

"Yes." Estes waited for Sera.

"Why does he want to see us? Is it because we're Jews?"

"He asked me questions about Gesia, and I answered them. He wants to try to understand what happened. It's a friendly invitation, Sera."

"If that's true, can I refuse?"

"Of course. I'll tell him you didn't feel well."

The children knew about Gesia's role in the assassination because the papers and periodicals printed her picture, and the Jews of Horodno spoke her name like a bad omen. They'd also witnessed Estes crying over the fate of her friend. Even the innocent stories Estes had told them struck her now as bombs she'd planted in her children.

Solly looked at her openly with Bernard's eyes, but Sera turned away and pulled the blanket over her shoulders. Estes said good night and put out the lantern.

※

On a chilly, gray morning, the five of them joined a line of petitioners formed outside. Jewish men talked amongst themselves. Two glanced up, then resumed their conversation. A husband and wife pushed four young children back and forth in two carriages. A young peasant couple, ripe with their farm labor, whispered to each other. The man twirled a broad-brimmed hat.

Sera frowned and glared at the building. Solly made silly faces for the children. Mama straightened out Estes's dress collar, and Papa examined the petitioners' feet, reading life stories in their shoes. Most waiting in the queue practiced their appeals, translating their Yiddish and hushed Polish into the required Russian.

The same clerk from her first visit opened the door and stepped outside. He wore a blue bow tie, the attempt at formality ruined by the lint clinging to his wool vest. "Exit permits must include registry of birth, military classification, and three hundred rubles. Land purchase or dispute, come back tomorrow morning. All other requests must be received in writing by this office two weeks prior to the consideration of your case." Half of those waiting in line grumbled and walked off. The clerk waved Estes, the children, and those who remained into the building.

"Wait for us outside," she told her parents.

"As long as it takes," Mama said.

Before Estes and the twins could sit on one of the benches ringing the exterior of the musty office, the clerk shouted, "Esther Leving Garfinkle, General Borishenko will receive you now."

✳

A rail-thin, middle-aged man carrying a pile of papers took Estes and her children to Borishenko's office. He placed the documents on a hallway table and knocked softly.

"Enter." A command, not an invitation. The attendant bowed and backed out. Estes went in first; the general stood and nodded curtly at her. She took Solly's hand, tugged him forward, and Sera stepped over the threshold after him.

"This must be Solomon and Seraphina." He indicated three chairs in front of his desk and held out a plate with two chocolates. "For the children." Solly took one, but Sera said, "No, thank you," and contracted her lips.

Determined to keep her composure despite her churning stomach, Estes laid her cane down and waited.

"Very handsome children, Mrs. Garfinkle. A young soldier, and your daughter as beautiful as her mother."

"Thank you, General Borishenko."

"Your husband hasn't shown up yet? I suppose it's possible he got in and out already, but with the vandalism to the rail line . . . Oh, you didn't know." He contorted his features to mimic sympathy.

"We've received reports of Easter rioting in Balta," he continued. "These pogromshichiki need an iron fist; otherwise, what's left of the People's Will and other groups will manipulate the confusion to launch revolutionary activity. I'm sure your husband will make it home, Mrs. Garfinkle, but it must be a source of intense anxiety for you. We'll keep Grodno safe. Right, Solomon?"

"Yes, sir."

The general had control. Estes despised him.

Borishenko lifted the blue scabbarded sword hanging on the wall from its hook and held the pointed end toward Solomon. "Easy now. Pull it off. Careful of the blade. It's sharpened to remove Turkish heads. Do you want to hold it?"

Solly turned to her. "Can I, Mama?"

Borishenko didn't wait for her answer. He laid the weapon on his desk, the hilt nearest Solly.

Solly reached for the handle, and with two hands lifted the sword off the desk. "It's heavy. Here, Sera."

Sera grasped it with her right hand only and extended her arm until the sword's tip hovered, almost motionless over the middle of the desk, her arm and the blade a single weapon aimed at Borishenko's heart. When a slight tremor appeared in her hand, she dropped the sword. The hilt struck first, followed by the blade, which scratched the desk's smooth surface.

Borishenko's eyebrows merged into one. "That's no way to treat fine steel." With his one hand, he eased the blade back into the scabbard. When he turned and replaced it on the wall, Estes glanced at Sera. Her daughter bore a hole in the general's back with her eyes.

When he faced them again, his frown had departed, replaced by a wry smirk. He rang a bell on his desk, and the thin clerk appeared.

"Take the children to the waiting area. We won't be long. Here, Solomon. Take the other chocolate. Share it with your sister." He eased back into his chair and waited until the children had left.

"Spirited, aren't they? Your daughter looks like trouble." He stroked his mustache.

"I searched for those letters."

"We'll get to that, Mrs. Garfinkle. Things are about to deteriorate further for your people. My sources tell me the committee looking into the pogroms will blame the Jews. What can you expect when the czar says it's gratifying to see them beaten? More exit permit requests flood in every day. Most we put through, but some, in your position . . ."

"Please tell me precisely what my position is, General."

"That depends on you, Mrs. Garfinkle."

"What more can I do?"

"Please, Mrs. Garfinkle—the Horodno Bookshop Lady." He looked at her and narrowed his eyes. "I wonder what Professor Micah taught you during those years? You know, of course, he worked closely with Belinsky at *Sovremennik* when he lived in Petersburg."

One cannot remain silent when lies and immorality are presented as truth and virtue under the guise of religion and the protection of the knout.

Borishenko read her mind. "A peddler of trash passed off as high ideals, Mrs. Garfinkle. Almost all villains think of themselves as moral. Whose side are you on? Your request to adopt the terrorist's baby—mawkish sentimentality for a bright woman. Our czar, assassinated, and you refuse to help. Don't you care that Russia's falling into anarchy?"

His tone suddenly changed. "I don't want to harm you or your family. We can discuss this in a more comfortable setting. I'm sure we can arrive at a mutually satisfactory arrangement. Would you dine with me tonight? I'll send my driver at six. I'd find great pleasure in discussing our favorite authors."

Eliza had warned her. "Thank you, but I prefer to meet here, General."

He looked glove slapped. When he stood and leaned across the desk on his one arm, his face loomed above her, transformed by anger into a misshapen moon. He enunciated as though he thought Estes partially deaf. "We don't need the letters. Just the information they contained. Names. We want the names."

Borishenko pulled away and sat down, still glaring at her. "I've tried to be civil with you, yet you stubbornly persist in your defiance. Are you willing to go to jail to protect these radicals from justice? Allow me to tell you what to expect."

7

Nothing stirred on Benzary Street, though a pogrom raged on the other side of the Kodyma. Some houses had white crosses as tall as a man painted on their doors. The Orthodox church spire, several blocks south, rose above all other buildings. Along the riverbank, next to a bridge, observers lounged, just as the blacksmith had described.

An intimidating chant rose above the screams. "Blood! Beat the Jews!" The mob began to charge across the bridge. Bernard prayed for God to collapse the span and plunge them like Pharaoh's army into the cold water below.

If we don't look out for ourselves, who will?

"The Gottmans are at the east end. Quickly, let's go."

They walked three astride, surprised by a group of men who emerged from between two houses in front of them. These marauders hooted and smashed windows with bricks. Leib started like a spooked grouse and reached into his pocket. Bernard pulled him and Joseph off the street and behind a leaning woodshed.

"They must have hidden on this side of the river to get a head start on the rest. Stay a minute here, then we'll walk boldly to the Gottman's. They'll think we're pogromshichiki. Freida's should be the last house on the left. Remember what we came for, Leib."

They could see the terror on the street. One of the vandals, with a bloodied Jewish prayer shawl around his neck, swung an ax at a wooden door until he made a splintered hole. He reached through and unlocked it. His companions rushed in, laughing. Moments later, the upstairs windows shattered from the inside.

"Get out! Get out!"

"Out! Out! Out!" voices mimicked. A feather mattress landed in the street and burst open. A woman with her clothes half torn off staggered out the front door. She covered her breasts and screamed as pogromshichiki carried her back into the house.

"There's daughters, too." A score of rioters pushed and shoved their way into the house. Something flew out from the second floor and landed beside the mattress with a sickening thud. A baby, its skull crushed, moved its legs convulsively, then lay still.

Bernard gripped Leib and Joseph's shoulders. His dry mouth made it difficult to speak. "There's nothing we can do here. Too many of them. We have to get to Freida's."

They continued along Benzary street, trying to walk confidently, like the hunters, not the hunted, past rioters holding torches and Jews forced out of hiding into the jaws of the mob. Rioters held Jewish men down and cut their beards and peyes, mocked an old rabbi praying, beat others pleading for mercy. They smashed Seder plates, fed quilts, books, and furniture into street fires, crammed silver into their pockets. Glass shattered. Men fought and grabbed stolen items from each other.

They walked through hell, Joseph and Leib with their eyes locked straight ahead, but Bernard glanced back once in the direction of a desperate scream. On a front porch, four men held a young girl's limbs apart while a fifth assaulted her. Perhaps even younger than Sera, she cried for her mother and father to save her, pleaded with the men to stop, called on God to intervene, her prayers unanswered, and Bernard also turned away. He couldn't descend any lower. What good was his weapon when he was incapable of using it?

They passed beyond the black, oily smoke, goose down, and horror until Bernard stopped in front of a house with green shutters. "This is it!" He pounded on the door. "It's Bernard Garfinkle. Esther Leving's husband. We've come to help. Freida. We've come to help."

A window opened a crack. "Bernard? From Horodno?"

"And my two friends. Quick, Freida. Please."

A moment later, the door opened. A younger Doris stood in front of him. Behind her, a man with thinning hair held the hands of two young women.

"My husband, Hirsh, and our daughters."

Hirsh let go of one of the girls and adjusted his glasses.

"I'm Ledl. This is my sister, Eleanor."

The same intense alertness in their eyes as Estes's.

"Later!" Leib pulled a curtain aside and peered outside. "Is there a back door? Our horses are behind the blacksmith's."

"Yes, but what if they turn north themselves," Hirsh said. "It's unpredictable. It might be safer to stay." He looked frightened.

"Blood! Beat the Jews! Blood! Beat the Jews!"

"Listen to that! They're continuing down the street. We have to go now," Bernard shouted.

Freida led them out with Bernard just behind, followed by Ledl, Eleanor, Hirsh, Joseph, and Leib. They passed through the kitchen and out into a narrow yard. Bernard stepped around a pear tree draped over a moss-covered table.

They passed through an opening in the fence, overgrown with vines. Chained dogs barked and lunged as they walked quickly down a narrow alley. Bernard held the poker at his side and asked God for strength. Behind him, a cloud of ruin rose above Benzary Street.

They exited the alley and Bernard spotted the blacksmith shop to their left, not more than a hundred arshins away. He yelled with immense relief, "Almost there!"

Drunken pogromshichiki stumbled into the street and blocked their path. "No! No!" Freida screamed.

He counted seven. Four held bottles and had women's undergarments wrapped around their heads. They all carried cudgels, hammers, and ax handles. One of them stepped forward.

"Trying to sneak away?" He grinned, revealing yellowed teeth framed by a wispy moustache and beard. He took a long drink. "Bad timing, Jews, caught in the open. And with three women too."

The pogromshichiki spread out across the road. Leib raised the blacksmith's poker above his head and raced forward, screaming. Bernard and Joseph followed.

Fear showed in the leader's face. The line broke and scattered. Bernard turned and yelled to the others: "Just a bit farther."

Freida, Hirsh, and Eleanor linked arms. Ledl, the sentry, stood behind them with one arm on her mother's shoulder, the other across her brow as they started forward. Moments later she shouted. "They're back!"

Wispy Beard had quickly gathered more men. Some waved their weapons and others held theirs aloft, ready to swing. Bernard began to pray.

Leib reached into his pocket and displayed the revolver. "I'll shoot the first man who comes any closer." He knelt on one knee and steadied the gun with two hands. He shut one eye and peered along the short barrel with the other.

"I bet it's not loaded. Come on." The mob surged forward.

The gun's retort dropped Wispy Beard in a heap. "The bastard shot me!"

The pogromshichiki did not run away this time. Leib got off three more shots before the wave crashed upon them. Bernard had never hit a human being, nor had anyone ever struck him in anger. His father had taught him violence was a sin, but when a cudgel struck him in the side, he wielded the iron without hesitation. Out of the corner of his eye, he saw Joseph use his weapon like a club. Leib disappeared in a pile of howling men.

Bernard struggled to keep his balance and stabbed wildly at his assailant's eyes and throats. He would die. Freida cried out behind him. They would all die here.

If everything has to be balanced, what did I do wrong? He nearly toppled over but grabbed a man's long beard with one hand and righted himself. He planted a foot on a fallen body and ducked under the blade of a short-handled hoe, which scraped his scalp. *What will happen to Estes and the children?*

He braced to ward off the next blow and deliver more of his own. *That which is despicable to you, do not do to another,* his father whispered. Bernard slammed the poker on a hairy arm, and a man screamed. Bernard bellowed, "An eye for an eye, Father!"

A response came, not from his dead father, but from the huge blacksmith swinging two hammers. "An eye for an eye!" the blacksmith shouted. "I'll take them all!" The bear and his small army had joined the battle, and the mob of pogromshichiki parted and suddenly thinned out. They ran in all directions, abandoned their weapons, and left behind companions with fractured limbs and bloodied heads. The Jewish savior raised his hammers to the sky and roared.

The pogrom flame blew out as suddenly as it had started. Bernard, his friends, and Freida's family stayed in the blacksmith shop until workers repaired the last of the damaged track into Balta—three nights.

The Battle of Blacksmith's Crossing gave the Jews of Balta a measure of bitter revenge. Benjamin and his desperate men had prevented an even worse slaughter.

When more troops arrived the morning after the riot, the commander had orders to shoot looters on sight, but the pogromshichiki had already stolen or destroyed most of the Jewish property, assaulted men, raped women and girls, and killed twelve, including one baby. On the other side: broken bones, cuts, and concussions, four rioters shot in the legs, and three others dead, each from skull-shattering hammer blows.

Bernard and Freida went with a troop escort to find out what the Gottmans could salvage from their house, but the mob had smashed everything of value, even the table in the garden. They had hacked the pear tree down to a jagged stump, twined two branches into a cross, and stabbed it into the ground.

8

E stes lay in bed listening to the children's steady breathing. When she'd rejoined her children and parents after her interview at the Office of State Security two days ago, she'd managed a composed face. She lied to them about a pleasant meeting, and Solly agreed. Sera had frowned, but at least she didn't argue.

No one but herself and General Borishenko knew she'd cracked like a thin branch under his foot when he'd shown his fangs. He made her look at pictures of unwashed prisoners in raggedy clothes, their heads shorn to ward off lice. He described exile to Siberia—the impossible weather, unbearably brutish work for an intelligent woman, the isolation from her husband and children for years, think of the effect on them— and the names had tumbled out of her in a shameful confession.

She'd wept about it with Eliza, who did not judge her. But what would Gesia have thought about her friend-turned-informer? Estes had condemned those four people to precisely what she'd wanted to avoid for herself, maybe worse. Her tongue burned when she whispered their names before bed and again when she awoke in the morning.

One of Borishenko's lackeys had appeared at the bookshop today. He pretended to browse, but she caught him staring, and he quickly turned back to the shelves. On his way out, he walked by the counter pretending to read the newspaper he held upside down. And yesterday, she'd walked up the hill and found their kitchen drawers and cabinets open, clothes in her bedroom scrambled. More intimidation.

Writing in her journal no longer felt safe. Who knew when they might search her house again, or what could be considered subversive? Estes vowed to remember everything, though. Important memories wouldn't vanish for her like the fading image of the sun behind closed eyelids. Someday, she'd be a serious writer and turn these painful events into a story.

Borishenko had not arrested her, but her cooperation did not satisfy him either. He'd forbidden any travel, and she obviously remained under surveillance. Now that he had the names, how long would he watch her?

Her rejection had stung him, but after a time, didn't he have to move on to more important things? A leech attached to her skin once when she waded into a Niemen pool. She knew then to push its mouth sideways. If only she could shed Borishenko by flicking him off too.

The following afternoon, when a uniformed cadet asked her where to find books by Lermontov, Estes rose stiff limbed and led him to a second-level shelf of Russian poets. She lingered there a moment after the cadet left and pulled down a thin volume of Lermontov's early work.

"Forgive Me, Will We Ever Meet Again?" brought up a different wave of guilt—this time for how she said goodbye to Bernard at the station with only a carefree kiss on the cheek, not the kiss of a wife who sends her husband into the jaws of a pogrom. Some of the horrible reports from Balta said two people had died, others said as many as forty. Estes returned to her post nearly doubled over with anxiety. *Fifteen days since Bernard boarded the train.*

That night, Estes read *Alice in Wonderland* aloud. Solly posed for Sera, who drew his portrait with charcoal. Papa smoked his cigar. Most evenings passed this way, the uncertainty too much to bear by herself.

When a key turned in the downstairs door, the twins raced through the hall and took the steps two at a time in the dark. Estes limped barefoot after them. Her parents each carried a candle behind her.

She wrapped her arms around Bernard with the twins crowded in between. "Thank God!"

Mama and Freida laughed and sobbed as they embraced.

Sera and Solly yelled in unison, "Welcome home, Papa!"

✳

"Now this house is like most others in the Pale," Estes told Bernard. They'd stay at the Levings' tonight and go up the hill tomorrow. Papa had made space for their narrow mattress on the shop floor. The Gottmans had taken her old room, Freida and Hirsh in one bed and their daughters in the other. The twins slept with their grandparents.

Estes held Bernard's hand while he talked faster than usual about their trip, leaving out details about the pogrom but lingering on the return home. "Joseph sat with Eleanor and Leib with Ledl. They talked and held hands for hours. Eleanor even slept with her head on Joseph's shoulder. He kept looking at her as if he couldn't believe his luck."

"His young cousin will be heartbroken. Do Freida and Hirsh know he's not a Jew?"

"He helped rescue their daughters. They didn't say anything when Ledl kissed Leib on the mouth. After surviving a pogrom . . ."

In the candlelight, she examined the wound on his head and asked if he had others. He pulled up his shirt, and she kissed the ugly, raw scrapes across his chest and side.

"I'm ready to leave Russia. I've seen things, done things, Estes." His voice broke and he began to weep.

She held him. "Yes. We'll leave." She hadn't wanted him to suffer in order to reach this point, but she felt immense relief. They'd have to be cunning, though. Bernard didn't know about Borishenko yet.

"Russia will never accept her Jews," he said. "Of that, I'm now sure."

PART IV

SERA

1882–1885

And if you wrong us, do we not revenge?
If we are like you in the rest, we will resemble you in that.
– William Shakespeare

To the Border
June 1885

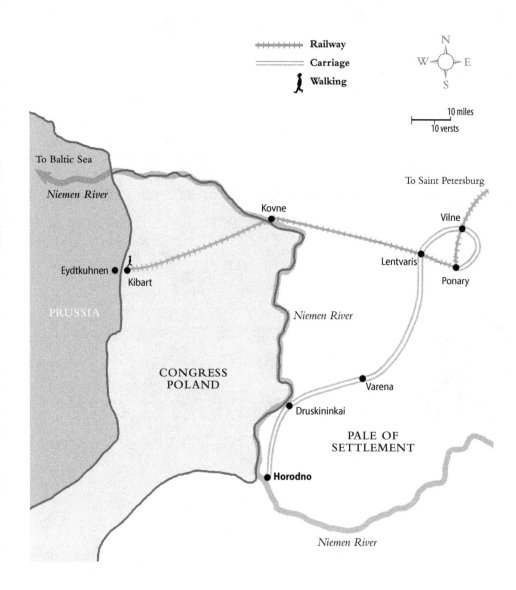

Railway

Carriage

Walking

N
W E
S

10 miles
10 versts

To Baltic Sea

Niemen River

To Saint Petersburg

Kovne

Vilne

Lentvaris

Ponary

Eydtkuhnen

Kibart

PRUSSIA

Niemen River

CONGRESS
POLAND

Varena

Druskininkai

PALE OF
SETTLEMENT

Horodno

Niemen River

I

On May 3, 1882, the czar's commission on the pogroms recommended new laws concerning the Jews in the Pale of Settlement. Banned: from moving into rural villages, except to existing Jewish agricultural colonies; from the purchase or lease of land outside towns; from working on Sunday or other Christian holidays.

Though Jews who had settled in a village prior to 1882 could legally remain there, even then, devious actions of town officials hounded many from their traditional homes. If they moved for a time from one house to another in the village, left to serve in the army, or the police never properly registered their original residence, they could face expulsion. Everyone knew these restrictions, known as the May Laws, would get worse. The czar's handpicked commission had concluded that the Jews had brought the pogroms upon themselves through their exploitation of Russian society. Only severe regulations would put them back in their place.

In July, two months after these laws had further demoralized the four million Jews in the Pale of Settlement—around half the global Jewish population—Eliza Orzeszkowa was scheduled to speak in Horodno's public library.

"I have something important to tell you, Estes," Eliza said. "Come, it's a beautiful evening. Let's stroll. We have time before my talk."

Estes locked the shop and took Eliza's arm as they began a slow clockwise walk around the square.

"We share something else now, besides our love of books. They've seized the presses and placed me under surveillance."

Estes suppressed her first reaction—fright. She needed to show Eliza her own strength, especially after Estes had given up names. Especially after her friend's bold speeches and articles condemned antisemitism and hateful rumors—that Jews plotted to excavate a network of tunnels under churches, burn Polish houses, and murder Christians while they slept.

"Here we are, the two notorious women of Horodno," Estes said. "What reason did they give?"

"They accused me of publishing under another's name, arousing unnecessary passion, and associating with radical elements."

"Will they close the bookshop?"

"I doubt it. As I said—a perfect spot to watch dissidents, refugees, and intellectuals, the lion stalking its prey at the watering hole."

"Did Borishenko . . ."

"He's not interested in meeting me again. I suppose he knows he won't intimidate me or receive anything useful."

Eliza left unsaid—*why would he bother, when he has an easier target.* Estes glanced over her shoulder. A thin man with baggy clothes, about twenty-five paces back, glanced away. He'd been lingering around the bookshop when they came out. "We're being followed."

Eliza turned and approached the man, who jammed his hands into his pockets. Estes followed and stood one arshin back.

"Pavel Manivitch, what a coincidence to find you behind us."

He blushed, removed his hands, and bowed from the waist. His sparse hair fringed a bony scalp.

"Give my best to your wife and children."

His shoulders sagged. "Pani, I don't tell them anything. Only that you spend your days writing."

"I understand, Pavel. I'll inform you if my routine changes."

He bowed again.

Estes and Eliza walked away. "Pavel has eight children. Desperation drives him to spy on a neighbor."

They left the square and walked toward the library. Families gathered on the front steps of their houses. Men pointed to items they'd dragged out for sale. On the street, a frail woman in a torn shawl held out trembling hands. Three gaunt men with long hair and beards stood next to her, holding bowls. A disheveled girl, waist-high, pulled on Estes's dress. She gave the girl a few coins. The girl bowed, and seconds later a score of desperate children surrounded Estes. The needy, including the new refugees, had overwhelmed the Jewish aid organizations since the pogroms. She and Eliza emptied their purses and pushed through the crowd.

They climbed the library steps to the second-floor lecture hall. Estes scanned the rows of wooden chairs. Bernard stood and waved. When she reached her family, Solly took her hand. Sera kept hers in her lap, her eyes fastened on Eliza, who walked to the podium. Leib, Ledl, Joseph, and Eleanor sat in front of them. Estes spotted Chaim and Shlomo, her parents, Freida and Hirsh. Everyone she cared about had come for Eliza Orzeszkowa.

Estes checked the back of the hall for an agent, and Jacob Rosenblum, sitting four rows behind, lifted his hand. This time, he held her gaze when she returned his greeting. Nonplussed by the attention, she looked away first.

Eliza spoke with authority to her rapt audience, and many wept throughout her talk. Estes, along with everyone else, stood and clapped when Eliza delivered her final remark: "I, for one, and a few more are ready, even if we perish, to stand between the raging wave and the doors of the victims."

2

By the spring of 1884, Alexander III had placed further limitations on his Jewish subjects. What his ministers had initially described as a temporary slap to the predatory Jew had turned into a brutal and endless lashing. But just one more painful year and their family would be away from all of this, away from Russia.

After she checked on the twins, Estes hobbled back to bed and stretched out beside Bernard. "I don't want to see that man, but it infuriates me to let him toy with us." That afternoon, for the sixth time since the March day in 1882 when she'd last faced him, Borishenko had called her family to his office. Like the other occasions, the four of them waited several hours before the clerk dismissed her without an interview. They had arrived prepared, with books and sketch pads. When they left, she felt both anger and relief.

Somedays, the possibility of their escape seemed too dreamlike, and she needed to review their plan with Bernard, as she did now, though it hadn't changed. They'd slip away on a Friday night, when the bookshop would be closed for Shabes the next day. Eliza and Leib would get them to Gródek, thirty versts east of Bialystok. There, they'd board the train to Minsk. Borishenko watched the Grodno station, and probably surveilled the other route stops in the gubernia's cities, but a shtetl like Gródek? Very doubtful he watched there, Bernard assured her again.

Through Minsk to Odessa, where a steamer would take them to their new lives in America. At first she had questioned the idea of fleeing across the Russian Empire rather than racing the short distance from Horodno across Congress Poland to the western frontier. The Suwalki province looked as thin as a goose's neck on their map. Bernard had convinced her that the terrible roads, impassible in wet weather, and the guarded border made that option much riskier. He thought Borishenko would never look for them to the east.

Jacob Rosenblum would arrange everything ahead of their escape— forged identity papers and exit passes, train tickets, an overnight stay in Odessa, and ocean liner passage. His position as a crown rabbi gave him access to all manner of documents, real and fake. Of course, she and Bernard needed to keep this plan hidden from her parents and the children.

"I wish we didn't need to be dependent on anyone," she said. Eliza and Leib were like family, but Rabbi Jacob Rosenblum? He never came into the bookshop anymore. Since the encounter at Eliza's speech, she'd only seen him on three occasions: twice in passing on the street, and once during a talk on Pinsker's Auto-Emancipation at the library. As Jacob's scholarly reputation had grown, so had his collection of acolytes. Each of those times, a crowd of admiring rabbis surrounded him, and she didn't think he noticed her.

An owl's "whoo-whoo" sounded in the forest. "Do you have any regrets, Bernard?" What had he asked of God when she'd watched him that morning at his father's grave, his lips moving in a silent prayer?

After Balta, new worry lines had creased his forehead, and it had taken a long time before he smiled again. When she'd tearfully confessed how easily Borishenko had extracted the names of Gesia's comrades from her, Bernard didn't add to her self-condemnation. He told her she didn't have a choice. Estes knew otherwise.

She tried to get Bernard to tell her about the Balta pogrom, but for months he avoided mentioning that event. One night she discovered him outside, tear-streaked, a bottle of wine in his hand. He revealed the horror, all of it. Principles were one thing when safe at home, another in a pogrom. Hours of prayer and long solitary walks broke the fever and gradually filled in the depression Balta had left in his spirit.

"No regrets, Estes." He pressed his mouth against hers and rested his hand on her hip. She felt him against her thigh, but her worries made it impossible to respond as he wanted. For him, though, sex relieved such tensions, the period after Balta the only time in their twelve years of marriage he'd been the one to turn her down. She took his hand and moved it with hers to his hardness. "Have you ever done this to yourself?"

"Yes."

"Did you think about me?"

"The first time we met."

She reached into their drawer. She filled her palm with oil and lubricated him.

He murmured, "My God."

"Even God can't save you now."

3

E stes wanted a quiet affair, with just the four of them, to celebrate the twin's eleventh birthday. Before they even cut the cake, Sera stood and said, "I wish General Borishenko dead! It's his fault—the awful laws and people leaving. Why does he force us to go to his office but never meets with us?" She left the table and went outside.

When Bernard brought her back, Solly served them each a slice, but Estes's dismay about Sera's words made it difficult to swallow.

Days later, Solly chewed on his lip and concentrated on reading *Twenty Thousand Leagues Under the Sea.*

"Join us anytime you want," Estes told Sera.

Sera nodded but made no move to put aside her drawing. When the children went for a walk with Bernard, Estes checked the books Sera kept by her bed, all untouched except for her bound journal. They'd given a new one to each child, and Solly used his to practice English and write stories—fantastic affairs about trips to the moon or strange creatures living in the Niemen. When he'd begged Sera to illustrate for him, she drew a giant serpent with one bulging eye, sharp teeth, and tentacles wrapped around the Leving's Shoes sign.

In Sera's journal, Estes didn't need the short captions to know what the illustrations portrayed: Grandpa in his shop, Grandma working in the kitchen, Mama teaching Solly, Papa and Uncle Leib at the distillery. The scenes of daily life reassured her until she came to the last four. *Revolution* showed a man throwing a bomb under the czar's carriage. In the next scene, the czar lay on the bridge, dead. *Pogrom*, with murdered Jews laid out like wares at market, brought bile into her throat. *Borishenko's Sword*, the blade suspended in the air, a line running along the middle of the forged steel like an arrow, drew her to the last page. In *Revenge*, the general's sword skewered him through the neck. His head flopped on his chest, and his tongue lolled out like a rain-soaked worm.

*

The pogroms seemed over by the summer of 1884, but just when everyone thought the violence had finally ceased, a mob threw ten Jews from roofs and hacked them to death in Nizhnii Novgorod. Estes couldn't believe what she could bear since they'd committed to leaving.

Horodno's Market Square, so congested with residents and refugees this early in the morning, no longer surprised her, but she warily approached the three officials outside the bookshop. Borishenko's men hadn't been around for weeks, although their presence lingered like night soil after it's transported from sight.

One of the men, with hollow cheeks and spectacles, said, "I'm Lieutenant Smyslov. By order of General Borishenko, please keep the bookshop closed while we conduct our inventory." He gave her a piece of paper with the general's signature in bold strokes and oversized letters. The other two men unloaded empty crates from their wagon. Estes put the key in the door, ashamed of how readily she complied.

As the two workers went shelf-by-shelf and removed books like spoiled fruit, she ached to throw them out and free her imprisoned volumes.

Smyslov followed his men, gave orders, peered at his list, and made marks on his paper. Estes concealed her distress as they tossed Marx, Chernyshevsky, Bakunin, Herzen, and Belinski—the revolutionaries— into the crates.

As the carnage spread from politics to art, from Russian to French, from English to German, Estes ignored the pain in her stomach. When poets went down, she didn't flinch. The verse of Baudelaire, Shelly, and Keats joined the philosophers and champions of liberty—Paine, Locke, Mills, and others from across the continent and America, writers known for their ideals, not their national allegiances. When the officials hauled the books that she, as self-appointed curator of enlightenment and knowledge in Horodno, had chosen over the past ten years to the waiting wagons, her eyes betrayed her.

"Don't attempt to replace any of these volumes," Smyslov told her. He unfolded a tattered paper. "The Office of State Security has deemed the confiscated volumes to be a threat to the welfare of the state. This doesn't mean other books are cleared. They may be subject to future seizures as conditions dictate." The lieutenant clicked his heels and departed.

The gaps in the shelves, like patches of her skin ripped off, made her sick. She doubled over the waste can and threw up.

❋

Bernard clucked, and Young Ferd eased along the riverbank trail. Last month he found Alte Ferd too weak to stand, staring at him with bloodshot eyes. He brought Estes and the children out to say goodbye. Solly threw his arms around the horse's neck, and Sera ran her hand over his coarse mane.

"Too tired to endure another winter," he'd told the twins.

Why didn't Russia's Jews give up like the old horse? So many now flooded the cities, expelled from their homes, hungry, desperate for work. Families fished along the crowded river path, often empty in the past.

Bernard dismounted and walked beside the horse. Men with tangled fishing lines blamed each other for the snags. A group of children watched as a catfish flopped on the bank. A young woman clubbed it with a rock until its tail stopped quivering.

Two old Jews approached, and Bernard remembered the wild ride out of Meerispol and the arguing brothers. Mordecai and Isaac, Misnaged and Hasid, stopped and stared at Bernard for a moment, then simultaneously embraced him.

"You're a long way from home."

Mordecai gripped Bernard's arm. "They ordered us out. Said we caused unrest among our Christian neighbors. There isn't a Christian within ten versts of Meerispol. They gave us two weeks to pack up our home of four hundred years, our birthplace."

Israel wagged his finger in the air and tapped his head. "We kept all the Shabosim, Seders, births, deaths, and weddings, but the mud we gladly gave away. We all scattered, Hasids and Misnagdim, some south to Odessa, others to Brody, Vilne, or here. Tomorrow we take the train to Warsaw. Once we settle, we'll send for our families."

They embraced Bernard again, and he wished them luck. The brothers walked away with their arms around each other's shoulders.

*

The family's last full summer in Horodno passed, and the leaves began to turn. Sera drew in her room while Bernard and Solly dug up the potato harvest and put the tubers in a sack. Estes remained at the table in the evening light.

The book censors had come again today, and she wanted to close the shop for good. "No. Sudden changes will draw suspicion," Eliza argued, and Bernard agreed.

This time, they'd seized old *Sovremenniks*, Yiddish folk tales, and what Lieutenant Smyslov called "amoral affronts to decency." The censors threw this strange meal, with its incompatible flavors, haphazardly into the crate. Smyslov held Madame Bovary between his thumb and index finger. "Dangerous times," he told her, dropping the book like something odious. "So much worthless drivel, decadence, insidious foreign influence. We must have Russia and Russians first."

What could she say to this man, with his hatred of ideas? *I think what I want. My thoughts give me power.*

Sera joined her at the table with art supplies and concentrated on a drawing. Without looking up, she said, "You cut a picture out of my journal. You censored me, Mama."

"Yes, Sera. It's not a moment for work like that."

"Are you afraid, Mama? Of Borishenko?"

"Can't you see we have enough challenges right now without you needlessly bringing more."

Sera's hand froze. She quickly gathered her materials and rushed back to her room.

Dangerous times. Family and survival have to come first.

After the twins had gone to bed, Estes held out her glass and Bernard filled it with wine. "I'll be so relieved when all this deception is over. I wish we could tell the children. It might help Sera to know. And I lied to my parents, Bernard."

"They have to go first, Estes. Otherwise, Borishenko might detain them out of spite, or to force your return."

"I told Papa we needed him to explore our new home and convinced both of them we'd follow soon after. If they learn we have to sneak out . . ."

"They won't. And in six months they'll be on their way. There are so many shoemakers in Horodno now, and no one has money. It's for the best. Herman's business is half of what it was."

"When did they grow so old, Bernard? How did I miss it?"

4

That winter, Joseph converted.

"Perfect sense of timing," Leib teased at the distillery. "You're going in the wrong direction. Don't you know any better than to run into a burning building?"

"I'm a fireman, Leib."

"You don't need a circumcision, Joseph. You converted in Balta."

"I want you all to come to the purifying micky."

"Mikve, Joseph. Study your Yiddish. Eleanor will suspect you're fertummelt if you don't know a knish from a shvantz."

Leib reached inside Joseph's shirt and exposed the chain and cross. "At least you keep it hidden now. What kind of Jew takes a cross to his bris? One who breaks glass at a funeral? Sits shiva at a wedding? Works on Shabes?"

"It's only for luck."

"Oy, Joseph, trying to play it both ways. Save the piece the moyel nips off. If it doesn't work out, stitch it back on."

Joseph's jaw set. He pulled off the chain and held it tightly in his hand. His voice quavered. "'If you marry a Jew, you're a walking ghost to us,' my mother told me."

The distillery crew dropped the cross into the Niemen that afternoon. The silver chain danced for a moment in the wintry sun, uncoiling in the lazy current before sinking.

A month later, Horodno's Great Wooden Shul hosted a double wedding. God, for unfathomable reasons, had brought them pogroms and May Laws. The lives they'd known would never return. Not here. Yet, today, they celebrated.

The rabbi held up a burning candle, and the flame wavered like a drunken dancer. The ceremony ended with glasses smashed on the floor. The couples kissed, Joseph and Eleanor shyly, but Leib and Ledl with their arms wrapped around one another and their lips locked so long the rabbi looked away.

The congregation stood and cheered, which broke the spell. Leib displayed his most wolfish grin. The sisters hugged, and Leib threw his arm around Joseph's shoulder.

※

The Jewish exodus from Russia accelerated, and Chaim's family left soon after the wedding. His sister Mazel and two younger brothers, all with their own families now, crowded the platform. His father hunched over and coughed up phlegm.

"Damn Shershevski's poison mill," Chaim said.

Bernard moved closer to his friend. He didn't want to miss any final words, although the mates had said their goodbyes on Chaim's last day distilling vodka. Leib had kept it light with toasts and teasing. When the second whistle blew—a stern rabbi calling his class to order—a sudden, heavy silence fell on the platform. Travelers hauled bags on their shoulders, held children, embraced, and made bold promises about meeting again soon.

Chaim grabbed Bernard. "In Warsaw, we'll work on exit passes or find another way out. I'll write."

They boarded before the third whistle, and as he headed through the aisle trailing the others, Chaim waved.

※

Weeks later, another departure. The dreary sky and miserable March weather matched Estes's mood. The presence of Borishenko's man, one who also took his turn as spy of the bookshop, didn't help. This separation was only temporary, she reminded herself. A necessary step in their plan to escape Russia. Spring and then summer would come. Still, the look on her mother's face almost made Estes scream, "Don't go!"

Mama, her eyes moist, led her away from the others. She made Estes promise again that they'd follow in four months. Otherwise, she'd come back across the Atlantic and carry them out herself.

Too many brave goodbyes. Aunt Freida's family also traveled west with the elder Levings, except for Ledl, who would remain in Horodno with Leib.

"Work on your chess game, Joseph." Leib's voice cracked, but he regained his composure. "I hear they have a club in New York. Try not to lose right away."

"Come join us, Leib, and you, too, Shlomo."

Mama and Aunt Freida had their arms around each other as they boarded the train. Papa, still on the platform, complained. "One thousand rubles for the visas, train tickets, and a ship from Hamburg. Can you believe it? Make life impossible if we stay, make us pay to leave." He'd barely boarded when the third whistle sounded, and the train pulled away.

Estes stayed on the platform with Bernard, Solly, and Sera until the rumbling sound of rolling steel faded away.

✳

After Chaim and Joseph departed with their shares of the distillery profit, the czar raised taxes again, this time to ninety percent. Bernard had stopped smuggling. Much too risky now. The censors, moreover, continued to pillage the bookshop, so Estes brought her favorites home and reread cherished passages before giving them away at market. Their family lived with less.

Bernard lifted his face to the sky and whispered the Shema before entering the cemetery next to the Great Wooden Shul. Alone with the dead, he knelt in front of his parents' graves. He pictured his father as he was before the consumption—the calloused hands wrapped around his own, his lifted brow making some point, his voice so often full of mirth. A cottony ball of dandelion seed landed near his foot. He waited for his father to speak and hoped for something profound—a fourth principle.

It's time, Bernard. We'll go with you.

He took a jar out of his pocket, bent over, and scooped up a handful of earth from each grave.

5

Bernard joined Estes and the children at the bookshop, and they all walked to the library. He'd go back to the distillery for Young Ferd and the wagon later, so they could drive home.

"It's perfect, Bernard," Estes said about his plan to start an evening chess club. "For appearances. Doesn't the square feel strange without the Leving's Shoes sign? A man from Kiev sits in Papa's work chair, and three children share my old room."

He touched her shoulder and whispered, "Soon enough, another family will live in our home too."

Estes studied her children. Solly's arms swung freely with his loose-jointed stride. Sera, who marched along with short, efficient steps, had recently asked for their permission to attend worker discussion meetings held in private homes. Leib had told them about these sessions, but what would it do for their family, with their departure so near, except bring more scrutiny? Instead, they'd enrolled Sera in a class for promising artists.

When the library door closed behind them, silence replaced the noise from the street. Four men concentrated on their chess games at a long table set up in the foyer. Estes wondered aloud if Leib would show up.

"Leib does everything like nothing else exists. Now it's the worker's meetings."

Bernard and Solly joined the men, and Estes checked instinctively for Moshe, but another man stood behind the checkout counter. She and Sera went to the back of the library and entered the same, narrow room where the Russian reading class had met all those years before. Estes counted eleven easels.

A young man, balding, with the bristly beginnings of a beard, greeted them. "You must be Sera. I'm Yacob Jablonski. I'm so glad you came. The vivid drawings your mother showed me are remarkable without formal training. Mrs. Garfinkle, we artists work in a limited space here, but given Sera's age, you're welcome to stay and observe."

Estes felt Sera's tension. "I'll browse, Mr. Jablonski. Thank you." She resisted glancing back as she left.

Over the following sessions, Estes collected a few impressions: Jablonski's prominent display of Sera's drawings by the entrance; Sera's excitement about this class, more than she had ever shown for books and learning from Estes; and Meyer Levinson, the handsome young man, Estes guessed around eighteen, a foot taller than their daughter, bending over Sera in private conversation when class ended.

Estes strained to hear them, reminded of her own parents' surveillance when she and Bernard had first met. She was sixteen then, and Sera was just twelve now. This must be nothing more than two artists interested in each other's work. Still, she worried about the way Sera smiled at Meyer and her habit of quoting his nihilistic utterances that eerily resembled Bazarov's in *Fathers and Children*.

Estes decided to invite the young man to a family dinner. They could assess his intentions and, if necessary, control the situation. Sera immediately agreed. "You'll see what an honest and well-educated person he is." When the date arrived, Meyer appeared with an armload of gifts—charcoal and another sketch pad for Sera, a thick volume of Dickens for Solly, and a framed picture of the Niemen he'd painted for Bernard and Estes.

The young man appeared amused when Bernard recited a blessing, unaware it was a compromise between the lengthier prayers Bernard would have preferred and Estes's secular desires. Sera never took her eyes off Meyer. He *was* handsome—long brown hair, a Roman nose, a strong chin.

Their daughter wasn't alone in her adoration. Meyer was also quite taken with himself. Estes and Bernard made eye contact—*this fellow is insufferable*—but, for Sera's sake, neither of them challenged him or even tried to redirect the conversation. They listened politely, while Meyer asked nothing about the bookshop or the distillery. He slouched in his chair and showed no interest in what they thought.

Meyer sat up, though, when the discussion turned to art. "For my ninth birthday, my stepfather took me to Warsaw. He recognized my talent and wanted me to observe Chełmoński and his friends in their Realist Forge at the European Hotel. He'd finished *Indian Summer*—the peasant girl with her dirty feet contemplating the fleeting season. It wasn't a stale portrait but real art of the people with life in flux." Meyer's face suddenly flushed with emotion. "Yet, the authorities want to strap their autocracy onto our backs. The time is coming when the masses will rise up, and no amount of censorship will stop us."

Following dinner, they shared reading Dickens aloud. Even Bernard, with his rudimentary English after a year of Estes's tutoring, took a paragraph. When the book came around to Sera's friend, however, Meyer said someone else could take his turn, and Estes suspected he didn't read English. What else explained a generous gesture from such a conceited young man? Meyer yawned and glanced about the house the entire time.

When the evening finally ended, Sera walked out with their guest. Through the window, Meyer looked excited when Sera pointed toward town.

"Did you enjoy dinner tonight?" Bernard asked Estes when they were alone.

"Yes. The kugel was excellent, but the Meyer rather disagreeable, and too large a portion. What was I thinking? Nothing about this evening has been reassuring. If everything else were perfect, I'd still leave Horodno just to escape from Meyer."

"He's too focused on himself to cause any real harm."

"Maybe, but how does Sera tolerate him?" Their daughter was probably just flattered by the attention. Estes pushed aside the troubling image of her headstrong Sera, now transformed into a devoted follower, ready to do whatever her leader asked.

6

April 14, 1885
My Beloved Daughter,

Good news! We survived the journey. Freida and Hirsh stayed in New York with Joseph and Eleanor when we continued on to Indiana, Pennsylvania. Uncle Simon bought a large house there, plus another building big enough for Herman's business and a hardware store for Bernard! Papa has already set up a corner to make shoes. I think about your promise every day. I miss you and Bernard and the children too much. There are so many immigrants, we don't feel like outsiders. We count the days until we are all reunited this summer.

Love, Mama and Papa

While Bernard and the children went out to brush Young Ferd, she read the letter once more. In transit for five weeks, she'd read it multiple times since it arrived several days ago, but she couldn't read away such an obvious breach. "We count the days until we are all reunited this summer." Mama had included the address and instructions about trains from New York.

All the precautions—giving up writing, hiding her old journals, their methodical planning. Maybe Borishenko didn't monitor their mail, but why, right after the postman delivered Mama's letter, had he summoned them to report to his office?

Bernard and the children returned. Sera sat on the living room floor and sketched while Solly sprawled next to her with a book. Estes led Bernard back outside, away from the twins.

"Perhaps tomorrow, he'll really interrogate us?"

"Even if he read the letter, our plan remains a good one. This is an opportunity for us if he actually shows himself. We'll study our adversary like the chess champion studies a position and still have time to adjust if needed."

Maybe, but she spotted a flaw in Bernard's analogy. Fallen pieces can be set up again for the next game, but in this struggle, Borishenko wouldn't give them a second chance if something went wrong.

✳

On the way to the Office of State Security, Estes tried to keep her mind off the impending meeting and concentrated instead on the pain in her foot. Sera and Solly held hands and walked in front of her and Bernard.

"Will the general meet with us this time? Maybe he'll let us hold his sword again, even though Sera dropped it. He gave us chocolate too."

"This isn't about that, Solly. This isn't a family picnic." Sera acted so much older now. "Meyer says the revolution will wipe out the Borishenkos. He's an evil man, and all you talk about is his stupid sword and some cheap chocolates."

When they stopped in front of the building, Sera put her brother in a headlock and tousled his hair, a bit roughly. He reached for the top of her head, but she immediately swatted his hand away.

Bernard put a hand on each of their shoulders. "Remember what we talked about."

"Answer questions only with 'yes' or 'no.'"

Estes waited for a maxim from Meyer Levinson, relieved when none came. The boy seemed to have lost interest, a welcome development. He had only exchanged pleasantries with Sera before the last class.

Inside the Office of State Security, the humorless gatekeeper called out two names. A middle-aged man with bowed shoulders like a water carrier and a heavy-set woman who gripped his arm to stay upright shuffled to their meeting. A Russian dressed in a black suit wrote notes in a book. He snapped it shut when his turn came. The Garfinkles waited, and just as Estes concluded this must be another false meeting, the clerk called her name.

Borishenko did not stand to greet them. Her eyes swept the room—the sword, samovar, neat desktop, just as before. The general's sleeve still pinned to his uniform, the medals. Two more bookcases had been added, filled with some of her forbidden texts.

The children sat between her and Bernard, and Borishenko observed them in silence. He did not offer tea, nor acknowledge Bernard. Solly stared at the floor. Sera looked past the general, perhaps at the sword on his wall. Bernard kept his hands clasped in his lap.

"What a pleasure to see you again, Mrs. Garfinkle. It's been much too long. We've been so busy, and I apologize for any inconvenience. I must thank you for the loan of these books." He waved at his full shelves. "It's important to understand the enemy."

"Loan? Do you intend to return the volumes you borrowed, General?"

"Mr. Garfinkle, you married an erudite woman, as I'm sure you're aware. And you know why you're here?"

"I can assure you Estes didn't save the letters from Gesia Gelfman."

"Of course. I have no doubt she destroyed them. When that happened is another question. Did you ever read them?"

"Estes read them to me. Communication between friends. Gesia was our midwife."

"The names Mrs. Garfinkle recalled were quite helpful, by the way. We have dealt with all of them."

Estes wanted to ask what happened to them. *Olga Markinova, Ivan Karlovitch, Mikail Petrovitch, Ekaterina Tumanova.* She glanced at the twins. Solly's serious and attentive expression didn't change, but Sera looked at her with widened eyes.

The general again let silence cover the room.

"Now, there's also the matter of a Leib Fetterman. One of your workers, I believe, Mr. Garfinkle?"

"Yes."

"He's been associating with radicals. A discussion group to improve the lives of workers, they call it. Talk usually triggers action."

Bernard said nothing.

"It might help your family's situation if you kept us apprised of Fetterman's activities and statements." Borishenko waited for a reply.

Bernard pulled in his lips, released them, and spoke slowly. "We talk about making vodka, General. I don't pry into my workers' private lives."

"Think it over. It would be a shame to close the best vodka distillery in Grodno."

He stood and walked behind them. He put his hand on the back of Estes's chair. She leaned forward to increase the distance between them.

"Now that your parents have emigrated, Mrs. Garfinkle, you must miss them. Of course, we let them go. Take it as a sign of my goodwill. Did you promise to join them this summer?"

"Will you let us go, too, General?"

"I want to help you. These anti-Jewish laws will continue, and conditions for your family will deteriorate. Predictions about the eventual solution to Russia's Jewish problem may be correct on two points. Some will starve here, and others will emigrate, but regarding the optimistic belief that the rest of you will convert and assimilate, I must disagree. Gelfmans will rise up in all our cities, spreading dissent in minor distilleries and great factories." He stepped behind Sera's chair and spoke into her ear. "And in art classes like yours, Sera."

Sera pulled away from him and Solly twisted half-around in his chair. Estes and Bernard stood and faced their interrogator.

"She's only twelve, General, and doesn't understand any of this. Is there something else you want of us?" She could have reached out and ripped off the medals hanging like chandeliers from his chest.

Bernard pressed Sera's shoulder down when she began to rise.

"I'm giving you a way out, Mrs. Garfinkle, a path to reunite with your parents. I've shown goodwill by not arresting you for those letters. Do what's right for your family. We want information—about certain people who frequent the bookshop, what they're reading, associates and activities of Leib Fetterman and Meyer Levinson. If you help us, you'll be helping yourselves. You'll die in Russia unless you cooperate."

He returned to the other side of the desk, reached into an opaque glass jar, and pulled out a chocolate. "What a good son. You must be very proud of him. In a few years, he'll make a fine soldier." He stretched his one arm out and held the candy in front of Solly.

Solly stood between his parents. "No, thank you, General Borishenko."

Sera pushed Bernard's hand off her shoulder and rose next to her twin brother.

7

Summer arrived in June with oppressive humidity and violent wind. Hours before the sun peeked above the horizon, Estes and Bernard lay in bed, too hot to sleep. The gusts from the south provided little relief.

In exactly twelve days, they'd be on their way. Since the debacle with Borishenko last month, she wished him real harm. Bernard believed God gave the commandments for such moments, but she found no comfort in his theology.

When Borishenko ordered them to come in for photographs, they'd stood in front of the Office of State Security, the camera on a tripod in the middle of Police Street, the photographer bent under a black shroud. A second man rerouted people behind him. Even Solly hadn't managed a smile.

Now, heat lightening momentarily revealed her son peering into the bedroom through the open door.

"What is it, Solly?"

"Sera made me promise not to tell."

Bernard sat up. "It's important to keep a promise unless it causes greater harm than breaking it."

"But how can I know?" he cried.

Estes rolled out of bed, passed Solly, and looked in on Sera, reassured to find her daughter asleep. *Why was she under a blanket on such a night?* She went closer and tapped the hollow gourd with imperfect features.

Between choked sobs, Solly told them, "Sera left to meet Meyer near General Borishenko's office."

Bernard leapt from bed. "How long ago?"

"I'm not sure. Less than an hour, I think."

"Wait with Solly. Maybe I can still catch her on the road."

"We'll all go," Estes said.

They hastily dressed, and Bernard hitched Young Ferd to the wagon. Wind-blown dust pelted Estes's face and, even with Young Ferd's fast trot, the familiar ride seemed to take forever. Landmarks appeared as eerie ghosts when lightening flashed in the southern sky. No sign of Sera. Past Market Square, Bernard secured the horse to a post on Police Street, a block north of the Office of State Security.

"On foot from here."

Estes struggled to keep up as the cursed wind blew her sideways. Another blast of light revealed Sera across the street, in front of the Catholic basilica.

"There she is!"

Sera had one arm raised, her fist closed. Night swallowed her again, and glass shattered. They started across the street, angling toward the church, before a deafening explosion sent them all to the ground.

Estes pushed herself onto her hands and knees and screamed, "Sera!"

An orange tongue of flame, a demon's taunt, answered, darting through a jagged horse-sized opening blown out of Borishenko's wall. A roiling wave of debris and smoke spread out from the blast. Sera emerged from the growing plume of destruction, coughing and gagging.

"Thank God!" Estes stood and embraced her daughter. Alarmed citizens exited nearby houses. Fire bells rang.

Bernard rushed them away through the gathering crowd of panicked residents. Estes kept her hand on Sera's back. When they reached the wagon, Estes wiped the grime off Sera's face with her sleeve while Bernard checked her for injuries.

Estes hugged her again, then gripped Sera's shoulders and studied her face. "Are you hurt?"

"No, Mama." Sera's shoulders sagged and she looked down, with her hands at her side.

"What were you thinking? You've ruined everything!"

Sera straightened, looked right at Estes, and said with conviction, "I had to do something."

"Listen," Bernard said. "A time to talk about this will come, but here's what we have to do now. Solly and Sera, take the wagon back. Pack one duffel each. You'll find them under our bed. A change of clothes for travel and one extra item only. We'll be home soon. We're leaving Horodno."

He hoisted Solly into the driver's seat and Sera climbed up beside him. The wind roared.

"Quickly now."

Solly shook the reins and Young Ferd clopped toward home.

"We need two horses and Eliza's carriage immediately, Estes. Leib will pick them up from her shortly. Eliza will confirm our secure route to Vilne."

"Vilne, but—"

"We'll trade for fresh horses on the way and Leib will pick up Eliza's on the way back. We leave this morning."

"What if she's not home?"

"She'll be there."

"How can you know? What about our plan?" She couldn't believe this was happening.

"Trust me, Estes."

The angry wind whipped smoke and fire across Police Street. Bernard ran east, away from her and the spreading catastrophe.

When Estes left Eliza's house, the shock settled in her chest. She said goodbye to her mentor's decisive tone and erect bearing, to Market Square and her old house, to the Horodno Bookshop. Halfway home, breathing hard and sweating from exertion, Estes stopped. Sick to her stomach, she took in the clang of bells and the razing of Horodno.

✳

"Cut it all, Bernard."

He gathered her waist-length hair like a sheaf of wheat and buried his face in its thickness. "If each strand represented a year of your life, you'd be older than Methuselah."

"It's only hair." She turned around and looked at his naked chin, settled back, and awaited the scissors. As Bernard cut, Solly collected the hair into a bucket. Next to her brother, Sera folded her arms across her chest as the bucket filled.

"This is all your fault, Sera." Solly had never spoken to his sister so harshly. Sera, who never let any slight go unanswered, did not respond.

Bernard kissed Estes's shorn head. "Round as a ball."

She scarfed herself, and when she did the same for Sera, her daughter squeezed her eyes shut and the muscles of her face hardened. Sera's appalling action and their dire situation had opened a chasm between them.

"I almost forgot." Bernard retrieved a brown leather cap and gave it to Solly. "For our adventures."

Their son turned over the cap in his hands and admired the stitching. He pulled it on. "No one will know it's me, Papa."

"Sera, bury the hair in the garden. Both of you—water the horse. Put out hay and grain. Shlomo will come for him this afternoon. Keep watch and let us know as soon as you spot Leib." He waited until they'd gone outside.

"Jacob says our guide in Vilne is the best. And he gave me two more contacts just in case his first choice isn't available."

"Can we believe him?"

Bernard looked at her sharply as if searching for something. "I'm absolutely sure."

She couldn't let fear and distress overwhelm her, not now, so she forced herself to repeat their inn stops and traveling distances. "Three nights on the road into Vilne. So much for all our advance scheming. How did you change our plan so quickly?"

"Emergency escape strategy."

"You never told me we had one."

"Set up after the meeting with Borishenko. Our friends agreed to be available every day until our planned date. In case we thought he might arrest you."

"But how would you know?"

"Eliza has a contact. But that's not important now. She arranged to have horses and her carriage always ready to go. Thank God our helpers stayed in place, even on this crazy morning. No one could have ever predicted this. Perhaps if we'd confided in the children, if they'd known about our plan to leave, this never would have happened."

"You should have confided in me, Bernard."

"I didn't want to worry you unnecessarily. Anyway, we can't risk using the forged exit passes now because the *Lady Odessa* doesn't sail for three weeks—much too long to hide. Jacob will keep the receipt for our berth—a useful decoy. We don't know how much added scrutiny this mess will cause, but why would Borishenko suspect we had any involvement, or that we've left by carriage for Vilne. We'll be out of the country before he even knows we're gone."

She pulled her hands from his, ashamed and indignant that he thought she needed protection.

"I'm sorry, Estes."

Now wasn't the time to talk about her feelings. Solly alerted them as Leib approached. The four of them each grabbed a bag and left the house.

Bernard had stuffed in an oilcloth, large enough to wrap around the four of them, and nestled a jar of dirt among his clothes. Dirt! Her parents waited in the future. His resided here forever.

Solly brought a braid from Alte Ferd's mane, and Sera took two filled sketchbooks. Estes left behind all her journals, years of observations and thoughts about life and her place in it all. Only *Jane Eyre* would travel west with her. She'd need her courage.

The growing cataclysm at daybreak brought up nausea again, this time mixed with rage. She had a sudden urge to slap Sera, to draw out some emotion, but their predicament and her own complicity stopped her.

"Going my way?" Leib hopped down and swung open the door of Eliza's carriage. He secured the four bags on top and settled into the driver's seat. The horses headed northeast, and the family's escape began, barely two hours after the explosion.

✳

Just an hour from Horodno, they encountered the patrol. Estes saw them approaching in formation, their leader in front, the soldiers riding in pairs behind. No place to hide, no other road to turn off. It would all end here.

She waited for the command to stop, the questioning—what would she tell them? But the men never slowed their cantor, and in a moment they had passed. Bernard leaned back and yelled, "They must be on their way to help with the fire. They're not looking for us."

She hoped he was right. But how would they know for sure unless they were caught by a more curious patrol or a prying town policeman? For three days she maintained her vigilance, even when they stopped for the night. They passed dense forests, lakes, bogs, and fields of grain, with only light traffic on the road. Solly rested with his head on Estes's lap. Sera leaned against the carriage and stared without interest at the passing scenery. Bernard spent time up top with Leib, and the countryside rolled by.

Eliza Orzeszkowa's name worked magic at her safe inns. The first night, in the spa town of Druskininkai, a taciturn keeper smiled and offered his two best rooms when Estes mentioned the Polish writer.

The next night, in Varena, a middle-aged couple bowed and called them special guests. In the morning, they chewed on hard biscuits and got back on the road with fresh horses before the other guests stirred.

The third day's journey was the longest, ten hours to Lentvaris. When they reached their lodgings, the Jewish matron exclaimed, "Eliza Orzeszkowa, so good to the Jews!"

8

As at the other inns, Estes and Sera shared one room, Bernard, Leib, and Solly another. After they settled, their host delivered trays of food and wine. Later, Leib took out his small chess set, and he and Solly sat on one of the beds and played.

After Solly went to bed, Bernard went to check on Estes and Sera. His daughter slept facing the wall. Estes sat on the edge of the bed, studying one of the sketch pads Sera had packed.

He sat next to her as she slowly flipped the pages—a chronicle of life in over a hundred drawings: Herman's hands with the deft fingers that could shape leather into comfortable shoes; Doris and Freida cutting vegetables in the Levings' kitchen, Freida's eyes focused down on the cutting surface, Doris's fixed on her sister; Bernard leading Young Ferd from the barn; Solly with an armload of firewood; the faces at a Leving Shabes, candles on the table casting each in light and shadow; Estes looking up from a book—ordinary scenes culled from their life, yet remarkable when drawn with such intricate detail.

Estes repacked the sketch pad, and Bernard led her outside, his arm around her waist. They looked for a few minutes at the stars without speaking. *Estes must be in shock too.* How had they missed this?

"Tomorrow, we meet our guide out of Russia."

"A euphemism for a smuggler, Bernard. If they're not looking for us, why couldn't we get on the train here and go directly to the border instead.

"A lot could have happened in three days. We just don't know what's going on, and crossing the border on our own without getting caught . . . We could look for help, but no telling who we'd end up with."

"I should get back to Sera." Estes embraced him and said goodnight.

When Bernard returned to his room, Leib was studying a position on the board.

"Let's play, Bernard. It will take your mind off your troubles."

"I can't concentrate, Leib."

"Who knows if we'll ever play again."

"A reason for you also to get out of Russia."

Thus far, Bernard had avoided talking about what had happened. It was already risky enough for Leib, escorting them almost to Vilne, but after they emptied the wine bottle, the story came out.

"I heard a bomb started the fire. Blowing up Borishenko's office! Consider the courage it took." Leib grabbed his wrist. "Our enemy is ruthless and irredeemable. I should have thought of it myself."

"Does such a vicious act make us any better than them?"

"Yes, we're better. Don't become confused by tactics."

"But the deceit, the fire, people homeless, maybe some burned or dead." Sera had driven a thorn deep into his flesh, and he didn't yet understand his daughter's sin.

Leib turned both hands up. "Unfortunate, but not Sera's intent. I'd blame Borishenko. Let's review your plan."

When Bernard finished, Leib whistled. "Rabbi Jacob Rosenblum and his smugglers. It's the quiet ones who surprise you. It makes me happy to think about you, Chaim, and Joseph in America." He reached into his pocket, took out the revolver he'd used in Balta, and pressed it into Bernard's hand. "But you have to get there first."

Bernard pushed it away. "Thanks, Leib, but no. We'll be across the border soon. Who would I shoot?"

Leib cataloged a long list of potential targets. Later, when Bernard fell into a fitful sleep, he dreamed of the Great Wooden Shul. The survivor for centuries, despite nature and man, billowed smoke and fire.

In the morning, when Bernard peeked into Estes's room, she had her arms around Sera, who nestled against her. He flashed his fingers twice. Twenty minutes later, they gathered to say goodbye to Leib. When his friend offered to guide them across the border himself, Bernard had an answer. "Return Eliza's horses and carriage. What will you call your distillery?"

"The name won't change, but it will be strange without you. They might take it away from us, but our real work now, and Ledl agrees, is to organize. When Jewish and Russian workers join the common struggle, the czar's days are over."

His friend's zeal, the conviction in his voice, his unyielding eye, reminded Bernard of the most dogmatic rabbis.

"Won't another czar just take his place?"

"It's possible, but nothing could be worse than what we have now."

Leib embraced them all and climbed up behind the horses. Framed between two clusters of towering pine, Leib Fetterman waved and vanished from their sight.

✳

They timed their departure to arrive after dark. The matron's young driver took them into Vilne. The entire way, he dropped loosely connected thoughts, like wheat from a torn sack. Bernard cut him off mid-sentence, pressing several coins into his palm.

He'd memorized the directions Jacob had given him, starting from the Vilne cathedral. A golden cross topped the adjacent white bell tower. He held Sera's hand as they walked on a worn cobbled street dominated by cigar smoke from outdoor cafés. A policeman slumped on his horse and yawned. A cluster of soldiers laughed among themselves.

They followed alleys bounded by centuries-old buildings and eras of architecture—Roman, Gothic, Renaissance, baroque—held together by crumbling mortar and unified by the smell of decay. He glanced over his shoulder to spot Estes and Solly, fifty paces back.

He opened the heavy wood door of a three-story building and waited inside with Sera. When Estes and Solly arrived, Bernard led them up the winding stairs to the top floor. He knocked on number nine, and the door opened a crack.

"Who sent you?" a man asked in Yiddish.

"A friend from Horodno."

The middle-aged man peered down the dingy hallway before waving them into his apartment. Bernard's first impression of Jacob's best smuggler—short, fleshy, bald, with a belly that hung over his belt—did not reassure.

"Lev," he said, sticking out his hand. He cut off Bernard's introductions. "You have something for me?"

Bernard handed him a leather packet, and Lev ushered them to a torn sofa. Two dirty lanterns illuminated a knee-high table.

He looked at Estes. "Bad foot, eh?"

"Just lead us safely out of Russia."

"That's my job." He sat across from them in a rickety chair and spread out the contents of the packet, which included a wad of rubles and a note from Jacob. He read it aloud. "Lev, take the very best care of my friends. Everything they need is enclosed: identity cards, open rail passage from Tilsit to Hamburg, and four tickets for the *Ocean Voyager*."

He held up a sealed envelope. "What's this?"

"A letter for us from Rabbi Rosenblum."

"Uh-huh. Is your name really Saul Garry? It doesn't matter. This will be a tricky one, with children, and I've done hundreds of crossings. Only one time, my passengers lost their nerve at the border and came back." His eyes shifted between Bernard and Estes.

"Look here, an advance payment." He picked up the rubles. "Is there more, just in case? Never hurts to be prepared."

"You've been well paid to guide us to the border. If you do right by us, we won't forget."

"Fair enough. Rabbi Jacob sent us a smart one. Now, about choosing our route—sometimes I follow the river to Jubarkas, but my favorite is southwest to Kibart. I have certificates to cross the bridge into Prussia there, but those border towns are so tiny the Russian guards recognize everyone who lives there. If you could just stroll across the border, I'd be out of a job."

Bernard gathered up the documents, slid them back into the leather packet, and stuffed it into his pocket. He'd keep it against his body, even when he slept.

"We're not going anywhere near the checkpoint," Lev said. "We'll have some walking to reach the Liepona River." He looked at Estes's foot. "River, ha! A stream no wider than this room, but the most unfortunate torrential rains this month have made a hell of a mess. Historic flooding, they call it . . . Hey, wait a minute." He scratched his head. "You folks left four days ago?" He picked up a Russian newspaper from the floor. "This arrived today. The first news out of Horodno since the ruckus down there."

He studied them, looking back at the paper several times. "I take everyone the rabbi sends, but just suppose this has anything to do with you. A hefty reward complicates our situation."

"They'll be searching elsewhere," Bernard said.

"Maybe, but something this important? I'm not talking about the Russian border patrols. Predictable. Not much motivation, and they can't pursue you into Prussia. And I'm not worried about the tiny stations, but they're probably watching a big one like Vilne, with all its connecting trains. You folks were smart or lucky coming in by carriage, and at night, but if I'd known about you, we could have met in Lentvaris and saved a bit of time and trouble."

He shook the paper. "Even without this, the authorities in Horodno most likely telegraphed about you anyway. But we can slip out of Vilne easily enough. It's the bounty hunters and thieves on the border. Scoundrels. Too bad the one they captured didn't hold out a few more days and give you time to escape."

Sera covered her face and groaned.

Lev examined them again. "You're different than the picture, though. Took my sharp eye to match you up, and only because you're all together. Too bad about the foot, but you're lucky Jacob uses me. Don't worry. You'll arrive in the promised land. I've got my contacts bought off, as dependable as a gold ruble, but we'll have to do something about the limp. Even a well-fed bear might be tempted if we stick our head in his mouth. Best take some rest before we leave. But first, eat."

Lev brought over four bowls and spoons and set up a sloppy table. He passed around unappealing-looking beets, a cream sauce, and stale bread. Bernard broke off pieces and passed them around. Everyone but Sera managed to swallow a few bites. No one tried the beets.

Lev led them to a room with two beds, no windows, and the smell of dead rodents. "Double up. I don't often host whole families. It's the husbands that sneak across and send back money for exit passes or just disappear. Here's a basin to wash up."

He pointed at two chamber pots. "You fill them. I'll handle the emptying."

Without undressing, Sera fell on one bed, Solly the other.

Bernard and Estes rejoined the smuggler, who leaned back on the couch and yawned. "Can't sleep, huh? I understand. I'm just doing some figuring. Given the events in Horodno, we might need more compensation than you thought, Mr. Garry." He sprang up and passed the rumpled newspaper to Bernard. "In case you're homesick."

"I'll be back." He went to the door. "Preparation for the trip." His footsteps faded on the stairs.

"I don't trust him."

"Jacob sent us."

"What's in his letter?"

Bernard slowly exhaled. "He said to wait until we reach America to read it."

Estes sat next to him on the sofa, the newspaper between them. In the front-page picture of their family, Bernard and Solly stared at their shoes. She looked west over the eye of the camera. Sera glared, her brow furrowed.

The caption said: *Missing! Fugitives! The Office of State Security is looking for these persons of interest related to the recent tragedy in Grodno. A reward of three hundred rubles is offered for information that leads to the location of the Garfinkle family.*

"Lev! He's gone to the authorities. We have to leave."

"It's a risk, but he's our best chance now. He's a smuggler, not a bounty hunter. In his own way, he takes pride in his work." Bernard flipped the paper over. "We should try and get some rest."

"Go to the children, Bernard."

"Estes . . ."

"No, I want to read this."

FIRE! GENERAL BORISHENKO DEAD!

On June 25, before dawn, a crude bomb exploded in Grodno Gubernia's Office of State Security, killing General Borishenko and starting the conflagration that burned one-half of the city. Officials believe the bundled sticks of dynamite thrown through the window caught the general by surprise. A short fuse to the blasting cap didn't give him enough time to react before the bomb detonated. A witness reported hearing the window shatter and the explosion a few seconds later. It's possible the Crimean War hero, who gave an arm for his country, bravely grabbed the dynamite in an attempt to throw it back. Borishenko, renowned for his long hours and strict enforcement of the law, was also an avid book collector. His office library, along with a can of lamp oil, provided fuel for the blaze.

GRODNO DESTROYED

Fierce winds whipped the fire, which began on Police Street, into a mountain of flame that ripped throughout neighborhoods north of the Niemen. In three tragic days the inferno destroyed six shuln, ten churches, and the home for orphans, along with two-thousand houses spread among twenty-two streets and alleys. Writer Eliza Orzeszkowa, whose own house was consumed, has taken charge of the relief effort. Homeless residents have moved into the local barracks, which are empty for the summer. Churches and shuln which escaped the destruction have also provided temporary shelter. Miraculously, only three fatalities have been reported, though scores of people are being treated for burns, some life-threatening.

INVESTIGATION

General Pavelvitch, who is leading the investigation, reports that Meyer Levinson, a radical known by authorities to espouse extreme views, is in custody. He was injured in the explosion and captured not far from the scene. Levinson, eighteen, confessed immediately that he built and threw the bomb alone. Detectives, however, after several days of intense interrogation, discovered that an accomplice is still at large. Esther Garfinkle, proprietress of Horodno Books, and her daughter are wanted for questioning. Mrs. Garfinkle, who is crippled in one foot and uses a cane, was an associate of Gesia Gelfman, one of the assassins of the czar.

The paper identified the destroyed businesses and houses of worship. It didn't mention the names of the dead. Old? Too slow to get out? Infants among them? She needed to know. How else could she understand the enormity of what Sera had done?

"The Choral Shul survived, except for the attached prayer house, and so did the library. The book and shoe shop are both gone. The entire square, all the businesses and homes—ash," she said quietly.

"The Wooden Shul?" His voice choked with emotion.

This is what he cares about now? She swallowed the bitter resentment that rose in her throat and glanced back at the page. "The Great Wooden Shul burned to the ground."

9

Estes woke up on the sofa. Hours might have passed. Her neck had stiffened. Sleep noises came from the bedroom. She stood unsteadily when footsteps sounded on the stairs.

Lev came in with another man, a younger version of himself but thin with a full head of hair. "My brother, Max. He's a mute. I got all the words, and he got the brains."

Max blushed. Estes nearly sobbed with relief.

"We're leaving soon. We'll pick up the train in the morning."

"You said they'd be watching."

"In Vilne." He scratched his belly. "You paid me to worry. Gather your family now."

Five minutes later, they stood by the door with their bags.

"Two things. First, this will go best if you trust me completely. I don't usually tell my clients this. Best to keep things strictly professional, but since you folks have special circumstances . . . My brother and I do this because they arrested our parents for political activity and murdered them in prison. This isn't just a job. We live to help folks in your situation. It's a slight measure of revenge for what happened to us.

"Now, the second issue. The Russians are looking for a family of four, so Max will lead with our small bag and the two children each carrying their own. Mrs. Garry goes with me, and Mr. Garry, you're the caboose with two bags. Mrs. Garry, you won't use a cane because I'll be on your left like this." He put an arm around her waist. "Your left hand on my shoulder. That's good. Lucky we're the right height. Okay, let's go." Lev opened the door and paused at the threshold. "Keep us in view, Mr. Garry. Smile, everyone, you're leaving Russia."

⁂

A light rain fell as Estes slid along a muddy alley ripe with the stench of garbage. Lev supported her, and she appreciated the slow pace without any luggage. She didn't need to look back. Bernard wouldn't lose them. Ahead, Solly took his sister's hand, and Estes imagined him trying to pump life back into her. Sera's usual bold walk had turned into a defeated trudge, but they'd drag her across the border if necessary. Lev guided Estes by her waist when they changed direction. *Was any part of his story real?*

Max, in the lead, avoided the major streets and stuck to a warren of crisscrossed alleys. They passed a few scruffy cats indifferent to the baying of dogs and walked for thirty minutes. When they emerged into a square across from a sprawling inn, he led them into the attached barn. She spotted two wagons with slatted wood sides through the open back doors. Beyond the wagons, a narrow road trailed into the woods.

The smugglers walked two horses out from a stall and hitched one to each wagon. "This is where my brother leaves us," Lev told them. "He'll be on the train from Vilne tomorrow and will signal me before we board at Ponary if he spots any problems." Max patted Solly on the shoulder and departed.

"I'll spread some dry hay in the back. Each of you grab one of those leather blankets. If the young lady would hop on with Mr. Garry, and Mrs. Garry and son with me, we'll be on our way."

It had stopped raining. She and Solly snuggled for warmth and lay back against their bags. "Solly, would you like me to read to you?"

"It's too dark, Mama. You won't be able to see."

"I don't need the book. It's about a determined young woman. It's the first story that convinced me girls could be brave, too, and it's the first book I shared with your father."

"Before he could read?"

"Yes."

How many times had she read this to Solly? Yet he pretended he'd never heard it before. Another of their games. She ruffled his hair and closed her eyes.

"There was no possibility of taking a walk that day. The cold winter wind had brought with it sombre clouds, and a rain so penetrating, that outdoor exercise was now impossible."

Estes recited through the remainder of their two-hour journey, laying out the plot and tone, if not the exact words. Under the circumstances,

Charlotte Brontë wouldn't mind her editing. The familiar story and clop of Bernard's horse behind them made her hopeful.

"Some tale," Lev said as they approached the station. "I wish I could hear the rest."

Two boys, Solly's age, came off the platform and approached Lev. Without a word, he put a coin into each of their palms. The boys unloaded the wagon and drove the horses back the way they'd come.

✳

An hour after sunrise, a soft rain started again. Wisps of fog rising from the track matched the slate-gray sky. They had the Ponary platform to themselves. Estes, Lev, and Solly stood, looking for the approaching train. Bernard sat on a bench with an arm around Sera.

Solly covered his ears when the loud whistle sounded. Max popped his head out of a window and beckoned Lev, who refused the conductor's help and clambered up. Solly passed him their bags, grabbed two steel bars to pull himself off the platform, then reached his hand out to Estes. Farther down the platform, Bernard boarded behind Sera.

The heavyset conductor took the tickets from Lev and smiled with recognition. "A few hours to Kovne, four more until the afternoon run to Kybart. Hang onto your bags. Going to Prussia?" His eyelids twitched.

"Privacy?" Lev asked.

"Yep."

Lev pulled out some bills, and the conductor stuffed them into his pocket. They followed him past a few dozing passengers. In the next car, Max gestured to Bernard, and Lev ducked across the aisle into a compartment with two cushioned benches. He sat on one side and Estes and Solly on the other.

"They're good with Max." Lev scratched his stubbled chin. "Too bad so many stops on these two lines. But you still might be in time to cross over before dark."

"Wouldn't it be better at night?"

"Some agents might say yes, and they're the ones that lose clients. I told you, the Russian patrols are easy to avoid. Max and I will lead you to a crossing, but after that, you'll be on your own." He smacked a fist into his other hand. "You won't see them, but they'll intercept you before you make it near the border station—nocturnal predators. They have some arrangement with the Prussians, a payoff in exchange for free rein at night. During the day, they disperse and hide. Better for you to stay concealed in the woods and cross in the morning."

"Mama, can we read some more?"

"Yes. And now I can see." She pulled *Jane Eyre* from her bag.

"Wouldn't mind hearing a bit more, myself," Lev said. "Who did you say wrote it?"

"A woman wrote it, pretending to be a man," Solly told him.

"Well, if that doesn't beat all."

✳

Lev ushered them through the Kovne station. Estes tensed when two soldiers standing by an exit door looked at her and Solly, but the men half-saluted the smuggler and continued their conversation.

They avoided the brown puddles scattered across the rail yard. She glanced back. Max walked next to Bernard, who held Sera's arm. Would anyone take this girl, with her headscarf and eyes on the ground, for the one in the photo?

Lev entered the broad street at the far end of the rail yard. Houses with white walls and red roofs rose above narrow shops, and laundry hung from recessed balconies. He took them around the side of one of the houses, up four steps, and fished a key from his pocket.

Estes adjusted her eyes to the relative darkness in the dank hallway. Lev fumbled with another key and cursed when it fell and clanged on the brick floor. She put both her hands around Solly's shoulders and held him tight. Bernard, Sera, and Max crowded against them.

Lev got the door open, stood aside, and motioned them in. "This is our home for the next four hours. Max is going back to the station to keep an eye on the departure time and make sure it's all clear for us."

Lev grabbed plates and utensils from an open shelf and set them on a thick slab of wood with four stumps for legs. He removed cheese, corn salad, and apples from his bag. "Hope you folks don't expect hot food. In my line of work, it never pays to be too particular."

All but Sera sat down on one of the damaged chairs with broken spindles and cracked seats.

"Hey! Get your daughter back from there. This is my safe house, but it lowers our odds if you advertise yourself."

Sera had wandered over to the window and pressed her head against the glass, crying. Estes got up and pulled her away.

"I want to trade places with the people who died in the fire."

Estes held her and Bernard joined them.

Lev rapped his fork against the table three times. "If you feel bad now, how will you feel if you get us all captured? I've learned something about guilt. It used to plague me until I wised up to it." He ran a hand over his scalp. "I don't know exactly what happened down south, but it doesn't take a scholar to figure most of it. You got led astray by an older boy. You're not the first one."

"No! You have it all wrong. It was my idea. I asked Meyer if he knew how to build a bomb. I encouraged him. I picked the night. Now he'll take the punishment for both of us. I never imagined anything like this could happen. I didn't even expect General Borishenko to be in his office."

Bernard spoke softly. "Did you see his light?"

Sera nodded.

"And you signaled Meyer to throw the bomb?"

"Yes, Papa."

"So you've got some things to answer for," Lev said. "And you will, but not by harming yourself or drawing attention to us. It won't be so easy. Make a vow to do more good than the harm you've done. Start by grabbing something to eat and stop worrying your parents." He shoveled a forkful of corn salad into his mouth.

IO

Sera's grief, her confession, and Lev's sermon, brought their daughter back to them. During the long wait in the safe house, she wrapped one arm around Solly and listened to Estes read *Jane Eyre*.

To Estes's disappointment, though, the train arrived nearly four hours behind schedule. Max had come back once to write out—"mechanical problems." By the time he returned to escort them to the station, she realized, if they accepted Lev's advice, they'd spend one more night in Russia.

Bernard and Sera sat half a car's length away from them. She and Solly watched the rain-swollen Niemen without speaking. Her first walk with Professor Micah and encounter with Bernard had occurred on the banks of that river. As the tracks curved away, she strained for a last glimpse. She closed her eyes and tried to ignore Lev's snoring.

Estes awoke to Lev's gentle shake. "Twenty-minutes until we arrive in Kibart. I'll tell you what I told your husband back in Kovne: The soldiers won't bother us here, either, because I've bought their commander. You're just another refugee family crossing illegally. More rubles in his pocket. Read this. Max bought it while he kept watch at the station." He handed her a rolled newspaper.

HUNT ON FOR SECOND ASSASSIN

Sera Garfinkle, who fled with her family, is the second suspect in the bombing attack and murder of General Borishenko. Garfinkle, just twelve years old, is accused of acting as Levinson's lookout on Police Street and signaling him an all-clear before he threw his deadly bomb.

General Pavelvitch reported that Odessa is being searched. "We have evidence she and her family may try to exit the country there, so we're watching the port closely. We won't cease our investigation into this heinous crime until we bring all those responsible to justice."

"They're interrogating rail station managers and conductors between Horodno and Odessa. A perfect—" Lev puckered his lips as if to blow a kiss "—ruse. Here you are with me instead."

Assassin. That's what they called Gesia.

"Jacob Rosenblum must have cost you a fortune."

She didn't tell him Jacob refused to take money from Bernard.

"The station is practically on the border," Lev said. "We'll put a bit of distance between us and the checkpoint before we enjoy a wonderful hike in the woods."

She stayed silent, not trusting her voice.

"How's that book end? I mean, with Rochester and Jane?"

"We both want to know the ending of things, Lev. You'll have to read it someday and find out."

✳

Just as Lev had said, no trouble at the rail station. He carried Estes's bag and put an arm around her waist. She reached for his opposite shoulder. Solly held her hand on her other side. Lev broke away to chat with two policemen. They extended their hands, and he laid a ruble in each.

Lev bustled back. "Like feeding pigeons." He spun around. "Look at that, will you? Folks seeing this for the first time can't believe it. The czar used to tour Europe from this spot. Built this station just to house his special train."

She pulled Solly away from him.

"Hey, you're limping badly, wait for me. No interest in seeing the sights now, huh?"

Travelers struggled to load bulky bags onto waiting wagons while their drivers stood by. "Most of them will spend the night in Virbalis, a few versts east, and hire their guides there. The lucky few have exit passes." A driver gave Lev a lazy salute. The Garfinkles and their smugglers climbed into a wagon, and two spotted mares pulled it away. Sera held Solly's hand, and Estes gave Bernard a slight smile. Ten minutes later, when the driver pulled over, Lev handed him a ruble.

"Remember who pays your bills, Mendleson."

"Just one, Lev? There's four of them."

Lev handed him another and slapped his hand when it returned for more. The driver handed down their bags and headed back toward the station.

"Max will lead, and I'll be last. Rough going ahead, so watch your step. Mr. Garry, I'll take your bag. Help your wife now. It'll be faster than her limping along with the cane. This here is Kibart's farm. We skirt the field over there and move into a stretch of forest. A one-hour walk. We go north, then west to reach the crossing."

"I'll take Mama's bag." Sera picked it up and pulled the strap over her shoulder. "I can manage two."

"Thank you, Sera."

"I'll help if you get tired," Solly offered. Sera nodded at her brother.

The exertion, after several days without much sleep, took all of Estes's concentration. Bernard's familiar arm provided support, but the uneven, rain-sodden terrain made her feel more crippled than using a cane on Horodno's streets ever had. In front of her, Solly and Sera maneuvered around rocks, muddy holes, and exposed roots.

Trees screened the setting sun, and their bags caught on hanging branches along the shadowed path. Max alerted them when he spotted obstacles. When the land sloped to the west in a gentle descent, Bernard kept her upright as she slid in the mud. She tried to calculate how long they'd been walking. Her foot caught on a rock, and numb with pain and exhaustion, she nearly fell. Bernard encouraged her, and she dragged her foot forward. *One more step.* As dusk turned to dark, Max halted.

"This is the place," Lev said. "It's flat enough to sleep, but a difficult spot to cross with the steep banks and all the flooding. In the morning, just follow the trail three hundred paces north to where it winds down to the river. It's easy there, and once you step on the other side, say goodbye to the czar." Lev stuck his tongue out and blew air through his lips.

"Walk south and follow the Liepona upstream, right into Eydtkuhnen. That's your sanctuary. They don't like the Russians and won't care about your past or why you're fleeing. You'll be in woods for the first verst or so, then open fields the rest of the way. When you reach the border station, ask for Sergeant Muller. Tell him I accompanied you and show

him your train tickets and ship passes. Some rubles will also be helpful."
Lev shifted from foot to foot.

Bernard handed him some bills, then shook his hand and Max's. The
brothers blushed when Estes and the children hugged them.

"That's enough. We've got to go. You folks keep the blankets."

Max started down the path. He stopped, turned, and waved, visible
in the rising half-moon. "Don't suppose you'll tell me how that book
ends?" Lev asked, and without waiting for a reply, added, "No, I didn't
think so." He turned to go.

"Wait." Estes pulled *Jane Eyre* from her bag and handed their smuggler
the three hundred and fifty pages of Brontë's transcendent prose she
knew so well—Jane's suffering and isolation, plucky courage, flight from
Thornfield, near-death on the moor, reunion with Rochester.

Lev tucked it against his chest and stared at her a moment. "So long,
God bless, and good luck in America." He followed his brother into the
woods.

Downstream, a triangle of moonlight rippled on the Liepona, an
arrow pointing west. A good omen, she hoped.

✳

Wrapped in the leather blanket and wool sweater, Estes snuggled
against the children between her and Bernard. The endless night moved
too slowly. She slept fitfully and woke to the tapping of rain. Bernard
had already covered them with the oilcloth. A crack of thunder and the
sudden fiery light made her sit up. The rain increased, then exploded
in a wind-driven torrent. Bernard pulled her back under the oilcloth.
Nothing she could do but wait for morning.

The downpour slowed to steady rain and finally stopped. The oilcloth
had helped, but rivulets of water seeped along the ground and wet her
in spots. When the first birds sang, she looked out. The hazy moon in
the early dawn revealed Bernard stuffing his rolled blanket into his bag.

"Tight fit, but it might be useful." He shook out the oilcloth and
secured it with string to the outside of his bag.

With growing anticipation and anxiety, she kissed her children, still
asleep beside her.

Bernard passed her a hardened loaf of bread and laid their leather canteen on the ground. "We can fill it again when we cross. I'll scout ahead and be right back." He darted into the forest.

Sera stirred and Solly yawned. "Where's Papa going?"

"He'll be back in a minute. We're leaving Russia now." She broke off chunks of bread and insisted they eat and drink. Baths, hot meals, and beds waited in Eydtkuhnen.

She removed the cane from her bag. Without hanging onto anyone, she'd take her last steps out of Russia. She helped the children pack their blankets and jammed her own into her bag.

Sera gazed across the river. Solly pulled on his cap and stood next to her. Pockets of mist clung to the ground. Estes looped her arms around her children and nuzzled the backs of their heads. "A new life for us all." She squeezed them against her. Sera stroked the back of her hand. Estes murmured how much she loved them.

"We won't ever return, will we?"

"No, Sera. We'll never come back."

＊

After a minute of fast walking, Bernard came to the easy descent Lev had described. The stream spread out, knee-deep, with a nearly flat exit on the far bank. To the north, he saw no movement. Upstream, two figures made their way slowly along the eroded bank on the Russian side.

Refugees like us, looking for a place to cross over. But where are their bags?

Bernard hurried back. Before he reached the camp, he left the trail and crawled stealthily through the brush, scratching his arms and face in the thicket. He regretted not taking Leib's pistol.

Why did Bernard come back off the trail? Estes froze when two men struggled into their clearing. Mud covered their boots. The children leaned back into her. One of the men had a gaunt face and blond beard, the other a large head with an oversized square jaw. He smiled and displayed a mouth full of blackened teeth.

The gaunt one spoke first in Russian. "Well, how about this. Just when I thought we had nothing to show for our night's efforts. See," he looked at his companion, "if we had crossed upstream like you wanted, we would have missed them."

She considered telling them that they weren't alone, until he pointed the gun at her, an ugly, vulgar thing.

"Now, listen carefully, ma'am. I'm not going to shoot you unless you scream or try to run. Come here and give us a closer look."

When she didn't move, he waved the gun back and forth impatiently. "You don't speak Russian? I'll try German. That's closer to Jew talk." He motioned them forward. "Komm sofort her!"

She pulled the children behind her.

The intruder switched back to Russian. "Okay, if that's the way you want it. That your cane? Where did you come from?" He looked puzzled a moment. "Hey!" He reached in one pocket, then the other, and pulled out a folded paper. He studied it intently. His eyes darted back and forth several times. His gun hand began to shake. "I can't believe it! Look at this picture."

"The older one has long hair."

"She cut it off, stupid oaf! See, she's lame, like they told us."

"But there's four of them in the picture."

"Jews," he sneered. "Lady, take the scarf off the girl and that dumb cap from the boy."

Estes held Sera in place with one hand, Solly with the other.

"Rip them off," the gunman ordered his partner.

Sera wrapped her arms around Estes and pressed against her back. "Mama, don't let him hurt us."

Estes screamed, "Stop!"

Doubt crossed the big man's coarse features, but then he smiled and started toward them.

"Not one more step!"

He looked back at the leader.

"It's only a woman. You're useless. I have to do everything myself."

Her voice wouldn't be enough to stop this one. "Do what you want with me, but let my children go."

"I give the orders, Zhydovka!" He strode past his companion.

He expected a helpless victim, but she intended to surprise him and grab the gun. "I won't let him touch you."

Bernard burst out of the brush. He smashed into the gunman and knocked him to the ground. All his years lifting heavy horse hooves and shoveling grain in the distillery bore down on his foe as he dug one knee into his enemy's back and grabbed for his gun hand. The gun fired, and Sera screamed. Bernard bent the thin wrist back with all his strength until it snapped. He threw the weapon in the brush.

Blood dripped from a wound in Sera's right hand. Estes sank to the ground with a burning pain in her chest and landed in a sitting position. A revelation struck her like a second bullet. *So this is what I would die for.* She slumped on her side and laid her head on the rain-soaked earth. *So close . . .*

II

Bernard searched for the second man, who'd already disappeared. The one with the broken wrist cursed and staggered into the woods as Bernard rushed to his family.

Sera sagged across her mother's body. "Stay with us, Mama. Please stay with us."

Between sobs, Solly said, "Papa, what should I do?"

"We need bandages. Grab clothing from our bags, anything we can use. Quick, Solly!"

Bernard pulled Sera away and ripped open Estes's dress. A fist-sized red bloom stained her linen corset and the chemise underneath. A smaller crimson patch showed on her side. He undid the busk snaps and swallowed an impulse to scream.

Pale, eyes closed, but still breathing. Alive.

Solly handed him cotton undergarments that Bernard folded and pressed against the two pinky-sized holes. He wrapped one of his shirts over the bandages, pulled Estes to a sitting position, and secured the sleeves in back. He told Solly to wrap Sera's hand.

Bernard lifted Estes in a fireman's carry and implored the twins to keep up. As they splashed out of Russia, he prayed for strength. They raced through woods and across flooded fields just as Lev had described.

When he looked back, Sera held her hand up, and a trickle of blood ran down her wrist. Solly pushed her along and they both wept. *Why take this life now? If you meant for us to fail, we should have been captured in Horodno.*

When he spotted the Prussian border station in Eydtkuhnen, Bernard fell to his knees and screamed for help.

PART V

SPIRITS

You've got to go on living, even if it kills you.
– Sholem Aleichem

Between 1881 and 1914, around one-and-a-half million Jews emigrated from the Russian Empire to America. The vast majority never looked back. Repression, revolutionary upheaval, and starvation beat down any nostalgic inclinations. Most Jewish immigrants settled in cities, and many stayed in New York, the major point of entry. Some, though, with the help of relatives, made new lives in towns away from the coast.

Thanks to Estes's resourceful Uncle Simon, who died five years ago, at ninety-three, Bernard Garry's house in Indiana, Pennsylvania, had a basement and five bedrooms. The one he'd fled in Horodno, thirty-four years ago, would fit on half of one floor. Bernard had renovated the house himself, and the overhead electric light he'd recently put in, a simple bulb under a plate of glass, delighted him. His town had brought in electricity before some of the big cities. He pushed the switch with his thumb. Not enough illumination to read, but atmospheric. He loved that word.

Bernard placed the lemon cake, hot water, tea bags, plates, and utensils on a silver tray and carried it out to the coffee table. He straightened the cushions on the sofa and brought over his favorite caned chair. He stretched to relieve some new aches in his back. Not too bad for sixty-four. He sat and relaxed for a moment. No need to rush. It would be a tiring day, and he worried about her stamina. When he'd suggested they reschedule their trip to New York, Estes had patted his arm and smiled in silent dismissal.

After a few moments, he opened the bedroom door and helped her out of the leather chair where she spent hours each day reading and writing. Estes didn't use her desk anymore. With the help of her cane and his arm, she moved slowly and eased onto the sofa. A plum-colored sweater contrasted with her white hair, still kept short after all these years.

Bernard poured tea and cut two slices of cake. He passed her the publisher's proposed dust jacket and a pen. "With the interview at *Harper's*, *Spirits* could do well." Bernard avoided eye contact because, with this memoir, Estes cared nothing about sales. He imagined her squint, the one that could squeeze juice from a shelled walnut.

"Have we done right by them, Bernard? Have our lives justified what they lost?"

"You've brought pleasure to so many with your writing."

He took their suitcases to the car. Rain splashed on the running boards and windshield. He cranked the Model T, went back to the house, and escorted her out to the passenger side. She didn't walk into town anymore, and the rail station, only five blocks east on Philadelphia Street, was farther than she could manage.

On the train, a smattering of pessimistic travelers still wore disease masks, although the third wave of influenza, which had killed millions worldwide, most young and healthy, had subsided that summer. A young couple across the aisle immediately rushed away to the next car when Estes coughed.

Bernard wanted this trip as much as she did—a Shabes with family and old friends, and a few days later, the interview with *Harper's*. Inquiries had also arrived from *The Bookman*, *The Atlantic*, and lesser journals. Estes had left these arrangements to him. Maybe he shouldn't have accepted *Harper's* offer, because it, like the others, didn't meet her first requirement—a female editor. Still, at least *Harper's* new chief had used the term "brave women."

After changing trains in Altoona, they settled in for the long ride across hilly, green Pennsylvania. The pain medication made her drowsy, and when Estes closed her eyes, Bernard pulled the invitation and her response from his traveling satchel.

June 8th, 1919
Dear Mrs. Garry,

It is with anticipation that I inquire regarding your interest and availability to be interviewed by one of our staff writers in New York. We at Harper's have followed your career and admire your body of published work, including your novels, essays, and poetry.

Although it takes place far from our shores, your memoir is an American story with brave women, relevant today as we near the precipice of dramatic change.

We at Harper's would be most gratified to include a chapter along with your interview in an upcoming issue.

Respectfully,
Mr. Thomas Wells

He smiled when he reread her response.

June 18th, 1919
Dear Mr. Wells,

Your offer does interest me, with one condition. My husband Bernard, my first and most loyal reader, must be included, because we lived most of Spirits together. Perhaps you meant to use another word in place of precipice to describe our hard-fought victories for universal suffrage. It comes from the Latin praecipitium, which means abrupt descent.
Sincerely,
Esther Leving Garry

As the leafy landscape passed by, the swaying of the train triggered a memory of another trip to New York, not long after Herman and Doris had died within weeks of each other. When had he started using death to measure time? Fourteen years ago, the day Sera told them she loved Emma Gladstone, a labor organizer and suffragist, he'd fumed about it during their return home. When they passed through a snow squall, the large flakes landed on the train's window like wet paper, then dissolved. He tried to let his emotions melt away, too, but as soon as they entered their front door, he exploded.

"It's just not natural! Why would she make her life any harder? And besides, this woman, she's not even Jewish."

Estes thumped his chest with the side of her fist. "Tell me what's natural, Bernard! Someone who prays to an imaginary being with little boxes bound to his body? Separating life into kosher and treyf? Denying the vote to women? Is God a man in your mind?"

Stunned by her anger, he still made no move to retreat.

"Who are you to say whom she can love?"

He slept on the couch, rose early, and left for his hardware store before she came out of the bedroom. When he came home, she retreated into her study. After five days of mutual avoidance, she came to him. "One can overthink, Bernard. Please forgive me."

Now, he loved Sera's partner like a second daughter.

*

The train pulled into Penn Station before dusk. With its palatial floor and immense vaulted ceiling, the station could have swallowed every shul in Horodno. He never felt prepared for the explosion of light, blaring horns, engine exhaust, and rumble of trolleys on the street. Bernard always sought out and welcomed the earthy scent of the curbside horses, who waited placidly in their traces as modernity rushed by.

Fruit peddlers, newsies, and young bootblacks, with smudged faces and boxes slung over their shoulders, waved their caps and shouted at pedestrians. A busty matron wearing a pleated dress and feathered hat looked askance at a trio of younger women with short, colorful skirts and cloches. A disfigured veteran with war medals and a slash for a mouth begged for change. Wealthy men carrying umbrellas and newspapers, some in tuxedos and top hats, others in three-piece suits, pressed trousers, and felt fedoras, ignored him.

How did so many people live without quiet, the night sky, verdant fields? Solly and Sera greeted them, maneuvered around the crowd, and flagged a taxi like veteran New Yorkers. On the way to Chaim's, Bernard replaced his cap with the yarmulke he pulled from his pocket. He'd always worn it in Horodno, but now he put it on selectively—for prayer, shul, Shabes, and the other holidays. An American Jew.

The annual Shabes reunion had grown over the years, and three generations squeezed around Chaim's walnut banquet table with its inserted leaves. Chaim's fiery red hair had transformed into a thin, silvery-white fringe. A ring of baldness framed his yarmulke. Years ago, his family had left their dingy East Side tenement on Hester Street, which was packed with tiny sewing shops. Joseph, his belly bulging with affluence, had traded his belt for suspenders. Shlomo, who had never possessed the exuberance of youth, had changed the least, and Bernard found comfort in that sad, steady countenance. After years of struggle, his three landsmen had a successful furniture business. Bernard admired the dovetail joints in the intricate corner hutch.

After the main courses, Sera's Emma sliced a brick of halvah for dessert with a steady hand, each cut piece the same thickness. Her lithe frame, warm smile, and black curls hid the toughness she needed to battle unscrupulous capitalists.

Two bottles of sweet red circled the table in opposite directions. Silver clinked against glass, and the animated conversations and laughter tapered into quiet.

Time for their personal exodus stories, told every year, imprinting a memory like initials carved in trees for those too young to remember or born since, in America. Solly, who'd turned an interest in biology into a research career at Columbia University, spoke first about that awful trip across the Atlantic. Only the growing distance between the ship and Russia had sustained them through the rough seas, boat sickness, and cramped quarters.

When they reached New York quite broken, Estes's near-perfect English and storytelling ability helped them thorough the inspections and inquiries. The customs officials assigned "Garry" as their permanent American name. For days, the earth still heaved, and they took refuge with Chaim's desperately poor family crammed into that tenement.

"During those days of recovery, we had visitors," Solly said. "When our grandparents saw Sera's bandaged hand and learned what happened in Horodno . . . well, you can imagine."

After all the stories, and after Joseph recited Kaddish, it was time to honor the dead. Over the years, the tiny flames had spread across the table until the dead outnumbered the living. Some of the candles clustered together, though those they memorialized had not known each other in life. Gesia Gelfman flickered with Rabbi Menshein; Bernard's father glowed next to Estes's parents. Friends, teachers, and relatives mingled across families and generations.

Years had passed after the escape from Russia before Sera would attend the Shabes or speak about the past. Horodno still burned for the four of them, but it burned hottest for her. She'd struggled as a painter until after the Triangle Shirtwaist Fire, when a philanthropist had taken an interest in her series on women immigrants.

Estes put her hand over Sera's bullet-scarred right hand—the one Sera painted with, the one she'd used to signal the all-clear to Meyer Levinson, the one that had saved Estes's life. The bounty hunter's bullet had changed its trajectory after shattering her daughter's wrist and exiting her palm. So, instead of striking Estes's heart, it had ripped just below the skin before exiting through her side. When the old Prussian army doctor at the border station dressed Estes's wound, he expressed amazement at her luck. When he came to check on her the following days, he'd held out his thumb and forefinger with a small space between. "So knapp," he said each time.

Estes and Sera lifted a single candle together, touched it to another, then recited in unison the names of Gesia Gelfman, Gesia's four comrades, Meyer Levinson, and the seven victims of the fire.

Estes lit a candle for Eliza Orzeszkowa. Most years, just reciting the names of her people brought them back to her. This Shabes, she needed to tell again the stories of friends who'd helped them escape.

"Eliza took a terrible risk giving us her carriage. The authorities questioned her, but what could they do to a Polish hero, a famous author, the leader of the recovery effort. She was the first woman nominated for the Nobel Prize in literature, imagine . . . the same year as Leo Tolstoy. The entire city showed up for her funeral. Eliza wrote to us every month for years. That's how we learned the names of those who died in the fire that day and those who succumbed afterward. That's how we learned what happened to Jacob and Leib."

Her voice trembled a bit. "Jacob Rosenblum saved our lives. When the authorities interrogated him, he directed them to Odessa. He must have been persuasive, because they spent weeks searching that city while we escaped in the opposite direction. When they realized the extent of his lies and forgery activities . . ." Estes breathed deeply before resuming. "Jacob knew the danger he faced because they executed Meyer Levinson a week after he confessed to throwing the bomb." Bernard reached out, and together they lit Jacob's candle.

With children at the table, she left out some facts that Eliza had shared: how the Russians denied Jacob visits from his distraught parents and rabbinical colleagues; his dreadful last months of solitary confinement, the beatings and mock executions; the guards' derision when he requested kosher food; his hunger strike; how Avram Rosenblum, called to retrieve Jacob's body, didn't believe the battered, gaunt form was his son. Avram hanged himself a week later, and Jacob's mother, Maida, died soon after.

Estes had included all of this in *Spirits*, but she left out what happened when Bernard raced to Rabbi Jacob Rosenblum the morning of the fire. He hadn't shared it with her until the family reached America. Estes pressed him for details because she had to feel that moment herself.

Jacob had lived in one room of a boarding house for single rabbis. A wall of religious volumes, a twin bed, and a desk filled the space. Jacob, wearing only his white tallis katan and black trousers, gave Bernard the emergency documents, and the letter to be opened in America. They stood facing one another in the doorway, and Jacob's eyes watered as he gave the final instructions. Bernard embraced him and left quickly.

Jacob followed him into the smoky street and yelled at his back, "Bernard, I did this all for her." When Bernard looked back, Jacob had retreated inside.

By the time they read his note, Jacob languished in prison. Estes used her remorse as a reminder of her foolishness. The condescension and excessive pride had been hers all along, not his. How had she failed to see?

Their Shabes ceremonies varied from year to year, but they always ended with Leib. Joseph described their friend's courage in Balta. Bernard told how Leib, imprisoned three years for helping them flee Horodno, returned home to find Ledl dead from a cholera outbreak and Garfinkle's Spirits seized by the Russians.

Shlomo had the final words. "In 1906, my brother, Commander Leib Fetterman of the Polish Socialist Party, went to Bialystok to protect the working-class parts of the city. When thugs, aided by czarist troops, began murdering Jews, he organized a self-defense unit. Outnumbered, he set up barricades and stole weapons before leading a desperate counterattack to drive them off. Leib saved hundreds of lives and died in that battle."

Shlomo retrieved his fiddle case from beneath the table and played the tune he'd written twelve years ago for his brother, "Leib's Charge." He didn't slow down to emphasize the sadness, like he did with most other songs. This bold and frantic reel raced from beginning to end.

Final toasts and promises to meet again next year left unsaid what Estes knew—the cancer of the breast had spread, and this would be her last Shabes with them. Next year they'd light a candle and lift a glass to her memory as well.

✳

They stayed with Solly for three nights and returned to Pennsylvania immediately after the *Harper's* interview. Back home, Bernard removed her boots and massaged her foot while she stretched out on the sofa. She closed her eyes, and when he covered her with an afghan, she smiled.

"Thank you, Bernard."

"Why do you think everything happens the way it does?"

"Because of what came before."

How did she manage without God? Not just religion, with its rules and forms, but God, the creator, the first before. After they'd arrived in their new home, Estes had finally started to attend shul and sit by his side. When he'd given it up for her during their life in Horodno, he'd imagined this time would eventually come.

Jews came in from nearby towns that lacked enough men for a minyan. This new kind of rabbi, between Hebrew prayers, spoke to them about the Torah, in English. She did not repeat the prayers, but she also refrained from any comments later. She went with him for one full year, through Solly's bar mitsve, made the acquaintance of other women, and then stopped attending. She'd hugged him, which didn't lessen his disappointment. "I'm just not interested in religious worship, Bernard."

Struck by the inevitability of loss, he watched her chest rise and fall.

Estes lived to read the *Harper's* article, the excerpts from their interview written with warmth and insight. The lengthy review catapulted *Spirits* onto *Publishers Weekly*'s bestseller list.

She wrote and shared her last essay with Bernard. When her strength waned, she put her pen down and asked him to bring Eliza's *On the Niemen* to her. They looked at the inscription together: *To Estes, my friend and fellow writer, a woman who never accepted her place. Professor Micah would be so proud! Love, Eliza*

After Bernard read aloud the first twenty-five pages of Eliza's masterpiece, Estes requested other offerings. He searched their shelves. A thumbs-up from her and he read. A thumbs-down verdict he sent back to shelved obscurity.

He began *Jane Eyre*, but she stopped him after a few chapters. Gothic romances belonged to her past, she told him. She requested, instead, pages from Joyce's *Portrait of the Artist as a Young Man*, and one chapter of the avantgarde *Ulysses*, serialized in *The Little Review*.

"If only I had more time, Bernard. My next novel would be full of interior monologue and stream of consciousness."

He wept and Estes held his hand. Shouldn't he be comforting her? They settled into a volume of Emily Dickenson's poetry. He practiced reading with expression while she slept, so he could brush on color with a deliberate pause or change the tone at the right moment.

Family and friends came and went. Estes said goodbye to each of her grandsons. Bernard forced himself from her side to give Solly and Sera time alone with her. After an hour, he went back in and placed a glass of water she wouldn't drink and food she wouldn't eat on the bedside table. He arranged her covers, raised and lowered the blinds, overheard bits of conversation.

"Your father will need help . . . proud of you . . ." She ran her hands through Solly's thick hair, gray at the temples, and caressed Sera's old wound. The twins got into bed and held her while she dozed.

Bernard took the final watch at her bedside. She gathered her strength and wrote out instructions on the front inside cover of *Spirits*.

Please, my dearest Bernard, no religion at the funeral. Ask everyone to bring a favorite poem or story to share. Keep what you need from the sales of Spirits *and donate the remainder for the new public library. Read to me when you have time. I love you.*

He promised. "Is there anything else you want me to do?"

She flipped to the back cover. With one hand, she shielded her last written words to him then shut the book like a coffin lid. "Read this when you want an answer, Bernard."

He wasn't sure if she heard the final poems he read, until she faintly squeezed his hand.

※

Shortly after her death, he gave the hardware store to the grandson who had moved with his young family into Bernard's house. When Bernard woke at six each morning, he washed and prayed the Shema. Even his most intense concentration did not bring him back to the ecstatic state he'd discovered after his father's death. Maybe he'd lived too long in the world, and time had calcified his perceptions like handprints in mortar.

Every day, he made the half-mile trek to the cemetery and read to her. Afterward, on his way to the hardware store, he walked down Philadelphia Street and checked the progress on the Esther Leving Garry Library. He read the sign under the marquee in front of the movie theater. Garry's Hardware bought up matinee tickets and gave them out to customers. "You have to spend money to make money," Bernard had instructed his grandson.

He passed the fire station, the two-cell jail, and shuttered beer joints where sad drunks used to commiserate during the day and angry miners at night. He read the strike messages posted at the union hall where, years earlier, John Lewis had implored the county's miners to stand in solidarity for a living wage.

He loved everything about the hardware store: the largest picture window in town, with "B. Garry's Paint and Paper" in white block lettering; the creak of the old floorboards, with their dirt-filled cracks; the aisles of paint products, arranged brushes and rollers, tools and supplies to fix a leak, wire a light, live a modern life. Displays of roofing and flooring materials hid the basement door and the rickety stairs, which led down to a storage area, always damp in summer, where buckets of tar, felt paper, linoleum, and bundles of shingles stacked on pallets reached the cobwebbed ceiling.

He waited on customers, carried heavy rolls up from the basement, and arranged new displays. His taught his grandson the skills to run the business.

Bernard accepted condolences and teared up when customers passed on remembrances of how Estes taught a husband or wife to read, the books she gifted to their children, and how proud she'd made them feel about Indiana, Pennsylvania.

A few women who'd lost husbands to the war or influenza lingered in the store. He sensed they waited for a sign of interest from him, as he'd waited for Estes years ago. He could only offer formal respect, though, because he felt Estes still with him, like a phantom limb.

Spirits remained in the drawer of his nightstand. Not yet, he told himself, about reading her last words. She didn't comment on this matter, but she did speak to him when the states ratified the nineteenth amendment. *March!*

✳

August 27, 1920

For seventy-two years, beginning with the Seneca Falls convention and continuing until August 18, 1920, American women fought for the right to vote. Some, like Estes and Sera, joined the National Women's Party, a militant organization.

To celebrate ratification, Bernard wore Estes's rectangular "Jailed for Freedom" pin just above his left breast. It resembled a prison door, with crosshatched bars and a heart-shaped locket. Alice Paul herself had awarded them to the women who endured prison, forced feeding, and beatings as a result of their heroic picket of the White House, three years ago. Sera and Emma wore theirs too.

He moved along with the small but enthusiastic group of suffragists and supporters whose loud cheers had drowned out Al Smith's brief welcoming speech. Six mounted policemen led the procession. A single automobile followed, carrying the renowned leader, Carrie Cattman Catt. Two lines came to him from Estes's last piece, the one he published after her death.

> *We must stand for the rights of all women, and men, too, from many races, religions, and nationalities. We must not appeal to men's worst instincts.*

It had deeply troubled her that Catt had campaigned for support from white men by arguing that suffrage for women would keep blacks,

Indians, and immigrants in their place.

You're not the only one with principles, Bernard.

He sighed. *Can't we just celebrate this moment?*

Sera looked at him strangely and took his hand as if helping a child when they crossed over to Fifth Avenue. On his other side, he linked arms with Emma Gladstone. The ranks of marchers swelled, as did the onlookers filling the sidewalks. In front of the Waldorf-Astoria, he looked up at the towering corner structure. Sera reached her hand across his chest and pressed the pin. His heart fluttered.

＊

April 15, 1946

All these years, he visited her every morning. In winter, he often shared news of the family, as he did on this day. It was Pesach, which usually ushered in spring, but a surprise snowstorm the day before had left a small drift against Estes's gravestone and melting patches on the ground. On rainy days he stood with an umbrella and recited a poem. Through the long summer, he brought a folding chair and read short stories. In the fall, he read a novel. The Esther Leving Garry Library had all the famous volumes. It didn't matter where he started, or if he finished. Over the years, he'd introduced her to Marcel Proust and Virginia Woolf. She wouldn't mind that he also indulged in Dashiell Hammett and Jack London.

I love the words, Bernard. You read so beautifully.

He never mentioned world affairs. Why trouble her with unimaginable horrors. And how could he even begin to describe the enormity of the cataclysm? With the perspective of time, Bernard could clearly see, now, that the interlude of reform when he'd been a boy had offered only brief sanctuary from the deadly course of history. The pogroms back in '81 and the repression which followed had restarted a doomsday clock for Russian and European Jews.

In Horodno, twenty-five thousand Jewish residents were murdered. In Vilne, Kovne, Kiev, Balta, Odessa, and a thousand other cities and towns, only a few gaunt survivors remained to bear witness. He should have died of grief, himself.

"What a Seder we'll have tonight," he told her, hiding his sorrow. "Our youngest wants to practice the questions with me."

Your hands are frozen. Go home and warm up. We'll talk later.

"Not yet." Bernard needed to remember the dead—so many now. He ran his hand tenderly over her stone and glanced at the space reserved for him. Part spirit already, he felt brittle as a hollow reed.

He left the cemetery and tried not to shuffle like an old man. With gathering purpose, he lifted a foot off the ground and planted it firmly, still a stepper. He had a date with his five-year-old great-granddaughter, Esther.

When he arrived home, his extended family greeted him as though he'd been gone for years. His household had grown in the past two days, with four generations of Garrys. Three tables, with places for thirty, crowded the dining and living rooms.

Solly and Sera had assured him the meal would be kosher. His children, wrinkled with age themselves, made him feel too ancient to worry about details. He resisted the urge to go into the kitchen.

"Tea, cookies, and books!" Esther shouted, running to him. She stepped on a small stool and reached one of the hooks in the closet to hang up his coat. With her tiny hand, she took his and proceeded to his bedroom. Pointing at the corner table with two cups and saucers, a plate of cookies, and pot of tea, she said, "I helped carry it in for our party."

He eased into his chair and patted the child-sized rocker for her.

"Not yet, Great Grandpa Bernard. First, help me pour."

He guided her hand while she filled the cups.

"A cookie for you and one for me." She sat and slurped the tea with an exaggerated "thp!" and giggled when he did the same.

"Let me hear you read the questions, Esther."

"That's too easy. I want to read something by Great Grandma Esther." She put her cup down and picked up *Spirits* from the bed.

"I thought I left that book in my nightstand."

"But we can't read it in a dark drawer, silly."

He stroked his chin, considering her point. "We could if we had a flashlight."

She laughed, took a bite of cookie, and opened the book to a long-ago Seder—Estes as a young girl, her parents, Jacob Rosenblum.

She read with expression; her firm voice, coming from such a tiny body, mesmerized him.

"Wake up, Great Grandpa."

Disoriented, Bernard glanced at his watch.

"You've slept through a whole chapter. And guess what? I found a message from Great Grandma Esther to you on the back cover too. Look." She flipped the pages and held the book up in front of him.

Why hesitate now? He fiddled with his glasses. *A fourth principle, dear husband,* she'd written. A second line, with three exclamations, slender fingers pointing to the sky, left no doubt.

This was a commandment.

Live, Bernard! Live!!

Glossary

Most of the Yiddish words in the novel follow the YIVO Institute for Jewish Research recommended transliterations. Where readers might be accustomed to a more common form, I relied on the updated *Joys of Yiddish* by Leo Rosten. In those instances, the YIVO spelling follows the definition.

Yiddish

Adonoy: My lord

afikoymen: Matzo hidden during a Seder and searched for by children

alef: First letter of the Hebrew alphabet

aleykhem: Aleykhem sholem (and unto you, peace); response to sholem aleykhem

alte ferd: Old horse

alte moyd: Old maid

ayen: The sixteenth letter of the Hebrew alphabet

babka: Fruit-filled dough with fluted sides

baleboste: Homemaker, mistress of the house

bar mitsve: Religious ceremony for a Jewish boy when he turns thirteen

beys: Second letter of the Hebrew alphabet

bobeshi: Affectionate name for grandmother (bobe)

bobkes: Goat droppings; worthless or trivial

bris: Circumcision ceremony

Chumash: A Torah in printed form, as opposed to a Sefer Torah scroll (Khumesh)

chupe: Wedding canopy (khupe)

dibek: Evil spirit

drek: Excrement

Eyn-Sof: Infinite, boundless God

feh: Expression of disgust (fe)

fertummelt: Mixed up, confused (fartumlt)

gimel: The third letter of the Hebrew alphabet (giml)

goy: A gentile non-Jewish person, sometimes used as a pejorative

goyim: Plural of goy

gut morgn: Good morning

Haggadah: The story of Jewish bondage and escape from Egypt, told at Seder (Hagode)

halvah: A sweet dessert with honey and ground sesame seeds (khalve)

Hasid: Adherent of Hasidism (Khosed)

Haskalah: Jewish Enlightenment movement in the nineteenth century (Haskole)

ilui: A child Talmudic prodigy (ile)

Kaddish: A Jewish prayer; called the Mourner's Kaddish when recited for the dead (Kadesh)

kahal: The mostly autonomous Jewish town governing body, abolished 1844 (kool)

kashrut: The body of Jewish law dealing with food preparation and consumption (kashres)

ketubah: Jewish marriage contract (ksube)

keyn eynhore: Uttered to ward off bad luck or the evil eye

khapers: Men hired by Jewish leaders to abduct Jewish children for the czar's army

kheyder: A Jewish elementary school with religious and Hebrew instruction

kiddush: Blessing over wine during Shabbes and holidays (kidesh)

kleyngelt: Small change, as in *Do iz dayn kleyngelt* (Here is your small change)

knish: A dumpling, slang for vagina

kugel: Pudding of noodles or potatoes (kugl)

lamed: The twelfth letter of the Hebrew alphabet

l'chaim: A toast offered with raised glass: to life (lekhayim)

lebn: Life

matzo: Unleavened bread

Mayse-Bukh: A book of religious stories and Yiddish folktales from the sixteenth century

mazel tov: Congratulations (mazl tov)

melamed: A teacher

mentsh: Human being, decent person

meshuge: Crazy

meshugener: A crazy man

mezuzah: Prayer parchment in a case fastened to the doorpost as a sign of faith (mezuze)

mikve: A bath used to achieve ritual purity

minyan: The ten Jewish males required for a religious service (minyen)

Misnagdim: Orthodox Jews opposed to the Hasids

Misnaged: Singular of Misnagdim

moyel: Person who circumcises male infants

nu: An interjection whose meaning depends on context and intonation: well, so?, no!

nun: The fourteenth letter of the Hebrew alphabet

oy vey: A Jewish expression of distress or woe

Pesach: Passover (Peysekh)

peyes: Sidelocks

Purim: Holiday commemorating Queen Esther's rescue of the Jews from annihilation

putz: Insult, slang for penis: also shmok, shvantz, shvents (plural), shmekl (pots)

rebbe: Hasidic grand rabbi (rebe)

rugela: A sweet pastry (rogele)

rugelach: Plural of rugela (rogelekh)

Seder: Literally "order." The ritual on the first night or first two nights of Pesach (Seyder)

Shabes: Sabbath

Shabosim: Plural of Sabbath

sheyn ponem: Pretty face

Shema: Literally "hear." The first word and title of the famous Hebrew prayer (Shma)

shiva: A seven-day mourning period for the dead after the funeral

shmundies: Slang for vaginas (see also knishes, yentzes)

shofar: Ram's horn blown in the synagogue during the High Holy Days (shoyfer)

sholem: Hello, goodbye, peace (sholem aleykhem: how do you do?) (see aleykhem sholem)

shpilkes: Literally "pins." Sitting on pins and needles, nervous, agitated

shtetl: A small market town with Yiddish-speaking Jewish residents

shtot: Bigger than a shtetl; small city

shul: A synagogue

shuln: Plural of shul

Sukkos: The Festival of Tabernacles or the Feast of Booths (Sukes)

tallis: Prayer shawl (tales)

tallis katan: Worn by orthodox men, the corner fringe a reminder of duty to God (tales-kotn)

Talmud: The massive collection of Jewish religious law and commentaries

Tanakh: An acronym for the three parts of the Hebrew Bible (Torah, Nevi'im, Ketuvim)

tefillin: Two small leather boxes containing Torah verses, worn at morning prayer (tfiln)

Torah: The five books of Moses (the Sefer Torah is the handwritten scroll) (Toyre)

treyf: An animal not slaughtered according to ritual laws, and any food that is not kosher

yarmulke: Skullcap worn by observant Jewish boys and men (yarmlke)

yeshiva: Academy for rabbinical and Talmudic study (yeshive)

yentzes: (See shmundies)

Yiddish: Literally "Jewish." The language of Ashkenazic Jews (Yidish)

Yom Kiper: High Holy Day of atonement

Zohar: The most important book of Cabalism, written around the thirteenth century (Zoyer)

Russian

arshin: A unit of measure; one arshin equals twenty-eight inches

funt: A unit of weight used in the Russian Empire, equal to .9 lbs. (also lb. in Yiddish)

gubernia: A territorial and administrative unit of the Russian Empire

knout: A whip to inflict punishment

kopek: Monetary unit worth one hundredth of a ruble

pogromshchiki: Those who attack Jews during a pogrom

ruble: The basic monetary unit of Russia

sdacha: Change, as in *Vot vasha sdacha* (Here's your change)

spasibo: Thanks

verst: A unit of distance used in the Russian Empire, equal to 1.07 kilometers

Zhydovka: Antisemitic pejorative term for a Jewish woman

Polish

Pani: A respectful form of address to a Polish women

Zydzi: Jews

German

Komm sofort her!: Come here right now!

so knapp: So close

Historical Note

Horodno Burning began with pieces of family history—the arranged marriage between my great-great-grandparents, Estes and Bernard, at ages 12 and 14; escape from service in the czar's army; pogroms; a harrowing trip from the Pale of Settlement to America; a reverence for books; and radical politics. Ultimately, these fragments inspired me to write a novel about literature, freedom, and Jewish survival, in which real events and historic figures appear alongside the imagined.

Horodno in the novel has an altered and simplified street layout loosely resembling the real city of the late nineteenth century, which developed around the Niemen River and rail line. The Choral Shul (known today as the Great, New, or Choral Synagogue), public library, Shershevski's tobacco factory, the train station, Catholic Basilica, Sophia's Church, the railroad and foot bridges, Efron's sawmill, Boris and Gleb Orthodox Church, and Eliza Orzeszkowa's house all existed, though I changed the details of these landmarks for fictional purposes. The Great Wooden Shul and the Market Square emerged from my imagination, based on other wooden synagogues and town markets found throughout the Pale of Settlement. Shershevski's tobacco factory did become the biggest employer in Horodno, but several years later than described in the story.

The names of the most important towns in the novel are identified by their Yiddish transliteration: Horodno instead of Grodno, Vilne instead of Vilnius, and Kovne instead of Kaunus. Chimilenski and Meerispol, shtetls that feature in Bernard's 1882 trip to Balta, are fictional representations. Otherwise, I relied on historic descriptions and maps to portray the cities, towns, and train routes of that trip, and the family's 1885 escape.

In *Horodno Burning*, I wanted to realistically convey the brutality of the pogroms after the 1881 assassination of the czar. Those assaults and the repressive May Laws that followed initiated a catastrophic turn in Jewish history.

A terrible fire in the summer of 1885 did destroy half the city. The fire station where Bernard volunteered after his father's death is fictional, but the city finally erected a stone fire tower in 1902, which still exists today, as a museum. The Russian Orthodox morality campaign, the Office of

State Security, General Borishenko, and the bomb that started the fire are also fictional but reflect the repressive atmosphere and revolutionary response of the times.

I don't believe chess master William Steinitz ever visited Horodno. In 1867, when he conducted the simultaneous exhibition in the novel, he still played in the swashbuckling romantic style of the period. By 1873, he had introduced a new scientific analysis to the game.

Eliza Orzeszkowa, beloved by the Jews for her fierce opposition to antisemitism, was the first woman nominated for the Nobel Prize in literature. The city erected a statue honoring her memory and converted her house into a museum.

Gesia Gelfman's hiatus in Horodno is fictional. The historical Gelfman rebelled against her father, ran away to Kiev, joined a collective, and studied midwifery. As a member of the People's Will, she played a secondary role in the assassination of Alexander II. Her death sentence while pregnant and her courage in prison, despite impossibly cruel conditions, made her a cause célèbre across Europe.

Pale of Settlement Timeline

1648–1650   A Cossack revolt against the Catholic church and the Polish nobility traps Jews in Ukrainian lands. Thousands die in the Chmielnicki pogroms.

1768   The Haidamak Cossack uprising kills many thousands of Jews in Uman and other towns.

1772–1795   These violent rebellions weaken the Polish-Lithuanian Commonwealth, and a partition takes place in three stages. In their land grab, Russia inherits the largest Jewish community in the world.

1791   Catherine the Great bars her Jewish subjects from inner Russia. She restricts Jewish residence to the newly acquired territories, which will become known as Congress Poland and the Pale of Settlement.

1796   Catherine the Great dies; Paul I becomes czar.

1801   Paul I is murdered; his son, Alexander I, becomes czar.

1804   Commission calls for the removal of Jews from small villages within three years.

1807   Relocation halted, first by concerns about Napoleon, and then by the economy.

1812   Russia defeats Napoleon's invading army.

Bessarabia incorporated into the Pale of Settlement.

1815   Russia creates Congress Poland from ten Polish provinces. In practice, the treatment of Jewish subjects residing in this puppet state resembles the treatment of Jews in the Pale of Settlement.

1823   Over twenty-thousand Jews expelled from the countryside in Mogilev and Vitebsk Gubernias.

1825   Czar Nicholas I, Alexander's younger brother, seizes control of the Russian Empire after the failed Decembrist revolt.

1827   Jews expelled from Kiev. Nicholas I introduces military conscription quotas which include Jewish boys and men twelve to twenty-five years old. The czar inducts around fifty thousand Jewish children during his reign. Harsh conditions and a twenty-five-year service, toward which the years prior to age eighteen do not count, lead to death or conversion for many. The Russians make local communities collectively responsible for fulfilling the quota of four to eight recruits for every one thousand people on the tax rolls.

1835 Statute passes, which Jews mostly ignore, directing Jewish schools to teach in Russian. The Pale and its provinces are formalized. More cities and towns ban Jewish settlement.

1843 Nicholas I orders the expulsion of Jews from within fifty versts of the Russian Empire's western frontier. In 1858 this is amended, so only new settlement is banned.

1844 The kahal, the nearly autonomous Jewish self-government organization, is officially abolished. The Jewish community is still responsible for taxation and fulfilling the czar's conscription quotas.

1845–1851 Measures directed at Jewish dress and appearance vary from region to region and include a tax for wearing yarmulkes in public and a ban on wearing side locks.

1855 Czar Nicholas I dies; his son, Alexander II, launches his great reforms, which include expansion of the empire's rail system.

1856 Alexander II suspends conscription of Jewish children.

1855–1859 Alexander II opens universities to Jews and permits essential Jewish merchants to live outside the Pale of Settlement.

1859 Odessa Pogrom

1861 Alexander II abolishes serfdom. He allows Jewish doctors and university graduates into the interior of Russia.

1863–1864 Polish Rebellion is defeated. Russia suppresses the Polish language and culture and steps up its Russification strategy. Expanded rights of Jews in the Pale extends to Jews in Congress Poland.

1865 More Jewish skilled workers are allowed to reside beyond the Pale of Settlement.

1866-1867	Two assassination attempts against Alexander II fail.
1871	A second, more violent pogrom, occurs in Odessa, twelve years after the first.
1879-1881	In a two-year span, the radical group, the People's Will, tries to assassinate Alexander II four times. They finally succeed on March 1, 1881.
1881	Pogroms explode across Ukraine and elsewhere, and continue for a year, then become intermittent before ending in 1884. Czar Alexander III, a fervent antisemite, begins to roll back his father's reforms. Jews start to emigrate in larger numbers. Between 1881 and 1914, 1.5 million Russian Jews leave their homes and settle in the United States.
1882	Measures called the Temporary or May Laws include new rules limiting Jewish rights of residency in the Pale of Settlement. Other restrictions against Jews are added in successive years and remain in effect until 1917.
1884	Jewish participation in various professions is decreased or banned.
1886	Jewish attendance at universities in the Pale of Settlement is capped at ten percent of the student body, five percent for universities outside the Pale, and three percent in Saint Petersburg and Moscow.
1891-1892	Twenty thousand Jews are expelled from Moscow.
1894	Alexander III dies; his son, Nicholas II, rules Russia until 1917.
1897	Census counts 4,899,000 Jews in the Pale of Settlement— ninety-four percent of the total Jewish population in Russia and twelve percent of the general population of the Pale. Ninety-nine percent name Yiddish as their first language. Jewish nationalism leads to the first Zionist congress.
1903-1906	Pogroms, even more violent than the 1881 outbreaks, erupt in hundreds of towns and villages.

1905	The first Russian Revolution fails.
1905–1916	Russia publishes several thousand antisemitic books with the support of the czar.
1914–1918	Over a million Russian soldiers are killed in World War I.
1917	The provisional Russian government officially abolishes the Pale of Settlement. The Bolsheviks seize control.
1917–1920	Civil war erupts between the Red Army's workers and peasants and the anti-Bolshevik groups. Widespread violence toward Jews (especially on the part of the White Army, Ukrainian rebels, and criminal gangs) far surpasses the pogrom waves of the late 19th and early 20th centuries and kills fifty thousand.

Suggestions For Further Reading

Antin, Mary. *The Promised Land*. New York: Penguin, 2012.

Assaf, David, ed. *The Memoirs of Yekhezkel Kotik.* Translated by Margaret Birstein. Detroit, Michigan: Wayne State University Press, 2002.

Berk, Stephen M. *Year of Crisis, Year of Hope: Russian Jewry and the Pogroms of 1881-1882*. Westport, Connecticut: Greenwood Press, 1985.

Chagall, Bella. *Burning Lights*. Translated by Norbert Guterman. New York: Schocken Books, 1962.

Dubnow, Simon. *History of the Jews in Russia and Poland from the Earliest Times Until the Present Day*. Philadelphia: Jewish Publications Society of America, 1916.

Engel, Barbara Alpern. "Gesia Gelfman: A Jewish Woman on the Left in Imperial Russia." In *Jews and Leftist Politics: Judaism, Israel, Antisemitism, and Gender,* edited by J. Jacobs, 183-199. Cambridge: Cambridge University Press, 2017.

Engel, Barbara and Clifford N. Rosenthal, eds. and trans. *Five Sisters: Women Against the Czar*. New York: Routledge, 1992.

Figner, Vera. *Memoirs of a Revolutionist*. Translated by Camilla Chapin Daniels et al. Dekalb, Illinois: Northern Illinois University Press, 1991.

Freeze, ChaeRan Y. and Jay M. Harris, eds. *Everyday Jewish Life in Imperial Russia: Selected Documents 1772-1914*. Waltham, Massachusetts: Brandeis University Press, 2013.

Gitelman, Zvi. *A Century of Ambivalence: The Jews of Russia and the Soviet Union, 1881 to the Present*. New York: Schocken Books, 1988.

Klier, John Doyle. *Russians, Jews And The Pogroms of 1881-1882.* New York: Cambridge University Press, 2013.

Nathans, Benjamin. *Beyond the Pale, The Jewish Encounter with Late Imperial Russia*. Berkeley: University of California Press, 2004.

Petrovsky-Shtern. *The Golden Age Shtetl: A New History of Jewish Life in East Europe*. Princeton: Princeton University Press, 2014.

Samuel, Maurice. *The World of Sholem Aleichem*. New York: Alfred A. Knopf, 1943.

Stites, Richard. *The Women's Liberation Movement in Russia: Feminism, Nihilism, and Bolshevism, 1860-1930*. Princeton: Princeton University Press, 1978.

Acknowledgments

This novel exists in part because of the support of my wonderful family. Patricia, my clear-eyed wife and best friend, provided feedback and encouragement. Our daughter Hannah closely read and helped shape the final version (although I did not always take her suggestions, as she reminds me.) Our son Aaron read an early draft and urged me to continue. My sister Rachel Grossman served as a model of courage and resilience. Grandson Leo Porter Freed-Thall and his zestful approach to learning inspired me, as did the interest and warm support of daughter-in-law Jeanette Aaland Brun. Daughter-in-law Jillian Porter, a professor of nineteenth-century Russian literature, offered specific and immensely helpful feedback over the years.

A hearty thank you to the Kyles and Freeds for the many years of kinship and their interest in this project, and to my amazing mother-in-law Jeanette Freed, who celebrated her one-hundred-and-first birthday in 2020.

Thanks to my cousins for all the fascinating conversations, and to our loyal friends in Fletcher, Vermont, with whom we've spent every New Years, howling at the moon and sharing stories. Gracias to old comrades scattered throughout our Green Mountain State, and across America, for the many adventures we've shared. Pieces of these conversations, stories, and adventures found their way into this novel in altered forms.

A bow to the members of the Burlington Writers Workshop who reviewed early chapters: Wendy Andersen, Barbie Alsop, Cathy Beaudoin, Peter Biello, Martin Bock, Dennis Bouldin, Cynthia Close, Alexey Finkel, Deena Frankel, Jim Gamble, Margaret Grant, Mark Hoffman, Kerstin Lange, Walt Mahoney, Natasha Mieszkowski, Riki Moss, Erin Post, Lorraine Ryan, Sondra Solomon, Danielle Thierry, Al Uris.

Thank you to the YIVO Institute for Jewish Research for the critical information they provided. YIVO possesses the largest collection of materials about the history and culture of Eastern European Jews in the world, some twenty-three million items. The only prewar Jewish library to have survived the Holocaust, it relocated from Vilne to New York City in 1940.

The Yizkor (memorial) books for Jewish communities destroyed during the Holocaust, and the Grodno (Horodno) volume particularly, proved invaluable. Edited by Dov Rabin and translated by Jerrold Landau and Batya Unterschatz: *Grodno, Volume IX, Encyclopedia of the Jewish Diaspora,* can be found at: http://www.jewishgen.org/yizkor/grodno/Grodno.html#TOC.

Thank you to the AWP and the Vermont Studio Center for their excellent writing programs. Thanks also to the Historical Society of Indiana County, Pennsylvania for their assistance with the setting of the novel's denouement. I also appreciate the translation help with Yiddish, Russian, German, and Polish graciously provided by Alec Eliezer Burko, Sergei Motov, Cullen Forbes Robertson, Stephanie Rost, Norbert Palej, and Stella Sławin Penzer.

I met Stella, a Holocaust survivor, when she was ninety-six years old. She translated one of Eliza Orzeszkowa's speeches for me and shared some of her own thoughts about the Polish author. Stella escaped the Warsaw Ghetto in 1942, and miraculously survived the war in Ukraine. I'm grateful to her daughter, Martha Penzer, for her interest in this project.

Deep gratitude to those who read full drafts of the manuscript and provided invaluable editorial comment: Karin Ames, Lee Blum, Liz Blum, Terry Cleveland, Rose Eggert, Ann Fisher, Alice Golan, Kat Hudson, Ken Post, Rabbi Jan Saltzman, and George Sibley. And to the editors and mentor who helped push this novel to the finish line: poet Rebecca Starks, who wisely encouraged me to keep revising when I thought I had finished; Lex Williford, my compassionate writer-to-writer mentor from El Paso, who believed in my book; and Victoria Barrett, whose editing suggestions led to an improved structure.

Thank you to Rootstock Publishing and Mark Greenberg, Courtney Boynton Jenkins, Samantha Kolber, Bernie Lambek, Stephen McArthur, and Tim Newcomb for bringing *Horodno Burning* into the world with integrity and meticulous attention to detail.

Horodno Burning is dedicated to the memory of my parents, Marvin and Harriet, committed civil rights and peace activists who showed their children and grandchildren what it means to be astonished by life.

About the Author

When he's not cutting next winter's firewood, pulling weeds in the garden, or off on an adventure with his wife, Patricia, **Michael Freed-Thall** is probably staring at his computer waiting for inspiration. When he retired after thirty years as a teacher and principal in Vermont schools, he took up writing. He became active with the Burlington Writers Workshop, co-edited one of their yearly anthologies, and published four short stories. The Vermont Studio Center accepted him into their week-long summer writing camp, and the Association of Writers and Writing Programs chose him to participate in their Writer to Writer Mentorship Program. These opportunities helped him finish his first book, *Horodno Burning,* a novel about literature, freedom, and Jewish survival. Learn more at michaelfreedthall.com.

Also Available from Rootstock Publishing

The Atomic Bomb on My Back
Taniguchi Sumiteru

Blue Desert
Celia Jeffries

China in Another Time: A Personal Story
Claire Malcolm Lintilhac

An Everyday Cult
Gerette Buglion

Fly with A Murder of Crows: A Memoir
Tuvia Feldman

The Inland Sea: A Mystery
Sam Clark

Junkyard at No Town
J.C. Myers

The Language of Liberty: A Citizen's Vocabulary
Edwin C. Hagenstein

A Lawyer's Life to Live
Kimberly B. Cheney

Lifting Stones: Poems
Doug Stanfield

The Lost Grip: Poems
Eva Zimet

Lucy Dancer
Story and Illustrations by Eva Zimet

Nobody Hitchhikes Anymore
Ed Griffin-Nolan

Preaching Happiness: Creating a Just and Joyful World
Ginny Sassaman

Red Scare in the Green Mountains:
Vermont in the McCarthy Era 1946-1960
Rick Winston

Safe as Lightning: Poems
Scudder H. Parker

Street of Storytellers
Doug Wilhelm

Tales of Bialystok: A Jewish Journey from Czarist Russia to America
Charles Zachariah Goldberg

To the Man in the Red Suit: Poems
Christina Fulton

Uncivil Liberties: A Novel
Bernie Lambek

The Violin Family
Melissa Perley; Illustrated by
Fiona Lee Maclean

Walking Home: Trail Stories
Celia Ryker

Wave of the Day: Collected Poems
Mary Elizabeth Winn

Whole Worlds Could Pass Away: Collected Stories
Rickey Gard Diamond

You Have a Hammer: Building Grant Proposals for Social Change
Barbara Floersch

9 781578 690671